# buffalo road

## A Yellowstone Park Love Story

## bett bone

### NATIONAL PARK ROAD SERIES- BOOK 1

This is a work of fiction. All the characters, organizations, and events portrayed in this novel are products of the author's imagination or are used fictitiously.

Published by Bettina Carter, Edmonds, WA 98026
https://bettinacarter.com
ISBN 13:978-0-9983576-1-4 (trade paperback)
ISBN 13:978-0-9983576-0-7 (eBook)
Library of Congress Control Number: 2017902888
Product of the United States of America

# THE NATIONAL PARK ROAD SERIES

Fall in love with some of our most precious, public national treasures. Unlike many other federally funded institutions and buildings, our parks have been set aside, preserved and protected for anyone and everyone—of all ages—to use and enjoy.

The wisdom of preserving these lands goes beyond their natural beauty, wildlife habitat, recreational and family enjoyment, and special memories, to another unintended benefit and bonus—more essential than ever today—knowledge. Knowledge and answers.

Answers to understanding how our planet functions, past and present; clues to the beginnings of life on earth; seeing what "green" and "natural" truly stand for, from the microscopic primitive life forms that color hot springs, to the massive etching of a supervolcano over Yellowstone, teaching us the earth is not static, but continually renewing, shifting, changing and recycling in ways we still don't fully grasp, but must understand to make good future decisions for our children.

Each book will introduce you to a park with such a unique personality it becomes a main character of the story. Like any character, they have a background of complex forces that shaped them into who they are in the present, from the geologic upbringing of the region, to dramatic climate shifts and stresses that molded them, and the stories of the First People to interact and adapt to the everchanging land.

Though works of fiction, these prehistoric beginnings are carefully researched, so you may fully appreciate the tour of the roads in and around, and leading to the heart of the present day park.

You will be guided by another love story, an entertaining light romance, with more new friends to share the trip and the laughter.

The National Park Road Series starts with the first national park in the world!

Please enjoy Buffalo Road: A Yellowstone Park Love Story.

For mom

and

Laura K


and for Yellowstone NP

@ 144years old in 2016 on the 100th Anniversary of the

National Park Service

# Prologue

IT WAS A ZOO out there.

An unfenced zoo with wildlife on all sides. The human wildlife species were known as tourists.

On the first day of a long anticipated vacation in Yellowstone National Park, Dana and Jenny were already becoming wise to the habits of that predatory camera wielding group. All it took was a rumor, a pointing finger, even sudden brake lights could create a mad feeding frenzy.

And the words "treed black bear"? Floating into an open car window? Chaos!

A flock of tourists had abandoned cars to block the narrow, raised two-lane road. Doors left wide open, kids left to stayinthecarjustaminute, they ran with cameras and tripods dangling to capture that most precious object—the Great Vacation Photo.

The children—wily veterans of just how long adult-minutes lasted and tired of missing the action—waited the required minute before spilling out to chase after their errant parents.

From their blocked vehicle, Dana and Jenny waited and watched with resigned humor. Until a herd of buffalo lunged up the opposite shoulder behind the distracted parents, and a massive bull led his herd toward the cars, cutting the amazed and now terrified children off from their parents, and left in the open.

The children's screams and echoing yells from the parents angered the bull. He lowered his brutal, shaggy head angling a cold, black eye to threaten a small girl, mere yards away. She was too frozen with horror to run.

"Oh, God. No!"

Dana lunged from the car, running through fleeing children toward the herd, shouting and clapping her hands. But the big bull stood firm. His huge, muscled, upper torso twisting the horned head, he swung to pin this new target with his black-eyed glare.

The beast snorted, stamped and moved a few paces forward, forcing Dana to attempt a dodge past those deadly horns to grab the girl and leap over the drop-off, with the child cradled in her grasp.

She almost made it.

She saw the head swing in her peripheral vision, felt the blinding pain crush her shoulder as she jumped for the far edge of the road. Her world tumbled and spun and went red with battering pain, then gray with numbing shadows

Darkness blanked all Dana's senses.

# Chapter 1

FEW TOURISTS HAD begun their vacation to Yellowstone as hopefully and happily as Jenny Morales and Dana Revson. The excitement level went from a long simmer to a bubbling boil as they drove south toward the park beside the Yellowstone River. They could barely contain the joy of *almost* being there; or their envy of the people living year round in this vast valley of the sparkling river, framed with stunning mountain ranges.

No matter how many books, brochures or pictures they studied the past year, eagerly planning the trip, *nothing* had prepared them for the emotions that gripped them when they wound through the town of Gardiner. Easing around that last sharp curve, they confronted the fifty-foot high historic arch that had greeted visitors for over a century. It celebrated the 1872 Congressional Act that made Yellowstone the first national park—not just in the nation—in the world!

Made of local basalt, the gateway arch had a simple grandeur and meaning that made them pause and think of the forefathers that had preserved all this for them. It stood as a symbol that could make the heart clutch as it did when the stars and stripes waved against a cloudy sky in troubled times. Simple, strong, steadfast stone guarded a national treasure of natural wonders and mysteries.

The arch did not face the town—avoiding being lessened as just another of man's attractions. It stood alone, facing the distant mountain ranges, river valleys, and spacious skies, with an invitation to even more wondrous eons of geological wonders and mysteries sequestered inside.

The words engraved on the arch had a deeper impact on them than all the overused, superlative, marketing language they were so accustomed to.

"For the benefit and enjoyment of the people."

So simple, yet so powerful in meaning.

For us, they thought awed.

For our future children, they realized.

Reverently, they drove beneath the gateway and crossed open grassland to the entrance booths, sharing a smile, eyes already glowing in anticipation, as they received maps and began their long-awaited adventure.

Climbing slowly, the road followed the glittering ribbon of the Gardiner River as it tumbled past ever changing rock faces, a different color and form on each side, around every turn. The last steep switchback was walled on one side by a cliff of compressed volcanic ash, 'tuff' Dana called it, and suddenly they were up in Mammoth Village.

The site of the original Fort Yellowstone in the late 1880s, the village now served as year round headquarters for the Park Service. Some of the original buildings from that earlier period remained, including the site now used as a Visitor Center. While the women admired the old buildings, they moved by quickly. Nature, and its architecture, were what they had come to admire; the works of man to be left behind. The terraces of Mammoth Hot Springs glittered invitingly just beyond the tourist center.

Dana hummed with excitement when she saw them, urging Jenny to an open parking slot at the foot of the terraced edifice in front of a separate, but distinctive, limestone monolith. She was jumping from the car before Jen had finished parking.

Joining Dana on the board walk, Jenny laughed, asking, "What is that?"

"Liberty Cap. It was named for the hats of the early French Revolutionaries."

A hat? Jen looked up at the tall, narrow thirty-seven foot tall blunt-topped column, and snorted. With a wicked grin and gleam in her eye, and mischief in her voice, "It doesn't look much like a man's hat to me, more like ...," she trailed off with a suggestive wiggle of dark eyebrows, but her more serious minded buddy wasn't listening.

"It is believed to be a remnant formed by an extinct hot spring when the plumbing in the area changed over time." Dana then explained the Mammoth Terrace limestone deposits came from an inland sea located here back in dinosaur days. The limestone combined with the hot spring waters of Mammoth to form calcium ... something or other. Jenny frowned at the technical words.

"A chemically concentrated calcium carbonate," Dana repeated slowly. "Travertine."

Travertine? Jen recognized that term from her home decor magazines.

Dana explained that both travertine and marble were formed from limestone, though marble was baked underground with intense heat and pressure, while travertine precipitated, usually in caves.

"You know, after the chemicals are dissolved in water, the water drips or evaporates away, leaving new rock."

"Right."

As Jenny's eyes start to cross, Dana hurried to add something familiar sounding—that the chalkier travertine deposits were used for anti-acids, among other things—before clarifying that the similar chemical processes were why the terraces looked like chalky veined marble.

Jenny had never taken any more science than required in college; neither had her college roommate. Jen never regretted it; Dana clearly had. She had become fascinated with geology and prehistory recently, and was now trying to teach herself those disciplines, and—like anyone with a new religion—felt compelled to share it all with her unwilling pupil.

Trying not to sound bored or impatient, Jenny finally broke in.

"So, let's climb up and check out those terraces."

As Dana leapt up the stairs of the boardwalk, heads turned. They turned to see long, sleekly muscled legs under khaki shorts; they turned to admire a tall, toned, form and lovely curves hinted at beneath her crisp white blouse, and appreciate sunlight striking life off wild, auburn curls. They turned to watch and share the beauty of her obvious joy and vitality.

Dana loved rocks, and they were being formed here before her eyes! Pointing, laughing, taking photos, she was as excited as a little kid. Excited as the child the serious, focused, woman had never had a chance to be, Jen thought, her heart softening to see her friend so carefree. Glad to see heads turned to look at Dana in admiration—not in recognition, anymore.

Sure, Jen had come on this trip to enjoy the geysers, the wildlife, and nature—though she was glad to see the gift shops—but mostly she came to explore and enjoy the vacation with her best friend. Dana was there for all the same reasons—except the gift shops—but with her new interest in geology, she was in heaven!

Jen caught up to hear Dana telling total strangers how the prehistoric limestone deposits, from the ancient inland sea, reacted with the hot spring minerals to create the dazzling white travertine terraces, complete with a tracery of rusty veins.

"The Greeks and Romans may have grandiose marble temples and staircases, but here we find a rare marvel. Curving travertine terraced steps, pools and cascading waters, created—not for the gods—but by them!'

The couple smiled and nodded at Dana, turned to give the view an awed appraisal, then turned back to nod and pat Dana's shoulder, seeming to express their thanks before descending the steps—but in a language Jenny could not identify.

Laughing between labored breaths, Jen climbed further up ramps and stairs as Dana waved, urging her to hurry to yet another viewpoint. The six-thousand-foot elevation was challenging Jenny's sea-level lungs. Finally catching her friend, and her breath, she looked to see what the excitement was, wondering where the Dana—normally polite, but cool and reserved with the public—had gone.

Then taking in the view, Jen had to admit the pictures they saw had only hinted at the reality before them. A circular reflecting pool perched on the side of the mountain. The brimming pool mirrored a brilliant blue cloud-puffed sky. Scalloped white and caramel travertine terraces curved and stepped down the slope, like tiered pedestals designed to display the pool crowning the top. Jenny raised her camera and captured the moment at Minerva Terrace with Dana's glowing, grinning face in the foreground, admiring the cascading pools of shimmering water and her freshly made rock.

After taking the picture, Jen turned to head back down the steps.

"We will pass here every day, so let's hit the road. You can see these rocks later. I want to get deeper into the park and get some close up pictures of wildlife."

As they headed down the stairs, they saw the wildlife had come to them.

The roads were silently filling with more of the wonders that were Yellowstone.

GARRETT HEARTH DID NOT rile easily, or often, but right now he felt like a wolf stalking off with his ruff still raised in annoyance. Pulling his cap off to cool his head, he tossed it onto the passenger seat of his truck. Cupping a large palm over his head, he calmed himself, smoothing it over the gold hairs down the back of his head, keeping blue eyes narrowed and focused on the winding road ahead.

He usually loved his work and enjoyed his clients.

14

But today was not turning out to be one of those days.

Hearth Homes of Livingston, Montana, his local construction company, had a reputation for quality work and an owner with a steady, soft-spoken manner.

Usually. Not today.

Today the owner was steadily growling softly and grumbling to himself, venting steam in the privacy of his truck, as he headed north for home after meeting with a potential client. If his current mood was any indication, the man would never become more than that—but Garrett had an uncomfortable and unwelcome dilemma.

Hearth Homes had built its reputation and steadily growing success on referrals. Today's meeting had been with a man that had gotten his name from one of Garrett's favorite and best clients, to bid and build a home near Jackson south of Yellowstone. They hadn't met before today. Garrett wished it had remained that way. He hadn't figured out yet how he could turn down the job without offending his favorite client, and it was putting him in a rare foul mood. The late summer traffic in Yellowstone Park was not helping.

Tourists were great for business; the locals loved to see them coming in droves. But they all were ready to breathe a sigh of relief at season's end when they got back their long, quiet stretches of road, blanketed only in crisp snow—instead of motor homes—the odd tire tracks overlain with deer, elk or coyote prints.

Garrett had always loved Yellowstone.

He slipped down into the park often. It had some of the best fly-fishing in the country, with the Yellowstone River being the only free-flowing river in the U.S. (that had never seen a man-made dam). The trails in the back-country wandered through eons of geologic history and at least ten thousand years of man's pre-history. He liked to come down on crisp dawns just to watch the sun rise, see and hear nature stir, without the clutter of people's voices and vehicles. It was a marvel to see the wild animals able to go freely about their lives, in a world reminiscent of the past.

But he tended to avoid the park on late summer afternoons when it was buried in great herds of people—when he had a choice. That had been the plan today, but—

Brake lights flashed suddenly in front of him. He cursed softly as he slowed around a curve where the road sloped steeply into the Hayden Valley, easing to a stop. Probably buffalo this time, he thought, drumming his fingers on the wheel. The wolves were further east, in the Lamar Valley mostly, and weren't likely to be seen much this time of day, anyway.

A herd of tourists covered the road. They had left all their cars in the middle of the narrow road, blocking traffic in both directions. Garrett shoved his car into park and turned off the ignition. This jam would take a while to clear. Tipping his head back against the seat, folding his arms across his chest, he closed his eyes, seeking peace and patience.

Screams snapped his eyes open, his head forward. But, not screams of delight at a wildlife sighting. He had his door cracked open before he'd finished assessing the situation.

That was terror! Those were children's screams!

A herd of buffalo had joined the crowds on the narrow, raised road.

He jumped from the truck. From this vantage point he couldn't see the kids, but he heard their shrieks from the far side of the herd. Grabbing emergency flares from behind his seat, he started pushing his way forward between lines of stopped cars. He didn't bring his rifle into the park—didn't believe guns belonged here—so the flares were the only weapon at hand to help if he needed to scare off dangerous animals.

Just as Garrett reached the front cars blocking his side of the road, he saw most of the herd break up and lumber back down, returning to the valley side of the road. He could see the shrieking children now, fleeing away from him, and the herd. But—

What the hell?

A flash of white shirt, khaki shorts, flying red hair? A woman charged right into the face of a massive bull! Before he could even yell, he saw the massive, brutal head lower and jerk, tossing the woman from sight. Garrett's gut flipped and rolled.

"NOOOO!" Helpless onlookers screamed.

The bull's head came back up, bright with a red stain glistening on its horn.

Ducking behind the monster, Garrett jumped to the ravine side of the road, snapping and tossing flares at the bull's feet to stop it charging after its prey. Leaping off the road edge, scrambling to keep his balance, Garrett plunged downhill to where a crumpled body lay.

He didn't check behind, just rushed hell bent toward the body, fear bitter in his throat. Blood was already spreading across the back of the white shirt. She lay on her face, strangely twisted. She didn't move or even twitch. Swearing, praying, running, he

16

didn't know his tears streamed down as fast. She lay there on the bottom like a bloody pile of rags.

"DANA! Oh God, oh no. NO! DANA!"

Those agonized shrieks came from his right, close behind him. As he galloped and stumbled downhill, he was conscious of tourists plunging frantically over the edge to the left, also. They were hysterically screaming something else, in a foreign accent.

GRETCHEN?

Almost at the bottom of the gully, he thought he heard a child's wail, saw a tiny sneaker kicking from beneath the crumbled body of the tossed and torn woman bleeding out in a field of wildflowers.

WHEN GARRETT PEEKED into the room, he saw a little brunette sitting beside the hospital bed, tears rolling down swollen red cheeks. He paused, hesitating to invade her private misery.

The brunette held her palm carefully beneath a still hand— the only undamaged hand—which bristled with IV drips, oxygen clips, and other apparatus. She seemed to be trying to comfort without disturbing any vital lines. She appeared to be desperately hoping to anchor her friend to life.

He heard her murmured pleadings between sobs.

'So sorry, Dana. I was so impatient. I rushed you. So, so sorry. My fault. All my fault. We wouldn't have been there. Not then! If I just hadn't rushed you." Her breath shuddered as she begged, "Please, please, come back ... so sorry, oh, God, Dana..."

Garrett was turning away, not wanting to witness the guilt and pain, when she must have sensed his presence.

Long hair swirled as she turned her head, settling like dark chocolate silk on her shoulders to frame a delicately boned face, heart shaped, and eyes a shocking blue between damp black lashes, though the portrait was distorted, swollen and blotched with her grief.

She gasped out a quick, "No, don't go! Stay. Please." She hiccupped, trying to halt her tears.

He tried desperately to recall her name. They had met, briefly, in the chaos of the rescue vehicles. She was the woman's friend. They had come to Yellowstone together. Jenny ... something. She gave him a faint smile warmed by watery blue eyes, but her chin quivered. She had to swallow before speaking again.

"You're the one, aren't you?" Another swallow and sniff. "That helped us?"

"Yes," he answered softly. "Should I come later?"

She glanced down at the gift-shop flower bouquet he had grabbed on the way up.

"No. Please. Come in. She... Dana," another swallow, her control faltering, "hasn't woken yet ... at all!" Then Jenny lost control again, crying harder. She tried to stop, as he stood there awkwardly, holding his flowers, but when he stepped forward to pat her shoulder, the dam seemed to burst harder.

"My fault!" Her moan was sheer misery.

"No, hush now. I'm sure it's not." He patted more, stepped closer to grab tissues from a box, pushing a huge wad at her.

"It is," she insisted. "My idea. I had to go. I didn't listen...I had to rush!" Her voice cracked between sobs. She seemed to need to tell someone—and Dana couldn't hear her. Garrett patted and listened.

"We planned a year. So excited. Our first day ... It was my fault. We wouldn't have been in that spot, at that time, if I hadn't been so impatient!"

"Hey, now. Don't blame yourself. It was just one of those freak accidents," he comforted her. Though Garrett personally blamed the parents. Just to get a bear picture! But hell, who ever expected things to go so bad, so fast. Thank God the little German girl survived with just bruises, a cracked rib, and a slight concussion. It could have been terribly worse!

It was an incredibly brave thing the woman on the bed had done!

The woman, Dana. Incredibly brave lady, and . . . so incredibly stupid! God! He'd felt his gut clench just edging behind that shaggy beast. She'd run at him head on! Man, she had some ....well, nerves of steel.

Her friend, Jenny, seemed like a nice lady. Pretty as a pixie, too, but a pretty miserable pixie. He felt for her. She shouldn't blame herself like this. She was still sobbing. Hard. He should do something. He'd patted her, but maybe she needed a hug? He could do that—or run.

Looking around, finding a place to set his flowers down, he pulled a chair close to sit beside her. Wrapping his arm gingerly around her shoulders, he nudged her head against his chest. Trying to soothe her, like he did his little sister, he patted her back, then moved his hand in slow soothing circles.

She leaned into the comfort, but never let her palm slide from beneath Dana's hand. Slowly the sobs lessened and she began to breathe again—though the breaths were pretty shaky.

He tried to think of something to ask to help her get her composure back.

"So, tell me about her. Dana. What does she like?" He thought she mumbled 'rocks' against his damp chest.

"Sorry, what was that?"

She lifted her head, swiping at her eyes before blowing her nose, then calmer, said it again.

"Rocks, she likes rock."

"Oh ... that's nice." I guess, he thought, confused. "Music? Rock music?"

"Rock music, too." Her answer seemed distracted. She brushed back dark strands of hair that had become plastered against damp, dainty cheeks. Jenny fell silent, gazing at her friend with eyes blue and brimming with unshed tears, before seeming to realize she had forgotten to finish answering his question.

"She likes r-o-c-k-s," she spelled it out, "like layers of rock, like in the Yellowstone Canyon."

"Oh! Geology rocks. Well, that makes sense. Sorry. Is she a geologist?"

"No."

"Oh."

They both looked at the woman in the bed for a while, listened to the beeps and buzzes of the machines that monitored her brain, blood pressure, and other mysterious functions.

Most of the damage was to the upper left side of her body and, hopefully, wouldn't be as bad for her head, as it appeared right now. She'd hit it hard. Not on the bull's horn, but on rocks as she had tumbled downhill, unconscious, unable to shield herself. He'd heard they were afraid it might swell, or ... well, they didn't say all they feared, just that they were monitoring her.

The bull's horn, though just catching Dana, had broken ribs and torn a hole, from under her armpit, back across her left shoulder toward her neck. Muscles and tendons ripped. A real mess! Her left wrist and lower arm were shattered. Broken because, even unconscious, Dana had kept her arms wrapped around a small child, protecting her as they crashed downhill. Her hand had shielded the child's head, clutching it to soft breasts, while Dana's wrist and arm hit the rocks instead, crushed cushioning the girl.

Garrett knew this.

He had wept himself as he'd tried to gently ease the panicked child out of the tangle of broken limbs that had saved her. He had uncurled slender fingers from the child's skull, knowing he was probably causing greater damage to her savior. He'd had to do it. He'd had to hurry to free the child, both to check her and to stop her struggles from shifting the woman too much. He had needed to position the woman so he could apply pressure, before she bled out from her wounds, because, amazingly, she still lived!

Garrett couldn't blame himself—or tried not to—for the extra muscle and tendon he might have destroyed. No choice—it was that or her life. He couldn't blame himself any more than Jenny should blame herself. But tears had run down his cheeks as he'd moved her; whispered desperately to her.

"Sorry, sorry, so sorry, God! Please hang on, babe," he'd pleaded. He was not ashamed of those tears.

The paramedics said his actions had saved her life. So far, anyway. After passing the child to her parents, he'd compressed her wounds as well as he could, whispering encouragement she didn't hear, until the helicopter had come with help. Even then he remained kneeling, keeping the steady pressure while the paramedics took her vitals and started to prep her for the medivac to a hospital in Livingston.

While he'd knelt, waiting for the rescue flight, it felt as if a lifetime passed, praying desperately that her lifetime would not. She was too young, too brave to die like this. He'd heard comments from gawkers on the hill above. One idiot said he wouldn't touch an injured person for anything. 'No way. And get sued?' Garrett ignored him, the guy was probably related to the jerk he met earlier that day—same type. Garrett wasn't a doctor, but he was there first, and knew basic first-aid. He had to do anything he could. How could anyone not?

Garrett looked now at the bleached face on the hospital pillow. A tiny bridge of freckles marched across her nose, so vivid in contrast, they looked like little brown paint splatters. Her face was so lax he was sure it looked different from usual. The firm jaw line, straight nose and high cheeks, spoke of good bones. Her eyebrows arched softly, matching the dark auburn color of eyelashes and strands of hair that curled free and bright from the turban of bandages covering her head. Her lips were, well—not rosebuds—more like squished plums, to be honest. Torn, bruised and misshapen, they looked too dry and cracked. Automatically, he reached his hand into his pocket for lip balm, then withdrew it regretfully, empty. She didn't need any of his germs, right now.

Poor thing. Poor lovely thing, he realized—even like this—still, white and beat to hell.

She had appeared long, lean, and athletic in the quick glimpse he had when she charged that bull. His shoulder jerked at the visceral memory. He saw again the sunlit flash of her glistening auburn hair, then the red blood glimmering on the bull's horn. His stomach rolled.

Her friend sat staring silently at the bed; he sat and stared with her. They both waited, both hoped, then waited and hoped some more for Dana to show some sign of coming out of the coma. The bustle of sound from the hospital corridor behind them just seemed to further emphasize their own isolation, and the stillness inside the room.

Garrett wondered what color the woman's eyes were. He asked Jenny.

"Green. Gorgeous green," she smiled sadly.

Garrett sure hoped they'd open again. He also hoped this woman, Dana, did end up suing him. She would have to live and have her brain and spirit back to do so.

*Open those eyes, girl, please. Do it for me.* Reaching over, he brushed a finger gently over the bruised and still cheek. "Keep fighting, Dana," he said softly, then turned to give Jenny one last pat on her shoulder. "Hey, I have to go now," he said apologetically. "Here's my card, cell number. Call me? Anytime. Let me know how she is, okay?"

"Sure."

"I'll be back around, unless they move her back to your state..."

"I'll call you," Jenny promised, and he left.

He hoped when she called, it would be good news. It didn't look too promising, at the moment.

"HEY, BOSS! WAY to go! Says here in the newspaper that you're a Hero!"

Garrett just shook his head, striding back to the coffeepot at the rear of the site's construction trailer.

"And what a looker you saved! Whooeee! You saved her, boss. Doesn't that mean you get to keep her?"

Garrett checked, came back and snatched the paper from his plumbing sub-contractor's hand.

"Let me see that!"

A full-color photo of Dana centered the front page, with a picture of the child Gretchen, and one of himself, to the side. After

21

quickly noting he looked grumpy in his photo, his eyes were all for the one of Dana. The features he had seen in the hospital this morning, with their hint of promise, even slackened, now bloomed to life in the photograph. The beauty revealed caught at his gut, as he saw the vibrant, smiling face for the first time.

He hoped not for the last.

It hurt physically to see how much of the life had gone out of that face; just a ghostly impression lay back on the hospital bed. He wasn't a praying type of guy, but he'd do it to see that life come back to Dana.

"....Don't ya think?"

"What?" Garrett set the paper back down and returned to get his coffee and plumbing blueprint.

"I said, don't ya think you two look good together? In the pictures. A fine looking couple, don't ya think?"

Garrett's face and voice were grim as he said, "She might not make it." His lips couldn't find a smile as he added, "I think I just want to see her get well and look like that again. Come on. Let's get some work done today, you slacker."

Garrett stepped outside the construction trailer, pausing on the steel stairs, to say another silent prayer. *Open those green eyes, babe.* He took a sip of coffee, then followed the plumber out into the framework of the new building.

After checking in on his most vital job sites—after missing the whole day before—Garrett found he just couldn't concentrate on all his paperwork and the bids that needed doing, worried it was getting late; he wanted to get back to the hospital before visiting hours ended.

WHEN HE RETURNED to the hospital room that night, he wasn't surprised to see Jenny's back still seated in the chair facing Dana. He would have been surprised if he hadn't. What did surprise him was her lack of welcome, after what they had shared that morning. She didn't even turn when he said, "Hey". Though keeping her back to him, he heard a quiet "hi" in return. Okay, he respected her space. He took a seat on the other bed, behind her. He could see Dana from there. She hadn't moved, as far as he could tell, from the last time he had seen her.

"She wake yet?" He asked as gently as he could.

He saw the tension in Jenny's shoulders as she shook her head in a wordless negative. Scared to death, numb, probably exhausted too, by now, Garrett thought. He knew she wouldn't leave or rest until Dana woke up, or moved, or spoke.

"Has the doc been by?" A nod. Yes.

"But he wouldn't tell me anything." He heard the anguish. "Just said Dana's hanging in, not getting worse." Or better, Garrett finished Jenny's thought.

"Hey, little Jenny, come on, be strong now. I don't know you two, but it seems clear to me that Dana's a fighter. No question. I bet she'll scold you for not getting any rest worrying over her."

The one shoulder shrug in response told him this was probably true.

"Listen, I'd get you a hotel room nearby, or give you the keys to my place, to use the guest room as long as you need ... Now just wait, quit shaking that head and let me finish ... But, I know you won't leave her.

"This is a small town; we know each other here. I've contracted renovations at this hospital, so I know the key staff. I'll talk to them before I leave tonight and make sure this bed I'm messing up is yours until they transfer Dana. I guarantee it." He would buy it if he had to. "So when you need to, just climb on up here, get some sleep. I'm starting to worry about you. Remember, your friend isn't going to be happy if the minute she wakes, you zonk out on her. Okay?" He saw her head nod down and heard a sniffle. "Promise me?"

"Yes. Thank you, Garrett. For all of it."

"You're welcome. Anything you need." He paused then added, "I've been wondering, where's Dana's family?"

Jenny just shook her head.

"They couldn't get here yet?" Jenny shook her head again. Her voice sounded choked when she finally added, "She has none. She never did."

Garrett thought that over for a few minutes, then excused himself and went to find the head nurse. He arranged the bed for Jenny easily enough, but he had a lot more trouble with his second request.

"No, Garrett, I'm sorry, I can't. It's not just rules, there are laws now," the head nurse told him, clearly regretful she couldn't help.

"Who do I need to speak to?"

"Well, we could call the administrator, but ..."

"Get him on the line, would you, please?"

The savvy head nurse made sure to hand him the phone while it was still ringing.

23

"Hey, Bob? Garrett Hearth here. Aw, cut that hero crap. I saved a hero, a heroine, is what happened. Listen, the reason I'm calling is that you can be a hero, too. Now don't uh-oh me, this is easy. That poor heroine is an orphan, did you know that?

"Right. Well, here's the problem you can solve. The only person in the world here for her now is her best friend, Jenny. Anyone can see those two are closer than natural-born sisters ... I know you know where I'm headed with this, and you are going to go there with me, Bob.

"Yes, you are. I know about that law, but there's no one close to her who has the information about Dana's medical condition. What if she has allergies, or you need to know something to pick the best treatment? You need a family-type member involved, and you know that person is Jenny. It's no less than torture withholding information from that poor girl. Legal liability? Yeah sure, I've heard of it. That's what they have in all those big city hospitals. Not the way we do things in this town. We're all family here.

"Okay, if that happens, I'll sign a legal statement that I swore to you that Dana and Jenny were blood relatives. And I'll back date it, sure.

"Thanks, Bob, you're a hero, give her Doc a call and make sure he understands the deal. Thanks. Oh, and thanks for the bed, too. Yeah, the bed. The nurse will explain it all to you tomorrow; just get that doctor to call her tonight.

"Yes, I owe you. A rec-room at cost? Sure, no problem."

By the time Garrett got off the phone, his earlobe ached. With the nurse standing by to hear which way the conversation went, he felt like one of those cell phone posers doing their big wheeler-dealer act in public. But Garrett was dealing for a good cause. He could hardly wait to tell Jenny.

Giving the nurse a thumbs up, and a wink, he scooted back down to the room.

"Jenny, you and Dana are sisters—blood relatives."

Thinking it was a question, she said, "No, but we are as close as sisters."

"Not what I meant, dear." He winked at her. "I made a deal with the administrator, don't tell on us. We agreed you two are probably blood sisters, so they will involve you in Dana's medical information, and start updating you. He's calling her Doc right now to give you her real status. So remember, you're sisters with different last names."

Damn. The brunette started crying again!

He hugged her. Patted her back again. Got his shirt soaked again. But he felt better to have helped with a few problems for the poor little rainy thing.

After Jenny calmed, he moved to Dana's bedside. Garrett stood for a long time, hands in his pockets, gazing at the silent figure. Finally, unable to resist, he leaned forward and ran his hand softly down her cheek, tucked an errant curl behind her ear, whispered to her softly.

"Open those green eyes for me, babe." After waiting for a response, and getting none, he turned to Jenny.

"You mentioned before that Dana wasn't a geologist, just a rock lover. You didn't ever say what she does."

He watched the smile dissolve from her face, replaced by a grim line. She turned her back to him again before answering, her voice flat.

"She's a professional athlete. A gymnast." Jenny's voice caught on a sob, before she could level it out and continue. "She was a U.S. Champion decades ago—probably on your cereal box—Dana Revson was once a familiar name and face. Now she teaches at her own studio, performs in public exhibitions. Parallel bars are...," another catch, "were her specialty."

Garrett felt the gut punch land hard.

As a young lad, he'd been in love with that girl on his Wheaties box. Little wonder Jenny hadn't been able to look at him when she told him. *An athlete? Hell.*

He'd just watched the Olympics, amazed at the strength and grace of the U.S. Women's routines on the parallel bars. He had not been able to imagine the torque and stress it must place on the delicate shoulders, arms and wrists of the athletes when they executed handstands and pirouettes as gracefully as if their bodies weighed no more than a feather. That picture tried to mesh in his mind with the memory of the mangled body he'd found at the bottom of the meadow, the ripped shoulder tendons, the...

Bile rose in the back of his throat. He fled the room, sped down the hall to the restroom, where he could smash his fist against the concrete wall, rail at the unfairness and tragedy of it all.

My God! Would the athlete hate him for saving her for . . . what? If she survived? It was how she would feel about herself that terrified him. He could not go back to the room right now with so much pity and horror showing on his face. It would just make it worse for Jenny—and, he admitted, he lacked the courage.

AS SHE SAT in silent vigil after Garrett left, Jen felt her throat tighten again, eyes finding more water somewhere to well up, as she stared at Dana's flat, sedated features on the pillow. They had been *so* happy. How could it all go so wrong?

Digging listlessly in her purse for a damp wipe to cool and clean her face, her hand bumped against her camera. Pulling it out she turned it on and hit the memory button desperate to see Dana's face lit once again with joy and laughter—and life!

The picture that came up was of Dana standing before the reflecting pool on Minerva Terrace. So happy and glowing. Would she ever be able to print out that picture without her heart breaking at the fleeting moment of joy? One of the last pictures she had taken of Dana before—

Jenny shivered. She couldn't think that way! She had to believe Dana would recover; she had to concentrate on believing she would see her friend like that again. She had to, because if she didn't, Dana might not make it. Determined to quit her bawling, she would focus all her thoughts and strength on that positive picture and outcome. To believe, to will, as hard as she could, in a bright future for Dana. This was her job, while her friend slept and healed.

"Please, God," she whispered another plea for her fallen friend. Exhausted from grief and fear and guilt, Jenny finally crawled on the bed, turning so she was facing Dana, so any movement would wake her. Clenching her teeth to hold back the weeping, she tried to see only the image of Dana's laughter as she surrendered to a restless, tormented sleep.

# Chapter 2

GARRETT STEPPED OUT on his covered porch to greet the day at dawn. Blowing the steam off his coffee, he took a tentative sip. Savoring the rich aroma and heat in the crisp morning air, he gazed across the sage studded grassland to the Absarokas. The mountains were a dark, wavy, navy silhouette against the rising sun, just now breaking over their domed and pointed peaks. This was his favorite morning ritual. No matter how long he lived here, the quiet and the beauty of these immense spaces still nourished something in him. Narrowing his eyes against the sun's morning exuberance, he let his senses breathe and absorbed it all.

The low, bright rays reached out and captured him standing beneath the eaves. The sun's fingers sparkled in the hairs beneath his hat that were the golden blonde of a palomino's mane. The hairs on his forearms glimmered like wheat shining against the taut, bronzed skin. The sun's touch slid down the lean, jean clad hips, long rangy legs, and feet encased in work worn and dusty cowboy boots. Garrett's face flickered in and out of the shadow of the cowboy hat that rested as comfortably on his head as the construction hard-hat, or baseball cap, he often wore.

His silhouette was that of a working man, in his natural habitat: ranch wide shoulders, range lean waist and hips, muscled arms under denim, and the strong, well-formed hand of a man that could create magic with tools, resting on his hip. Garrett was all substance; his clothes weren't worn for show any more than his life was lived for it. He was a man comfortable with himself and his accomplishments.

An impatient snort from the corral had him setting down his coffee, and strolling down to toss a bale of hay to his horses, rub their velvety noses, and converse softly with each, in the quiet of the new day.

Heading in to shower his thoughts caught on the fragile, battered redhead at the hospital. He wondered if she had opened her eyes yet, if Jenny would call with good news today. He would just have to wait, to hope for the best.

After his shower, he tossed bacon in a pan and grabbed his blueprints. Rolling them out across his kitchen table, he secured the corners with the salt and pepper shakers and a couple of unusual rocks he had found and used for paper weights. The rocks were geodes, smooth, normal looking rounded, palm-sized rocks on the outside, but inside they hid a surprising jungle of amethyst colored crystals. The bacon started to sizzle and tease him with its aroma as he grabbed his notepad, worked over his plans, and began making notes for the day. As the aroma of breakfast filled the room, he caught himself gazing at the geode resting on the corner of his blueprint. That lady liked rocks; she might like this one. His concentration broken, he rolled his plans, gathered his notes, and got up to finish making breakfast.

Maybe he should take one of his rocks to Jenny. Then If Dana opened her eyes, she could look at the beautiful crystals buried inside. She'd probably enjoy it more than the flowers he had taken her the day before.

When he left for work that morning, along with his work papers and sack lunch, he optimistically put one of his special rocks on the seat of the pickup truck.

"JEN, LOOK OVER THERE!" Dana had called, bounding down the wooden steps from Mammoth Terrace, pointing. "Unbelievable! There's a whole herd of elk coming between the buildings! And look, *babies!*"

Below in the village of Mammoth, rangers were rushing about erecting bright orange cones and barricades. Cars were stopping and tourists crowded the barricades. They hustled down the terraces to gather with the other excited camera-toting tourists, all completely awed to see these majestic animals wander into the center of the town's green lawns as if they owned them—which, according to the ranger's actions— they clearly did!

A warbling wail came from a tiny elk calf that looked like it was all legs and hadn't quite learned how to operate them yet. Temporarily separated from its mother, it warbled another cry that had Jen, Dana, and half the crowd wanting to grab it up to cuddle. The mama cow waited patiently, pausing at the base of the steps of the Terrace Grill for its baby to catch up, then casually crossed the street near the crosswalk in front of a stopped line of cars. No movie stars could have received more attention, or been photographed by so many admiring fans, walking the red carpet, as these two elk were crossing to the rich green lawns. Even seasoned tourists, stepping out a store door, stopped and gasped at the majestic animals suddenly and quietly surrounding them.

Jenny and Dana tried to count the various grazing groups of elk scattered across the roads and lawns, and had reached the high thirties when they spotted a sight that made them lose count. A regal bull elk, with a truly massive rack of antlers, strolled over to ease his bulk down under a shady tree were he could watch over and guard his harem and children. Even lying down, it looked like two tall leaf-less trees sprouted from his head. They had seen many trophies on the walls of the local bars and restaurants in this part of the country, but nothing to match this old, but obviously prime bull elk—wise enough to keep his herd, and his own head, in the protection of the park. Delaying the plan to move on, the women settled in to watch the elk.

Nothing really prepared a person for the novelty of this ringside seat, for the reality of Yellowstone. It just developed before one's eyes, naturally, on its own schedule. So amazing for the first morning of their vacation.

After the big bull finally led his family off, they made a quick stop in the Visitor Center, then skipped the rest of the sights around Mammoth Hot Springs, to revisit later, taking the road south along the west side of the park. Climbing again, they came upon the Hoodoos. The formation looked like a giant had smashed some of the limestone mountains into huge blocks, then rolled and tossed them down into a jumbled, awkwardly balancing pile, as odd as their name. A short one-way lane ducked off the main road to weave in the scary tumble, a remnant of the original 1899 stagecoach road in the park, according to the detailed guidebook they had picked up after the elk had wandered away. The short loop through the jumble brought them back facing the opposite side of the canyon. Here again they saw a completely different perspective as they faced the high golden cliffs of the Golden Gate, as it rose up to Bunsen Peak.

In the colorful display of gilded cliff, it was easy to see how the park had received its name. They were just beginning to understand the uniqueness that made Yellowstone so treasured that it became the first preserved national park in the world. Around every corner, even on either side of the road, it changed its rock faces, shapes, its colors and marvels; it might have lakes and swans to the right, buffalo to the left, basalt walls, golden mountains, geysers blasting and rivers and springs boiling, or elk dropping in with their babies—endlessly fascinating, endlessly new and changing. It was hard to imagine a person could begin to enjoy or absorb it all in one lifetime of journeys.

They were learning the first lesson of Yellowstone—slow down and savor.

Their original plan to spend the early days getting to the furthest sights first, saving locations closest to the north entrance—most convenient to their hotel in Livingston—for later in the trip, might have been efficient, but became laughable. They might have missed the wonder of being surrounded by a herd of elk! As they continued south, the list of all they passed and wanted to return to spend more time, was growing with each mile.

Rising from a canyon, they entered an immense area of grassland and ponds—the Swan Lake Flats. The vista once again dramatically changing. suddenly. Dana grew more excited as they approached a site she had thought about and studied all the prior winter. She could barely wait to stop at Obsidian Cliff.

The cars began to slow and jam up, just before they reached their destination; there must be wildlife sighted somewhere ahead. As they inched forward, Dana spotted the dark cliff rising two hundred feet on the left side of the road, but as they came alongside, her view was obscured by the roof of the car. The small pullout across the road, intended to view the cliff and volcanic glass exhibits, was jammed with parked cars. Jenny hesitated, but Dana waved her on. There was just no room for them to stop. But Dana eagerly explained the importance of the cliff to Jenny.

Paleo Indians had visited here to obtain the black volcanic obsidian for their spear points, dating back to at least 8,000 B.C., if not earlier. The points had been chemically traced to Yellowstone's Obsidian Cliff. Later archaeological finds, in the early centuries A.D., had also been traced here, including a cache of stone points that had been discovered in the Hopewell Mounds in Ohio. It was hard to fathom that before 1,000 A.D., stone from this cliff made its way over 1400 miles overland from this source, or twice that distance, if the trade goods had traveled by river!

Dana had wanted to stop and absorb the ancient history of a cliff that was so important to prehistoric hunters and early trade networks that had stretched across a nation, centuries before Europeans stumbled on the Americas—and another four hundred years before they stumbled on this site.

The cliff itself was closed and restricted. Too many visitors wanted just one tiny rock sample as a souvenir. With about three million visitors each year, the cliff needed protection. In 1996,

30

Obsidian Cliff became a National Historic Landmark in recognition of its ancient value and history. The small pullout was the closest they could have come to enjoy and learn more of the site, taking pictures for their own souvenirs.

As they passed by, Dana gave a small sigh and twisted to try and capture a view of the cliff through the rear window. The sun striking the cliff face picked out black glittering sparkles, where cracks and recent erosion exposed the fine black glass beneath the weathered matte-black surface. Turning to silently gaze across the road at Beaver Lake, and the meadows surrounding it, Dana said she wasn't looking for wildlife, but vividly picturing an ancient and rich culture that would have camped in summer lodges among the lush grasses and freshwater ponds in distant prehistoric times, while quarrying the black glass cores to knap their tools and spear points.

As Jenny maneuvered through the tangle of cars to continue on to Norris, she promised her disappointed friend, "We *will* come back, every day, Dana!"

We have to go back, was Jen's first thought when she woke, before realizing she was in a hospital room, not in Yellowstone with her friend. Reality was as harsh as the morning light that showed the same still and lax countenance on the bed beside her. She hadn't meant to sleep so long, afraid she might miss some slight movement, or some need of Dana's. But there was nothing to see. Nothing had changed. There was nothing Jenny could do except to wait and watch. Wait and hold thoughts of a vibrant Dana firmly in her mind, the images and memories used like a force to bind Dana to life.

They had never made it back to Obsidian Cliff; Jen felt the weight of that broken promise now.

The doctor entered the room as she was telling Dana how sorry she was; telling her to get up so they could go back. Momentarily embarrassed for speaking out loud to a comatose friend, Jen realized she should be ashamed for not doing so all along. Dana needed to hear about her interests, be reminded of their experiences, to bring her back here, back to life. Not silence, not Jen bawling her head off! Geez! What was she doing? Jen needed to share and celebrate their friendship out loud more than ever! Even if Dana was letting Jen do all the talking, for once. Dana could get even when she woke. Jen smiled at that thought as she left to make way for the doctor's examination.

Thanks to that dear, sweet Garrett—such a nice guy—the doctor gave Jen a full briefing after the examination. Some of the things he said made Jenny cringe and realize the damage was extensive and maybe permanent, as his words began to sink in.

"Possibly some permanent crippling," Jenny whispered the awful words, then gulped in a great breath of air, nearly shouting her questions.

"But, that means you expect her to live! Is that what you are saying? Is she going to make it?"


PROBLEMS THAT CRIPPLED progress developed for Garrett right from the start that morning.

The home with the most urgent completion date always seemed to be the one that experienced the greatest delays. Today, as he waited at the site to meet the delivery truck with his roof trusses, he received a phone call from his normal supplier—instead of his delivery. The roof trusses had not arrived. They had been offloaded in Billings by mistake. The supplier was apologetic, but honestly admitted he wouldn't be able to free a truck up to pick up the missing shipment for a couple of days. The short summer building season was always a frantic time in these mountain regions.

Garrett had worked his crew on this job overtime to complete the framing, so they would be ready for the trusses today, after a prior delay had put them behind schedule. The crane and operator that Garrett had rented to place the trusses would be arriving soon. His crew had finished everything else needing to be done until then, so they were taking an early lunch, waiting for the materials.

Garrett swore under his breath, and not so softly, after getting off the phone. He couldn't afford the time delay, or the added expense of having his crew and a crane idle for days. Sudden delays were an unpleasant—if not an uncommon occurrence—in the tightly scheduled ballet of a contractor's world. Each delivery of special order materials, or prearranged labor or equipment subcontractor, had to arrive on cue for the job to flow smoothly. A hitch in any phase increased the pressures in each step to follow. This house had been out of sync from the start.

Doffing his hat, he scrubbed his fingers in his hair, hoping to stimulate his brain to find a solution for the current crisis. Then he palmed his head down, smoothing hair, and soothing himself, before resettling his hat. Heading over to his pickup, he pulled out the files and plans that rested on the front seat, his impromptu office. Pulling out his phone, he settled on the seat, his door open to a cooling breeze, as he began to call around.

He managed to make arrangements with the equipment rental company to cancel the crane and operator before they left for the site; arranging to rent a flatbed truck and driver instead. The crane was rescheduled for the following morning. Giving his crew the afternoon off, he headed into town to meet up with the flatbed driver, and ride with him to Billings. He'd need to locate and pay for his trusses there to get them back on site by tonight. It was a good two hundred mile roundtrip drive, and with the added time to locate and load, he wouldn't be back until very late—at great added expense, he added to himself, but he couldn't let his client down, despite any delays or added costs.

Reaching for his lunch sack, to eat his sandwiches as he drove into town, his hand came in contact with the crystallized rock. Damn! He wouldn't be able to deliver it to Jenny, or check on Dana, until tomorrow.

Garrett was in Billings, hot and exasperated, but finally watching his trusses being slowly loaded, when he received the call. He immediately wished he hadn't left his pickup in Livingston—but it wouldn't have mattered. Even if he could have left right away, he wouldn't have been able to get there in time.

He recognized the Washington state area code on his caller ID even before he heard Jenny's hesitant voice asking for him.

She quickly informed him that the doctor had been in that morning and assured her that Dana's condition had stabilized. No, Dana hadn't opened her eyes yet, Jenny told him, but they were keeping her sedated on purpose. She didn't fill him in on any other details, just thanked Garrett again for everything that he had done for them and apologized that they wouldn't be able to see him again before leaving. Dana was being transported within the next half hour back home to her hospital in Washington. Jenny had just wanted to give him a call before she finished checking out of her hotel, to follow her friend back home by car. She gave him her cell number again, adding her home phone number, in case he wanted to call and check on Dana's progress. Thanking him yet another time, she assured him that she was sure Dana would want to call and thank him personally, once she was able. Thanks for everything. Goodbye.

Garrett mumbled his best wishes and closed his phone, shoving it back in his pocket. He stood, hands stuffed in his jeans, staring at his trusses being loaded, thinking about what he was feeling.

Glad that Dana's prognosis was better and she was stable enough to be moved. It would be better for both women to be home for Dana's continued care. But, hell, he felt empty, hollow, cheated somehow.

The woman had suddenly come into his life, and just as suddenly left it. He told himself he was just bummed he was unable to deliver the crystal geode for her enjoyment. But his gut knew it for a lie. He felt guilty for being so disappointed that she was being transferred away. He shouldn't feel that, think that. It meant she was better. That should be all that mattered. He should be happy. But he had never had a chance to see her open those green eyes; he'd never had a chance to say goodbye. *Or a chance to say 'hello" to the brave beauty.*

He glanced down and kicked a clod of dirt with his boot, uncomfortable with himself.

His feeling of hollowness persisted throughout the long afternoon and the long ride back. His silence finally got to the driver, another local he had known casually for years, who wondered what he was brooding about.

"Is it the delay, man?" he was asked.

"Nah," Garrett answered briefly.

Another twenty silent miles passed, then the driver tried again.

"What's eating you, man?"

"Nothing. Just thinking," Garrett replied, then added with forced enthusiasm. "Hey, I heard the lady, that saved that girl from the buffalo in Yellowstone, is well enough to transfer home."

"Man that is cool. That was one damn brave woman, you ask me! Glad she's better and going on home," the driver responded with true happiness.

"Yeah," was all Garrett could find to say.

JUST SHY OF MISSOULA, Jenny was thinking of pulling over to crash for the night—before she had a vehicular one! It wasn't all that late, still light out, but sleeplessness and worry had drained her reserves. Without her friend's cheerful chatter to accompany her on the drive, she was having trouble keeping awake and alert. Dana should be home by now, under her own doctor's care, so Jen could relax her vigilance—but not while driving seventy-five miles an hour.

She saw the Motel 6 sign and then a familiar Starbucks Coffee sign, and that did it. Gratefully, she exited at Reserve Street, one of the last Missoula exits heading west on I-90. Swinging in for some coffee from her home state, she decided to dine later at Famous Dave's BBQ Restaurant. She and Dana had happily pigged out there on their way east. It might make her feel closer to her friend tonight, and she needed the nourishment. Tomorrow she would be home and head straight to the hospital.

After checking in, Jen drove to the restaurant. She was a little startled by the boisterous, happy atmosphere, though it had appealed to them the first time. But after the silent, tense vigil in Dana's room, and the quiet of her drive home alone, she felt disconnected from all the noise and gaiety.

This was a college town. Many of the tables, she noted, held the fresh, exuberant faces and voices of college age kids. She smiled a little, remembering how she and Dana, college roommates, had shared many such evenings, sharing excited dreams of futures with the world laid out at their youthful, expectant feet.

As she quietly ate her meal, her eyes wandered the other patrons. At a back table, four young men enjoyed their meal, long-neck beers, and each other's camaraderie. They also had that fresh energy, but their bodies had an athletic maturity and solidness that marked them as older. Faces deeply tanned, muscles rippling under their casual t-shirts, they shared a broad-shouldered outdoorsy look. At first, Jen pegged them as soldiers on leave. They shared that kind of bond—and seriously toned bodies, she wasn't too tired to notice—but their hair seemed too long. They were hot, that was for sure! And they had the self-confidence to go with those broad shoulders and ... smokejumpers! Jen bet that was what they did. Didn't they train around these parts?

They reminded Jenny of Garrett, in a way, with their strong, sexy, sure good looks. Now there was a man! Handsome, capable, mature and confident, and so damn nice—even without being their personal hero!

Jen recalled a casual comment she had made on their drive here from home, just a few days ago, that had pulled surprising revelations from her friend. Dana would joke around with her, but rarely discussed her serious thoughts about men and relationships. Just how had that conversation gone? Jenny tried to recall what had happened just days before. It seemed now like a lifetime ago—Dana's lifetime, almost!

Jenny had been driving, and they had just curved around Butte and started uphill. They were talking about the books they had brought to read. Yes, that was how it had started.

Dana had brought mostly geology and history books, which seemed way too serious and heavy for enjoyment, especially on vacation. Jen had brought a collection of small paperbacks—all romances. She'd casually offered to share them with Dana, so she'd have something lighter and pleasant to read at night. Dana had thanked her, but passed on the offer. When Jen had teasingly asked if she were anti-romance, Dana had replied she was all for romance, it was just the books she would pass on.

"All romance book plots are basically the same," Dana pointed out. "Boy meets girl. They hate each other first, or have some insurmountable problem, then, suddenly, they fall madly in love and marry at the end."

"What's wrong with that? Sounds like fun to me," Jenny had laughed.

"It just doesn't work for me," Dana replied simply, as she had turned to gaze out the window at the unusual stacked boulder formations in Butte Pass.

"Why not?" Jenny pressed, but assumed her friend was already lost in her fascination with the geology of the area, and no longer tuned in to her. Even to Jenny's eyes it looked like some ancient giant or god had rolled up a bunch of snowmen, then left them to petrify into antic gray stone columns. They seemed to balance in defiance of gravity.

The silence, as they wound up the pass, was interrupted only by the low rumbling strain of the container freight trucks they passed, that crawled to the summit so slowly it seemed as if some were about to lose momentum and roll back to Butte. They had just passed the summit and were speeding down the other side when Dana spoke again.

"It's just such a waste of time, is why, I guess."

36

Focused on her rear view mirror, Jenny had no clue what Dana was talking about, and didn't dare distract herself by asking. She was feeling like a rabbit trying to sprint in front of a herd of stampeding buffalo; all those slow, heavy trucks were now hurtling downhill, coasting at speeds way beyond the limit, and swaying dangerously on the sharp curves—and they were all chasing Jenny! Trying to take the dizzying downhill curves at a reasonable speed with only two lanes to leap between, it seemed that every time Jenny glanced up there was a steel toothed grill filling her mirror, climbing up her rear bumper. When the road finally leveled and flattened, and she'd felt she could breathe again, she finally turned to question Dana.

"Why, what? You lost me back there."

"You know, all that fighting crap first. It's such a waste of time, it irritates me."

"O-kay-y," Jenny drew out the word as she tried to remember what they had been talking about before they went over the pass. Books, romance novels. But Dana had already turned back to study the landscape and lapsed back into silence.

Later, in words so soft they could hardly be heard, still gazing out her side window, Dana spoke to herself, it seemed.

"I don't want to fight for someone's love, anymore. I don't want to invest any more of my life in relationships that don't look like they will belong to me."

Jenny held her breath, not daring to say anything that might stop her friend's flow of words. Dana rarely spoke like this— of deep feelings or private thoughts. Her polite, smiling personality seemed to openly share her joy and thoughts with the world. But that was the surface Dana—the athletic performer—not the real Dana underneath. Not the quiet, introspective, serious, and sometimes coolly distant Dana—the orphan.

"Anyway," Dana had turned toward her and stated firmly, "I don't see why they have to fight like cats and dogs first, or two-year olds fighting over a toy. Why waste the effort trying to love a man you start out hating? I won't. How far to Bozeman?"

Jen hadn't been willing to let Dana close back up so quickly or easily, ignoring Dana's last question, she answered the other comment.

"I think the point of them fighting so intensely at first is that old thin line between love and hate thing. The idea that if someone stirs your passions enough to feel such an intense reaction, there is a reason. They mean too much to each other just to ignore, to

37

let it go, so they fight their way through to the real reason for their passion—to love..."

"Happily ever after," Dana inserted in a mocking tone. "Yeah, I know the theory. I just get irritated at them wasting so much time getting there, instead of just grabbing their happiness and skipping through all the false pride at the beginning. That's just not my recipe for romance, is all." Reaching out to pat Jenny's arm, her voice had softened, "Hey, I know you love those books, devour them. I'm not giving you a bad time, but I'll just stick to my own books, okay? But thanks, anyway."

Jenny had thought that was all she would hear on the subject from Dana, but just before the Bozeman exit had come up, she had heard another pensive comment addressed to the scenery.

"I just need to look into the eyes of the man I desire, and watch how his look into mine. I think I'll know if the warmth and affection in his words and actions, match the warmth in his soul—if I can see into his eyes. Lots of men have charming manners and eyes that can laugh, but have a wall at the back. I should know, I've looked in the mirror at my own all my life. I won't waste more of my life without someone to belong to, when I find him, Jen," Dana had promised, then the orphan had sighed, and admitted, "If I ever find someone to belong to me alone."

Jenny dabbed the corners of her eyes with her napkin, trying to return to the happy clamor of the restaurant, but regrets still choked a hard knot in her throat. They had almost stopped in Bozeman to visit the museum and spend the night, but were so eager to see Yellowstone, first. If she had just turned off the exit, they wouldn't have been at the wrong place, at that horrid time. If they had just stopped, Dana wouldn't be fighting now to get back to life with a chance to open her eyes and look into the love and belonging that she had needed all her life!

Jen thought of the way Garrett had brushed his fingertips so gently across Dana's still cheek, whispered softly, 'Open those green eyes for me, babe.' His voice had been so tender that, even worried as she was, Jenny had shivered with goose bumps.

When Dana spoke of a relationship without storms, Jenny thought her friend would trade peace and security instead of excitement and passion. She hadn't been able to imagine it. Now she could picture it easily. Garrett seemed like the kind of man that could have given Dana both. Him, or a man just like him. A man that didn't live hundreds and hundreds of miles and at least four mountain passes away. Not an insurmountable problem, but not easy, either. And there were two other minor problems to the fictional romance that Jenny was visualizing for Dana. Dana had never seen Garrett, and, Jenny hadn't told him that Dana might be permanently crippled, or worse. Who needed other conflicts, she asked herself, when you had those problems to deal with?

Forcing herself into a lighter mood, Jen tried to grab her new positive attitude and hang on tight. One thing was for sure, Dana was going to be really, totally upset when she found out what kind of guy she had bled all over!

And she *would* find out. Jen grinned all the way back to her hotel.

The doctors had reassured her that Dana was healing and should regain consciousness about the time Jenny arrived back in Washington. She'd see her friend tomorrow, and start teasing her about the gorgeous guy she would have seen, if she had just opened her eyes a little sooner.

The subject of Jen's mischief was on his porch the next morning, while darkness still lingered.


GARRETT HAD BEEN bushed enough to manage a few hours' sleep, but the rest of last night was haunted with disturbing dreams of a red haired, green eyed woman—and not the good kind of dreams a guy wanted.

His earlier hollow, uneasy feelings had followed him to bed and tangled him in his sheets with a stream of chaotic nightmares. Pictures had flashed in his head, like stop-action film, of him trying to run to Dana's rescue. But he ran and ran, never getting any closer, as each screen flashed and a time clock ran madly. He shook that horror off only to flash on a picture of her lying broken and bleeding in his arms, her skin peeled open, inner parts raw and exposed. Then it switched to one where he was looking up at a helicopter hovering overhead, descending slowly, but the blood and heart pulsing under the pressure of his palms stopped suddenly, before the rescue vehicle reached the ground.

"No!" He jerked up in bed. "It didn't happen like that!" He shouted himself awake. Rubbing his forehead he stretched to grab a glass of water, whispering to himself, "She lived! I know she did." Shaking off the lingering terror, before curling back down in bed, he had been half afraid to sleep. He hadn't had nightmares like that since he was a little kid. Even just lying there awake, his thoughts had coiled with tension and worry.

Wondering, now, if Dana was home with her own doctors; was Jenny back yet? He worried that Dana might have gotten hurt worse in the transfer; Jenny had been so stressed he was concerned she might have had a car accident on the long drive back.

Hell! Stop this. They're fine, or you would have heard ... then it hit him.

No. He wouldn't have heard. Why would anyone call him?

Damn. He wasn't a worrier by nature. What was wrong with him? He checked his clock. 4:18 A.M., too early to call anyone, especially Jen, she needed all the rest she could get.

Realizing he wouldn't get any more, he had given up and gone out to turn on the Northwestern News channel. Dana had made headlines before; if there was any further news about her, this is probably how he would hear it. When nothing alarming scrolled across the screen by the time he'd finished brewing himself a pot of strong coffee, he told himself everything was *fine!* Twice. Then headed off to for the shower to soak his head.

He gave his horses a special treat. He cleaned their hooves and gave them each a bucket of oats and a nice juicy apple. Patiently, he curried and groomed them while they munched on their morning hay. The long, gentle, brush strokes brought him easier, matching thoughts. He pictured himself comforting and stroking tangled red hair back from a pale forehead, brushing his fingers across a soft white cheek, soothing his thumb across the rusty trail of freckles over her nose . . . His buckskin snorted, and shifted, twisting his neck back to cast him a wall-eyed stare.

"Hey, who asked your opinion? Mind your own business, Corky, or no apple for you next time," he threatened, grinning, giving the horse a finishing pat.

Getting into his truck, he left early for the site. He'd be grateful for all the long, hard hours of work they'd need today, catching up. It would keep his mind from straying; keep his fingers from making the call it was too soon to make.

What if Dana woke up and Jenny wasn't there yet?

He couldn't, wouldn't, imagine how hard that would be on Dana. Hell! He wished Jenny would just call and tell him Dana was okay! But he would just have to wait patiently—or impatiently. He'd give her two days, he bartered with himself. Or maybe, two days since she had left, that would be tomorrow afternoon ... or tomorrow morning—

JENNY MISSED Dana's first words. It was just as well.

# Chapter 3

WAKING IN A PANIC, Dana tried to sit, and screamed long and shrill; tried to lay back, and rasped a collection of every known curse. She passed out from pain without ever opening her eyes.

The local doctors had reduced her pain meds after the transfer, to bring her around to accurately assess her problems. They wanted to speak to her about what hurt.

Clearly, what hurt was pretty much everything!

As she had experienced severe head trauma, the staff had hoped to check her ability to speak.

Dana had expressed her feelings very eloquently—if not elegantly. Hopefully, she would have a more extensive, and much less colorful, vocabulary when she *was* feeling better.

The same local practitioner had both Jenny and Dana as patients; she knew the pair well. She was on hand again the next time Dana woke briefly, asking "Where am I", able to greet and reassure her. The doctor told her she was at home, in the hospital, after an accident, and that Jenny was fine and would be there shortly. Jenny would tell her all about it as soon as she arrived.

" 'kay," Dana whispered, already skidding back into sleep.

She didn't really understand why she was there, but it must be okay; Jenny was coming. She was so tired, she must not have gotten any sleep lately. Her body hurt all over. Did she go sailing off the high bars again and miss the mat? That would teach her to not forget her spotter, she knew better! A nap sounded nice while she waited; Jen would tell her what idiotic thing she'd done this time. Dana just hoped there hadn't been an audience and her professional pride remained intact.


THE DOCTOR AND surgeons had decided it might be best for Jenny to ease her friend back over details of the traumatic experience, while they listened from the hall; allowing them a sense of privacy, but ready to act if needed. Jenny had already called, and agreed. Just in from Montana, she was dropping their bags at her house. After grabbing a quick shower and fresh clothes, she would arrive shortly.

As soon as Jen placed her warm hand over Dana's, those long-sealed eyes opened groggily, their green as murky as a stagnant pond. Her hair was a flattened, oily tangle of red curls bound up in bandages. She looked fantastic to Jenny—purple, green and yellow bruised face, lumpy lips, and all!

Dana croaked, "What happened? Did I fall? Wait ... the vacation. Is it over?"

Jenny squeezed her hand, pleased. Dana's brain was working, so far so good!

"You remember the vacation then, Dana?"

"Not really," Dana sighed.

The doctors had been concerned that the battering on Dana's head might have caused problems, or she might just have blocked memories from trauma. They had advised Jen to take her through slowly, see how much she could recall with help, but not tell her too suddenly. Pulling her chair closer, Jenny got comfortable. Tucking dark wings of hair behind tiny ears, she leaned forward in her chair, so they could see each other's faces better. Her steady blue gaze silently assessed her friend for a while before she thought to ask, "Hey, do you want some water?"

"Just a gallon, or two," the scratchy voice answered.

Reaching for the large cup and straw, she was thankful Dana's humor seemed to have survived, also. Then, holding Dana's hand, she slowly took her step by step through their recent trip. When reminded, Dana remembered the hotel, the charming town of Livingston, the drive south down along the Yellowstone River.

"Then we got to the entrance and—"

"Stone arch," Dana volunteered, "Basalt, beautiful. For the people ..." she breathed around her swollen and cracked lips.

"Yes! Wasn't it something?" Jenny's dimples flashed in her smile of delight. Her friend was finally starting to do more than just whisper agreement.

She saw a slow smile cross Dana's face before her eyes popped wide, and with the first tinge of excitement in her voice, Dana blurted, "Elk and babies!"

"You remember Mammoth. Wasn't that amazing? And, weren't they cute?"

Dana tried to nod, winced, and just said, "More water."

Jenny refilled the cup and slowly continued their journey. When she got to Obsidian Cliff, she saw a frown etch deep furrows on Dana's pale forehead.

"Did I miss it?" she asked in a small voice.

"The cars blocked everything, remember? We couldn't stop."

"Oh, yeah. Go back."

"Ah ... right," she answered softly, glad Dana could recall, but sad she'd been unable to keep that promise. Jen forced fresh gaiety into her voice, clasping her friend's uninjured hand in both of hers. "Then we had a picnic. Do you recall that? We went to that wonderful, ancient ranger station and found a picnic table at the edge of the campground. There were bear warnings posted everywhere! Even those notices bolted right onto the top of the picnic tables! 'Watch out for bears! Don't leave food out!' We had peanut butter sandwiches, and all kinds of things that were listed as being the most attractive to bears. We gobbled our lunch, looking over our shoulders as we swallowed. Do you remember what you told me?"

"What?"

"You set the camera on the table and told me, very firmly, that if I saw a bear to be sure to take a picture first, then I could run like hell!" Jenny's laugh was merry as she saw the faint smile on Dana's face.

"Did you?"

"Take a picture?"

"See a bear?" Dana asked.

"Oh, no, but while you were still eating I walked down to the historic ranger station, and came tearing back to get the camera...," Jenny paused, tensed, afraid and unsure what reaction this memory would bring. She had not meant to address this yet, but the words had just tumbled out of her mouth thoughtlessly while—

"Like a kid, excited!" Dana leaped in. "Your first buffalo!" She actually smiled at the memory, without any reserve, or even any catch on that fateful word.

"Right." Jenny blew out the breath she'd been holding. "You remembered!" *And didn't fall apart*, she noted privately.

There had been a huge buffalo grazing in a grassy meadow across from the Ranger Museum's parking area. Jen had run back to grab Dana and the camera, thrilled at her first buffalo sighting. Laughing at her excitement, Dana had warned her not to get too close. Jenny had worked in behind some sturdy tree trunks on a hill above the buffalo to get her shots, nervously peeking over her shoulder all the time, making sure a bear wasn't sneaking up behind her after scenting her peanut butter breath.

Meanwhile, Dana had brought the car down and backed it into a parking slot, so they had a safe place to view the buffalo through the front windshield. Well, view the rear of the buffalo, anyway. For the next half hour they watched it graze happily, totally oblivious to their presence behind him. A recent late summer storm had greened the bottom of the meadow to an almost springtime brilliance. The big shaggy buffalo was clearly in his idea of heaven, munching the new greens, moving a few feet, feasting on more, his tail busily swinging side to side to swat flies. From their viewpoint, he had looked more like a big shaggy dog, wagging its tail happily. They laughed, enjoyed the sight until the buffalo grazed away, then continued on.

"Happy as a fuzzy puppy, wagging his tail," Dana laughed, coughed in pain, and settled for a subdued, lumpy smile.

Though Dana's words followed Jenny's memories, she blanched at the guilt that returned. She'd spent long hours waiting beside Dana's bed, wondering if maybe they hadn't seen the buffalo as a placid, happy pet, or fuzzy version of a cow, maybe Dana wouldn't have ... But, those were wasted regrets. Jen had others.

She knew Dana hadn't jumped from the car because she thought buffalo were harmless. Just the reverse! She had clearly recognized the extreme danger to the children, and run straight into it, while Jenny had just sat frozen, terrified, like everyone else!

Except Dana. And later, Garrett.

Looking up at her friend, she shook off the remembered terror, amazed Dana could think of a buffalo and smile, even try to laugh, at how funny it had seemed then. Had she blocked the other memories so thoroughly? Jen wished she could stop now; she had to continue for her dear friend's sake.

"Ah ... then after our picnic we took the road across the park to Canyon."

"Later," Dana said.

"Yes, that's right. We decided to do that later so we could spend a whole day, do some hikes around the rim. So," Jenny paused a moment, sighed, hearing the shakiness in her voice. "We turned south toward Yellowstone Lake. Do you remember the horse corrals we passed?"

She saw a frown come back to Dana's face as her eyes seemed to narrow in concentration and confusion. Jenny just held her breath now, and waited.

They had just turned uphill, where the raised road was more like a bridge between a gully on the inner right-hand side and herds of buffalo grazed a vast lower meadow to the left, when the cars had stopped on the grade.

Jenny watched, not breathing, surprised to see a smile cross Dana's features before recalling that, at first, they had both laughed at the antics of the photo-hungry tourists.

Then Dana gasped, tried to lunge up in the bed, her good arm flailing.

"NO! No! The child, the child!" she began to scream, thrashing. "No! N-O-O-O-o-o!" Her eyes were open, but not focused anywhere in the room.

"Dana! Oh God. Someone quick, help me! She's hurting herself!"

Jenny lunged, frantically slapping the call button, even as the doctors, listening unobserved in the hall, burst in to restrain and care for the patient.

"It's okay, honey. Okay," Jenny wept as she captured Dana's hand and held it tight between her own. "The child is okay. Dana, listen, please! It is okay, the child is okay. Dana, shush now honey, the child's okay. You saved her!"

None of Jenny's words could breach the terrible memories screaming in Dana's mind.

The doctors held the patient down until the sedative started to work, then eased her back down in bed, reconnecting the tubes she had torn loose in her frenzy.

"The child, that poor little girl ..." Dana's anguished words wound down to whispers as she finally lost consciousness again, to Jenny's blessing this time.

Shaken to her soul, crying, Jenny refused to let the doctors also sedate her. She needed to be prepared and ready when Dana woke again. If she could just quit shaking. Still trembling, Jen finally was able to stand and leave the room on wobbly legs, seeking an orderly to set up a video machine in Dana's room.

She needed to be doing something; needed to help, to be ready when Dana woke next time. Thank God for that tape!

She should eat, but she couldn't. Just the thought had her stomach turning over. But thank God she did have the tape! She would get everything ready, then sit by Dana's bed and wait. Just wait. Soon it would be better. She would sit and concentrate on that. Only that. And wait. Already things were better. Dana's head seemed okay. She could recall so much.

Too much.

Jen had to constantly block the horror of those moments from her own mind; she couldn't imagine the pain and terror that memory held for Dana. But she had the tape. It wouldn't erase those moments from Dana's mind, or heal the damage caused, but it would help.

Spotting an orderly, Jen chased him down.

Once she had, all she could do was wait, and pace, and wait, chewing her lip raw, watching over her friend. And waiting.

AFTER MAKING SURE his crane arrived and the truss work was proceeding smoothly, Garrett was able to spend most of the day at his other job sites. Roaming around checking up on his other crews and projects suited his restless need to do something useful, to quit listening and waiting for his cell to ring.

Returning to the problem site that afternoon, he joined his crew and started the roof sheathing as the last trusses went into place. They took advantage of the crane to hoist most of the roofing materials into place, then worked late into the evening sealing in the roof, until the light began to fade. After the crew headed home, he drove over to check a final site, where his office trailer was located.

Rolling sore shoulder muscles, he checked out the plumbing contractor's work, noting the inspector's sign off, stapled to the framing. Taking it to make a copy for his files, he closed himself in his tiny office in the construction trailer, determined to stay put until he had dealt with the problem he had nearly forgotten about. But he couldn't just sit around waiting to hear from Jenny. That would make him crazy.

So he would deal with what he could and should—the bid for that jackass.

It was hard to believe he had imagined that *he* had problems on that fateful day. Mere days before, yet it seemed almost like a different lifetime, now.

Jim and Sarah Wentworth, his favorite clients, had thrown a house warming party for their wealthy friends to showcase their new home and its builder. It had generated a number of referrals for Garrett—referrals had been the source of his business success. One call referencing the party had sent him to meet a man south of Jackson, Wyoming, early that terrible day.

46

He had scheduled the appointment early, hoping to avoid the worst traffic on the only direct route to and from his destination, south through Yellowstone Park. Passing through Jackson Hole, he arrived early and decided to walk the site before the client arrived.

It was a stunning property, heavily wooded, along the Snake River. He took his time, listening to the birds waking and singing their greeting to the day in the fresh, woodsy air, accompanied by the crisp splash of water in the river. He familiarized himself with the setting, identifying the best home site to create the least alteration to its natural beauty. Taking pictures, he made notes of his questions regarding surveys and utility easements.

He could hardly wait to see what the architect had done with the house plans. But wait he did.

He had returned to his truck to await the client, due any minute ... and waited ... waited ... then waited some more. An hour had passed when, after trying the man's number several times, getting only a busy signal, Garrett had stepped over to his truck to leave when a shiny, silver, high-end SUV plowed up to stop beside him.

The blackened windows hid the driver. When the car door opened, first to emerge were a brand new pair of highly detailed boots—that no cowboy would be caught dead wearing—followed by crisp creased slacks and a beefy body contained in a bright polo-shirt, a designer emblem embroidered on its pocket. Gold flashed on thick, well-manicured fingers and wrist, a thick neck supported a ruddy grinning face of the same width. Thinning hair that slicked back from a salon-tanned forehead was an unlikely shade of black for a man of his obvious years. Hitching up his slacks, he took a stride toward Garrett, hand already extended when he stopped, turning back to pull a set of plans out of his vehicle. He turned back to Garrett with a hearty, unapologetic grin, booming out a greeting.

"Glad you could make it, Gavin buddy!"

*I could?* Garrett blinked, too stunned to even correct his name.

He watched the man stretching out that jeweled and manicured paw again, then suddenly dipping into his pocket instead, pulling out a cell phone, watching Garrett cheerfully as he spoke into it.

"Hey darling, miss me already?" He tapped the rolled plans against his leg, his chuckle deep and intimate.

47

Uncomfortable, Garrett's fingers twitched to grab the plans and go look at them elsewhere, while the man spoke to his wife. He felt like the worst eavesdropper as the man murmured to her to keep the sheets warm as he'd be back soon. Well, that explained the delay! The man's wife probably didn't appreciate the meeting interfering with their romantic vacation.

Garrett's eyes never leaving the plans, he was relieved when the man flipped his phone closed, dropped it in his pocket, and tapped the plans on his palm saying, "Now. Where were we, buddy?"

Garrett extended his hand for the plans and got a bone crushing handshake instead.

Right. That's how far they had gotten. Forcing his grimace into a grin, he nodded and said, "Great property you have . . ." Pausing when his client held up a hand and fished his phone back out of his pocket.

"Ben! Well how the hell are you, buddy? No, just got in last night. Yeah, we'll have to get a game of golf in." He swung the plans back and forth—practicing his swing while he talked. Garrett's eyes followed.

"No, left the wife and kids at home. Man's got to have a little fun, heh, heh."

The curves the plans were drawing now in the air were clearly not the wife's, Garrett suspected wryly—nor were those warm and waiting sheets.

"Bull!" Suddenly the plans stabbed at the air. "Don't tell me he won't take my deal! What the hell did I hire you for if you get weak in the knees the first time someone gives you a little flak? You tell that sum bitch who he's trying to play hardball with. I'll ruin him. Fine! You do that! Just handle it!" Clicking off, he immediately re-dialed. Looking up at Garrett with a smug grin, he held up the plans, one finger raised as if to ask for another moment, then he was talking again, shouting orders at someone, the plans now thumping Garrett's truck like a club being used on someone's head.

Garrett folded his arms over his chest, turned his head away, and gazed at the wooded lot that had seemed so pristine and serene earlier. Teeth clenched, he tried to blank out his expression and hearing, rousing only when a tap on his shoulder from the plans made him realize he was being addressed.

"So. Heard some great things about you fella. Saw the Wentworth's house, so you'll do. But listen, great meeting you, Gavin, but I gotta run. Time is money you know! Heh, heh. Give me a call." He was already turned heading back to his car when he suddenly stopped. "Almost forgot." He shoved the plans at Garrett, whose gut screamed at him to turn the job down. Now! But his conscience, nagged by the client referral, made his hand clasp them.

"Just look those over and get me a bid pronto," the man instructed, before backing his fancy SUV over a patch of delicate wildflowers, then gunning off between the trees.

Garrett opened the door of his truck, set his clipboard on the passenger seat, and tossed the unopened plans on the floorboards. Climbing in, he glanced at his watch and swore. Carefully he pulled his door closed without slamming it. The traffic heading back through Yellowstone would only be the next of the day's headaches.

Back then.

Back when he thought *he* had problems.

A thought that shamed him now. Still ... the bid needed to be dealt with.

And he was waiting again. But with more dread than impatience this time.

Checking his cell one more time, seeing no message from out-of-state, he forced the worry out and focused on something he could act on, something he could control. And the perfect target for his frustration.

Finding the manila folder in his in basket, where he had stuffed his handwritten field notes, he dropped them on his desk along with the still unopened architectural plans. As he booted up his computer to bring up all his digital photos, he was shaking his head again, still baffled that his favorite clients, Jim and Sarah, could even have the man as an acquaintance, much less a friend they referred to him. He had almost given them a call, but hadn't figured out quite how to ask them why they had sent him such an asshole. They were the nicest people, he didn't want to embarrass them, or let them down, but he knew he had to find a way to avoid taking this job. It would ruin more than his digestion. He'd worked hard to build his reputation and referrals. Taking the job on the Jackson site was sure to destroy them one way or another—and give him nothing but grief.

Scrolling down to locate the pictures he had taken of the site that day, he didn't need to look up *which* day he sought. That terrible date was—and forever would be—burned in his memory from the tragedy that followed.

Forcing all other thoughts from his mind, he started working out the materials and labor and off-site costs for the bid, careful not to miss any potential expenses, making sure to add in premiums for having to deal with such a jackass. If he got stuck with the job, he knew already that he would earn them.

As he worked he felt an evil grin crease his face. He thought about how he might file the completed bid under A for Asshole. Seemed fitting, easy to remember, but his professionalism just wouldn't go quite that far. Maybe R for Rude? What was the guy's real name anyway? He paused to check. Jenkins, Ralph Jenkins.

Perfect! He could file him under J for Jerk and call him RJ—if he was ever unlucky enough to have to speak to him again—or *not* speak to him, as the last meeting had turned out. Garrett could just see the man's chest puffing with more hot air to be called RJ, never knowing his contractor was calling him Rude Jerk instead.

Garrett smiled at the sweet mental revenge, and labored over the more specific getting even. He had a bid to fax. A bid he had no desire to win, so he would price it accordingly. Exorbitantly!

After sending the bid off and filing it, he felt cleansed, facing the rest of his paperwork with renewed energy. He proceeded to update the construction journals for each of his other projects, from his notes. Printing out each of the progress reports, he completed the papers for the banks involved with each job. As each completion target was met, he filed for the portion of each construction loan due for that phase. He would run to town tomorrow and drop off the funds requests at the banks, then take his bookkeeper the lists of subcontractor and crew payments due on those phases, to process as soon as the funds were transferred into the Hearth Homes account.

It was very late when he completed all the paperwork that he liked to handle personally. It was a hassle, but he needed to stay on top of his projects; the extra paperwork was his way of doing so.

Tonight, however, it had just been busy work. Before heading home, Garrett released himself to personal issues. Bringing up his internet connection, he typed Dana's name into a search engine, pulling up several links to her business and to events where she had performed. Clicking on a sport's magazine link, a picture came up, of Dana gracefully airborne on the parallel bars, with the article

It made his heart ache. It made his lips tighten, his throat hurt, and his eyes burn. He saved the download, but had to shut the computer off and turn away. He had hoped he could hold the pictures of her flying through her air ballet on the bars in his dreams, but the pain told him it would not chase the nightmares away—only make them worse. Shutting off the lights, he headed home to try to sleep. He knew Dana could never be the same as in that picture, no matter how he wished and dreamed for a miracle.

THE CHILD LOOKED LIKE an angel in her fuzzy-knit bed jacket against the stark white sheets of the hospital bed. Her dark blonde hair had been precisely parted in the middle, and braided on either side, with pale pink ribbons woven in. A soft fringe of bangs covered the bruises on her pixie-like face. Huge amber eyes glowed, overwhelming pale cheeks and a tiny rosebud of a mouth.

Gretchen gazed seriously and earnestly into the camera as her parents, crying and smilingly, framed either side of her bed.

"Danka, Miss Dana." The soft, sweetly accented voice said.

"My name is Gretchen. You saved me from that mean buffalo! I love you. My mommy and daddy love you." She crinkled her nose a minute, translating her thoughts. "My brother thinks you're very pretty. I do too." She added shyly, a soft blush pinking the round cheeks.

The tape rolled while the little one was clearly thinking of what else she wanted to say. Her mother whispered in her ear.

"I have to go back to my home. I can't see you." A worried little frown creased her forehead. "The hospital people say you are too sick." Her lips quirked down, but her little voice firmed. "I want you to get well, Miss Dana, so I can see you again and thank you again." Then her sad expression suddenly brightened.

"My daddy says I can come see you sometime. In the airplane! So please get well so I can say thank you. Did you like the flowers my mommy and daddy sent? The teddy bear was from me. I hope you like it," she added, shy again.

"I love you Miss Dana. Bye-bye." She gave a little wave and a tooth-missing-in-the-front grin, that was so adorable, both Jenny and Dana were crying when the videotape ended.

"She's such a little doll, so precious," Dana sobbed and smiled at the same time. "Oh thank you God, she's all right! I just can't believe she's okay. I'm so happy! Why can't I stop crying? I never cry, you're the crier, Jen."

51

"Relief." Jen got up and turned off the set, feeling it herself, then went to give Dana a careful hug, and more tissues.

"You know, her parents don't speak much English, but that little one's amazing. She was speaking for her whole family." Jenny explained. "They left me a business card and I will email them tonight that you've woken up and your brain seems okay. When they had to leave, the doctors were still afraid of swelling and damage, so they will be very happy."

"It was so thoughtful of them to make that video before they left for Germany," Dana got out between her tears of relief. "I never would have believed she was really okay, if I hadn't seen for myself."

Jenny nodded, so thankful she had the tape, especially after Dana had to be sedated earlier. She had made sure it was set up and frozen on the still image of the little girl, before Dana ever reawakened, so it would be the first thing she would see. And, it had worked. Dana seemed more relaxed now, ready to hear whatever bad news the doctors had for her own prognosis. They would be meeting with her in the morning to go over her injuries and medical status. Everyone had felt that Dana's mind needed to accept the trauma and be reassured the child was really safe, before she would be ready to deal with her own physical concerns.

That had proved so true. Jenny said a silent thanks again to little Gretchen for her tape, as she listened to Dana try to begin to face the rest.

"I remember the cars stopping. We were laughing at the herd of tourists rushing to take pictures. We thought whatever it was would surely rush off in fear, unseen, from such an unruly crowd." Dana's lips tightened, but she didn't flinch now, from the memories.

"It was funny until the buffalo herd jumped on the road, the kids, the screams. I remember running, an angry black eye, grabbing the girl, pain, sharp pain, everything was spinning and then...nothing." Dana's eyes shifted to Jenny's, capturing them in a direct gaze, her soft voice firmed.

"Tell me, Jenny. Now. I must know what happened. I need to hear it all."

Jenny couldn't stall any longer, but she couldn't look in Dana's eyes as she recalled that horrifying time. Gazing at her hands twisted in her lap, her voice was shaky as she told Dana how she had seen the bull toss his horns; seen Dana go flying and disappear over the edge, out of her sight. Everyone screaming.

52

Jenny had jumped from the car, run to the side and looked down at the bottom of the hill...

"There was a man," her voice stumbled, chin quivering, "Oh God, if it hadn't been for him..."

The ache growing in Jenny's throat cut her words off. Tipping her head back, she tried to keep the tears filling her eyes from spilling. Breathing deeply through her nose she tried, for Dana's sake, to regain her control. As the lump clogging her throat eased, she was able to swallow, sniff, and begin again.


"There was a man ... "

# Chapter 4

" ... A MAN NAMED Garrett. Garrett Hearth. He...," Jenny swallowed, a fragile smile trembled at the corner of her mouth. "Such a wonderful man," she breathed, "he ..." As memories rushed at her she faltered, eyes blinking rapidly, head tipped up again, trying to keep the moisture welling in her eyes from rolling down her cheeks. Lips tightening, she fought for control.

"He ran after." Ducking her head, Jen took a moment then tried again. "After the bull, ah," seeming unable to say *gored*, "hit you off the road, he ran up, and jumped after you. No one else could move—or did. I remember shrieking your name, over and over. Everyone was screaming something. Except that man. He tore downhill to do something to help. But ... from above, when I looked down and screamed to you, you...," Jenny lifted eyes glittering with tears and a wordless plea for her friend, "you didn't move. You didn't even move! What could he do? What could anyone do? You just lay there, a...," Jen lost her struggle for control, sobbing, "a bloody pile of clothes, and I thought ... Oh Dana, I thought you were dead!"

"Gross, huh?"

Dana's soft attempt at a joke just made Jenny sob harder and lunge for her perhaps wanting, needing, to give her a hug and give, and receive, comfort. But Jen didn't seem to know how or where to hug with all the wounds. Raising her good arm, careful of the tubes, Dana pulled Jenny's head down to the bed where she could pat it and soothe her, aware her friend felt guilty for thinking her dead. Poor Jen. The horror she must have gone through in those moments, before she knew her friend was still alive. Even barely. Dana was glad she wasn't there! Well, she had to add, aware there anyway. It was hard to listen to; she swallowed a lump lodged in her throat.

"I didn't do anything!" Jen sobbed against her side. "I just stood there and screamed!"

"Hey, hey, it's okay, Jen," Dana soothed. "What could you have done anyway, huh? It's okay."

"He did." Jenny hiccupped, trying to stop her tears. "He did. He saved you!"

"Hey, Jen, please calm down," Dana repeated, wishing she could wrap an arm around her distraught friend. Instead, she tried to tease and ease her from her tears.

"Hey, you were freaked. I know I would have been. And you know how you are like that. I wouldn't have wanted your clumsy hands on me, you know! Now would I?" She tipped her head back a bit so Jen could see her teasing smile.

That seemed to work. At least it coaxed out a watery chuckle. It was a long time joke between the two that when something scared or freaked them out, Dana acted, and Jen froze or dropped everything she touched.

"Get me some more water, will you please, Jen?" Dana knew the chance to do something for her, no matter how small, might help her friend regain her composure.

With a last shudder, and deep breath, Jen filled a cup, put a long straw in it, and handed it to Dana. She fussed with the covers, adjusted the bed a little so her friend would be more upright, then pulled her chair to an angle where Dana could see her more easily, before trying to recount the rest of the events in a less emotional state.

"The man, Garrett, pulled the little girl out from under you. She was okay, mostly." Jen flicked reassuring blue, almost dry eyes up to Dana's.

"Then," Jenny looked back down at a tissue she was shredding in her lap, "he took off his shirt and pressed it against you, trying to stop the awful ... bleeding, until the helicopter came with the paramedics. It seemed like a very long time. It seemed like forever, but... They wouldn't let me near you, they kept me away..."

"Thank God," Dana said with mock horror, earning a brief shaky smile from Jen.

"He saved you, Dana! The paramedics said if Garrett hadn't stayed with you, stopped the bleeding... Well. Umm, so they rushed you by copter to emergency in Livingston hospital. You were unconscious for days! No one knew if. . . Everything was so torn and crushed. They operated on what they could. They were afraid of brain swelling and, ah, damage...maybe...," the last low words trailed away.

Jen's face brightened. "Then the crisis passed and though you were still sedated, they could transfer you back here. That was late yesterday. I drove the car back and got in today. And here we are. Here you are, thank God! Alive and ... ah, awake. The doctors want to tell you about the injuries, and stuff. Oh good, here they are now." Jenny finished with relief.

"I'll just grab a bite to eat and be back when they are through." Jen fled the room.

Dana let her escape. She knew how hard the recital had been and suspected her friend hadn't wanted to watch her hear any more bad news. That was okay. She wanted a chance to hear and absorb it in private first, anyway.

Dana hadn't been able to feel the terror she had seen in Jen's eyes as she retold the tragic accident. It was like hearing her talk about something that had happened to a stranger. She only recalled her terror for the child, and the black gimlet eye in that massive furred head blurring just before a short, sharp pain. Nothing more.

But she felt fear building in her now—a queasy terror of the unknown—as her doctors filed silently into her room. Jen had said something about crushed things. Not good. And there were several doctors—she only recognized one. Something was clearly very wrong beneath the bandages that swathed her whole left hand, arm, neck, shoulder, and head. As an athlete, Dana already knew from her own body awareness and pain that things were not all where they belonged.. And she feared they might never be. But she'd rather face the truth, than wonder.

As the doctors formed a semi-circle around the foot of the bed with their clipboards, she tried to prepare herself for the verdict, unconsciously, and unwisely, squaring her shoulders to face the news. Yeoow! The severe shock of pain at even that small motion told her the news was going to be very, very ... unpleasant.

And it was not unpleasant. It was bad!

Her pain medication had been held back so she would have a clearer head when the doctors spoke to her—unfortunately.

One of the doctors, she thought the neurosurgeon, had stepped forward to the head of the bed. "First, let's just do something about that awful head dress we've given you." He chuckled a little. "Not a very fashionable hat, is it?" He asked jovially, looking into her green eyes.

She would have been more cheered if he hadn't used a pen light to gaze at them.

"I'm not much of a stylist," he continued his attempts to cajole as he tried to unwrap her head bandage without yanking out too many of her snarled red curls. "Oh, much better!" He pronounced with a grin.

Dana might have grinned back if he hadn't taken out a tool and measured her head after saying it.

"Well," he stepped back, with that smile still pasted on his face so Dana couldn't tell what he was really thinking or seeing. "We will have to put another little head band on there, of course." He winked at her, "but it won't be so big. Maybe we can have the nurse jazz it up for you? We'll see if she has a pink bandage. More fashionable, don't you think?" He teased, trying to put a smile on her pale face.

"I've never really been fond of pink with my color of red hair. It clashes." Dana answered soberly, dousing his light attitude.

"Please," she pinned him, then turned those green eyes, that serious pale face, to the rest of her doctors, "just give it to me straight, okay?"

So they did.

Dana listened stoically. Her head felt light, but she didn't think it was from the temporary removal of all those bandages. Her stomach rolled, nausea churned and rose in the back of her throat, as she listened to their words, the harsh verdicts. She tightened her swollen lips, and took it all in silently, gathering the crucial information. She would think about it later, when she was alone. She would remember they were talking about her—not just a patient—later. She couldn't let herself feel it now. Let it sink in later—much later. Her body desperately needed healing. She'd hold off the fears, the thoughts, to give it more time—if she could.

She had suffered injuries before, many times in her profession, but never faced anything like this. Her strong will, the lessons learned in the past, should help her focus that will on letting her body do what it could by giving it the rest it needed, holding back the stress, until she could deal and act to start to help to rebuild it. So she didn't resist in any way when the doctors, concerned the news could put her into shock, mercifully renewed and increased her sedatives, before leaving her alone with her shattered body.

She welcomed the oblivion.

When Jenny returned, she was told by the head nurse to go home and rest. Her friend would need her more the next morning.

BY THE NEXT MORNING, when Garrett still hadn't received any word, he quit worrying about the future Dana would have to face.

The sick feeling in his gut had him worrying, once again, that the lovely redhead would have no future, at all.

It was way too early to call her friend, he convinced himself. After breakfast for himself and the horses, he forced himself to delay again. Still too early for most folks, he told himself as he got in his truck and headed into town with his paperwork. Besides, he recalled, with a different time zone, it was an hour earlier in Washington State. And it was too early in Montana for Garrett to hear bad news, if he must—it would always be too early.

Driving past the hospital in Livingston, he couldn't help wishing she was right there, where he could see her himself, instead of hundreds and hundreds of miles away. Pulling into the bank parking lot, he pulled out his cell to check for messages, forgetting he had checked just twenty minutes prior.

Nothing. Hell! He wished he knew if Jenny was just too busy with Dana awake now—he hoped—or too scared to call him with bad news.

Maybe she has just completely forgotten about you, dude!

That was a more comforting thought. Both the girls probably wanted to forget everything about their trip to Montana. Who could blame them? But he was tied to Dana. In more ways than he could rationally explain to himself. Her future was tied to his future. Somehow, he knew that; he needed that in some way. If he could make it happen, he would. If Dana had a future...

Refusing to let himself drift into negative thoughts, he closed his eyes, tried to mentally send her his wish for strength and health, and... Jumping from his truck he tightened his lips and tried to yank his mind back to business. Gathering his paperwork, he strolled into the bank to meet with his loan manager.

GAZING OUT THE window, early that morning, her head turned away from the door, Dana heard the soft tap of heels come down the corridor then stop abruptly at her room. Only Jen would wear hard soled heels in a hospital. Turning her head slowly on the pillow, she let her friend see that she was awake.

"Come on in. It's safe," Dana said in a subdued voice.

Jen slipped in and stood where Dana could see her, raising a silent inquiring eyebrow.

Dana caught herself on the verge of shrugging. "Well, the good news is that nothing is paralyzed or in danger of being amputated. Beyond that...," Dana sighed heavily. "Beyond that, everything depends on how things heal and knit, physical therapy, and so many other variables, that there's just no point in getting stressed over it. They just won't know anything for certain for some time—

"But," a tiny spark lit Dana's green eyes, "they *are* sure I don't have *any* brain damage. I have a what-ever-they-call-it scan to prove it to anyone that tries to claim otherwise!"

"Ah," Jenny smiled, "so the next time I tell you you're crazy, you'll just whip out your scan?"

"Exactly!" Dana claimed, trying to push up against the pillows.

Jenny rushed to help raise the bed and help her sit upright.

"So," Dana grinned, shakily, "since I obviously won't be in training for some time, I've decided I deserve to be indulged. I want you to go out and smuggle some Starbucks Coffee Ice Cream in for me. And don't chintz! I want my own container for myself, so get extra for you. Then you're going to sit down and we're going to have a girl talk. I want to hear everything you know about that 'wonderful man' that saved my life."

"Got it. You want your 'jamies too, for this pajama party?"

"You read my mind. I'm already getting tired of having my butt hanging out of this gown. When I count all the days I didn't know it was hanging out...well! Bring my older ones though, we'll have to cut one of the shoulders out."

"Anything else?"

"You need to ask?"

"Okay, I'll smuggle in a king size Almond Joy bar for you also, just don't squeal on me if you're caught."

"Moi?" Dana gave her most innocence look, and smiled until Jenny left and she could sink back into her silent brooding.


GARRETT CAME FLYING out of the bank as if he had just robbed it, wrestling to pull his phone from his jean pocket as he jogged to his truck. Jumping in, slamming the cab door, he flipped his phone open, punched a button and held it to his ear, waiting with little patience. He felt the phone vibrate in his pocket while he was inside and jumped straight out of his chair, startling the bank manager and abruptly ending their friendly banter.

"You should have all the papers you need there. Any questions, call. Gotta run." By the time Garrett tacked a "thanks, bye" on, he was already pushing though the outer bank doors.

He had one message—from one of his foremen. Well, hell. Biting down his frustration, he dutifully returned the call, keeping the conversation as brief as possible. He would swing by the lumberyard and pick up the requested supplies before he dropped off the papers at the bookkeeper's and left town.

But that had done it, flipped his switch, he was acting like a mad man. He couldn't convince himself to wait any longer to bug Jenny. It was after ten in the morning in Washington State by now. Taking a deep breath, he punched in her cell number. He had gone beyond wondering if Dana was awake yet—or worrying about the future she would face when she did—to the fear he had felt beside her, waiting for the rescue team, hoping she was still alive. The ringing stopped and an automated voice answered informing him the voice mailbox was full. He tried her home phone number next, holding his breath as it rang.

When the message machine answered, he blew out a sigh of relief.

"Jenny, it's Garrett from Montana, I...," the dial tone sounded. "...need to know she's okay," he groaned to empty space. Slapping his phone shut, he dropped his forehead down to bounce hard before resting on the steering wheel. He felt tortured, cut off ... scared. Clenching his jaws, he raised his head, breathed in deeply through his nose, trying to control the pain and panic that twisted through his gut. He opened his phone again, switching it from vibrate to the loudest ring available, then placed it in his shirt pocket. Starting the truck, he put it in gear and headed off to complete his town errands.

By the time he reached the highway south out of town, he had almost convinced himself he was overreacting. He turned the radio on, volume cranked up, but he couldn't have named what songs played, or even hear the noise over that of his thoughts, on the long drive back to the construction site.

"HIS NAME IS Garrett. Did I tell you that? And damn, I forgot to call him again! Oh well, he has my phone number. Anyway, he's a local construction contractor in Livingston." Lowering her voice, Jenny grinned, "Lots of muscles, you know?" Not earning a smile from Dana with that comment, she continued on more seriously with her account. "He seems to know everyone, and is much respected. He was coming back through the park, got caught in the jam, heard the screams and ran up just as the buffalo tossed you. I heard he threw flares to stop the bull from chasing after you, but I didn't see that part. I was ... well, frozen, staring, well, never mind that part." Jenny shook herself.

"Then he plunged down the hill and kept you alive until the paramedics came." Leaning forward, she pinned earnest eyes on Dana's. "He is such a nice guy, Dana. You just can't imagine. He came by to see you in the hospital. Even brought flowers! I...I'm afraid I was feeling so scared and guilty that..."

"Guilty! Why?"

"Well, the vacation was my idea. And if I hadn't..."

"Jen! You idiot! I wanted to go as much as you. More probably."

"That's what Garrett said, but...I was so scared. Dana, I started crying all over the man!"

"No!" Dana started laughing, then stopped abruptly, trying to breathe her words out through pain. "You probably scared the hell out of him!"

"Oh, yes, I'm afraid I did. But he didn't run. He patted me and got me a tissue."

"This, of course, made you cry harder," Dana added knowingly. She chuckled at Jenny's shameful nod. "Oh, that poor man!"

It was no secret that Jenny was very emotional and notorious for crying like a heartbroken two-year old once she got started. Any attempt at comfort just made her bawl harder with floods of crocodile tears. Most men ran to save themselves from drowning once Jenny got her waterworks going.

"Oh yeah! Your savior, that poor man, pulled up a chair and started hugging me and rubbing my back, until I'd completely drenched his shirt!" Jenny laughed as hard now as she had cried then.

Dana looked like she was trying hard to hold back her hilarity. Her hand was holding her side as if to protect it from pain as she burst into an aborted giggle. "I was just imagining the look on that helpless man's face. It's just too funny! And ...,' she gasped for breath, "I don't even know what he looks like!" Which seemed to be even more hilarious to Dana—and catching.

Jenny was laughing so hard now she was wiping tears from her face. And she *had* seen the look on his face. The words pathetic, panicked, ready to bolt, barely began to describe him, it was comic! Jenny tried to stop laughing before she wet her pants, but when she and Dana got going like this—

A nurse stepping into the room to take Dana's temperature couldn't help but start chuckling herself.

"What's so funny? What's the joke?"

"Oh, God." Dana managed, trying to catch her breath. "No joke, just my crazy friend here. The guy that saved me came to the hospital and she lost it and threw herself on a total stranger and drowned him in tears."

"Did he run?" the nurse grinned.

"No!" Dana said amazed, "He just stayed and took it, apparently." Clapping a hand over her mouth she tried to keep from setting off more giggles.

"Wow!" The head nurse grinned, impressed. "Hey, wait a minute. Did you mean that guy back in Montana that stopped the bleeding?"

"Yeah," Jenny admitted. "What a cruel reward, huh? He was such a sweet guy."

"You know, I heard about him." The nurse sobered and spoke seriously, resting a gentle hand on Dana's good shoulder. "One of the paramedics that came to transfer you was with that park rescue team. He told me the paramedics originally thought the guy was your husband or boyfriend."

Puzzled, Dana quit grinning, "Why would they think that?"

"Well, he said the guy worked so desperately to save you, and ... ah, when they got there, I guess the guy had tears pouring down his face." She patted Dana's shoulder and smiled at her.

There was a hush in the room while Dana took this in, then suggested practically, "It was hot that day, it was probably just sweat."

"No, Dana. I saw it too," Jen added softly. "He was really choked up. I'd forgotten."

Dana tried to pass it off as a joke to hide how moved she was. "See Jen, you don't have to feel so bad now about getting him all wet?"

"Well, that time anyway." Jen gave a guilty little smile. "I'm afraid I gave him a soaker the second time, also," she giggled.

"That must be a brave man to go back for more torture," the nurse said in parting, whisking the empty ice cream cartons out of the room with a wink.

"So he came back?" Dana asked. "Oh, Jen! Sounds like he had a little crush on you, huh? No wonder he is so wonderful. Come on, confess all!" Dana tried to wiggle her eyebrows, but her head bandage ruined the effect.

"Oh, I think he had a BIG crush, all right, Dana."

"Reeaally? Tell!"

"He was really nice to me, Dana. He got the hospital to let me use the other bed in your room so I could sleep without leaving you. Then he got the administrator to tell the doctor I was your blood relative so they would release your medical condition to me. That was a big comfort!" Jen sighed with relief, then seeming to mull it over, murmured, "Well, kinda. But he was the most kind and considerate guy I think I've ever met." Sighing with a dreamy eyed smile, Jenny added, "He was like a big brother to me, Dana."

"Sounds like more than that to me," Dana teased.

Jen went quiet and gazed steadily at her friend for a while, before continuing softly.

"You should have seen the way he looked at you, Dana. Like he was... enchanted or something. No, don't snort at me, I'm serious! The way he touched you ... he stroked your cheek and asked you to open your eyes so tenderly, it gave me shivers."

Dana couldn't help herself, *she* shivered, fascinated. "Really? He did?" She could hear the softness in her own voice.

"Oh, yeah. He called you 'babe'. Not the yucky cool-jock kind of two syllable 'Ba-Be', but a sexy, soft, yummy 'babe'." She lowered her voice to recreate the word with a soft slow hum. "God! It was yum! He stroked your check and whispered, 'Open your eyes, babe'. Very sexy!" Jenny's dark winged eyebrows danced up and down.

A blush stole up Dana's cheek as if she felt that touch, unable to restrain a pleased smile. "Darn! And I missed that?"

Jenny taunted, "That should teach you not to sleep when a guy's trying to be sweet and sexy to you!"

No doubt! She gave her friend a playful scowl and challenged, "And YOU let them transfer me before Prince Charming woke me? Some nerve, Jen!"

Jenny just shrugged and gave her a silly grin.

"Well?"

"Well, what?"

"Well, what does he look like?" Dana demanded.

"Oh," Jenny thought it over for a while, "he's kind of hard to describe..."

"Try, brat!"

"He looks okay. Blonde and blue. Tall. He's really, really nice. Oh, and he's single."

"Hmmm." Dana didn't know if Jenny was playing with her or just trying to be diplomatic about the guy's appearance. In Dana's profession, good looking and built athletic guys were the norm, so she was less impressed by great looks than many women. A sweet guy that saved her life ... now that was impressive!

"I've got the newspapers from there at home. His picture is in them. I'll bring them by tomorrow so you can judge for yourself. "

"Thanks, and Jen? Another favor if you have time? Could you get all the pictures from our trip printed up and bring them to me?"

"Are you sure?"

"Yeah. I really need them. It wasn't all bad times. I need to see and remember the good ones right now."

"Sure. Okay. I get it. I'll get them done before I come back."

"Thanks. I'm bummed we didn't get our vacation. We'll just have to go back there!" Dana stated. She didn't notice that Jen hadn't made any comment before leaving the room.

IN YELLOWSTONE NATIONAL PARK, late summer was preparing to roll soon into fall. The tourists continued to pour in from the east, the south, and the west. But only at the northern entrance, at Gardiner, MT, did they pass beneath the great historic arch, as they had for over a hundred years, since it first announced the entry into the world's first national park. Except for this newest species in the area, now crowding all the roads and byways, the cycle of life continued on as it had for thousands of years.

The buffalo were gathering in great herds blanketing the open meadows beside the road. The battle was on for supremacy, when the wisest and strongest bulls challenged and claimed their victories. To either side of Buffalo Road huge storms of dust rose as bulls rolled and twisted in wallows, then rose to paw, snort, bellow, and charge each other for their rights. Sprinkled among the non-combatants were the bright butterscotch-colored calves of last spring, trying desperately to huddle beside their mothers. Yearling calves had taken on the darker brown coloring of maturity, though some still hovered as awkward teens with caramel-colored patches of down mixed in. They were the most confused and frightened of the group. As the bulls charged each other, chased away the weaker males and herded in the females, the yearlings nervously tried to follow their mothers while keeping a safe distance from the militant bulls.

The victors seemed to use the road as a defining and dividing line, herding their victories to the other side as they culled and claimed them. One yearling was shuffled with its mom to first one side of the road, then another, finally hesitating in the middle— as stalled as the tourists in their cars—as unable to determine the safest move with so many male bulls rumbling back and forth in such nasty moods. Vanquished bulls were fleeing, singly in shame, in all directions: through the woods and brush, into the refuge of the river, or trudging along the roads, leaving the scene of defeat.

In other areas of the park, it would soon be the bugling of elk, rather than the bellowing of buffalo, that marked the beginning of the mating season. The strangely beautiful, piercing calls of the proud antler-arrayed males fluted through the hills, catching the ear and attention of the sleek and elegant females gathered in clusters on hillsides and around ponds in the lush meadows.

It was the season for male mammals to call and gather in their ladies.

"HEY NOW, BOSS, would you stop that durned pacing back and forth? You're giving us indigestion!" complained one of Garrett's crew as they perched on coolers taking a lunch break.

Garrett scowled, then headed for the makeshift staircase, calling playfully over his shoulder, "I'll be back later to make sure you guys aren't slacking." He needed to find a project that he could do himself—pound a few nails, rip a few boards with a saw—and keep himself busy before he drove himself, and his crews, nuts. He couldn't just spend the whole day pacing and checking his phone for messages every ten minutes!

Putting his truck in gear, he headed home. His crews had everything under control on the sites. Garrett was just a nuisance today, micro-managing and getting in the way. He had been planning for some time to create some new grazing pasture for his horses. Today would be a perfect day to dig and set some fence posts and keep his body busy.

His mind ... well, that was hopeless until he got the call he needed, so he might as well get some work done in the meantime.

Sweat glistened on muscles rippling across broad shoulders, ran between the hard pecs on his chest, and followed the line of glinting golden hairs that arrowed down the bronzed washboard of his belly, as he strained to set a third post in the hard rocky ground. Garrett had long since stripped off his shirt to wipe away the sweat on his face and neck. His horses nickered their approval from the corral.

"Yeah, well you better be worth all this hard work," he called to them, swiping a hand through the hair on his head, lifting a gold thatch to catch a passing breeze. He headed into the house to take a break and get out of the hot sun for a while.

Reaching into the fridge, he pulled out a long neck and settled his hips back against the counter to take a long replenishing guzzle. When his head dropped back down after taking another deep drink, his eyes fastened on the phone on the kitchen wall. He stared at it for a moment, started to take a sip, but slapped the bottle down on the counter with a determined glint in his denim blue eyes. He picked up the phone and dialed a number from the emergency list attached to the fridge.

"Yes, I need the hospital administrator please," he snatched up a blank pad and pen as he waited.

"Bob, Garrett here."

"Hey, Garrett, how are you? Calling to discuss my new room you're going to build me?"

"Not yet." Garrett answered briskly. "I'm going to let you earn more brownie points first," he stated firmly.

"Uh oh. That doesn't sound good..."

"I need the name of the hospital you transferred my Yellowstone girl to." He heard a deep chuckle.

"Your Yellowstone girl?"

"Dana Revson." Garrett provided, a little impatiently.

"Oh, I know *who* you are talking about, buddy," Bob laughed. "I just didn't know she was *yours*."

Garrett didn't return the laugh or the friendly innuendo. "The hospital, Bob?" He bit it out tersely.

"Geez, Garrett! I'm looking it up, man. Hold your water." Bob found the file and read out the name of the hospital, including the address and phone number, before his good ole buddy bit his damn head off.

"Hope every things going okay with her," Bob offered.

"Yeah, me too. Bye."

66

DANA HAD SLEPT another four healing hours after her visit with Jenny when the nurse woke her to take a little food for dinner. She was hoping for something recognizable, like a nice beef or salmon steak. What she got was another tray of pureed mystery food, with sauce poured over it, and the inevitable quivering jelled-juice cube. Yum. No wonder she kept losing her returning appetite.

The nurse skillfully ignored her grimace and had just stepped out to get her medicine, when Dana was startled by the ring of a bedside phone.

It had never rung before. She glanced around; she was all alone in the room. Was she supposed to answer it? Managing to scoot over on the bed so she could reach it, Dana picked it up before it quit ringing, she figured it was probably an in-house hospital line.

"Yes?" She answered tentatively.

"Is this Dana's room?" A male voice inquired. There was a pleasant lightness and softness that Dana noticed in the deep tones. Always sensitive to voices, this one sounded like a deep male purr in her ear.

She couldn't explain why she didn't identify herself right away, but a static crackle indicated it might be a long-distance call.

"This is Dana Revson's room," she responded neutrally.

"Is she," then a pause, and a more pained and worried note. "Listen, I know you can't give me health details, but can you just tell me? Does she open her eyes now? Is she okay?"

Dana held her breath, eyes widening. It couldn't be ... could it?

# Chapter 5

THEN THAT INCREDIBLE male voice sounded again, more anxiously.

"Please, nurse, is she okay? Just tell me if she is okay."

Dana swallowed, how could she confess now?

"Are you a relative?" she asked professionally.

"No ... no... Just a friend ... but ..."

"Your name, please?"

"Garrett. Garrett Hearth."

Oh-my-god! Just as she had suspected. It was her hero calling!

Dana tried not to laugh giddily into the phone, feeling suddenly silly and shy, but a little imp and a desire to listen to his voice longer, lead her astray. She wasn't conscious of lowering her voice, of the playful husky tone that had crept into it. Garrett didn't notice at first, either, he was so intent on his mission.

"Garrett? The one who saved her life?"

"Ah ... well, I guess, but ... can I leave my phone number? So she can call when she's better? Or ready ... or, if she wants?" his voice trailed off.

What a sweetie, Dana thought. She wanted to know more about him, without giving herself away. He'd seen her when she was unaware; it seemed only fair, to turn the tables just a little.

"The paramedic report said that you were crying when they arrived. You two must be really good friends!" Dana, you dog, she chastised herself, but held her breath to hear his reply.

"Ah, that poor babe, she was so brave, so hurt. She's the hero, you know. Take good care of her. She saved that little girl's life," was his soft, sad answer.

Dana put her palm on her chest, trying to catch her heart before it melted all over the bed. And there was that yummy 'babe' Jenny had told her about! It sounded so good to hear. Much better than she had imagined.

Her voice was as soft as her mind, when she accidentally said out loud, "You have the sexiest voice, for a man." Whoops, Dana could feel her face redden.

There was a very long silence on the phone, before an abrupt and chilly reply.

"Listen, nurse, just tell Dana that Jenny has my cell number and to please call when she can. Thanks for the info." Click. He'd hung up!

Whoa, she liked that! Garrett had called for her, and when he thought the nurse was flirting with him, shut her down, wouldn't give out his number. Mucho points for this Garrett guy! She could feel herself half in love with her mystery man, already. The voice, the personality and tenderness, the consideration that Jenny had told her about, and ... Garrett had saved her life!

Dana didn't care if Jen was just teasing her about his looks, she was falling for a man whose insides she liked a lot—and that deep purr of a voice—oh, yes!

Or perhaps she was just suffering from drug induced giddiness? This was hardly her normal style. She prided herself on being cool, cautious, and analytical. A serious minded woman, she didn't flip over men. Normally.

Then depression swept over her. What was she thinking? He was just being nice. And she was no longer the normal woman that she was used to being. Dana had never had to worry that a man would find her attractive. She wasn't vain; she just knew she was always fending guys off.

Now she didn't have any attractions for a man. Scars crossed and puckered her upper body. Her once smooth, supple skin and muscles, were now mangled, misshapen. Men would still look at her as a friend, but the instant desire she was used to seeing, would no longer light their eyes. Or if it did, once she took off her blouse, that flame would gutter out fast!

Dana couldn't even begin to think about what these injuries would mean to her profession—or if she would still have her profession. Her doctors couldn't even tell yet if she would ever be able to raise her left arm at all, much less... Her arm and shoulder would be restrained for weeks, then with more surgeries, it would be months before she even had a basic idea of how well her left side would be able to function. First, she had to get through tomorrow.

It could be worse, lady. You could be dead!

She sighed. She was supposed to be a hero, like Garrett said. She wasn't feeling very heroic at the moment, but she felt good about saving the child—she wouldn't regret a single pain for that! And that was more than enough for her to feel good about right now, she determined. Pushing her whiny depression away, she would feel good and lucky for today.

And that voice! Now she had the sound of his voice to rumble sexily through her head. She could enjoy being his 'babe' for now.

But could she call him back? She chuckled, then gasped at the pain in her side. Not for a while, anyway. He'd recognize her voice as that flirty nurse's and hang up on her! She'd better have Jen return the call for her.

Her eyes did a double loop and roll, and she realized the strong medications were kicking in. The doctors had come this afternoon with grim news. Dana had agreed to a delicate but dangerous surgical procedure. The urgent surgery would be done early in the morning. The doctors said they wanted to keep her as motionless as possible until then. They were going to knock her out cold tonight and keep her heavily sedated until the procedure was over.

Dana nestled back against her pillows. She had forgotten tomorrow's concerns. She only had a chance to breathe 'babe' once, before she was dreaming.


LATE AFTERNOON SUNLIGHT slanted across a lush Yellowstone National Park meadow, silhouetting a pair of shaggy buffalo grazing lazily.

The gilded rays of low light threaded through a treed ridge picking out the matchstick clutter of dead logs scattered in the forest as they were everywhere throughout the park: tumbled on hillsides, lying like silvered bones in fields and along roadways, and jamming the rivers and canyons with new and tangled islands and dams after spring thaw. It was a natural sight, but visually surprising—even shocking—to park visitors accustomed to groomed and managed landscapes. Here the startling mass of fallen timbers weren't hauled off and cleared away until Nature chose to herself. It was a sight modern man rarely saw—a view lost to him since pioneers first came upon untouched lands and cut and cleared, removing all the downed trees to build and burn and removed all the debris. It was fire wood, fire hazard, but it was also habitat and cover for all the other creatures.

Nature had her own way of cleaning up the damage and deadwood of life, creating a fresh start, leaving only the priorities that mattered most in life and death: risk, strength, survival, and most of all rebirth and renewal. The dead clutter of the past burned away to prepare a clear path to the future. Nature's way of doing things was not always very pretty and not often very safe, but she always created new opportunities for the life that was ready to leap forward and grab hold and grow.

The summer of 1988 was known as the Summer of Fire in Yellowstone. There were fifty fires ravaging throughout the park until the snows of November did what all man's efforts could not, and snuffed the last one out. On Black Saturday, in late August of that year, over one hundred and fifty thousand acres went up in flames in one day, due to the tremendous winds Nature called to cull her land. Over two million acres of land lies within the boundaries of Yellowstone Park. That summer, thirty-six percent of it burned. All but a few of the large mammals survived.

Present day Yellowstone has the opportunists from those, and other, fires crowding right onto the roads.

The Lodge Pole Pine drops its cones to the ground to wait for fifty long years to open and spread their seeds. Renewal would be a slow process without the opportunity of fire used to burst the cones open and fling themselves far and wide in a newly barren, sun-blasted landscape to grow. The pines now cover the park with a solid blanket of fresh green rolling across the slopes and mountains, pushing out on the road rims for sunlight.

From disaster, new beauty is created.

Yellowstone Park is a testament to the changes wrought by nature and the promise of rebirth those changes of the future hold—without guarantee they will resemble either the present or the past.

As the dry heat of late summer rolled into fall, a flame could start, flaring into heat and fire from a bolt of lightning—or just a single spark.


"GARRETT? THIS IS JENNY. From Washington State?"

"Sure, Jenny. I remember you. How are you doing?" Afraid to ask the question that had tortured him for days. Days that seemed more like forever. He was pretty sure Dana was still alive when he had called yesterday evening and been connected to a room for her, but he still didn't know if she had ever come out of her coma—or ever would. He waited tensely for the little brunette's words.

"Dana ... Ah ... The nurse said that you called. I am so sorry..." Jenny's voice sounded ... shaky?

Garrett grit his teeth, preparing for bad news.

"I should have notified you sooner..."

Oh God! No! Garrett stumbled a few steps, dropping to sit on his tailgate, his free hand clinging to the edge. He barely felt the burn of the sun-heated metal on his palm, all his senses focused on the voice in his ear.

"...there was a chipped bone, a sliver that the doctors didn't notice until it started to migrate in the tissue. It...Well, it was too close to the heart and lungs ..."

His own heart and lungs seized, his guts plunged then rose back into his throat. Nausea and fear flushed through him as a cold sweat broke across his forehead and formed on his upper lip. He couldn't release his steely grip on the solidness of his truck to swipe at it. The voice on the phone receded as his jaws clenched, he tried to hold on through the ringing in his head.

The ringing. The phone. He must have cut the connection when his hand clenched. He couldn't talk now. Couldn't speak to anyone. Then he realized it was Jenny's number on the display. He punched it on.

"Yes?" His voice was raw and hard.

"I'm sorry, you must be busy," Jenny's voice rushed at him, breathless, apologetic. "I just wanted you to know. Dana made it through surgery today okay."

"What?" Garrett croaked, pulling in a deep, shaky breath.

"She's fine. They got the fragment out safely. She's sleeping again, but she woke after recovery. She reminded me to call you."

He tried to gulp down the lump lodged in his throat.

"She's awake?" He found he could breathe again. "I mean ... she will? She was awake? Talking?"

"Yes, that's why I'm so sorry! I should have notified you sooner. She woke a few days ago, but we've been so busy trying to see if she could remember. If her mind was ... Well, when she did recall, it was horrible. Luckily I had a tape from the little girl proving she was alive. So then she was okay." Jenny rushed to get the information out, seeming convinced she had caught Garrett at a bad time at work. "So she passed the surgery today and she's getting better. I'll call you in a few days. I promise this time. Bye."

"Jenny, wait!" A little embarrassed at the desperation in his voice, he added more casually, "Say ... if I wanted to send like a card, or something, where should I address it?"

72

Grabbing a pen from his pocket, he hastily inked Jenny's address on his forearm. She assured him she'd deliver anything to Dana then hung up.

Trying to stand, Garrett realized he was still a little light headed. Clothes drenched with sweat, he could smell the stink of fear on himself. But he could also smell the sage again, feel the slight draft of breeze on his face that brought the scent. He realized the sun was still shining and he could hear the buzz of a saw, the uneven rhythms of hammers and voices form the site. Sitting a few more minutes before rejoining the crew, he let relief wash the tension from his body.

A soft smile eased the haggard creases from his face. He felt a flame of hope burst free inside him, lighting a hot fire that sizzled along his tattered nerves until it exploded in his heart like a bright torch of joy and happiness. Merciful God! His Yellowstone girl was alive, awake and alert! The smile spread until it consumed his face.

He gladly suffered his share of ribbing from the guys that afternoon, before he could transfer the address to paper, and wash the ink off his arm. He often scribbled quick notes on his arm on site, but the out-of-state zip code stuck out like a sore thumb—not to mention his mile wide smile—causing plenty of leers, grins, and jests. He took it all well, never confessing its importance. Several of his crew saw the change in their boss, figured it out for themselves, and left the poor man alone.

Garrett showered, changed and took his truck into town later that afternoon to pick up some supplies. Stopping in at the florist's, he ordered a dozen fragrant yellow roses to be delivered by FTD to Dana's hospital. Next, he stopped at the UPS store and carefully packaged the crystal geode that had remained patiently on the front seat of his truck. Addressing it in care of Jenny's address, he debated over a card to send. Pawing through all the romantic cards, he decided they were way too mushy. Then he considered the selection of get well cards, finding most of them too cold. Finally, he selected one of the latter, adding his own note wishing Dana his best, hoping the crystal brightened her recovery. Hesitating just a moment, cursing himself as a coward, he signed the card "Love Garrett", with a flourish.

Then he chickened out again and sent his package and love-note by three-day delivery instead of rushing it to Dana overnight—to give himself a chance to get used to naming his feelings.

He had always thought guys falling in love at first sight was a little shallow. Lust, at first sight, sure! But, it wasn't lust for Dana's body he was feeling—it was hope, joy, prayers for her recovery. It was a desire to protect, to cherish the life of the amazing woman, almost lost because she rescued a child that was a total stranger. What man couldn't love such a woman? And she had a surface beauty, also. Oh yeah. Garrett wasn't going to deny he had been attracted to that! But he could get around to the lusting part when she was feeling a little better.


JENNY WAS WAITING with a big grin on her face when Dana woke again later that evening.

"How are you feeling, sleepyhead?" She asked cheerfully.

Dana tried to lift her head, getting out only a groggy, "Hey," before letting her head drop back.

"I'd crank you up, but the doctors want you to stay flat on your back the rest of the night."

"How'd go?" Dana mumbled.

"Boy, you must be dopey still. You asked me that after recovery. It went great! They got the fragment, then x-rayed again before they closed and made sure there wasn't anything else to worry about. There wasn't any more internal damage." Just a few more horrid scars. But Jen kept that thought to herself.

"Good." Dana's voice was listless. She must be worn out from the extra trauma and didn't look as if she had a drop of energy left in her body.

"I called him."

"Who?"

Wow, she was flat or fuzzy, Jenny thought before prompting, "Your savior ... Prince Charming? The Handsome Hero? Remember ... Garrett?"

"Never met him."

Jenny ignored that.

"I called him back. He sounded busy or something, so I just gave him the details fast. But ..."

"But, what?" Dana sounded irritated.

"He asked for an address. I think he wants to send you a card, or a surprise. I gave him my address, just in case you're out of the hospital then."

"Fat chance," was the muttered response.

"Hey, cheer up, girl! I shouldn't have teased you. I know you're tired so I'll go ahead and show you your surprise now,

74

instead of waiting until you can sit up and see for yourself. Look what he already sent to the hospital for you?" Jenny moved over Dana, so she could see the vase of gorgeous yellow rose buds that she held aloft. "And I confess, I read the card. It's definitely from Garrett. He says 'Get well'. Aren't they just gorgeous?"

"Mmm," Dana grunted, staring at the vase over her head, "Don't drop those on my head, I can't dodge."

"But, Dana ..."

"Nice. Now put them down. Now!" Jenny hurried to comply, Dana was never so sharp with her.

"They're great, Jen," her friend reassured, calmer. "Sweet. But for now, can you just tear a few petals off, and set them on my pillow so I can smell them? Thanks Jen, just so bushed...." Dana passed back out before she'd finished her sentence.

Jenny left more petals on the pillow, crushing one to release its fragrance. She brushed a curl from her friend's forehead, and examined the lines of stress on Dana's face. She'd gone through so much already. Dana would have such a long road ahead of her still.

Jen would need to pace herself, her enthusiasm, realizing what a toll it was taking on Dana. She needed to be ready to help Dana through all of the ups and downs to come. Glancing up at the lovely bouquet, she silently hoped that Dana would have another friend to help her through the long journey ahead. She was especially worried about what would happen when Dana had to face her different future, instead of just being focused on dealing with each day at a time, as they stitched her back together.

What would her friend do when she had to leave the hospital? When the doctors said they were done and had fixed everything as much as they could?

Jenny looked at all the casts, the bandages, the tubes that entered and surrounded her fragile friend; she thought of all the ragged scars crisscrossing the body beneath the bleached white sheets. Dana had always been so mentally strong, and so physically tough and healthy, relying on her body to not let her down.

Lifting her fingers to sniff the scent of the crushed rose petals, Jenny told herself those worries would just have to wait. She vowed that she would be there for Dana to help her through. But would Garrett?

He had done so much for them already. More than enough!

He'd saved Dana's life! Checked in on her in the Montana hospital, eased the situation for Jenny. He'd sent good wishes and flowers. He'd been kind and compassionate, and maybe that was all that he meant to be or do. Had she misinterpreted his interest in Dana, the bond she thought she saw forming? She'd been in a highly emotional state herself: she could easily have read more into it than was there. It was probably wrong for her to encourage Dana in thinking his attentions were special, more than that of a kind stranger.

In fact, maybe it would be better if Garrett just faded into the past, while he was still just someone Dana thought of as 'my hero'?

She knew Dana used that light term to hide her awe and embarrassment that she was indebted to some unknown stranger for being alive. Wasn't it better that he remain just a fantasy, a shining, untarnished star that would fade into the past, with the horror of the incident?

Would the reality of further contact, getting to know him as a person, hold Dana to those memories, and keep her from looking and moving forward? And if Garrett, the fallible man, hurt or disappointed Dana, even unintentionally ... Would that be one blow too many for the future Dana needed to face?

How could any man live up to the fairy tale Prince Charming in Dana's mind? *The fairy tale you put there*, Jen scolded herself, feeling she might have made a major mistake.

She'd just been trying to give Dana something else to think of—a bright spot as she became aware of the extent of the damage to her body. A distraction. Now she would have to correct that error. Try to undo her own well intended mischief, by not talking about Garrett, or encouraging Dana to think of him.

The graceful, fragrant roses looked so sunny and light against the thunderclouds rolling up behind them in the window. The deciduous trees, on the edge of the hospital grounds, were swaying in the rising breeze, flashing the silvery under sides of their leaves, warning of a storm to come. It had been sticky hot today. The evening storm, and rain it would bring, would be a relief, as long as lightning didn't produce any forest fires. Fall was drawing near, the fire danger was at its greatest after an unusually dry summer.

Jenny felt like all that had happened to them had been like a sudden strike of lightning, a sudden conflagration that destroyed the old life, reshaped the future in an unrecognizable form. Regrowth, renewal, how long would it take? What form, what shape?

Was Garrett like a firefighter that came in, put out the blaze and checked the hot spots to make sure the danger was over? Was that his only role? Then it was now time for the next phase to begin—the renewal, the growth that would cover and hide the scars of the past. Jenny would help Dana move in that new direction.


THE NEXT MORNING. Jenny was reminded that her friend always chose her own path.

"Show me the picture," Dana greeted her, as Jenny stared blankly at Dana's outstretched arm, still shaking the morning drizzle from her coat before draping it over the back of a chair.

"Hi to you, too. Wow, you look a lot better this morning! You have some color back in your cheeks today." Jenny noticed Dana's smile toward her roses, which had been moved to the bedside table. Ignoring that, she responded, "Pictures? I'm sorry, with that emergency surgery you had, I forgot all about taking the digital card in to have them printed. I didn't think," Jen faltered, "I wasn't sure you still might want to see them ... after you heard all the ... um, damage, and had that new scare."

Dana looked horrified. "You didn't take pictures of me all broken and bloody did you?"

"No! Of course not! Dana! How could you believe I'd do that! Or even think of it?"

"Oh, well it's just that when you said I wouldn't want to remember . . . Never mind. But the rest of the trip? Of course I want to see the pictures! We were having so much fun—short as it was. I still want to see my vacation photos."

Narrowing her eyes, Jen studied Dana closely. She did seem sincere and relaxed with the idea.

Recognizing the doubtful expression on her friend's face, Dana reassured softly. "You know, Jen, I don't regret the trip. I don't want to forget about it all. I told you, I want to go back again. I meant that."

"Seriously?"

"Yes," Dana laughed. "I'm dying to go back to Yellowstone!"

"You nearly died the first time!" Jenny muttered tersely.

"That wasn't the park's fault. It was an accident. That's all. I'm not going to let it keep me from going back and enjoying all the things I missed." Putting her hand back out, she asked again, "So, the picture?"

"When they're ready," Jen answered reluctantly. "I'll try to get them in for processing tomorrow."

"Great. But, I meant my hero's picture," Dana grinned. "You promised to bring it in today."

"Did I?"

"Yes! Quit stalling."

"I'm not stalling, I just forgot—

"Jen, don't even finish that sentence. I can tell by your face that you're trying to think up some fiction. Remember, I've known you for too long. What gives?"

"Well, the picture is in the newspaper. I reread the article last night. It's pretty, ah ..." *Gruesome, actually.* "It's pretty bad. I'll just cut the picture out for you, so you don't have to see that ..."

"Thanks for your concern. You can forget that. I want the whole paper, understood?" Dana's words were firm, her chin locked in her most stubborn expression.

"Fine. I'll bring it ..."

"You live ten minutes from here, Jenny. I'd really like to see it now. My curiosity is killing me. You wouldn't want that would you?" Dana used guilt shamelessly.

Jenny huffed out a breath. Lifting her arm palm up toward the window, she complained, "It's raining! You'd send me back out in that?"

"You should have thought of that when you deliberately tried to hide the paper from me." Dana held firm. "Besides, it's only one of those cozy, steady drizzles. I'd go myself, if they'd let me out of this damn bed."

She would, too, Jen knew. Dana loved to go out and walk in soft steady rains like this.

"Okay. I'm going! Anything else, your highness?"

Dana glanced over toward the door, then lowering her voice, and lifting her brows mischievously, added, "More candy bars? The food here really sucks!"

Jenny pulled on her damp coat, let out an exaggerated long-suffering sigh, and left to follow orders. It didn't look like this plan of hers to put Garrett in the background was going to work. If Dana caught her even trying to avoid the subject now, she'd be on her, and even more demanding.

"HEROINE, GORED BY BUFFALO, SAVES GIRL", the headlines read.

A large picture of herself, not one of her favorites, was right beneath the headlines, captioned 'heroine'.

"H-m-mph." Well that certainly felt strange, Dana thought. She scanned the article.

".... The adult female victim was rushed to the nearest hospital in Livingston, but was not expected to survive the ordeal. Dana Revson, the woman that sacrificed her life to rescue the young German girl, had just had her thirtieth birthday. The vacation to Yellowstone was meant as a celebration of that event according to her inconsolable friend, Jennifer Morales, who was unharmed in the incident."

Well! That felt even stranger! And very disturbing to read about oneself as if her life was already past! Gone. Over. She couldn't repress the shiver that crawled up her spine as if some ghost was just waiting to dance over her grave.

"Would you please call that reporter and tell him I'm really sorry to mess up his touching," sarcasm dripped from the word, "story, but unfortunately I'm still alive. And tell him to quit calling me a heroine, Jen! "

"Yes ma'am!" Jenny added, muttering as she tried to shake the rain from her coat and hair. "Now you know why I wanted to hide the paper."

Dana still felt creeped out by the words. She was alive, dammit! She ignored the rest of the articles and let her eyes rush to the other pictures, of the sweet girl, Gretchen, then a man's picture, captioned 'local man, hero'. She studied the flat, grainy black and white photo, trying to get it to tell her everything she was so curious to know about this man that meant so much to her, but was a total mystery—the man that kept the news report from being true.

The headshot appeared to have been snapped outside, un-posed. A three-quarter profile of the fair-haired man, with windblown hair, looked like a shot of a man noticing a picture being taken, and scowling and trying to turn away. Though the features were slightly blurred, not head on, it was a profile of a ruggedly good-looking man.

"This is him?" A note of wonder in her voice.

"Well, it doesn't really look a lot like him," Jenny cautioned.

"You mean he's not as good-looking as he seems here?"

"No." Jenny leaned to glance at the picture again, over Dana's arm. "I'm afraid he doesn't look a lot like that in person."

Dana turned to frown suspiciously at her friend's tone of voice.

"Okay," Jenny huffed, "He's w-a-y more handsome than that in person."

"You're kidding!"

"Not." Jenny shook her head sadly. "Truth is he's total eye-candy! The smiles-and-curls-your-toes type."

"But...I got the impression you were just being diplomatic when you said he looked good. This guy is a doll! Well, a nice rugged looking kind of male doll. Wow!"

Jenny just sighed.

"So why were you hiding it from me, Jen? Did you want to keep him to yourself?" Dana asked cautiously.

"Who wouldn't? But not my call, I'm afraid. He treated me just like I bet he treats his little sister, if he has one." Dana couldn't detect any disappointment or jealousy in her friend's voice, and was relieved. She'd been thinking of her hero as...well, all hers!

"He's a nice guy, Dana. He was really worried about you. It's too bad he lives so far away, or you probably would have seen him again." Jenny sounded like she was trying to warn Dana, for some reason.


GARRETT HOPED DANA had received his roses. He hoped she liked yellow ones. He'd thought about sending the more traditional red, but they had made him shudder, thinking of the bright red blood that Dana had spilled. He wanted to give her hope, wanted the soft sunny, yellow blooms to brighten her life, instead.

He thought of the other gift he'd sent that wouldn't have arrived yet. The one he'd signed 'love'. That was probably a mistake. He felt a little foolish now, but it was too late to call it back. He hoped she wouldn't be offended, thinking he was some forward awe-struck jerk chasing after her, trying to keep her from forgetting him.

Even if he was.

Just a chance, for her to get to know him. That's all he asked.

Maybe Jenny would put in a good word for him and help get him that chance.

# Chapter 6

NOT FOR THE FIRST TIME, Dana gazed with longing out her hospital window at late summer-blue skies and drifting cotton-ball clouds that set off evergreen forested foothills that she ached to hike.

Today she could almost smell the crisp pine and cedar scented air, almost feel the cushioned layers of softened bark and ancient needles beneath her feet. Almost. She saw herself stepping over massive roots as she wound her way upward around the cedar giants of the forest; she could feel their papery pin-striped bark beneath her hand. She heard the squirrels stop to make that funny, indignant, chucking sound to scold her invasion, as they raced up the trees storing their harvest. Birds called out in the treetops, the undergrowth and ferns rustled from other small creatures going about their business, and the soft drone of lazy insects bracketed the stillness. But, bound to her hospital bed, *almost* seeing, hearing, smelling, *almost* feeling it, was all she could do.

Her gaze slid down to the nearer trees edging the hospital grounds, soon to turn their leaves from faded green to bright yellows, and the brilliant orange on the maples. Then her eyes dropped to the deep-seated window ledge that had begun to look like a brilliantly colored and crowded garden center display shelf.

Tall vases of cut flowers abounded with cheery white and yellow daisies, ferns, baby's breath, spider mums, more roses in buds and blooms of white, red, pink, coral, peach, and more yellow—though she still treasured Garrett's the most, though it was now near naked of wilted petals. Carnations, both large and miniature, tossed out spicy prom-night scents from their large full-colored blooms or delicate tinted-edge swirls. Crowded between the vases were a variety of potted plants, brightly foil-wrapped and beribboned, or in colorful ceramic pots. She spotted violets and frothy white azaleas, exotic blooming cyclamen—she always killed those somehow—and budded begonias. A few potted ferns, and variegated ivies, and some other greens she couldn't name—

maybe herbs, from the blessed aroma in the room— filled in her personal indoor garden.

They were all so lovely and bright. They reminded her of Jenny's yard in the summer. She glanced back out at the rough barked pines and cedar scented trails, then sighed and focused on her garden center.

She needed to do something with all the flowers, sharing the cut blooms out to other rooms. She'd keep all the scores of cards that had poured in as word of her hospitalization spread. She'd save the special vases, and keep all the potted plants to keep her company through the long journey ahead, when the fresh flowers ceased to arrive to replace the dead.

She especially needed to do something about the tall elegant new arrivals. The white and fuchsia toned alstroemeria that still waved their freckled blooms from having just been set in place.

Dana heaved a great sigh that seemed to come from deep in her soul as she glanced down at the card in her hand, delivered with the bouquet. She could see the face of the well-wisher in her mind: the serious gray eyes, the silky blonde hair pulled tightly back into a model's bun. It was the same style Helen had worn since their days together on the college gymnastic team.

She had received many cards with offers to help in any way, but this card, this offer, was not one that she could just appreciate and file away. This card required a decision that she really wasn't prepared to make. But time was running out. Only denial, and the strange limbo her mind seemed to hover in, made her hesitate.

Dana and Helen had been the top two scoring members on their college team, regularly exchanging firsts at their meets. After college, Dana had gone on to coaching and a short stint on the national team, traveling to events all over; Helen had headed in a different direction. They had lost touch for a few years when Dana received a wedding invitation from Helen. Scheduled during one of her final competitions with the team, she had been unable to attend. She had sent a gift and her best wishes to her old teammate.

The newlyweds had moved back east and Dana received a few brief updates: a birth announcement, then a congratulatory card when Dana had opened her own gymnastics studio to train and coach others. A little over a year ago, Helen and her family had returned to the area. She and Dana had gotten together for lunch to catch up.

Helen was working as a legal secretary for her husband's law firm, and was the mother of an adorable, and rambunctious, preschool son. As they visited, Dana watched Helen's joyful smiles as she spoke of being a mom, replaying the exploits of her dirt-eating, jean-shredding, energetic, and healthy son. They admired pictures of the fat-cheeked, bright-eyed boy grinning from under a baseball cap that sat askew on his gilded head, wearing his grass-stained "Daddy's Little Dude" tee shirt.

Dana had to laugh at Helen's absolute pride and joy in her son. As an athlete, Helen had always been the most elegant member of the team. Never untidy, despite the exertions, Helen's hair knew its place, her body seemed trained to not even sweat. To see her proudly show off that picture of her stained and rowdy son, instead of carrying a groomed professional portrait in her wallet, told her how thoroughly Helen loved her little rascal.

When the pictures were tucked back in the wallet, and the conversation turned to their current jobs, she saw Helen's smile fade and a look of envy shade her eyes when Dana spoke of her work and studio. Dana suspected Helen wasn't very happy with her job behind a desk.

"You know," Dana mentioned carefully, "I've found that many of the mothers of my students were interested in gymnastics when they were younger, and still miss it. Since I already have all the equipment, I decided to have a Saturday morning session where the adults could just use it on their own, while I'm there in my office doing my weekly paperwork."

"Really?" Helen's eyes glowed. She leaned eagerly towards Dana, confirming her suspicions.

"Everyone has to sign a liability waiver, of course, and help spot each other. Otherwise my insurance would be impossible. It's just a self-serve kind of gym session," Dana added, noting Helen's increased interest. "A couple of my teenage students watch over the children in a play corner and let them roll around some mats, in exchange for their tuition."

"I'd still have to pay them extra to corral my boy!" Helen laughed. "But, luckily for me, Saturday mornings are official 'Dad & Tad' time for my boys. That's their special time to do things together. Soccer, baseball, fishing, whatever, but it's a 'no girls allowed' time for them to share. So please sign me up, Dana. I can hardly wait to get back on the bars and beam!"

In the year since, Helen had shown up nearly every Saturday. Dana watched her covertly as she did her weekly entries and caught up her schedules. She'd seen the early frustration, then the gradual re-toning of body and skills. Helen was now wowing the other attendees who watched her on the bars, like they did when Dana performed.

Dana also noted how cheerfully she answered questions and helped others, showing them techniques and encouraging their skill development. Her old teammate glowed with energy, happiness, and renewed confidence after those Saturday sessions. But, Dana noted with wry envy, she still didn't seem to glow with sweat!

As she plugged numbers in her computer and watched demand for her classes expand, Dana had thought more than once that Helen might be a candidate for an assistant part-time trainer—though she hadn't broached the subject with her yet. It was on the list she had prepared before closing down the studio for her vacation.

Each year, in mid-August, Dana's Studio was shutdown to give her time for vacation and to plan for the upcoming season that began with the return of the school year, and re-enrollment in her fall classes. During this time, Dana analyzed the prior year, did her planning, added courses, innovations, and events for the upcoming year. This year, with a waiting list for classes, she had been considering whether to expand, add additional equipment, and at least one other part-time instructor.

That had been her original plan during her vacation break. Unfortunately, it had been more break— or breaks—than vacation, or planning. Now all her plans for the future had been cast down like a game of pick-up-sticks, some pieces so shattered she did not know if she would ever be able to gather them in and begin again.

And now what?

School would be starting soon and she was incapacitated.

Not only did Dana not have a plan for the future, but she was unwilling to squarely face what that future might be, much less make any decisions that would acknowledge her uncertainties and fear. She knew this, yet she couldn't seem to deal with it. Every time she tried she found herself just turning over the charred ashes of the past, unable to even think about what came next.

The studio was closed—she rationalized—she could wait, drift a while, push this aside a little longer. Avoid, a little longer... The stiff card that crumpled in her clenched fist reminded her that it was past time to face her denials.

A sense of weakness and helplessness sweep over her. Leaning her head back on the pillow, she blinked rapidly to block the moisture welling in her eyes and threatening to spill out. Dana's throat tightened in anger. She hated feeling like this, being like this! Weak, helpless, indecisive ... scared.

What am I supposed to do? What will happen to me? Will I ever be well again? The questions screamed through her head in an answerless, repetitive cycle. One she just wanted to shove aside, deny and take another pill and silence. Running out of time, without a plan, no will to look at the future, Dana ground her teeth on her self-pity and the fear consuming her.

The hard edges of the crushed card, stabbed her palm. Her hand reached for the button by her bed that would shoot more pain killer into her bloodstream—but she managed to stop herself. Taking deep breaths, trying to regain control, she pushed the control to raise the bed, instead, grabbing tissues to dry her eyes and blow her nose.

*You're stronger than this!* Dana told herself over and over again until she began to believe, drawing in calmer and steadier breaths. Sipping some water to soothe the rawness in her throat, Dana carefully flattened the card, smoothing it on her lap.

Okay.

Reaching resolutely for the phone, she dialed the number written on the card, taking a last breath to steady her voice. She was relieved when an answering machine responded, unsure she was stable enough to carry on a conversation yet, but determined to take the step forward.

"Helen, it's Dana. Thanks so much for the lovely flowers and card. I ... I, ah, would like to take you up on your offer of help. Can you give me a call here so we can set up a time to visit ... soon? Thanks. Hug your boys for me. Bye."

*There!* That's better she thought, quickly hanging up before someone could pick up. She still had no idea what she planned to ask of Helen, but she'd started in the right direction. There were still ten days remaining before the previously scheduled re-opening of Dana's Studio for Gymnastics. For now, she had done all she was capable of—just one tiny step forward. Hopefully, she'd find some courage before the next step—whatever it was.

Dana picked up the book she had been reading, about a really tough trip taken a long time ago. Maybe the journal would inspire—or shame her—to find the courage for her own journey into uncertain territory.

BY EARLY APRIL 1805, when the 'Corps of Discovery' left their winter quarters at the Mandan Village Fort, they had been hearing tales of a 'Yellow stone river' from the natives—and mapped an idea of how it trended southwest from where it met the Missouri River (near the present day border of North Dakota and Montana). Yet Lewis & Clark remained firm in their decision to take a route northwest up the Missouri—that was their charter.

In light of all the trials, tribulations, and delays they encountered, due to the Great Falls and the portages and other obstacles, it seems like a dangerous error, today—if their object was only to reach the Pacific Coast before winter set in.

They had been tasked, however, by President Jefferson to map and claim the Louisiana Purchase, including all the drainage of the Missouri River. He was hoping for a northern tributary that would lead them into the rich fur trade resources above the forty-ninth parallel. Even when their boat party was temporarily joined by three French beaver trappers, planning to drop off at the 'Yellow stone river' where big beaver were found, the Lewis & Clark expedition was not deterred, sending only one lone man to scout, while they camped at the mouth.

They resumed the journey upstream on the Missouri, from its confluence with the river of yellow stones, on April 28, 1805. The next day, they had their first encounter with a great 'yellow bear'. The big humped grizzly, instead of running when Lewis shot it, chased him for seventy or eighty yards before it could be killed. They did not complete their loop north and westward, then all the way back down south to historic Three Forks, until the very end of July of that year, three months later—dangerously late to find horses and begin their trek over the many unknown ranges of the Rocky Mountains.

On the return journey from the Pacific, the Corps split up. Lewis headed north to return down the Missouri, still looking for that river route to the northern fur trade. William Clark, along with Charbonneau, Sacagawea, her year and a half old baby, and eight other men, left Three Forks around July 11th or 12th, and traveled by horseback, overland and uphill, to meet the Yellowstone River, just east of present day Livingston, MT, only sixty miles distant. Arriving on July 15th, 1806, Clark's party had to find trees to build new dugout canoes before heading downstream to the Missouri—eastward on that 'river of yellow stones'—to wait to meet Lewis. They arrived a good week before him on August third, less than one month after leaving Three Forks! Condensed versions of the Lewis and Clark journals do not include Clark's daily journals from

Three Forks to the Yellowstone because so little happened—apparently it was such an easy, enjoyable part of the journey, it was deemed boring.

Due to the perceived future importance to the nation of the fur trade, the bulk of expedition time, energy, and danger, was given to the northern Missouri route. At Livingston, Clark passed right by, and camped not far from, where the Yellowstone River took an abrupt turn south between a narrow gap cut between the massive Gallatin and Absaroka-Beartooth mountain ranges. It headed south to the wonders and mysteries of Yellowstone Park, where in the late 1800s, visitor's from across the land and around the world, would begin to arrive. The northern border of the future Yellowstone Park was only sixty miles south on the river from Clark that day in July 1806, and the geologic wonders of the Upper Yellowstone Valley started before that boundary. Making its way north, half that distance closer to where William Clark camped, the Yellowstone River passed through Paradise Valley, the location of Emigrant Peak and Emigrant Gulch. Less than sixty years later, when beaver fur hats and their trade value were long out of fashion, another wonder was found in that location in 1864.

To put it in a parlance of the time—'Thar were *GOLD* down thar!!!'

GARRETT'S APPETITE HAD come roaring back once he was relieved by the good news from out of state. He hadn't even noticed how long his worries had kept it at bay, despite his hard daily labor. Seeking a quick lunch, he stepped through the narrow door of The Saloon in Emigrant, his eyes trying to adjust to the dark interior of the narrow saloon, first opened in 1902. Garrett slapped the backs of the three old-timers that anchored the end of the bar most afternoons.

"Hey, where you been, you young runt? Don't you like to eat with us anymore?"

"He probably lost his appetite just looking at you, you ole coot," his companion chided, as they all turned to greet Garrett with grins and handshakes.

The three were such colorful characters they could count on a free bowl of chili, a long neck beer, and some chips to snack on from the bartender. The locals knew and enjoyed them and the tourists just loved to look at them, doing a double take as they entered the bar. The rough and rustic decor had nothing on the old-timers for western authenticity.

With their felt slouch hats, flowing white beards and mustaches, clean, if faded, flannel shirts and dungarees cinched with suspenders, they were reminiscent of the miners that had populated the original town that had flourished here in the late eighteen and early nineteen hundreds. Better than advertising, they drew tourists eager to soak up the nostalgia, picturing the trio there to stake and work a claim, or grab a rusty tin mining pan from the wall and step across the road to the river, looking for more of those shiny yellow stones among the dull sandstone ones.

Garrett enjoyed occasional lunches here, sitting on a bar stool, swapping pleasantries and telling outrageous fishing lies with the old-timers. He had his arms stretched out at least a yard, in the middle of one of these hilarious tall tales, when his hand was grabbed and shaken.

"Garrett, good to see you. I thought I heard your voice back here."

He turned to the tanned and silver-haired man that eased up beside him.

"Hey, Jim! Great to see you. What are you doing around here with these old goats?"

Casting a friendly grin down the bar, Jim motioned the bartender, "Give those 'old goats' a round on me," before turning back to Garrett.

"I was over on the restaurant side. Just slipped over here for the men's room and heard you entertaining the boys. I've been hoping to see you."

Jim was a handsome, well groomed, east coast CEO that had taken early retirement and moved west. While his denim shirt and jeans probably had designer labels, and cost ten times those worn by the local crowd, he wore them with a friendly open smile and just as casually. Unlike many wealthy retirees, Jim didn't try to wear string ties, cowboy shirts, boots, and big hats, and dress with phony western accessories that he hadn't earned. He was a regular guy that had retired with a huge bank account and wanted to live where a man's character mattered *more* than that bank balance. Garrett had come to know him well, and respected and enjoyed the man and his wife.

"So how's the new house working out?"

"Well, Garrett, my wife was just complaining about that the other day."

"Sarah? We can't have that!" Instantly serious, Garrett reached for the pen in his pocket, grabbing a clean napkin off the bar. "What's the problem?"

"She said you built the house so square and tight, and sealed it so well, that not even the tiniest bugs can get out."

Garrett blinked, then saw Jim's teasing grin, and relaxed. Jim's wife had been an executive back east also, a VP in charge of quality control for a high-end furniture manufacturing firm. He knew she would be scrutinizing all the woodwork and cabinetry and was extremely pleased to hear she was so happy with the quality of her new home.

"Yeah," Garrett drawled, "that is a problem I tend to have. Sorry about that."

"You should be," Jim chuckled. "Every time I step out the glass doors to the deck I'm so dazzled with my view of the mountains and the smell of fresh air that I have a habit of just standing there with the door open, breathing it all in. She told me to quit letting all the damn bugs in because they don't have any way to get back out! Seriously, we love the house, Garrett. You gave us everything we asked for and more. Actually, I'm afraid I owe you a big apology."

"How's that?"

"The other day I got a phone call from a man I can barely tolerate. I can't tolerate him, really, but he's loosely related to one of my wife's old friends, so I have to put up with him.

"He called me, sputtering and raging, saying he was sorry to tell me that I had been taken. He felt it was his duty as my 'good friend' to tell me about it so that I could sue." Jim paused a moment with a mischievous twinkle in his eyes, building Garrett's curiosity.

"It seems that he thinks that I was grossly overcharged by my building contractor, who is a crook, according to this guy." Jim's grin took any sting from the words. "Seems he got a bid from my contractor for a house like mine, and it was exorbitant. His word.

"So, I asked him how much his bid was and when he told me, I almost coughed up the muffin I'd just eaten. It was all I could do to keep from laughing out loud. Way to go, Garrett!" Jim clapped him on the shoulder. "If I'd had any idea that ass was going to call you, I would have warned you off, but I guess you got his number pretty quickly anyway. My apologies that he wasted your time. "My wife is just sick about it, she hates him also. She said to tell you to put us at the very top of your referral list and be sure to include our cell phones. We'll talk to anyone you want, anytime, and invite them to the house to see your workmanship to make it up to you for the badmouthing you're going to get from that ass. We're also getting a reference letter ready telling how you give much better quality than you charge for. We're more than pleased."

"I really appreciate that, Jim. I have to admit, I was a little ... ah, surprised. He said you referred him, but he didn't seem, well—" Garrett stumbled for diplomatic words, then gave up and grinned. "I filed him under 'Rude' in my computer," he admitted.

"He said I referred him? That jerk!"

"Yeah, jerk, that's the last name I gave him. Old RJ."

Jim threw his head back and gave a great joyful laugh, and another sound clap to Garrett's shoulder. "I love it! RJ! Those are even his initials. Wait 'til I tell Sarah. But let's forget him. Say, I hear you've been busy rescuing damsels in distress down in Yellowstone. Our own local hero. Tell me, do you know how that woman is doing?"

Jim listened with growing interest, then an amused smile as Garrett told him about Dana and her friend and how she was back home at a hospital and doing much better. The young man didn't realize how much of his emotional attachment to the woman he was giving away.

"I'd love to play poker with you sometime, Garrett."

Totally baffled at the change in subject, Garrett responded vaguely that he didn't play.

"Probably a very good idea," Jim grinned.

"Well, you tell that Dana of yours that we're all pulling for her to get better, the next time you see her." Jim winked, then added, "I better get going. Come up to the house for dinner anytime."

Garrett was thrilled the couple was so happy with their home. Really nice people, they deserved his best. He never had been able to picture them as close friends of Mr. Rude.

So the guy was badmouthing him now? Well at least it would keep his other hotshot friends away. Jim and his wife had solved his problem for anyone else. They'd defend his good reputation in the right circles. They sure were nice folks.

He thought of Jim's parting comment about the next time he saw Dana.

Will I ever see her again? Talk to her?

Hell, man, not if you don't even give it a try, he scolded himself with a wry grin.

"WHAT DO YOU THINK it could be?"

"Well, open it silly, then we'll know!"

Jenny shoved the package that had arrived at her home that day toward her friend. Her curiosity was rampant—as it always was with gifts. Jen was a confessed package ripper.

"It's heavy," Dana commented, as she tried to carefully peel off the wrappings one-handed. "Here, you do it. I'm too clumsy. I can't wait."

Jenny tore the packaging off, pried off the lid of the small box, then set it back in Dana's lap.

Peeling back layers of tissue paper, Dana stopped and just stared.

"What is it?" Jenny nearly shouted, unable to see what lay nestled in the paper.

"It's beautiful!" Dana's voice was filled with wonder. "It's sooo beautiful. Oh, how sweet!"

"What-is-it?"

"It's a geode, Jenny!"

"Huhn?"

"A type of rock."

"Oh. I should have known, when you got so excited. Not the diamond or gold type of rock, I suppose," she grumbled.

"Don't be ridiculous. This is much better."

Dana's delighted tone said she was serious. Go figure!

She lifted the stone, so Jenny could see it.

"Wow. That is kind of cool," Jen admitted, watching the sun glisten off faceted crystals embedded in the ordinary looking broken stone. "You could probably knock some of those things out and make some great jewelry."

Dana gasped, horrified, closing her hand around the rock and hiding it from Jenny behind her back. "Are you kidding? That would ruin it!"

Jenny just grinned, pretending she hadn't meant what to her seemed like a completely reasonable suggestion. Guess not.

Dana pulled it back out, apparently deciding it was safe, and turned it slowly in her hand.

"Precious stone," she murmured softly.

"Yeah, it's a nice rock—"

"No, I meant, that's what it means," Dana explained—at length, of course. "The word 'geode' comes from a Latin, or maybe Greek, word I think. The word meant 'precious stone'. Can you just imagine what the first person that broke one of these open thought? I bet they thought it was some kind of magic, something sacred. It's so ordinary on the outside, but then this, inside. It's like a clue to the mystery of how the world is formed. All these mineral crystals, growing in such perfect structures. We usually only see them as tiny chips glimmering in granite and other rocks." She rolled the rock in her palm, her eyes full of wonder and excitement.

"I think this must be amethyst, a purple quartz, but I'm not sure. I'll have to do some research. I know the crystals need to be sealed away from water, and have a hollow pocket of room inside the rock to be able to grow so large and symmetrical—"

"Dana, I have never seen anyone who can get as passionate about a rock as you, so quit drooling on it for a minute," Jenny interrupted, impatiently. "What about the guy that sent it? Are you going to call him, or not?"

"Oh. No. I can't yet. I'll have to write him a nice thank you note, like I did for the flowers. This is just amazing, Jen, don't you think?"

Jen thought that Dana was so immersed in her rock, she could roll her eyes without getting caught.

WHEN THE PHONE RANG in the hospital room a few days later, Jen answered, grinned, and shoved it in Dana's startled face. "Sure, she's right here."

"Ah, hello?"

"Dana, its Garrett. I just wanted to call and thank you for that nice note you sent."

Dana glared at Jen. It was unfortunate, but she really was going to have to kill her best friend for this. Jen just tossed a saucy grin and wiggled her fingers in a careless wave as she escaped out the door. Desperately trying to gather her wits, Dana rushed into speech when she heard him questioning if she was still there.

"Yes, I'm here." She cleared her throat nervously. "That was the most thoughtful gift, and the flowers ... really you shouldn't have, but I do appreciate them. Very much."

She thought of the card he'd signed with his love. She had slipped it under her pillow, not even sharing it with Jen. He'd probably just used the word casually, not intending anything, but she hadn't been able to resist pulling the card out several times, reading the words softly to herself. Had he meant anything? The possibility sent a tingle of warmth through her at each reading. It colored her reaction now, listening to the deep and smooth voice in her ear. Nerves leaping to life, shyness snuck up on her to tangle her thoughts and tongue.

"Good," he was saying. "It's got to be a drag to be stuck indoors. I thought they might help. So...," his voice gentled, "how are you feeling? Or should I ask?"

92

"Well, I'm feeling okay. Pretty lucky, actually, especially after the doctors gave me that long list of all the things I messed up! It's hard to believe there are that many connecting bits and pieces under your skin that you can break and crack and tear or yank, but ..." The rapid stream of words suddenly stopped. Her voice came back after a deep breath, softer, slower. "Umm, I ...," then another pause, his name came in a deep, soft breath of sound. "Garrett..."

With supreme effort, Dana had managed to bring her mouth to a standstill, halting the nervous babble. She hadn't been prepared to have the phone thrust at her, to be speaking to the man that had become the most important, most essential, man in her life. And even beyond saving her life, all those thoughtful attentions and gifts, sweet words, she could barely think of those now, when she had so much else of greater importance to express. How did she speak the words she wished to this man? A complete stranger, yet so intimately close when he had given her back the chance for each breath of air she now took, each thought she had, everything that she felt. Why was it so hard to find and speak the soft words of such deeply felt and vital emotions? She tried again.

"Garrett, I ..." She swallowed, and heard him heave a deep sigh. He was probably impatient with her stuttering silences, but gratitude and affection ran so deeply inside her she would never find the right words of expression. Dana was a face to face person. She liked to say serious words when she could see into a person's eyes, and let them see the sincerity in hers. But the poor man was on the phone now, paying for long distance to hear her breathe. She might never get the chance to tell him in person, so she gave him the only simple words she could find.

"I have you to thank for even being here, Garrett. I know I wrote you, but I just want to thank you again. I can't find the words I need though, to express such a deep gratitude, but...thank you, Garrett."

EARLIER WHEN SHE FIRST spoke his name, almost in a whisper, it had knocked the breath out of Garrett. He heard it, deep! He had felt the soft stroke of it more. Her hesitation after she spoke had given him time to absorb the sound, spreading warm and intimate inside him. He had never heard his name from her lips before. She had never rolled the letters across her tongue and breathed them in his ear before. The novelty of it surprised and charmed him. It captured him, like the mystery and wish to see her green eyes open and gazing into his. He had waited patiently for her to speak, and heard it again. His name had never had such a unique sound and flavor, or feel, as when it came from her voice, from her lips. Then she had spoken so earnestly, his sensual shivers had turned to tenderness.

She may not have had the words she wanted, but her low, soft voice shook with the intensity of her emotions, and shook him to his soul. He wanted to help her, tell her it was okay, no big deal, she had thanked him enough, but he stopped himself.

It *was* a big deal. They both knew it. It was her life—her precious life. Too important to casually brush off her heartfelt thanks.

"Thank you, Dana." He heard the sudden thickness in his voice, felt it in his throat.

"It was the greatest privilege of my life to be there and to be able to make a difference for you. You are a brave and special woman, and you saved the life of that young girl . . ." He meant to say more, but his throat was closed on the words.

The emotion clogged and charged silence lingered on, broken only by clearing throats, eyes silently blinking away excess moisture, deep shaky breaths of indrawn air.

Garrett found his voice again, first. Eager to lighten the mood, he ventured, with an amused tone in his voice, "You know, Dana, I was just noticing ... your voice sounds very familiar."

"Familiar?" Dana asked, her voice suddenly tense.

"Yeah," he drawled teasingly. "Now just where did I hear that voice before? Let me think..."

# Chapter 7

"I'M SURE LOTS of people have voices that sound like mine."

Garrett heard her gasp, then the defensive tone in her voice and grinned, knowing he had been right. On more comfortable ground now, he couldn't resist pushing his teasing.

"Nooo," he kept the amused drawl, "there's definitely something unique about your voice. I'm sure I've heard it somewhere before. If I could just pin down where? I'm sure I'll remember ..."

"Garrett, you know, I was wondering," Her voice much brisker than normal, "Wondering just where you found that rock? Do they sell those in gem shops? It's so amazing, I was curious—"

"I found it." He tried to keep from barking out a laugh at her diversionary tactics. "I've had it a long time, actually. I just thought you might enjoy it. But you know, I think I recall where I heard that voice of yours before. It's the most amazing coincidence."

"It is?"

"Yes, you won't believe this, but it was the first time I called your room! Can you imagine? What are the odds that you, and the nurse that answered in your room, would have the very same voice?"

"But that was over a week ago! How could you ..." Her voice trailed off at the deep rumble of his laughter.

"Well, you know Dana that is an interesting point. The answer is that her voice sounded like I had imagined your voice would sound, when I heard it. That's why it captured my attention. I'm afraid I might have sounded overly friendly to her, as I was so distracted thinking it was your voice I was hearing and ..."

"But you hung up on me!"

"Gotcha, babe."

She seemed to give up her farce, joining in his playful laughter.

"Okay. I confess. It was me. But I did have a good excuse."

"Okay," he said teasingly, "listening."

"I confess, I was... well, curious about you. And I felt a little shy. I feel shy now, just telling you this." Dana's voice had softened almost to a whisper. "You... what you did for me... how I looked when you saw me...I just..."

"Hey, I understand. I'm not complaining. I'm glad there aren't two voices like that," he lightened the mood, "that would be scary."

"What do you mean?"

"Well, you have a very special voice, Dana."

"I do?" She sounded pleased.

"You have a dangerously sexy voice." He said softly.

"Well, thank you, I think." Suddenly shy, "You have a sexy voice, also."

He choked with laughter, at that, boasting, "So all your nurses tell me!" When their humor over the shared joke died down, the awkwardness returned.

"You know, it feels a little creepy," Dana admitted. "I mean that you saw me in the hospital, when I didn't even know it, looking like such a ... zombie," she finished awkwardly.

Garrett, a little surprised by her honest admission, responded in kind before he'd thought it through.

"The first time I saw you, you looked dead!"

There was a stunned silence.

Garrett considered the benefits of old-fashioned phones; they had a nice strong cord, which cells lacked, that you could strangle yourself with. "But you looked terrific in the newspaper," he tacked on quickly before she hung up on him.

Her 'thanks' sounded a bit choked.

"I guess you're probably tired," Garrett offered her an out.

"Of what?" She asked innocently, he could hear the mischievous imp in her voice.

Talking to a bumbling idiot, he almost suggested. "I meant that I should probably let you get your rest."

"I'm all rested."

"That's good news."

It was hard not to laugh at the awkward conversation. They were as eloquent as two kids that had just discovered the opposite sex was different—in a good way.

"I'm not keeping you from something important, am I Garrett? A business meeting? A hot date?" Dana seemed to be getting even for her earlier discomfort when he had teased her. It was working.

"No! You're the only thing I have planned," he blurted. Damn, this woman was tying him in knots!

He heard a pleased chuckle, then her voice came back deeper, huskier.

"So, do you have me planned," she asked slowly, "for the business meeting .. . or the hot ... date?"

Gulp.

Lowering his voice, also, "Either one I can get an appointment for." Garrett's suggestive lilt drifted down the phone line, he seemed to be enjoying the game.

"Hmm. Just what kind of business did you have in mind?" She came back at him in a playful sexy drawl that made him laugh.

"My, you do sound like you're feeling a lot better!" he chuckled.

"I am," she laughed with him, "but I confess, I'm talking a talk that I can't back up ... yet," she teased cheerfully.

"Well, babe," he crooned, "you are pretty dangerous with just that voice. A guy could be happy waiting a long time for ... 'yet'."

"Ah, and aren't you the charmer!" she murmured.

"Not really. I meant that."

Silence.

"Ah-h-h," Dana sounded flustered again, "Garrett, I don't want to..."

"Hey, relax, you didn't promise me anything, Dana. I know that. You're just feeling your oats, flirting a little, having fun. I understand. It feels good to be alive, doesn't it? And I like hearing you laugh, playing with you on the phone. But, for me personally, well, my hot dates right now are all reserved for you. That works for me. No strings for you."

WHOA! DANA WONDERED how many guys she had known who would leave themselves out there like that. Her nervous reaction prompted her to joke away his seriousness, but he deserved more than that.

"You're a very nice guy, Garrett." Her voice was soft but sober. "Thank you. For that, and for everything you've done for me."

"Well, there is something you can do for me. And that is to work hard at getting well, okay? Can I call you tomorrow?"

"Yes, I'd like that. But call late. They're putting pins in my wrist tomorrow, so I'll be in surgery, or doped up, most of the day."

"I'll be thinking good luck thoughts for you all day then. Until tomorrow. Goodnight, Dana."

"'Nite," she hung up the phone with a soft sigh and laid back, smiling to herself. She could almost feel a purr deep inside her. This guy..., man, he did something to her! According to Jen, he was definitely all man! And a hot one, to boot! A nice, handsome hot guy in cowboy boots, who had saved her, and spoke to her in a soft, sexy voice Did it get better than that? Not in her experience; not ones so honest about their feelings. She had gotten to where she held most men at arms-length—she had better things to do with her time and efforts. But *this* man—

Dana wished she had found him sooner, when she was still in one piece. Tomorrow they would pin more of those pieces back together. She'd be a major celebrity again, from now on—every time she tried to get through security onto an airplane, bells would ring. Great!

But Garrett, her hero ... Well, he was a really nice man that probably just felt sorry for her. She'd savor the fantasy for now.


HER HERO WAS in a sorry state the next day.

A recurring nightmare kept Garrett from sleep all night. In his dream he was at the accident scene. He was moving Dana's wrist to free the child, but all the tendons, and muscles, and shattered bones in her wrist had voices. They were each screaming and shouting out at him in pain. He knew it was just a nightmare, but no matter how hard he tried, he couldn't get the horrid sounds out of his head to rest, or to ease the heartache of the pain he caused the poor brave lady.

Needing physical labor today, while Dana was going through her operation, Garrett was dismantling a two-by-four framework that had been bolted together to support a temporary power supply pole. Now that the electricians had been able to come and connect the permanent direct power line to the house, it was no longer needed. Straining, and cranking hard on his wrench, he finally freed the last bolt that had jammed from the grit and effects of weather over the last few months. As he pulled back, he paused to look down at his own broad-boned wrist, turning his hand, bending his wrist to watch the play of tendon and muscle under the sun-darkened skin. He could see the spidery veins on the underside that carried his lifeblood through the various tissues.

"Sprain your wrist, Boss?" A passing worker asked.

"No. No, its fine," he answered absently, thinking how he took this complex part of his anatomy for granted all the time. He gave it another twist then bent to pick up his tools and clear the boards and bolts from the area, and stack them out of the way.

What a damn shame, he thought. Would Dana ever be able to get on the parallel bars again? Would her wrist even work at all? He wished he could give her one of his, then snorted at the idea.

Wouldn't that look ungainly on her elegant little arm!

But he seriously wondered if he had caused the damage that they were trying, again today, to repair? He had tried not to feel bad for doing what he felt was necessary and urgent at the time, but knew in reality that he had just been suppressing the guilt. That was what the nightmares were about. He probably had hurt her more, unwrapping the child, but couldn't see how he could have done otherwise. It didn't make him feel any better, though.

Poor brave, babe, he whispered under his breath, praying that all would go well for her operation today.

"I'm heading into town for lunch," he advised his crew, "I'll be back in a couple of hours."

Getting into his truck, he made a quick call to his friend the local hospital administrator.

"Free for lunch, Bob? I'm buying."

"Well, can't say no to that. Sure you don't want to come by the house instead? See that recreation room I'm saving for you?" Bob teased.

"Maybe later. I want to pick your medical brain, today. Pick you up in thirty?"

"I'll be out front at the east entrance. See you then."

Once they'd placed their luncheon orders, Bob had a bit of news for Garrett.

"Got to confess, buddy. You don't owe me that much of a favor anymore for those Washington girls."

"Yeah, why's that?"

"Well, apparently they already had medical release forms for each other. Did it some years back. Just didn't think to bring them. That Jenny was nice enough to fax me a notarized copy, shortly after she got back. Sure got my butt off the hot seat! If you ever hear from her again, tell her thanks. It's a good thing I was just pulling your leg when I said I wanted a remodel at cost 'cuz you wouldn't have owed me anyway."

"You don't want to remodel?"

99

"Oh, sure I do. I want you to do the work too, whatever it costs. I want a quality job. I just like to pull your leg a little to get a deal."

"Hell, you knew I'd give you my best price anyway, you old dog. All you have to do is spread the word, if you like the job. Anyway, that other subject is what I wanted to talk to you about. The injured girl, Dana. There's something that's been bothering me ..."

Garrett filled his lunch partner in on Dana's additional surgery to get pins in her wrist. He inquired about the procedure, what could be expected with an injury of that nature, and whether he might have caused a lot of extra damage by his actions.

He didn't like all the answers he got, but at least he understood what kind of recovery times, and outcomes might be expected from the procedure.

After dessert, he turned the conversation back to other matters. Grabbing a paper napkin and his pen, he shoved them across the table.

"So, Bob, give me an idea what this rec-room project is about. We can do an indoor project this winter. So tell me, what's there now, and what do you want to change or add?" Many of Garrett's local projects started out as rough blueprints on a napkin.

And he was eager for any work distraction he could find today.

FLAT ON HER BACK, Dana found herself staring grimly at the ceiling of her room as the medical fog of her surgery cleared. Blowing out a breath she closed her eyes so she could focus inward. She couldn't afford any more distractions or denial about her life's work.

She had to decide now, before something else interfered with her ability to concentrate. Expand. Close permanently. Sell. Or something in-between?

Expansion had been the plan that Dana was toying with before vacation. She had slowly built a reputation and a devoted clientele until she was now so successful that she'd found herself with long waiting lists for upcoming classes.

She originally built her business in a way that had allowed her to give back to the community at the same time. Instead of spending her budget on advertising, she had invested it in local schools. She had worked with the local school district to supplement their cash-strapped physical education programs. She

100

provided free one-hour after school sessions, at her new studio, once a week each spring and fall, for five local elementary and middle schools. It gave Dana a way to introduce youth and their parents to gymnastics and her studio, offering the specialized equipment and training that the school district could no longer offer on budgets cut down to only rudimentary tumbling in their programs.

Dana knew that if she'd had to wait until high school to start training, she would never have been able to pursue her dream. While that had been a primary reason for offering the opportunity to the younger children, the benefits her business had received back had made her business the success it now was.

Even with that success, and waiting lists for her paying classes, she had never planned to cease her free school programs. She had decided from the beginning that rather than lobbying tax-payers to meet the need, using that same time to offer herself to the district, would be her choice; it had been gratefully received by the already stressed school board, and given Dana untold personal satisfaction.

Not every child would want, or wish, to continue training, but Dana firmly believed that every child deserved the chance, regardless of skills or income, to find out. She had never intended to use talent, or lack of it, to squelch interest in the sport either; she didn't use that qualifier to limit classes. Part of her concern about the waiting lists were the stalled dreams for kids that wished to continue training, or young applicants eager to pursue abilities—whether late-bloomers or early stars. She would increase class sizes first, though she had concluded that what she really needed was another trainer.

Several of her highly skilled older students would be capable of training her youngest school classes, in return for free advanced tuition and coaching by Dana. That plan, however, depended on her supervision and personal skills. That plan depended on Dana's health and fitness.

The business was due to re-open in just under a week; the longer it remained closed after that, the more the damage to her finances, programs, and its sale value as an asset. She was most worried about her students, but had to face the reality that with the potential health care costs she would be facing, she had to consider the value of her business.

Her business, her dream—

In thirty years, despite minor injuries, her own health was something Dana had never doubted or factored into the risks. What now?

If she only knew when, and what shape, her recovery would take. How could she decide without that knowledge? How could she break this cycle of indecision and denial, without those facts? How could she break this hopelessness that swept her each time she tried to wrestle with these realities? She hated this weakness in her mind, it made her feel even more out of control than the damage to her body.


"LOOK AT YOU!" Garrett chastised gently as he smoothed a hand down the neck of his buckskin, following it with a brush to get caked bits of mud from its coat.

"You are a mess. Your mane and tail are always all snarled and sticking up in spikes like some punk rocker! Why is that? I swear I just don't understand it. Look at Blue Moon and Flicka over there." The pair of horses he motioned toward wisely kept their well-groomed heads down in their hay. Corky was known to bite.

"They stand in the same wind as you, Corky, live in the same barn, same corral, but they barely look ruffled between currying. But you!" Garrett just shook his head sadly, trying to untangle another rat's nest hunk of mane.

"You always look like you just got electrified! I tell you, Corky, it's just down right embarrassing. That's what it is. People see you looking like such a mess all the time and they think I don't take care of grooming my horses. And what is with these spikes? You using hair gel to make them all stiff like that? I swear, one day I'll drive up and you'll probably have pink and green dyed hair spikes. That's no way for an old man like you to act. You're twelve years old! Are you going through some kind of mid-life crisis or something?" Taking exception to being called old, Corky snorted and shook his head, further entangling the comb in his mane.

"I've heard you nickering at that three-year old filly in the neighbor's field. Don't think I haven't seen the way you prance back and forth along the fence line, kicking up your heels trying to impress her." Garrett dodged the attempted nip on his shoulder. "Hah! Don't even try to deny it."

Giving up on the snarled mane until he could take Corky into a stall and halter tie him, he leaned against his flank and lifted a hoof to clean it with the pick, continuing his gentle scolding.

"Now, you're not going to catch the eye of any fillies looking like such a mess, trust me. The ladies like a guy that gets himself all spruced up for them. It's a sign of respect for them, see? That you make a special effort for them. You need to shine your shoes, see, like this." Garrett stepped in front of Corky and demonstrated, standing on one foot he swiped the dust off his cowboy boot on the back of his other jean clad leg. "See? Ow! Use your own leg, dammit," he grumbled, rubbing his knee where Corky had pawed at him. The horse stretched his neck out and lipped Garrett's cheek, leaving a slime of ground grass and hay on his face.

"Eeuww. Knock that off! I know I need to shave, but I'm not the one trying to spark some young filly. Well," stepping back to the side of his horse and running the brush in long strokes down his back, Garrett admitted, "I am actually, but not in person, so it doesn't matter how I look. Remember about that Yellowstone girl I was so worried about? Well, she went back to Washington State, but she's going to be okay. Yeah, what a relief, huh?" Stopping to lean his arms companionably across the buckskin's back, he gazed out at the mountains to the west were Dana had gone. "Boy, that was one courageous lady!" he sighed.

"I told you how she saved that little girl, right? Man that was something. And beautiful? Long and lean and a mane of red-hair like you've never seen. I've been talking to her on the phone and she's got this husky honey voice and a real sense of humor and—" His horse shifted and turned his head back to give Garrett a wall-eyed stare.

"Yeah, I think you're right, Corky. I've got a real case for her, don't I?" Going back to his brushing he added, "And I'm thinking I'd like to be kissing something besides my horses. Not that what you just gave me was a kiss, that was just horse spit and you and I both know it."

After finishing up his chores and grooming, Garrett headed inside to shower the horse smell and spit off of himself, even shaving. Barefoot, in clean worn jeans and a fresh shirt, he checked the time and subtracted an hour for Pacific Time. Still a little early. He'd fix himself something to eat before calling the hospital.

GARRETT'S CALL WAS a welcome relief from Dana's tortured thoughts about her business and future. The deep, sexy voice acted like a drug on her system. She found herself feeling lighter, escaping her worries in a giddy playfulness and laughter.

After reassuring himself that her surgery had gone well, he seemed hugely relieved and captured her mood, joining her in the play and fantasy, turning it his way.

"So Dana, it occurs to me that we have a lot in common. I'm a hero, you know. It was in the paper, so I have proof. And you are an even bigger hero. Same paper," he chuckled. "And we also both have sexy voices, of course, so we have quite a lot in common." His laugh turned into a seductive rumble. "So much in common, we should do something about that."

"You think so?" Dana tempted.

"I do, babe. You?" Garrett held his breath.

Dana lowered her voice to torment him. "Well, I *am* very grateful to you already, so maybe ..."

He cut her off, "Not interested in just gratitude."

"Oh. Well, okay," she teased boldly. "I was going to take you to bed and give you a whole night of grateful sex, but if you're not interested . . . forget I said it."

Garrett's laughter sounded a little choked, but he parried well.

"Nope, wouldn't take it anyway. I want you to take me to bed for my body, maybe my brain, but gratitude? Never."

"I see," she purred. "Well, if your brain is as sexy as that voice . . , you might have possibilities. Hey, hang on a minute," she interrupted so briskly he probably felt like a man hanging off a sheer cliff with broken fingernails.

"I'll be done in a minute, Jen. So, Garrett, I have to go. Jenny's back and can hear every word we say, so we'll have to quit the phone sex for now. By the way, I just wanted to let you know, you were grrreat! Bye." She hung up on his laughter.

"Hey! No fair! He never had phone sex we me when I called!" Jen pouted. "I've been cheated!" She pretended to be deeply wounded—then deeply curious. "So tell me, how was he?"

"I'm beginning to wish I knew! He's awfully damn cute on the phone. And that voice!"

"So tell, now!"

Eager for the girl talk, Dana filled Jen in on all the juicy, corny details, laughing mockingly, "... and then he turned me down for grateful sex! Can you believe that?"

Jenny's serious tone belied her twinkling eyes, "You know, Dana, I think you fell for the guy when I first told you about him. But, trust me on this, if you went to bed with him for his body, it would be gratitude sex anyway. That is one hot cowboy! And his butt? Oh my god, you wouldn't know which way to flip him! "

"Jen! Don't be so crude!" Dana scolded, then grinned, "Now, I am on drugs; I have an excuse and can get away with it. So tell me, which side would you pick?"

"Hmmm." Jen seemed to give it serious consideration, but her suggestions were—well, so suggestive!—they left Dana gaping with shock, red-faced, and almost too scandalized to speak.

"Jenny! You bad, *bad* girl!"

Jen shrugged, unrepentant. "So, are you going to see him again do you think?"

"Again? I never saw him the first time."

"Quit stalling, you know what I mean."

"I don't know," Dana sighed, "but it sure is fun to flirt with him on the phone at a safe distance. It keeps my spirits up, right now. Maybe, someday—"

"Well," Jenny looked at her watch, "you have exactly sixty-two days and ten hours to decide, because after that I'm going after him myself, on my next four day weekend!"

"Is that right?" Dana laughed a little uncertainly. "I'll let you know before then."


THE LIGHT-HEARTED BANTER with Garrett and Jenny the night before—at least, she thought Jen had been teasing—helped Dana regain her equilibrium to face the meeting the next day with her former teammate.

To her surprise, Helen brought her husband along. She soon found out why the lawyer-husband attended with his wife. Their proposal stunned Dana. She was unprepared for their eagerness to negotiate an outright purchase of her business.

Dana reacted a little like they had asked to buy her firstborn.

In a way, they had. She had dreamed and nursed Dana's Studio for years, and birthed a success all on her own. All the children she worked with were her children. How could she just give them up?

She couldn't. Not yet.

When Dana recovered from her first shock, she explained that to Helen and her husband, with a passion that they easily understood.

Helen had always admired Dana's talent and dedication to her sport. She had missed it, also, until Dana gave her the opportunity to enjoy it again. She deeply respected what Dana had accomplished, not only for the sport, but for the community, herself included.

Helen made the offer to buy out of a sincere desire to offer Dana a solution to her problems, so she could focus on getting well again. She would also love taking it over. Seeing her former teammate in the hospital bed—and the extent of her injuries—she secretly and sadly believed that Dana would never be able to fly on the bars again. But she could never say that to her. Instead, offering any form of assistance with the studio, realizing Dana wasn't ready yet to give up her dreams, or let go of her hope—and hope healed.

Confirming that the free school program would be honored, it was decided that Helen would take over as Dana's manager through the end of the year. Helen didn't want a salary now, but to use that money to hire part-time assistants. At year end, Dana could either reimburse Helen's salary in cash, or with a partnership percentage, at Dana's discretion. An option to purchase would also be prepared that could be executed if Dana decided to sell at some time in the future.

Helen's husband would immediately draw up all papers outlining their agreement and get them to Dana's attorney to review. If all went smoothly, Helen would be able to re-open Dana's Studio only a few days late.

As simply as that, her immediate problems were solved; the weightier decisions pushed back until she would be more capable of dealing with them. Helen was thrilled, and Dana felt as light as a thistle. When the happy couple left, Dana smiled, falling into deep and dreamless sleep for twelve solid hours.

She woke to excruciating pain in her newly reassembled wrist.

# Chapter 8

IT HAD BEEN A SPUR of the moment impulse.

Now Garrett waited to hear her response. He switched the phone to his other ear so he could wipe a sweaty palm on his jeans.

"You're flying in for a business trip?" Dana clarified.

Well, no, that wasn't exactly what he had meant to imply, but maybe she would be more comfortable that way. Garrett could think of something business related. He hoped.

"Ah, sure." He knew Dana had only flirted with him by phone because he was so far away. Safe. He didn't dare tell her he was flying to Washington just to see her. She might think he was coming to collect on some of their flirtations, and turn him away.

"My, what a coincidence," she was saying politely. Or was her voice cool, or even wary? He couldn't tell. Her next words sounded a little more promising.

"Will you have any free time while you're here?"

All of it? He switched the phone again to his dry hand. Must be guilt that was making him sweat so much.

"I plan to. Actually, I was calling to see what the hospital visiting hours and rules were. I thought I might drop by...," he swallowed at the silence on the other end of the phone. "If that's okay with you? Maybe smuggle you in some chocolates?" Flat out bribery!

"I love chocolates," Dana ventured shyly.

"What's your favorite kind?"

"Any kind that has nuts in it instead of fruit."

"Hmm. I would have taken you for a big fruit and vegetable eater."

"Oh, I am. I'm just a purist when it comes to chocolate. I don't like mixing my sweets with healthy things. It takes all the fun out of indulging."

"Well that makes sense. So, ah, it's okay if I come see you then?"

"Ahh...," Dana hesitated.

Wrong approach, he told himself, quickly changing to a question she couldn't answer 'no'.

"So what times are the visiting hours?"

Dana quoted him the schedule.

"Great, I'll see you then with lots of chocolate, fruit on the side. Say 'hi' to Jenny for me. Bye."

Garrett hung up before she had a chance to stop him, and exhaled all the breath he had held in one big gust. He felt a grin light up across his face. He knew it was a grin because guys just didn't get dopey dreamy smiles. Dodging the inconveniently mirror-like steel surface of his fridge, he reached in and pulled out a long neck beer and strolled out to his porch to catch the cooling breeze.

He had already looked up the closest hotels to her hospital. Pulling out his list he called and made reservations for the weekend, then called and made matching airline reservations.

Stretching out his dusty jean-clad legs, he tipped back his hat and his drink. He studied the early evening sun highlighting the Absarokas, picking out all the rugged details of the creek-scored and individually carved peaks.

Sipping his beer, he savored the scenery while pondering a good business excuse to use for his trip. An impatient whinny from the corral brought him back to his feet. It was time for evening hay and, based on the rumble in his stomach, time to rustle up something for his own evening feed.

As he tossed hay, he thought he'd give Gil, one of his foremen, a call to see if he wanted to stay at his place and take care of the horses while he was gone. Gil was always ready to swap his apartment for Garrett's place.

"That'll make you guys happy, wont it?"

Gil always spoiled the horses with extra carrots and apples, while Garrett was gone. He claimed he had to 'cuz the fellas were so plumb heart broke that you were gone, it was downright pitiful!'

Right.

Yup, he'd call Gil for sure before he fixed his own meal. Better yet, he'd see if Gil wanted a prime rib dinner at River's Edge, the newest and nicest bar and grill in the area. He'd heard their steaks were better than the rib house in town. A treat like that should ensure Gil was available when Garrett needed him. He could use a good dinner himself, and a friendly game of pool. He was feeling lucky.

"DO YOU SUPPOSE your stylist does hospital calls?" Dana asked Jenny as soon as she arrived for her evening visit.

Jen blinked a few times, put her hand up to her hair and immediately regretted canceling her last hair appointment.

"Thanks for the sly hint. I'll go into her salon next week. Any other insults you have on your mind, just say so."

"Well, you do look a bit bedraggled, for you," Dana chuckled. "You need to take care of yourself, Jen, and not worry about me so much. I don't expect you to tie yourself to this hospital bed with me. I know you're my friend and love me, so take a break, huh? It's boring, here. I know, why don't you go on one of your famous shopping sprees? Then you can come back here and give me a fashion show! While you're at it you can pick me up some silk pajamas, maybe a matching silk robe, with a Chinese design or something, whatever you think is hot, but covers everything."

"Well, you must be bored! Whatever happened to your long T-shirts and flannel pajamas?"

"I feel like indulging myself in a little luxury, I guess."

"You're due, for sure. I'll go shopping tomorrow, instead of coming by, before you change your mind again. It's about time you dressed like a woman, instead of a tomboy."

Dana's clothing choices had always been a frustration for her more elegant friend. Jenny also figured that with her poor body so bruised and torn, Dana needed to feel pretty again. Hospital clothes were hardly designer labels!

"And Jen, I really hadn't meant to insult your appearance, but since you brought it up—"

"I know, you just couldn't help yourself. You were born with a merciless teasing gene, Dana."

"I do wonder if your stylist does hospital calls, but for me?"

"I can see it might be a little tough for you to do one of your do-it-yourself haircuts," Jenny eyed the bandage on Dana's head, the cast on one hand, "but why not wait for the full treatment, hair and nails, when they unwrap you?"

"Did I mention that Garrett called?" Dana asked, full of innocence.

"That's nice. Hasn't he been calling several times a week?"

"Did I mention he said he might 'drop-in' and visit the end of this week?"

"DROP-IN? Doesn't he know *anything* about women? When's he coming? I'll drag my stylist here two days before, just to be safe. Oh, Dana! This is so exciting! And horrible, if we don't get you fixed up! How sexy do you want those silk pajamas to be? We need to get someone in here from Nordstrom's to do your makeup, and perfume...scent is so important, we need to ..."

"Hey! Jen! Time out! I'm in a hospital, on medications. I'm not allowed to put stuff on my skin, like perfume, and probably some of the other stuff you're planning. It messes up something, I forget what. It's on one of those instruction sheets. Anyway, I don't want to look like a ghoul! I just want some pretty clothes and clean shiny hair and nails."

"... and shiny nose." Jenny added, disappointed her total makeover had been put on the skids. But, she had to admit, Dana had always looked great with just her clean, shiny face, even that freckled shiny nose. "I guess anything is bound to look better to him than the other times he saw you."

"Thanks. I think. At least I won't look dead this time. So you'll arrange the stylist and the clothes?"

"With pleasure. So did he say why he's coming?"

"A business trip."

Jenny wrinkled her tiny un-shiny nose at that. "What business would a local contractor from Montana have in this state?"

"I don't know. I was so flustered, I forgot to ask him. I'm scared, Jen. I've never met him before! And the things I've said to him on the phone!"

Jenny could see the scarlet creep up Dana's cheeks. She just laughed. "You'll love him!" And I think he's already half-in-love with you, girl, she thought to herself. Oh, this was going to be so romantic! Jenny could hardly wait to watch.


SALVATION CAME IN the form of junk mail.

Garrett almost threw his excuse away.

It had been a physically demanding day. This was the first time he'd been off his feet and he had just settled on his porch in a favorite wooden rocker, not ready to get up and start his chores yet. Thumbing through the mail he'd picked up, he decided to open and read the circular he had received from the builder's association, of which he was a member. These bulk mailings were listings of different master builder events around the country, usually all too distant for him. They did, however, occasionally have notification of pending new legislation of note to members, so he decided he better read this one. He wasn't eager to get back on his weary feet yet, anyway.

"Well, would you look at that?" He laughed out loud, scaring away the magpie that had been inspecting his woodpile for grubs.

The last piece of his weekend plans had just fallen into place. His builders association was involved in a Home Show in Washington. The city and event dates just happened to match up with his airline reservations. He had an excellent excuse to check it out. It must be fate!

Garrett jumped up and headed down to the barn, whistling happily, head high, with a definite spring in his long-legged stride.

"Well, 'ole Corky, you mess you, I've decided I've had enough of your horse spit kisses. I've got myself a hot date with that lovely filly out in Washington State. I'm going to put on my best clothes and my best smelling aftershave, and show her some respect, like I was telling you. And you are going to miss me while I'm gone. Yes, you are, quit snorting and shaking your head. Now all of you, listen up. I want you all on your best behavior for Gil." He accepted a few more horse kisses from Flicka—she never drooled on him—as he doled out carrots, like celebratory cigars, all around.

No longer tired, he started a list in his head of any last minute details he needed to complete before jetting out of town.

"OH, DANA, JUST look at you!" Jenny was delighted to see the transformation, especially the gemstone sparkle it put in Dana's green eyes. "All dressed up and no one to impress. You look terrific, Dana. Do you think he'll drop in tonight?"

"Well, it's Friday night. I don't know what he had in mind when he said over the weekend. I'm just not taking any chances. Besides, after so long in hospital garb and flannel pajamas, I thought I might need some practice looking more elegant."

It never failed to amaze Jenny how Dana didn't realize how she always projected a cool, reserved, elegance. But it was a natural elegance that had nothing to do with clothes, because she dressed like a tomboy, to Jen's never ending dismay. And maybe it was better. Dressed up like this Dana was almost too lovely and eye catching for the reserve that she knew her friend used like a protective shield.

"I like the way your seamstress fixed this sleeve. It drapes over all the junk on my shoulder, but doesn't slither off. Does it look okay? Did she fix them all this way?"

"Yes, so don't be so anxious. You're lovely and it's brilliant. Maybe she should start a hospital fashion line?"

"Well, I'd recommend her," Dana said, as casually as someone who had never turned down big bucks for sportswear endorsements.

"So what's new? Didn't they do one of those scan thingies on your wrist today? Does it still ache?"

"Well, yes, to be honest. They said there was some problem with a blockage in the blood supply to it, delaying the healing. They have started me on some new drug to see if that can help, before they try any more surgery. They quizzed me with about a million questions that I couldn't answer, about reactions to all kinds of things I'd never heard of. And,' she sighed, "they keep forgetting I don't have a family medical history. Anyway, I'm not one to take drugs. How would I know about that stuff?"

"Beats me, but maybe it will help. I know you don't like the surgery. You know, Dana, that color silk is really great on you. Your skin looks like it has more color than usual. You should wear those colors more often."

"Maybe. I always thought I wasn't supposed to wear this color with my hair, and I'm not sure the color in my cheeks is because of it." Dana put her hands to her face. "They feel kind of warm."

"Probably just a blush from all those hot thoughts you're having about Garrett," Jen leered. "Still a little scared about seeing him for the first time?"

"I'm not having hot thoughts!" Dana coolly denied. "I'm just curious, is all. Wouldn't you be? Someone that saved you? Someone that had seen you, but you'd never seen him?"

"And what a sight he is," Jenny added knowingly. "But it's nothing to get so breathless about," she added, when she heard Dana wheeze as she sucked in a breath.

"So let's talk about something else, so you don't get so overexcited. Tell me what you think about... Dana? Dana, are you okay, honey? DANA! NURSE, NURRSSE! Quick! Hurry! She can't BREATHE!!"


GARRETT DIDN'T GET Jenny's message until Saturday morning. He'd shut his cell phone off at the airport and forgotten to turn it back on.

When he had arrived and checked in Friday evening, he'd looked longingly at the hospital as his taxi drove by, but decided it would be wiser to wait to see Dana on Saturday. He had felt he would have a better chance to visit with her longer, going in early the next day.

He took himself out for a pretend business dinner meeting to pass the time, then watched a dozen different cable channels he didn't have at home, until he finally managed to doze off.

Just preparing to leave his room for breakfast, he picked up his cell and remembered to turn it back on.

He had five urgent voicemails. All from Jenny. Dialing her back, he felt his gut lodge in his throat, dreading what news could possibly be so urgent.


NEWS THAT WEEK OUT OF YELLOWSTONE PARK was disturbing; protests had headlined news and media.

For years there were debates, some heated, over balancing the need of the park service to preserve a natural environment for the wild life with the need for the safety and enjoyment of the public. As park visitations increased annually, so did the difficulties for the park in that balancing act between conflicting priorities. Rangers dealt with the situation by attempting to train and tame the people, and keep the other wildlife wary and separated from them.

Unfortunately, bears enjoyed junk food as much as the public did, and when they became too accustomed to it they began to become dangerous for all those Big Macs walking around on two legs. There was nothing entertaining about watching a bear entering your neighbor's unoccupied tent during the daytime—the sounds of a bear huffing and sniffing around your tent in the middle of the night was too chilling to imagine.

The park service had attempted to require permanent hard-sided-only camping in a number of locations of normal heavy bear habitat. Permanent restrictions were finally in place at Fishing Bridge, where only the bears were allowed to fish for their dinner. But most other campgrounds had heavy warning signs, bear proof food storage containers and trash cans, and flyers about how to be bear aware. All bear sightings were supposed to be reported immediately to rangers, so they could track and be aware of what, if any, inappropriate behavior they were up to. A human-habituated bear could become a dead bear, and the park service wanted to be proactive and prevent that, if at all possible.

But some bears just didn't get the message—and neither did many of the tourists.

New problems had begun a few weeks earlier, in a campground that had a hundred sites for visitors to a nearby popular geyser basin. Also a favored picnic area, it drew many visitors to its historic ranger station museum. Despite warning signs posted throughout the area, and nailed to the picnic tables, it also became a popular location for two unwanted visitors—a pair of young grizzlies. They started showing up at lunchtime and checking out the interiors of empty tents. Rangers warned the tent campers to sleep in their cars at night and began looking for the pair.

Non-lethal methods would be used first. Initially, rangers attempted to get the bears to relocate on their own, assaulting them with loud noises and arm waving, shooting them with bean bags, and using Karelian Bear Dogs. But the pickings were too good and the bears were reported back in the campsites the next day. With a long holiday weekend and hordes of visitors imminent, they had to temporarily close down the popular campground while they tried to find and capture the bears. With all the other camp grounds already full for the holiday weekend, the public did not take any more kindly to being relocated, than the bears did.

A few years prior, a mother grizzly with cubs had entered a remote tent camping location, on the far northeastern boundary of the park, at night. She had killed one camper and attacked two other families, all while they slept in their tents. Yet people had woefully short memories, and, even shorter tempers and patience when on their dream vacations. Some loudly complained about the sudden, temporary closure of the popular museum, campground, and picnic area that weekend. But that wasn't what all the protests were about.

Carrying placards, wildlife and animal activists marched, protesting loudly with a lot of help from a sympathetic press.

Rangers had finally needed to resort to forcibly relocating the stubborn bear pair. Sedating them with tranquilizing darts, they would move them to an area where humans wouldn't bother them—or the reverse. Unfortunately, one young male grizzly accidentally died from an unexpected, and adverse reaction to the drug delivered by the dart.


THE NEWS WAS HORRID, but it could have been worse.

Dana had survived a terrible drug reaction that had cut off her breathing. But she did survive.

She should recover fully, off the drug. She would be in intensive care all day. Neither Garrett nor Jenny would be allowed in. It was to protect Dana from outside germs, in such a weakened state. Maybe Sunday, they could visit if all went well, the doctors had hinted.

Garrett met with Jenny and bought her breakfast while she brought him up to date on everything that had happened since they last met.

His business excuse for the weekend trip had been the annual Home Builders Show in the local convention hall. When he mentioned the event to Jen, inquiring if she had any interest in coming with him, her enthusiasm startled him. Clearly countertop styles and cabinets rated much higher in Jen's world, than the rocks that captured Dana's interest—except for use in lovely landscape borders, of course, Jen noted. Garrett was pleased and relieved and suspected she was just as desperate for a distraction while they waited as he was. He would enjoy Jen's company and opinion on new interior styles and products, but most of all, she was his only link to Dana. If there *was* any news, *she* would be the one contacted. He was going to stick to her like super glue.

Jenny confessed she usually attended the home show anyway, just to dream and gather new ideas. They'd busied themselves gathering brochures, checking out all the new green technologies and appliance and electronics introductions, and examined new flooring materials and the latest in custom baths and kitchens.

Jen had stopped suddenly at a model kitchen; Garrett studied it for his own reasons. The sales agent said the efficient but compact design was targeted to residence hotels or studio rentals. It had all the essential appliances of an upscale kitchenette, scaled to half-size. Garrett measured it for use in small cabins. It was an ideal size and, according to Jenny, had a great layout with all the basics. So Garrett ordered plans and supplier catalogs, while he was there.

Finally, as they shared a quick dinner at the food court in the convention center, Jenny got word from Dana's doctors that she would be moved tomorrow. They would be allowed a ten-minute visit late Sunday, but the patient would most likely still be sedated.

Still, it was great news. Dana was improving, until—

"WHAT? NO, PLEASE! Not again!" Dana wailed, after Jen informed her hero had come and gone while Dana was unconscious after her life-threatening allergic reaction.

"You think you're frustrated, sister? Imagine how Garrett feels! He even kissed you this time, and still you wouldn't open your eyes for your Handsome Hero. Imagine what a failure he feels like!"

Dana raised a hand to her cheek, a look of horror in her eyes.

"Sorry, Dana, I was just trying to tease you, but I guess that was a little cruel. But I figured I better spill it all now, while you still had a few sedatives in your system. He still left you this huge box of chocolates though, no fruit. And just because I'm feeling so sorry for you, I've only eaten five of them while I was waiting for you to come to."

Dana wanted to cry. She wanted to stuff her face with chocolates and cry. This was so unfair! She'd so looked forward to finally seeing her wonderful, hot, hero in the flesh—and for him to see her looking ... well, at least looking alive, for once!

"There is a bright side to all this you know," Jen said as she carefully selected her sixth chocolate. "If you guys do get together and fall in love, you don't have to worry that the first time he sees you in the morning with bedroom hair and no make-up that he'll run screaming from the room in fright."

Dana groaned, wishing she had enough energy to gag her best friend. "Gosh, that is just so comforting, Jen. Thank you for that. Now give me a handful of those chocolates and go away so I can be miserable in peace!"

"He took me to the home show."

Dana gasped. "See? Just one of the many benefits of being conscious! It must be so much more rewarding to take someone who can actually see and experience all the sights and sounds." Dana knew she was being a wee bit envious, maybe even a little bitter, but she just couldn't help herself. "You two must be getting to know each other quite well by now."

Jenny smiled; Dana was incredibly, viciously, jealous.

"He *said* his business trip was to go to the home show, get ideas and supplier information."

"Oh." Dana felt bitchy.

"Turns out that wasn't really the business that brought him all the way out here though." Jen bit into her chocolate, crunching the nuts serenely.

"Okay, I'll bite. *You, probably*," Dana threatened. "What was his real reason?"

"You. To see you. Oops, gotta run. See you later."

"Wait!" But Jen was already snickering her way out the door.

Well damn! Sounds like he'd seen her, all right. Probably with her eyes rolled up and her tongue hanging out! At least her hair had been clean.

She tried to visualize herself lying in bed looking like that, and her hero leaning over and tenderly brushing her tongue aside so he could kiss her.

She almost laughed—it was quite the comic vision—but hardly romantic! She groaned in shame. Even though she had never considered herself the romantic type, some things were just a lot funnier when they happened to someone else.

She was not in a humorous frame of mind right now. When the hell was she going to get to see him? She grabbed a chocolate and bit into it vengefully.

Hmm. Did he really kiss her? Or did Jen just make that up?


GARRETT GAZED OUT the window, as the plane took him further and further away from Dana. He had wanted to cancel his return flight, but he had responsibilities back home, and payroll checks to sign. One of his homes was due for inspection in a few days. He needed to get back and make sure every last detail had been completed so it would pass the checklist and receive the occupancy permit, the first time. Otherwise, his eager clients would be delayed moving into their new home. And that was not acceptable for Hearth Homes.

He spotted the Rockies through the clouds beneath him. They looked like row after row of dark teeth. It was a strange sight to see them from above, with summer almost ended, without their normal glistening caps of snow. t wouldn't take long now for fall storms to dust the highest elevations with their first layers of snow and ice so they didn't look so unfamiliar with those barren, glacially-scraped, dark peaks. Ragged, raw, naked, like Garrett's spent emotions from the weekend. A weekend that had started with such high hopes and expectations.

He sighed and turned away from the depressing sight. Putting his seat back, he closed his eyes and let his thoughts drift like the clouds massed outside the window, back to thoughts of Dana.

It was his own damn fault. If he'd only gone to see her Friday night when he got in, instead of trying to play it cool. He'd regret that for a long time—a lesson learned.

As frightening as it had been to learn what had happened to her; as disappointing as it had been to not be able to spend time with her; he was thankful that he had been there close at hand. He probably would have hopped a plane anyway for those few moments he needed to see for himself that she had come through okay. Needing those brief minutes to see her breathe, to touch soft warm flesh, to reassure himself and know she was still there. Even unconscious, he'd been startled by her beauty.

The swelling and bruises on her face the last time he saw her, were gone now. Her lips had regained their shape. Their lush lines and upward curled corners had made him smile, made him want to taste them, taste her.

The need, the connection, that bound them, had not faded for him, but was stronger than ever. Now that he had heard her voice, the joy of her laughter, felt the force of her personality and impish sense of humor, he felt more connected to her than ever. That same need to reach out to her, to touch, had consumed him.

He had forgotten anyone else was in the room as he had gazed down at her, touching her cheek lightly with his fingertips. He'd leaned forward to brush his lips across her face, breath her in, fill his senses with the warmth of her skin. When he whispered encouragement in her ear, the feel of her soft breath against his cheek reassured him, inspired him, to add tender endearments as well. He placed a final soft kiss on her forehead, then he'd had to leave her. Again.

There was no longer any doubt in Garrett's mind. He was solidly hooked by this woman. He didn't have the least desire to try to wiggle off the line, either. He needed to focus on what it would take to convince Dana she wanted to reel him in.

# Chapter 9

"I'VE HAD ENOUGH!" Dana declared the next morning to her team of surgeons and doctors—a meeting she had urgently demanded.

"I know you are all doing what you think is best for me," she paused trying to stay calm when she wanted to scream in frustration. "But this kind of life is just not working for me. There must be another way! I will not be a guinea pig for testing drug cures. I will not just lie about waiting to gradually heal while imprisoned in this hospital. I am not one of your geriatric patients. I am young, and fit," seeing eyebrows rise at that, she tried to motion with her left hand as she muttered, "Well, mostly fit," but her arm boomeranged as it was still tethered by her IV tube, just increasing her rage.

"Take this out now," she gritted through clenched teeth, "or I will rip it out. All of it!"

They all assumed, naturally, that her frustration and determination were the natural result of her adverse drug reaction—her anger was hardly a surprise. But Dana would never admit that it was a missed kiss that had tipped the balance and caused this rebellion. She wouldn't credit that as the cause herself. After all, she had a logical, scientific, reasoning mind. Her decisions were made accordingly. So what if she had missed her hero? It was a near death chemical reaction that created a logical adverse reaction in the patient, she posited. Call it Dana's Theory. Adverse treatment = adverse anger reaction in patient. Exactly.

Not to mention her seriously peeved pheromones!

After her IV and a number of other tubes and items, which probably hadn't been needed for some time, had been removed, Dana took a deep calming breath, and continued on with her meeting.

"I am not used to being on drugs. They make me sluggish and stupid, and a lot of other very unpleasant things." She tried to keep her tone calm and reasonable, but could hear the tremor in her voice. "I am used to exercising every day, getting my blood pumping and circulating that way. I know my body needs to get oxygen to the tissues and cells so they can heal. I'd rather get it done my way, than through a tube up my nose, or strange chemicals in my veins," she emphasized—reminding them they had nearly done her in. "So, I've had more than enough of doing this your usual way. Please, I'm begging you, put your heads together and find another solution. One I can live with."

No immediate suggestions were offered—hospitals probably weren't used to treating a lot of healthy people. Dana offered her team some encouragement.

"Listen, my body can heal itself—if it's not just lying around here rotting. And I am determined to get well! That's half the battle, right? I'm ready for some physical therapy. I'm used to pushing my body and sucking up the pain without resorting to pills. Let's make a new plan, maybe get some sports medicine people involved. We have to change course. Think outside the box ..."

All her tough resolve seemed to flee momentarily, as she turned sea green eyes near to tears on them.

"Please. Help me! I *really* need your *help*."


JENNY ALMOST PANICKED when she found Dana's bed empty when she arrived that evening. She ran to the nurse's station, but Dana's favorite nurse reassured her Dana was only out having tests done.

"But, there weren't any tests scheduled for tonight. Not that I knew of," Jenny insisted.

"True, but our impatient patient changed the rules today," the nurse chuckled, grinning. "I swear they've scanned and x-rayed every single part of her body today, with every fancy scanner and test that they can think of," she confided.

"Oh, she'll just love that!" Jen snorted.

"She seems to be taking it well. She's why they are doing it."

The nurse motioned Jenny to lean in a little closer, her voice lowered confidentially.

"I heard our girl came out swinging today and challenged those doctors to come up with a new treatment plan. Demanded it!"

"Really?" Jenny whispered, leaning even closer.

"Oh, yeah. She told them to quit with the pills, no lying around in bed. She wants some action, that girl!"

Jenny's eyes gleamed, pleased. "To tell you the truth, I'm surprised Dana took this as long as she did. She's a physical person. Always has been."

"That's what she wants now. We could hear her all the way out here. She's had it with that hospital bed! The docs are doing the tests so they can study and see what they can come up with, and ..."

The nurse straightened suddenly as an intern walked by the station, adding in a normal voice, "So come back in about an hour. Your friend should be back in her room by then." The nurse added a friendly wink.

Slipping into the room an hour later, Jenny found Dana in her bed, a troubled scowl on her face.

"I hear someone's been naughty!" she sang in greeting.

"I hope to be someday. At this rate I'll be too old to enjoy it!" Dana heaved a deep sigh, then turned to smile weakly at her friend. "It's good to see you, sorry I've been such a grouch."

"I didn't blame you. After all, to have to miss a hunk like that!" Jenny clutched a hand to her heart, over dramatizing the tease.

"Ah, payback. Okay, we're even now. Enough!" Dana's laugh sounded choked, turning into a sob.

"I can't take this anymore, Jen!" All the frustration Dana must have been holding inside flooded forth in tears. "It's been over a month. I'm sick of this bed. Sick of being told not to move ... not get up ... not even exercise my legs! They're okay, aren't they? Is there something they aren't telling me?"

"No, no, hey," Jenny wrapped her arms around Dana and let her cry and vent and get it all out. She'd been expecting this explosion. Dana never was one to cry, but she must be scared stiff wondering what her future held—or didn't.

"If my legs are okay, why won't they let me get up? I'm sick of being helpless—sick of being sick! I'm starting to hate myself, Jen. I don't have anything to do but lie here and feel sorry for myself. I hate that self-pity! What's wrong? This is *not* me!"

"I know, I know. I'm the crier. You're the action girl," Jen shushed and stroked Dana's hair as the storm wound down. "And you know, Dana, you took a step today to start to change all that. *That is* like you, you should be proud of that."

"But I only did it because I was sorry for myself for missing my hero!" Dana wailed.

Jen tried to hold back a laugh. "Well, whatever works for you, girl!" She wasn't sure if the sound Dana made was a snort of laughter or another sob.

"So, is there anything I can do to help? Besides letting you sob all over my shoulder? Not that I don't owe you more than a few rounds of that!"

Dana lifted her head and reached for some tissue, calmer now that she had shared her misery with her best friend.

"Yes. If the doctors don't come up with a new plan, I want you to kidnap me and take me home."

"Deal. But show a little patience Dana. You know you want to heal right."

"I will. But outside of antibiotics for infection, I'm through with all those other drugs."

"With you there, kiddo! You scared the crap out of me the other night!"

"Me too. And I ruined the only professional hair-do that I've ever had," she added with a tiny twinkle in her reddened eyes.

"You'll be okay now," Jen breathed, relieved. "Thank god your sense-of-humor bone wasn't the one that was broken!"


AFTER JEN LEFT, Dana was exhausted from the day's tests and the stresses her system had taken over the weekend. She was a little ashamed of her crying jag, but glad that Jen had been there to help her. Had she been so sedated all this time that all those emotions had lain dormant, along with her willpower and self-respect?

Well, that was all going to change now, Dana pledged. Tomorrow she would wake with a clear head. She had a lot of thinking and planning to do. And, she was getting up out of this bed, at least for a while, no matter what anyone said!

But, progress was excruciatingly slow at first.

Dana couldn't believe her well-toned athlete's body had turned to mush so rapidly without activity.

Early on, she was frustrated being held back from even the simplest activities. It wasn't as if she had planned to jog, or anything, she complained to her health care jailers; she just wanted to be up and around a little each day. She soon had to admit, privately, that even a few shaky steps to her bathroom were surprisingly tricky.

She was glad she wasn't attempting to stand when her doctor team came back prepared for their next meeting. They started by doing something they hadn't done before; they *explained* all those mysterious "h-m-m-s" and thoughtful notes they had scratched into her chart—their thoughts, never shared with her—which made up the majority of their "discussions" with her in the past. Usually followed by an encouraging smile and a coming-along-fine pat before leaving the room—and leaving *her* feeling like a glorified lab rat, wondering what the next experiment was that they were planning for her.

Now they were giving her the facts and truths she demanded—and yes, in fact, the truth *did* hurt.

Her left wrist and hand had been crushed and broken, there were other fractures; she knew all that, but  not the full extent of her injuries. Her head wound, her doctors explained, had caused a concussion and inner ear problems. Until her sense of balance and depth perception recovered, they had not wanted her standing up, unattended, to crash and cause more damage. She had to agree that was sensible.

In addition, the wound that curved under her arm and across her back shoulder had severed important tendons that, stitched together, needed to heal to support her spine before they let her start running around. It was not, they explained firmly, like a clean and carefully done surgical wound. The bull's horn had torn indiscriminately; she couldn't expect as speedy a recovery as from a planned incision. Her doctors also warned that their decision, to encase less of her body in a cast, had required Dana's cooperation in staying put—implying they could, and *would*, plaster her down if she didn't behave.

It was ironic that Dana had not realized the true extent of her injuries *because* they hadn't taken such severe measures initially. Her doctors had considered her comfort, left access to monitor and perform repairs and follow-up surgeries—wisely, she now had to admit—as long as the patient stayed put and followed doctor's orders. She should have noticed how normally simple motions, usually taken for granted, were so difficult. Just reaching beside her for a glass of water, had jerked and shot pain through unexpected locations. And she had railed at them for all the restrictions and delays to being allowed to get up and do the gentle exercise usually recommended after surgery. The term 'patient' seemed better applied to her doctors, than to herself, Dana realized with shame.

Now she was hearing not what she *wished* to hear, but what she *needed* to hear to assist in making good decisions on her healing. A sports medicine consultant and therapist had already been added to her team to study the latest round of tests. Her team had agreed to try to let Dana push herself to her limits—not just to their worries. For now. With supervision. And constant testing for results and progress. If passing tons of tests would keep her out of a body cast—and get her out of this institution—Dana would do it.

*Athlete to invalid, in a matter of minutes!* Now to start climbing back to recovery. How high would that mountain be, Dana wondered. Would it be wise to look up at that dizzying summit? Would she just spook herself, seeing how daunting a climb she had before her?

She had always been goal-oriented, but knew she'd never gotten anywhere without taking just one step at a time. She would start by making it part way up the mountain, picturing the task ahead as individual steps to reach an interim goal, like a base camp, one level at a time.

Like most young adults, Dana took her invincibility for granted, never seriously considering her own mortality—or fragility. Her body always gave her anything she'd asked; it may have taken hard work and conditioning, but ultimately she knew she could accomplish any goal.

Now, the game was changed. She would need to adjust not only physically, but emotionally, to new realities and uncertainty. She could not let fear of failure paralyze her, stop her from testing the future, worrying she might lose control. She'd have to climb those emotional rocks and chasms along with the physical heights.

Forget the summit. Just get moving, she told herself, get started up slow and steady and work through the rest of the problems as she climbed. One level, one base camp at a time, she'd gauge her progress by looking down at how high she had come and let that build her confidence back—rather that peering straight up at what appeared to be impossible heights from below.

With her new self-awareness and resolve, Dana began to outline the first goal levels she wanted to reach, breaking down the steps. Working with her doctors, they modified and adjusted some steps, but agreed to most of her new regime, with limitations. She must start slow and have a physical therapist oversee and approve all exercise—even a simple walk down the hall would require a chaperone until assured she had her balance.

Reluctantly, Dana agreed; she'd think of them as trainers and spotters, like she'd required as an athlete practicing new routines on the parallel bars.

BY THE TIME JENNY took her lunch break from work the next day, she had four voice messages on her phone. She had a pretty good idea who they were from.

1st message: "Jen would you go to my apartment and bring my laptop the next time you come?"

2nd message: "Hey, me again, grab my ankle and wrist weights while you're there, the smallest ones?"

3rd message: "You have my credit cards at your place don't you? Would you use one and get a wireless card for my laptop? Just use the card to order whatever is needed to set up wireless internet service for me. The office store can probably figure out what to get if you take them my laptop."

4th message: "—and Jen? Thanks! A lot! You're the best!"


WHEN HE TOOK his break, Garrett found a breezy message on his own phone.

"Dana here. Sorry I missed seeing you last weekend. I hope the business part of the trip went well."

Then he heard her chuckle and that deeper, playful voice he loved. "I guess I'll just have to make it up to you for the other ... won't I?"

He had to grin. He thought he might have just heard the first click of that reel starting to turn.

He'd pushed hard all week to complete urgent phases in his projects. The leaves were turning color and the weather cooling; at this altitude winter could come on suddenly and unexpectedly. It was still warm during the days, but the nights were getting frosty. He needed all his homes undercover, roofs completed, windows and doors in, and exteriors sealed.

Strolling the site perimeter, he was satisfied to confirm a completed checklist, except for one last priority—the ditch that carried all the underground piping for utilities and cabling into the house. The plumbers and electricians had finished their connections from road to house, the backfill materials had been delivered and were waiting in mounds beside the trench, and now Garrett was waiting. As soon as the inspector arrived, checked the connections and that everything, including the fill, met county codes, he could sign off. Then he would be allowed to backfill the ditch.

As he waited, Garrett's sharp blue gaze turned out across the high mountain prairie. All the grasses and sage were high and dry, as tan as the mule deer coming down in increasing numbers. The deer were so well camouflaged now, in the dry grass, that usually only their motion, or the "Y" of ears silhouetted on a ridge, gave them away.

He was pretty well camouflaged himself after climbing around the site. His leather vest and boots were already the dusty suede of the film that coated him. He bent to brush at lean jeans, swatting dust from his knees and butt. Removing his hat, he shook motes out of his hair, then blew to get the dust off his hat, before resetting it. Feeling a draft of breeze, he reached back to edge the soft collar of his faded flannel shirt higher, to protect his neck.

Before his trip west, the shagginess had been trimmed from thick blond hair, sun-streaked almost white against his summer bronzed face. He grinned wryly now, thinking of how he had never gotten the chance to make that good first impression on Dana. Though he missed the warmth of hair on his neck now, he didn't regret the trip. What he regretted was having to leave before she woke. He ached to be near her again, to touch her, to hear her voice.

A flicker of motion at the corner of his eye captured his wandering thoughts. Focusing carefully, he located a doe grazing in a far off field as she raised her head, with those jackrabbit ears, to study him.

He had nearly spilled his coffee in his lap this morning when he'd had to brake when a herd materialized and leaped across the road in front of him, headed to the river for their morning drink. They crossed and jumped the fence into the next field, leaping like oversized jackrabbits, then disappeared in the grass. The deer liked to graze the irrigated grasses on ranches that lined the Yellowstone River, giving tourists on Highway 89 a thrill when they realized that the grazing herds of horses and cows had whole herds of deer blended in.

The doe hopped off and disappeared in a hidden fold in the seemingly flat land. The only motion he detected now was the waving of the grass in the wind.

He didn't see any other deer on the move, or any signs of the truck of the inspector. He needed to get this trench signed off and backfilled before the ground started to freeze, preferably by tomorrow morning, so the last of his projects would be safe from the caprices nature could pull in these high mountain valleys. Up here the weather could care less what the calendar said; snow could come at any time.

Where needed, interior finishing on his sites could be done later, once the outside was sealed up snug. First, they had to be able to hook up the interior electrical connections to run tools and heaters for all the other work: pipes, insulation, sheetrock, floors, trim, cabinetry and countertops. Unless, of course, the inspector didn't get out here and they were delayed and couldn't finish the necessary exterior connection signoffs on this house until spring!

Realizing that he was starting to pace, worried that it was getting later in the day than inspectors usually showed, Garrett raked a hand through what remained of his hair and tried to soothe himself. His concerns about the weather weren't unreasonable, but, hell, it probably wouldn't freeze tonight anyway. It might not freeze for another month. He needed to relax and get a grip.

He'd been working hard—too hard—trying to make up for his impulsive trip last weekend. He wanted to keep this project moving and to get all his clients into their new homes as soon as possible, but he needed to simmer himself down. No point letting his emotions control him—regarding work, anyway.

There were a few other emotions he rather enjoyed letting run wild. Especially when it came to a specific green-eyed gal. What a fighter! Another scary medical crisis, yet she popped right back, even sent him a cheery, flirtatious voicemail.

She couldn't feel as upbeat as she'd sounded, but she sure tried to stay positive. He respected that. He knew Dana had gone through cycles of depression, been pretty down at times, Jenny had confessed that much last weekend. Anyone would in Dana's situation, especially if they faced reality instead of just trying to ignore it. He suspected she had even darker times than she confessed to her best friend; he admired the way she continued to fight back. That was the major part.

And, hey, if it made Dana feel better to flirt with and tease him? Well, he was game. More than! Glad to help the cause. All joking aside, he hoped she would change those games over time into something more—more solid, more lasting, deepening her connection to him. For that chance, that hope, he'd gladly leave himself vulnerable, lose a little of his emotional control.

Something Jenny mentioned last weekend gave him a new strategy to draw Dana closer to him; something he also hoped would be healing. Part of his impatience to get these projects under wraps had as much to do with his desire to free up some time this weekend, as the weather.

He planned to head down to Yellowstone Park for some down time. He'd take the trailer and one of his horses and treat himself to a soothing trail ride. The solitude and beauty of the Blacktail Deer Plateau at this time of year was just the ticket, and it worked in perfectly with his plan.

He was grinning, thinking about his grand strategy, even before he heard the crunch of tires on the gravel behind him. Turning, relieved, he waved to the inspector. If all went well he'd get his approval, and his wish to spend time in the park this weekend.


DESPITE ALL HER cautious planning, and an awareness that she needed to stay emotionally steady, Dana lost control of her expectations.

Waiting, excited, for her first escort down the hall, she pictured herself rising and striding briskly up and down, reveling in her escape from enforced bed rest. Okay, so she had ached and been creaky on the way to her bathroom, but such a short distance barely gave her a chance to straighten up and stretch her muscles. Once through that hall door her stride would lengthen and everything would smooth out, start ticking again. Dana was convinced of that.

And she was betrayed. By her own body!

Her spine didn't feel the same. Every step seemed to jolt something she couldn't recall having before. Was a bone in the wrong place? She found herself rising on tip-toe to stop the jarring, but realized her knees were so weak that they felt dizzy. Her first excursion was much shorter than planned.

Dana talked herself past the sweeping disappointment. What had she expected? She'd been lying around like a slug for weeks; she couldn't let down. She'd try to walk every few hours, a few steps further each time. She began to push to reach one higher room number down the hall, before returning to bed. The exercise was so exhausting that even with the added pain, without pills to ease it, she found she had no trouble sleeping hard and long. Refusing to surrender to the I-told-you-so looks of her caretakers, she was convinced to try harder to prove them wrong the next day.

When Jenny arrived that night with her laptop and the weights she had requested from home, Dana almost cried to realize how overconfident she had been. While she smiled and boasted of her walk to Jen, she managed to send her away quickly before she whined and moaned about the pain she was in. She needed to toughen up and quit relying so heavily on her friend for comfort and support. Jen needed time to live her own life; Dana needed time to work hard every minute without sympathy. She felt horribly selfish thinking of how much her dear, sweet friend had sacrificed, and would continue to, unless Dana forced—ordered— Jen to go home.

After sending her off, Dana opened her laptop and a spreadsheet to create an exercise program for herself; one more realistic than her original goals before her first attempts to walk any distance.

Over the next few days, she became a regular in the hospital hallways, gaining strength and stability daily. Between walks she got on the internet, searching all the sites she could find about rehabilitation. Checking on-line journals for JAMA and Nature, looking for scientific and medical breakthroughs that might apply, or at least give her hope for a full recovery.

Her doctors patiently answered questions, read her articles for any relevance they could apply and monitored for side effects of the increasingly strenuous exercise program that Dana had set for herself. Recognizing that taking control of her own recovery was the most promising sign yet, her doctors were pleased, knowing their patient's spirit needed to heal, as well as her body.


SHE HAD BEEN EVICTED! What kind of gratitude was that? Jen raged.

After she had delivered the requested supplies to the hospital, Dana had said a quick thanks, bragged about her walk, then told Jenny to get out and not show her face in the hospital again until Dana called her back.

Jenny felt used and unappreciated and ... *hurt*. After all the hours she had spent worrying by Dana's bedside, then the minute Dana had stood on her own two feet she'd told Jenny to get lost! Well, not like that, exactly, but that was how it had felt. Fine!

Jen tossed her purse on her couch, stepped out on her patio, and glanced around, hands on hips. It felt strange. She couldn't remember the last time she had been home in daylight hours. The lawn had been mowed by the neighbor boy that she hired, but the rest of the area—especially the flower beds—looked like crap. Instead of giving her home and garden the care and attention that it needed, she had been spending it all on her ungrateful friend. Well that was going to stop! She would have the whole next weekend to work on her yard now.

Why wait? Stomping inside to change into her jeans, Jenny decided to get started tonight. She hadn't made any other plans, except for visiting her poor, lonely friend in the hospital. She was definitely in a mood to rip and hack away at something. The weeds in her flower beds would do—her glare alone, should shrivel them to their roots.

Each night that week after work, working up a good mad, she tore weeds from her beds, unintentionally tearing off a few flowers also, muttering in rage about her ungrateful friend.

It was, therefore, extremely annoying when, almost finished with all the beds, Jenny heard the echo of her door bell. Rising and hastily brushing dirt from her hands, she stomped around the side yard to her front porch.

"I don't want to buy anything, join anything, vote for anyone, or change religions!"

Her harsh, angry voice startled the young man standing facing her front door holding a clipboard in his hands. Turning to the petite, extremely feisty brunette that stood braced, hands fisted on hips, mud on her jeans and artfully streaked across her face, he tried not to laugh at the bird's nest of leaves and twigs tangled in her dark hair.

"How about flowers? Do you accept those?" Sweeping his hand down, he focused her attention on the five pots of lush copper-colored chrysanthemums that rested on her porch, encouraging, "They're all paid for," with a smile.

Without a word, Jenny stepped up, signed the clipboard, and accepted the large card he handed her. He just laughed and said "You're welcome," before driving off.

The card had a simple picture on the front of two little girls with their backs turned to the camera, sitting on a log, holding hands. Inside the blank card was filled with very familiar handwriting. It told of how much she was missed, how dear, supporting and sacrificing of a friend she was. How appreciative and apologetic the sender was for stealing so much of her time, energy and support. It mentioned the flowers were offered as she knew her selfishness had probably ruined all Jen's from neglect.

"I had to push you away, Jen. I was leaning too much, letting you pamper me too much. Stealing all your time and life. I need to do the rest of the hard work alone now. You can't do this part for me. I'll work harder if I miss your company, so I can get out

130

and we can get back to old times. Much love and many thanks, your Dana."

So annoying! Jen thought, reaching out a finger to stroke the soft, spiky bronzed flowers, smearing muddy tears across her face with her other hand.

# Chapter 10

PERFECT WEATHER! Garrett whistled happily as he wound beside the sparkling Yellowstone River that played tag with the highway on the way down to Gardiner.

About one-third of the way south from Livingston, driving through Paradise Valley just north of Emigrant, he crossed over a curving bridge. Reddened willows and bright yellow aspen banked the river to the east and an art gallery and cabins sat back from the west side of the road. Garrett's eyes widened as he saw a massive moose drinking from a pond beside the parking lot of the gallery that carried its name.

"Look at that rack!" He admired the bronze replica that looked so realistic he expected it to raise its head to gaze at him, water and shoots dripping from its mouth, as he drove past the Moosehorn Gallery. It was impressive, but so realistic, especially with a dark bronze finish so closely mirroring a real moose, that Garrett worried some half-blind idiot hunter might try to bag it this fall.

His horse must have heard his voice; a muffled neigh replied from behind.

"Only another thirty miles, fella. Then we'll play," he promised Blue Moon, his blue roan Appaloosa.

That was one happy horse! Not too thrilled to climb into the trailer, but like a dog that saw its owner pick up a leash, he had pricked his ears and knew it meant there was fun soon to come. Garrett was glad the short and intensely busy summer building season was starting to wind down; he needed to get out and exercise the horses more.

Arriving at the Yellowstone Park gate, Garrett put the first part of his strategy in motion.

After handing over his stock permit and his own park pass, he ordered and paid for a National Parks Annual Pass in Dana's name. Surprisingly, Jen had told him that Dana still wanted to come back, was eager to, in fact. And Garrett planned to make it easier—for her to return to Yellowstone, and closer to him.

Next he made a stop in Mammoth. Running into the old stone fort building that was now a Visitor Center; he purchased a couple of other items on his list. As the former bachelor quarters for the army, the old building's ghosts probably sympathized with Garrett's plan, and with his yearning for a gal he was sweet on, that was so far away.

Stepping back outside with his packages, Garrett found himself surrounded by orange cones, park rangers, and the Mammoth herd of elk. He could hear his horse neighing from the trailer, in response to the bugling call of a huge bull elk that now owned the center of the road. With eight points on each side of a rack that spread as wide as Garrett was tall, the magnificent male was calling out to his harem.

Traffic and tourists were barricaded in all directions. It was close to mating season, and the bulls were highly unpredictable, so more area needed to be blocked than normally required. With elk spread over all the lawns at the center of the village, and the arrogant bull proudly claiming the middle of the main drive, it would be some time before anyone drove anywhere. It would take even longer for the rangers to get all the gawkers back out of the herd's way.

Garrett edged behind the barricade as close to his trailer as he could, grimacing when he heard a hoof strike the wall inside, along with the increasingly agitated sounds of his horse. When the closest ranger noticed him, Garrett pointed toward his rig.

"That yours?" The ranger took in his nod, studying the local license plates, and the commotion. "You have the blood test, permit for that horse?"

"Yup. Showed it at the gate. I'm a regular here."

"And we have to kick him out on a regular basis, too," a deep voice spoke from behind his shoulder.

Garrett spun to face the ranger with the voice as deep and dark as the obsidian black eyes that glittered over a blade sharp nose, and high, ruthlessly sculptured cheekbones.

"I'll handle this," the dark ranger warned, clasping Garrett's arm above the elbow with a large bronzed hand, yanking him a few feet behind the barricade.

"Speak of the devil," Garrett muttered, like a curse. "What the hell are you doing, here? Aren't you still a Glacier Park Ranger? Trying to get me thrown out of here?" He complained. "I can't believe they'd let a redskin savage like you work down here!"

The sharp, dark face of the tall ranger lit up with a handsome grin, brilliant white teeth flashing, black eyes gleaming with delight, "Hey bro', how've you been? Still an insulting paleface, I see!" Laughing, the two tall men threw a one-armed hug over matching broad shoulders, giving each other a friendly slap on the back that would flatten most men.

"I'm heading down to Blacktail Plateau, so I was just thinking of you. And here you are. The devil conjured up!" Garrett told his best friend. "Are you just here for a meeting, or are you working?"

"Working. Temporary assignment to this park, or I'd go with you," the smiling ranger replied. "I meant to give you a call this weekend and let you know I'd be based here a few months. We haven't done any hell-raising together for way too long, man."

"Hah! Seems to me you raise all the hell and leave me to soothe all the feathers," Garrett replied with a good natured grin. "That's okay, you're one hell of a lot of fun to watch in action. Guess I better put a notice in the local paper warning all the ladies to either run for cover, or start getting in line at the local watering hole. How many hearts did you break last time, anyway?"

"Hell, I'm getting old, Garrett, and I never break anything, anyway. Just borrow a few hearts for a little while," he flashed that mischievous grin that was as lethal as a weapon on the ladies.

"Yeah, tell me a few more, you rascal. So when you coming up to stay a few nights?"

"I'll let you know when I get my next schedule. Wish I was off today. I'd go with you."

"Well, try not to get me eighty-sixed from the park just because you can't come with me today, Ranger Ravenwolf." Garrett responded with a wry grin. Another angry neigh and the sound of hooves striking the trailer got the men's attention.

"Always ruining my fun, Garrett. You better get in there and calm him down. That Corky?"

"Nah, he'd likely flunk the drug test, that crazy horse. I brought the Blue, the one you found me, Rave."

"Ah. Should have known it was a Native bred horse with all that spirit. That's good. We had to close that trail a few weeks back for grizzly activity, I hear. So keep an eye out for sign, but that horse has that trail bred into his ancestors, so you have a good mount for that ride."

"Got it. Good to see you, Rave. Call me soon." Scooting between his truck and a parked car, he opened the door to the trailer. Slipping inside, he soothed his horse, gave him some water and oats, stroking him until his buddy called that it was clear to pass.

The herd had moved over to the hill behind the ancient wooden barracks, across the old parade grounds. As Garrett put his truck in gear and slowly moved off, he could see a recalcitrant group of camera-toting tourists chasing the herd—with rangers in close pursuit of the tourists. Some things never changed, he laughed to himself, then took the road south toward Norris. The sun should be in the right position for the next item on his list.

When he reached the meadow near Beaver Lake, south of Obsidian Cliff, the setting looked just about perfect. Grabbing his digital camera, checking first for wildlife, he strolled the meadows until he found the location to frame just the right shot.

With time and weathering, the outer crust of the cliff had abraded and dulled. From this vantage point, with the lush green meadows in the foreground, the sun struck the south end of the cliff. Wherever there were cracks or recent rock falls, the black volcanic glass glistened through the weathered surface like stars in a galaxy across the dark cliff. He took multiple shots to insure he had the perfect photo he wanted for Dana. When they had spoken of how Dana wasn't finished with her Yellowstone vacation, Jen had told him of the broken promise to return to see the cliff.

That had been weeks ago while Dana had been back in intensive care. Since then Dana had made amazing strides in her recovery. Each time he spoke to her she boasted of another accomplishment and how she soon hoped to be free of the hospital. He smiled as he got back in his truck, proud of the way she was fighting back.

Backtracking to Mammoth junction, Garrett turned east this time, toward Roosevelt Junction. Midway between the two was one of his favorite places in the park. He was sure Dana had never seen it, and he wanted to share it with her. Hopefully, in person someday.

The one-way dirt and gravel lane had been closed to vehicles most of the year due to washouts and the normal annual closure. Each year from early March through the end of June the plateau was closed as a park Seasonal Bear Management Area. Bears emerging from their hibernation dens in the spring had one thing on their minds—food and lots of it. A couple park areas, remote from much human traffic, were closed seasonally in areas bears were likely to find elk and bison that had died over the winter. Bears tended to aggressively defend their carcasses from other species that ventured into the area, especially after waking extremely hungry. The high meadows and woods of the Blacktail Deer Plateau were one of these restricted areas. But this time of year, the bears should be fat and happy, full of berries and pine nuts for their winter nap. But they had been known to go after hunters in the fall, so Garrett planned to remain alert and cautious, especially after Ravenwolf's warning. Besides, the best way to encounter any bear was through a pair of binoculars—Garrett had his on his saddle horn.

A seldom traveled route at any time of year, the high plateau was spectacularly scenic in fall, and perfect on horseback. Backing his rig onto the turnout, parking where the gate barred vehicles, he unloaded his horse, checked his gear, and swung up into the saddle.

The Blacktail Deer Plateau always put a wide smile on Garrett's face, ever since he'd first come here as a teen with his buddy on a backpacking trip. His Native American pal had given him a deep appreciation for its past to go with one for its quiet beauty. It was too bad Rave hadn't been able to come with him today.

Man had traveled this and other trails through the park since prehistoric times to hunt and gather the obsidian that was found in projectile points far beyond Yellowstone. After horses had arrived, and the buffalo disappeared west of the continental divide, this trail had been taken east to the bison hunting plains, as part of the historic Bannock Trail. Ravenwolf had explained that many western tribes, including the Nez Perce, Shoshone, and Kalispell, among others, used this route high in the mountains to avoid the warlike and powerful Blackfeet that held the Three Forks area and northern lands, jealously ruling the buffalo grounds east of the continental divide.

"Aren't you of Blackfeet heritage?" The young Garrett had asked.

His friend's delivery was that of a reporter of fact, impersonal. "Yes, but I'm also part Nez Perce, so it's like having ancestors on both sides of a Civil War. I'm not sure how I feel about any of that, yet. I was raised as a city boy in Missoula," the young man had studied the flames of their campfire a long while, idly stirring the ashes, eyes black and brooding as troubled thoughts seemed to battle in his head. "Well, you know, Garrett, regardless of heritage stuff, I just respect men that faced this wilderness, traveled such unbelievably rough terrain and distances to get food and hides to last their families through winter. The challenges they faced just blows me away!"

It had boggled Garrett's young mind, also. It still did.

The Bannock Trail had started in southern Idaho, following the Snake River plain northeast up to the Henry's Lake area, crossing Targhee Pass, named for a Bannock chief. It entered the current park north of West Yellowstone then followed creek drainages until crossing the Gallatin Range west of Mount Holmes, to come down Indian Creek. North over Swan Lake Flats it followed a route partially covered or paralleled by the current Grand Loop road between Indian Creek, north to Mammoth, then east half way to Roosevelt Junction. There it cut south of the Loop, up over the plateau that ran behind Crescent Hill on the dirt road trail that Garrett was on. Coming down off the Blacktail Plateau, the Bannock Trail crossed the Yellowstone River near Tower Fall, taking the Lamar River Valley east to Soda Butte, where the trails split to different hunting grounds. It had been most heavily traveled by horseback between 1838 and 1878 by native buffalo hunters, but had probably been a footpath of men traversing the area for centuries, or longer.

Garrett loved the history, beauty, and solitude. He figured Dana would love it too. He hoped to bring her here someday on horseback. For now, he had his camera and a book on the Native History in Yellowstone that he had just purchased in Mammoth for her.

The trail started uphill, opening out on one side to an upland meadow that was a favorite of professional photographers in the spring. Most of the wildflowers that covered it then had bloomed and gone now, but a few remained surrounded by a swath of cinnamon colored grasses that ruffled in a slight breeze. He tried to capture it on film, but doubted the subtle meadow's impact would show in his amateur photos. Still, he wanted to share it with her somehow.

The soft-soiled road wound up through studded evergreens, then sagebrush meadows. He only planned to go about halfway, to get up on top of the plateau and go as far as Crescent Hill. He'd turn back before the trail turned south and wound down sharply into the Elk Creek drainage to rejoin the road to Tower-Roosevelt junction far below, where a petrified tree was caged.

Crescent Hill. Now there was a Rocky Mountain joke, he mused. Crescent Hill was at over seventy-eight hundred feet elevation. Much higher than the infamous, stormy Mt. Washington in the east of New England. The loop road from Mammoth curved down below its base, as did the rivers. From the "hill" one could look down where the Lamar and Yellowstone Rivers branched,

137

look east out across the Lamar River Valley, or around to far distant blued mountains ranges of the Absaroka and Beartooth.

Today, Garrett's goal was just shy of where the curve of the earth could be sensed, as the sky and clouds rose up from underneath, behind and around a high meadow with dazzling fall color. Where it seemed that if you stepped outside this clearing that you'd fall off into space. Grasses, yellow and straw-like in other places, gleamed like sheaves of pure gold here. Aspen groves backed the gold meadows, forming a colorful fence, at the rim of the earth. Flaming orange, red, and brilliant yellow leaves were staked up by their peeled white bark trunks, picketing the plateau's edge. An occasional dark evergreen was posted in the brilliance, enhancing the play of colors against the blue vault of sky. He tried to capture all this, taking shot after shot while his horse waited patiently. He hoped to capture its god-like, top of the world feeling.

Garrett finally mounted, patting the big blue roan fondly on the neck, content with his plan well underway. It was such a gorgeous day. The air smelled sharply of sage and spiced tree leaves. Leather creaked softly as they rode along, his horse held its head high, ears pricked forward, with a happy spring in his step. Life was so good.

GLANCING OUT HER window, Dana saw that fall was coming on rapidly. It was one of her favorite seasons of the year.

A soft drizzle was falling, so gentle it hung like mist in the trees. The soft gray background seemed intended to set off the display of the brilliant yellows and oranges of the leaves. Lawns, greedily absorbing the welcome moisture, brightened into emerald tones. The whole landscape seemed to be dressing up in its richest and brightest colors and textures for the fall season, shaking off the sun-faded and dry seared rags of late summer.

Dana felt an urgent need to get out there, to walk in the soft rain today. She wanted to breathe real air, feel its crisp bite, smell the spiced musty scent of fallen leaves on the path beneath her feet. She wanted to stroll through the forest where the newly washed evergreens would release their pine and cedar perfumes.

Eager to get outdoors, she dragged her eyes from the tempting view to the task at hand. She reread what she had written on the card that pictured on the front a massive ancient cedar deep in the Olympic National Rain Forest.

Dear Gretchen, Thank you for the video. I can't tell you how deeply I appreciated it, and how glad I was to see you safe and well. Please thank your parents, also, for their thoughtfulness. My friend, Jenny, made sure your tape was played for me as soon as I woke and remembered what happened that day. Seeing you safe, and hearing your voice and seeing your pretty face, did more to heal me and make me happy than anything else. Thank you so much, dear Gretchen.

I plan to go back and enjoy all the wonders of Yellowstone just as soon as I can. I hope you will return to enjoy it also. We have many wondrous national parks in this country. In my state, on the West Coast, we have the one shown on the cover, with super giant trees, and glacier capped mountains. (It doesn't' have any buffalo, but it does have lots of elk.) I love it there, and would love to show and share it with you someday. I'm not quite ready yet, but I'm working hard. Maybe when you are a little older you can join me for a vacation there, or at another cool park?

I'd love to receive a letter from you.

Much love, your friend Dana

Dana hoped the sweet, young child had not been traumatized by her experience and would not be afraid to return sometime. She could only encourage her, and hope for the best. She added a postscript.

P.S. Maybe we can be pen pals?

Sealing her card in an envelope to protect the picture, she wrote Gretchen's name on the front; she'd need to track down her address somewhere. If Jen didn't have it, she would contact the hospital in Montana, they were sure to have it in their records.

Setting aside her writing materials, she swung her legs from the bed, eager to get outdoors for the first time in ages. *Desperate* to get outdoors, she corrected, and feel some freedom from this room, this truncated life she was living. She hadn't survived just to be an invalid.

She could hardly wait to get out and breathe deeply of some fall fresh air. It always seemed richer with life than any other time of the year. Slipping her feet into her hospital slippers, she reached for her robe, to cover her open-backed hospital gown that she wore while her pajamas were being cleaned, then she stopped cold.

"Wait! I don't have outdoor clothes!"

"ARE YOU INSANE?" Jenny shouted the minute the door to Dana's apartment was opened.

Dana had checked the peephole in her door first, of course, but she had been expecting this. Just not quite so soon.

The tiny brunette was in her full fury mode.

Only five feet two inches—barely—the petite brunette made herself look larger when she was angry: widening her stance, bracing balled fists on her hips, her elbows out and sharp, steam coming from her nostrils, thunderbolts from her darkening blue eyes, and violence from rosebud lips. In fury mode, Jen never seemed to notice the eight-inch height advantage her best friend had—Jen was a giant when she was mad.

"Oh. Hi, Jen." Dana gave her a delighted smile. "Come on in. Everything is a little dusty and messy, I'm afraid, but—"

Jenny slashed right through Dana's cheerful subterfuge, almost getting a dusty vase on the hall table in the same motion. "Don't mess with me, Dana! Not this time!" She stomped past then whirled on her friend the minute they reached the kitchen. "This is NOT funny!" She emphasized each word with a pointed finger that stabbed the air dangerously close to Dana's nose.

"Tea?"

"Don't tea me, either!" Jenny huffed, folding her arms across her puffed out chest. Glancing at Dana's sling, she sighed and muttered through her teeth, "Oh, sit down! I'll do it." Grabbing the kettle from the stove, she stuffed it under the faucet, making little growling sounds over the gushing water.

Dana sat obediently, trying to contain the smile she always got when Jen was in her fury, the smile Jen *knew* she hid, that always inspired even greater flares of anger. Chin down, her hand curled over the splinted wrist in her lap, Dana bit her lip, knowing Jenny's anger was well placed this time.

Slamming the kettle back on the burner, Jen turned and planted her hands back on her hips.

"W-e-e-l-l-l-l?"  She demanded.

# Chapter 11

JENNY WOKE THAT morning eager to spend yet another Saturday in her yard, now all the hard work was done. A slow, drizzling rain had greeted her. Unlike her best friend, she was not a fan, and had hoped for another sunny day, even if it was getting chillier now.

Oh well, at least it was watering in the mums she had finally found the perfect spots for and planted. She would always call them Dana's mums. Standing at her patio door, she congratulated herself on her freshly groomed and mulched flower beds, darkened by the dampness. The bronze mums were vivid spots of color scattered among the other plantings along the board fence.

With plenty to catch up on inside, she would settle for a cozy indoor day. Returning to her bedroom, she dug deep into her closet and pulled out thick warm sweats, fleece lined suede slippers, and the thickest wool socks that she could find to bundle up and guard her against the chill, damp day. Not very elegant, but for once she chose comfort over fashion since she wasn't going anywhere or seeing anyone today.

Shuffling into the kitchen, she made herself a mushroom crepe for breakfast, mixing a batch of fresh cheddar biscuits to go with it to warm her insides. Having the oven going today would make it warmer, and seem less chilly and damp. Pulling her biscuits from the oven, she opened her cupboards to lift down copper canisters of flour, sugar, and her other baking ingredients, arranging them neatly on the spotless counter.

She thought once again of the gorgeous glass-fronted cabinet doors that she had seen at the Home Show. Every year she went and looked and re-priced them, hoping they would miraculously fit into her budget. But they remained out of reach, as did the rest of the kitchen remodeling she longed for.

She would bake a cake today, she decided, maybe some brownies, also. She'd take some to Dana tomorrow at the hospital, confident that she wouldn't be turned away if she brought the home baked sweets that made Dana her slave. It had been weeks now, and she was going to check up on Dana's progress, whether her buddy liked it or not.

Finishing breakfast, Jen gathered a discouragingly large stack of unopened bills and mail that had just been thrown into an antique porcelain bowl since her return. She could sort through and get everything taken care of today while she baked, so it could be properly filed and get this mess off her gleaming mahogany table.

Turning on a soft classic radio station, she went back to her kitchen and began happily peeling and chopping vegetables to start a pot of homemade soup simmering, then started to prepare the baked goods. She carefully measured out ingredients and mixed, greased and floured her pans, and checked her oven was correctly pre-heated. Jenny was using the copper measuring spoon and cup sets that Dana had given her one Christmas. She carefully filled each measure, and used a knife to scrape the excess off so each cup would be perfectly level, thinking of how Dana laughed at her when she did that.

"You look like the fussy old, home economics teacher I had in middle school when you do that," she'd say. It didn't rattle Jenny. She strived to become a gourmet cook, enjoying all the details, precision, and flourishes, and Dana ... well, Dana was just a total heathen in the kitchen!

Jen chuckled as she mixed and stirred remembering the time she had stepped into Dana's apartment and found her in the kitchen—cooking, of all wonders! At least that's what Dana had called it. Jenny had actually smelled garlic in the air when she walked in. Thinking her attempts to train Dana were finally paying off, she'd snuck up behind her.

"Are you really chopping fresh garlic?" She'd asked from behind Dana's back.

Dana had whirled around holding a hammer in one hand, then set it down to pick up a pair of needle nose pliers. "Kind of," Dana had replied absently, then turned back to her task, wrestling with something.

Jenny slid her pan of brownies into the oven, placing it exactly in the center of the rack, then set the timer, shook her head, and dusted her hands on a towel, starting to laugh out loud at the memory.

Dana had apparently decided to 'bake' homemade garlic bread to go with her canned ravioli. Not homemade bread, of course, just the garlic part she was homemaking herself. She'd been foiled in that culinary feat, however, by the four-year old plastic budget bottle of garlic powder that had aged to a solid, unshakeable concrete-like mass in her cupboard. Always stubborn, and never one to let a self-assigned task defeat her, Jenny had caught Dana trying to wrestle the block out of the plastic tube with the pliers, so she could wedge it out far enough to smash it back into powder with the hammer.

That was so Dana! Jenny smiled; she missed her friend.

Sitting down at her dining table, Jenny pushed up her sleeves. Hours later she had just finished the last of her paperwork. The soup that had been simmering comfortingly all day, filling the air with wonderful scents and the smells of real garlic, warred with the almond cake and fresh-baked brownies that were cooling on racks. The rain was now drumming outside, and the sky was turning even darker as evening approached, when the phone rang and disturbed the cozy atmosphere.

"Hello. No, I'm sorry, she doesn't live her. I'd be glad to take a message, though." Jenny checked the timer on the cookies still in the oven while she was up, and gave her soup a stir as she listened on the phone.

"No-o, she isn't here. I told you," she repeated, getting annoyed. "Who is this? Doctor? Dana's doctor? But ... she's still there in your hospital ... yes." Jenny turned her timer off before it started to buzz, and cradled the phone on her shoulder to pick up her oven mitts.

"Yes, she is," she stated firmly, giving him Dana's room number. She pulled open the oven and slid the rack out. The cookies looked perfectly done and a soft golden brown.

"Of course she is! You checked? Well, she's probably out walking the halls, or in the exercise room." She wished he would get off the phone so she could set it down. Her neck was getting a kink trying to hold it with her shoulder and chin. Awkwardly, she leaned down and lifted out the cookie sheet.

"WHAT?"

Straightening too suddenly, the phone squirted off her shoulder and landed in the middle of a half dozen perfectly golden, and now gooey, squished cookies. Cursing, Jenny heaved the whole tray in the sink, muttering angrily that the caller must be some kind of crank, while she tried to extract the phone from the mess and wipe it off without disconnecting.

"Say that again," she demanded when she recovered the phone, realizing, too late, that dough was still stuck to the back, and now in her hair, and on her hand.

"Listen, I don't know who you are, mister, or what kind of joke this is," she snarled into the cookie-dough-coated phone, "but Dana wouldn't ever do that! She is a sensible, responsible woman and she would never jeopardize her recovery like that!"

Slamming the phone back in its cradle, Jenny said very bad words when she realized she had just splattered the mess further. Rushing through her bedroom, to clean up in the bathroom, the phone rang again. Very gingerly she picked the extension up with two fingers, lifting it to her clean ear.

"Yes?" She said warily. "Oh, thank goodness you called," she gushed when she recognized the voice of their favorite nurse and co-conspirator. "I just got a crank call. There's some guy impersonating a doctor at your hospital. You guys need to do something about him ... Oh ... He is? She DID?

Jenny listened in horror to the evidence. Her fury shifted to a new target. A target she was pretty sure she knew just where to find ... and murder!

"WELL?" JEN REPEATED now, much louder this time.

The culprit gazed up at her with wide puzzled green eyes, auburn hair curling damply around a pale sculpted face, looking as sweet and blameless as an angel with those freckles marching across her nose.

"It was a fever, maybe, I don't know how else—"

"You have a fever?"

"No!" Dana threw her arm up defensively trying to ward Jenny off. "No, not that kind of fever."

Jenny managed to slap a hand on Dana's forehead, regardless, even angrier when the skin beneath her palm was normal, even cool. "Explain!"

"Fall fever...cabin fever, I don't know which. Both actually," she shook her head at herself.

"Fall fever?" Jenny snorted. "Never heard of it. I suppose next you're going to tell me it's one of those new medical syndromes." Sarcasm was really too polite a word for Jen's tone.

"No. Yes. For me anyway. I don't get spring fever, well, not as much. I get it in the fall—" Dana's voice trailed off in a deep sigh. "I just wanted to go for a walk," she shrugged, then winced, reaching up to rub her shoulder.

Jen winced with her, but wasn't going to let Dana off the hook.

"You just wanted to walk ten miles to your apartment?" She stormed. "In the rain?"

144

WITH THE ESCALATING screech of both the tea kettle and Jen blowing off steam, Dana just buried her head in the palm of her hand and rubbed. The day's exertion, the noise, throbbing pains running down her shoulder and through her wrist, all migrated to her brain. She was so tired, she just wanted to lay down for a while—in her very own bed!

She couldn't even explain her actions to herself, much less her best friend.

The relief when the kettle was lifted off the stove was immense, along with the silence while Jenny fixed them both mugs of tea and brought them over to the table, taking a seat across from her. Clasping her hand around her mug, Dana dragged it closer, too tired to lift it yet. Her head hung down between her shoulders, letting her face absorb the steam rising from the cup like a sauna, easing her headache.

Jenny studied her like a delinquent that deserved whatever pain she was suffering. "You look beat to hell." Her expression said it was Dana's own fault, but she just sipped her tea quietly, her cobalt eyes watching and waiting for the rest of her friend's explanation.

After a few moments, Dana took a sip of her tea, nearly shuddering in delight. Still damp from the rain, the hot, honey-laced tea felt wonderful, soothing her throat, warming the chill inside her, reviving her a little.

"I didn't mean to ...," Dana cleared her throat, took another sip, and tried to speak louder, seeing Jen lean forward, straining to hear her. "I was going crazy. The fall leaves, the soft rain, I wanted to go for a walk. Be outdoors. I had fall fever, bad, and cabin fever worse. I got up to take just a short little walk on the hospital grounds. Not those sterile, airless, hospital halls, for once."

Raising sorrowful emerald eyes to her friend, she gestured helplessly, "But, I didn't have any clothes!"

Jen just raised her eyebrows over the rim of her mug and waited, blue eyes stern and unsympathetic.

"So I went down to the therapy exercise room. I knew no one was there today. I thought I'd just borrow the sweats and shoes I use there, so I could take just a small walk under the trees and through the leaves that I have been staring at for days from my window." She was whining, Dana could hear it in her voice, but couldn't help herself.

"I sat down on the bench, pulled what I needed from my locker. When I stood, I realized my underpants were wet from the bench, so I'd just stripped them off when I heard a noise. Someone was entering the room from the far side. I don't know why, but I freaked. I felt exposed, I felt like a thief, or something. I can't believe I spooked like that, but I ran. I didn't want to get caught, get stopped.

"So I grabbed up the clothes and scooted out the side door. But ... it slammed on my robe, pulled it off. The door locks on the outside, so I couldn't my robe out, or get back in. I was barefoot and just had my hospital gown on—" She glanced up, wondering at the choking sound Jen had made. She seemed fine.

"So I ran before anyone could see me, across the lawn and down the parking lot until I found two vans to hide between and dress. It was raining harder so no one was around out ... Jen are you okay? You sound like you're choking. Sure? Okay, so after I got the sweats and shoes on, I noticed the street was right beside the lot, and there was a bus stopping there, so I just kept going. I just ... left. It felt so good to get home, even for a little while. I only wanted a few hours; I was going back, honest. I just got here, I don't know how you found out so fast!"

"The hospital called me. They thought you'd be at my house," Jen stated, setting her mug down firmly and leaning across the table toward Dana. "I told them my friend was a very sensible and responsible person. They must be wrong. She would never do something as stupid as a hospital JAILBREAK!"

Dana didn't have enough energy to blush. Her face just went a shade paler. "Oh, god, Jen, I'm sorry. I didn't mean to cause you trouble—"

"And make me look like a fool?" Jen coached, heartlessly.

"Or make you look like a fool," Dana conceded. "But I still don't see how they knew so soon! No one saw me. Oh, did they see the robe? The person I heard in the therapy room probably—"

"No." Jenny interrupted slowly. "Someone, several some ones, witnessed your jailbreak and gave a very, very detailed description of the escapee to the hospital staff."

Responding to the puzzled frown on her friend's face, Jen seemed to smirk before saying, "Apparently your escapade was as, ah, stimulating, I guess is the word, as a thirty-six hour hit of Viagra for the witnesses."

"What? What!"

"Above the therapy room is a sunroom for the patients. A whole wheelchair-brigade of geriatric gents was on hand with a front row view when you escaped." Jenny's smile was as droll as her voice. Then she laughed as the horror grew in Dana's eyes.

"They described an inmate in a hospital gown, hop-skipping, barefoot, across the lawn and through the puddles in the parking lot. She had some bundle in her arms and was clutching a dark blue sling on her left side."

Color was starting to rise up Dana's neck, and heat spread across her checks.

Jen, the merciless, continued her report.

"They told the staff it was a lovely, young, redhead, with a slender body, and..."

"Oh, no!" Dana's hand flew up to cover her face.

"Oh, yes! And ... A very firm, very exposed, and I quote, 'a very bodacious naked butt bouncing beautifully out the back of her gown!' All the way down the lawn and across the lot."

Dana gasped. She could feel herself flame with heat and blush all the way down to her bodacious butt. She missed what Jen said next.

"Huhn?"

"They are a bird-watching club," Jenny casually repeated.

"That's nice." Dana's response was absent minded, absorbed in her own embarrassment, she didn't really care.

"They meet there to spot birds on the grounds' trees. There are about fifteen of them," Jenny continued for some reason.

"Fifteen ... great."

"Yes," Jen grinned maliciously, "and they always bring their high powered binoculars."


"MY, THAT SHORT VISIT home seems to have been good for you. Look at all that color in your cheeks. Oh dear, I said ... cheeks!"

The nurse dissolved in giggles. Finally, patting her chest, she took in a deep breath and very insincerely apologized. "Sorry Dana, but...," and she lost it again, in a burst of hilarity that had her grabbing tissues to wipe the tears from her eyes.

Glaring at her former favorite nurse, and her former best friend, who had promised her that no one would tease her if she returned to the hospital, Dana stomped off down the hall to her room, jaw tight and chin thrust out indignantly. Jen stayed behind to laugh her head off with the nurse, of course.

Dana pretended not to notice all the silver-haired men in wheelchairs that seemed to hover in the hall near her room.

147

Slamming the door to shut them all out, she crawled into bed still fully clothed in her hard earned damp sweat suit.

Just what she needed! A bunch of geriatric stalkers in wheelchairs!

Her window ledge had fifteen new floral bouquets, all carrying the logo of the hospital gift shop. She was absolutely not reading any of the cards from her binocular-bearing fans!


LATER THAT NIGHT, Garrett called. "Hey, I hear you left the hospital. Glad you're back safe."

"Did Jenny call you? Wait until I—"

"No, no. I haven't spoken to her. I just called the hospital earlier and they said you were gone."

"Oh, good," she wouldn't have to kill Jenny for telling Garrett about her humiliating escape. "So what's the weather like out there? Any snow yet?"

"Not yet. It's pretty brisk, though. It almost froze the last few nights, but we're still a balmy fifty degrees during the day. How is it there?"

"Lovely! All fall-crisp and colorful, and the soft rain that I love just drizzling down, makes everything seem so cozy."

She asked him about his projects and what he had been doing for fun; he spoke in great and entertaining detail, telling of Corky's latest tricks. He asked her about her progress, how her business manager was working out, what fun was going on in her world; he listened with clear interest. She savored the rich, sexy sound of his soft voice, letting it caress her, ease her cares away. She was totally relaxed and smiling happily when Garrett paused, chuckled, and then spoke with a wicked tease in his voice.

"So, I hear you have a bodacious butt. I'm not at all surprised."

Too busy grinding her teeth, trying to think up ways to murder her friend, Dana had been unable to respond at first, finally spitting out, "That Jenny, I'll—"

"Hey, not Jen. I swear, she did not talk to me. Some guy answered the phone in your room. Said he was delivering flowers for the woman with the bodacious butt. Naturally I was extremely curious and jealous and asked. Fortunately a nurse caught him in your room, and shooed him out, before taking the phone. I was greatly relieved to hear my competition was ninety-seven years old." His tone was light, he didn't seem jealous.

148

"So, are you going to tell me all about your great escape, Dana?" Gentle humor in his voice.

Since he had already, apparently, heard the worst, she sighed and told him the rest. Realizing, as she told her tale that she was already starting to see the humor beyond the humiliation, even laughing with him.

Garrett had chuckled at Jen's capture, then reminded her, "You have a special friend there, Dana."

Then he had tempted her, invited her.

"The next time you decide to escape," his voice lowered, "run to me, babe. I won't turn you in, or away."

A heartbeat passed. Then another, before her voice came back.

# Chapter 12

"THEN DON'T BE SURPRISED when I show up at your door, cowboy, and say 'take me in'." Dana's response started light and playful, but her tone dropped in register, and rose in heat."

"With open arms, babe. Come to me, anytime." Garrett's response was immediate, his voice husky.

After soft goodnights, Dana hung up the phone with a smile and a wistful sigh. He knew how to make things so easy and comfortable when she spoke with him; they seemed to share some bond as if they had known each other much longer. He had become a close friend, even though she'd never really seen his face—so far—but she could picture it. She could feel the timbre of his voice when he asked her to come to him, it had rippled like heat waves through her body.

She lay back and sighed, dreamily, continuing to think of him, to replay the tone and texture of his voice in her mind. She could feel the soft smile curve her lips, feel the warm glow inside, and an impatient, exciting sizzle that skimmed along her nerves, wanting to be near him. Very near!

Maybe it was better they hadn't met face to face, yet. His picture was handsome, but Jen insisted it didn't do him justice, that he was much more potent and better looking in person. Her friend's enthusiasm always left a little niggle of curiosity about what Jen's true feelings were about the man, despite her denials. Dana brushed the momentary twinge of envy—jealousy?—aside, returning to her thoughts of the man she was coming to known without the benefit of sight. And without that surface distraction.

Without the distraction of personal experience, Dana's judgment of the man inside hadn't been blinded or distorted by a handsome smile. Which was a good thing as his sexy voice and charming manner were distracting enough!

She felt she was learning more important things about him this way, though. What a good and supportive friend he could be, how wide and varied his interests were, and the sincere pleasure he seemed to take in listening to hers. Maybe he was rolling his eyes at the other end of the line, like Jen did whenever Dana got off on one of her tangents, but he seemed to take a real interest and even share it, like with the geode gift.

He had a great sense of humor—even when she wished he didn't—she thought with a wry smile. She chuckled at the way he had teased and ambushed her into laughter tonight over her recent escapades. So she could enjoy the humor of it also, instead of embarrassed hurt. Yes, laughter was part of who he was, how he dealt with the bumps in life, and helped her deal with hers. That sense of humor was important to Dana. It was a must in a man, as far as she was concerned—especially in a relationship, a potential lover, because, she smiled, that was exactly what she had planned for him.

They were good together, even without sight or touch, or, she added, taste or smell. They might be able to build a more intimate relationship together. He was a man that Dana felt she could trust and love. Even if it didn't work out long term, she had every intention of giving this man a hot and passionate—and thorough—trial run. She'd show him some bodacious butt, all right! And ... She expected to see some in return.

Chuckling at her wayward mind, Dana curled her arms around her pillow, sending herself to sleep with thoughts of him. Nuzzling her face deep, she imagined herself nestled on his shoulder, her cheek against a warm, bare chest. She sighed picturing herself wrapped in his arms, enveloped in a clean male scent, his heart beating under her palm in time with her breath.

His hard, muscular body would be pressed snug against hers, her breasts soft against his side, their legs tangled, relaxed after mind-blowing sex.

M-m-m-m, yes, she breathed.

He would draw her arm across his chest, his fingers gently brushing up and down in sated affection, occasionally lifting her fingers to his lips for a kiss.

Almost asleep, she instinctively stretched her head up to nibble his neck, rolling over onto his bare chest, her hair falling in a shimmering screen around his—

—Her pillow! Reality screamed with the pain in her crushed shoulder and wrist as she quickly rolled back to take the weight off them. Damn! In her dream she'd been all dewy, naked skin. There was no torn flesh, shattered bones, searing pain, or navy-blue sling!

Shifting, she tried to get comfortable again, and re-enter her fantasy as she dozed off. It took a while for the pain to ease enough so tension could start to drain from her muscles and let her sink deeper into the bed. The sheets beneath her began to warm from her body heat.

She saw a woman, herself, as she had once been: whole, unblemished, sleeping, warm and relaxed on her back, pale bared skin soft with sleep. Her man, Garrett, gloriously naked and male, gloriously awake, braced on an elbow beside her. His eyes stroking her, his hand reached to tease the hair from her face, his deep voice a whisper that vibrated her senses, saying, "Open your eyes for me, babe." Fingers traced her jaw, trailed the column of her throat, cupped and captured a breast, his thumb brushing, playing with her nipple. He smiled as it hardened beneath his caress, murmuring, "Open your heart."

Leaning in, he started his lips lazily along the same path. Kissing, nibbling, his tongue sliding like wet silk across her skin. When his mouth took her breast, his fingers danced tantalizingly downward again, until his hand spread wide, to smooth his palm across her belly. Her body responded to him with little quivers of nerves leaping beneath her skin, even before she wakened in her dream to breathe his name.

She tried to picture what his blue eyes would look like, visualizing them as they flicked half-lidded up to hers while he filled his mouth and senses with her breast. Imagined his gaze as full of intent and possession as the hand that clasped the curve of her hip.

He held her gaze as his hand rode down her outer thigh, curling beneath her knee. She felt herself turn liquid, limp, as he slid it aside. His eyes flashed a triumphant spark, as his hand smoothed her inner thigh, beginning to rise, roughened male palm scraping oh so lightly, as his hand moved up slowly, torturously to the heat at her core.

Her eyes closed, head back, she savored the slow game he played in her dreams, inch by inch, her body trembling with anticipation. Just as his fingers neared their goal, his tongue moistened her nipple, then he blew on the damp, helpless skin. Her nerves jumped, fire shooting straight down to where his fingers reached the heat of her. Before she could even catch her breath, his wicked mouth started down her body, following the path of his fingers, in a sultry game of follow the leader. Her belly melted and shook beneath his tongue.

Oh god, she moaned. She'd never get to sleep this way! But, she dove back into her fantasy, not wanting to miss a single moment.

GARRETT WASN'T SLEEPING, but he was not complaining.

He'd been thinking about Dana's bodacious butt all day, ever since the old timer had mentioned it. Garrett had tried to keep his thoughts of Dana—and his conscience—fairly pure and well-intentioned. But, hell, he was a man, and the other guy brought it up!

If half the hospital was fantasizing about her body, or staring at it through binoculars? Well, why should he hold back?

He knew his feelings for Dana ran deep, his intentions were honorable—most of the time. But today his thoughts had been just shy of outright rampant lust. He'd been feeling a little ashamed of himself, while he spoke with Dana, but then she had pushed him completely over the edge. On purpose!

He was sure of that. He'd replayed the conversation in his head, and analyzed it from every direction. She'd flirted and teased him playfully before, but he was convinced that this time, she had acted with purpose, meaning what she implied. He hoped—or prayed.

Well, it was actually more the tone she used, than the words, but still.

When she said she might show up at his door, when she said those words, 'take me in', his body had shot to life like an arrow released from a taut bow. It was the voice as much as the words, the tone she'd used on him. Her voice had dropped so low, so deadly sweet. 'Take me' she'd said, barely tacking the 'in' on the end. He'd heard it. She'd done it so he would feel it all through his body, and he had. She'd played him, knew it, and knew he knew and loved it. There was no other interpretation of her words, her tone, they were a pure undiluted invitation to sex.

Oh, babe, I'll take you... in, out, sideways, upside down! Anyway, anytime, you want me!

His reply to her had been much more gentlemanly and subdued than that, of course, but he suspected she knew just how much she was tangling his mind and tormenting his body parts!

Come to me, babe, I'll give you what you want. You ask, imply, I'll provide. Nice or naughty. Today, tomorrow, whenever, forever!

He was still fantasizing about her when he laid down to sleep.

He liked the picture of opening his door to a tall, slender redhead. With legs longer than heaven and hair the color of her

153

passions, and that sweet, sculpted, alabaster face. Her emerald eyes, well he still had to guess there, but he suspected they would dance with the same laughter and sensual charm of her voice. She had the face of a serene angel, lit with smiling lips and heat in her eyes, she would be as dangerous as a siren, luring him ... exactly where he wanted to go!

'Take me....' she'd say in that throaty purr, and his arms would be around her, that sweet mouth crushed beneath the need in his, before she could say more. He'd drag her across the threshold without letting go of her body or mouth, kick the door shut with his heel, and never let go of her ever again. Oh yes, he could see it, feel it, in every pulsing nerve of his body.

Sliding his hands down her back, nibbling and catching her lower lip, covering her mouth with a sweet, sucking kiss, he'd cup that famous butt in both hands, pulling her tight and snug against the hard side of his passion.

He'd taste her breath catch and vibrate with the hum deep in her throat, groan as she molded closer, and softened in his arms.

Oh, yes!

That was how it would start; he'd already imagined a score of hot scenarios from there. He'd dream a score more. If she came to him—when she came to him—they'd try them all, and any she fantasized, and pick their favorites. Sounded like a worthy lifetime occupation for them. Now he just needed the girl. Woman, he corrected, remembering that voice.

It stirred more in him than his fantasies.

He remembered the sight of that hair colored like the leaves of autumn. Autumn, so dear to her, and now to him. He'd seen its glory spread across a pillow; he'd seen and stroked the fine bones and lovely lines of her face—in the hospital—but it was his pillow he placed that memory on now, his face hovering above those lips, ready to taste, to brush, to kiss, to take her in. She would be his.


JUST BEFORE DANA left the hospital—legally, through the front door—her favorite nurse dropped a package in her lap as she was wheeled, like an invalid, to the entrance.

"That just came in from your beau. Please don't tell him you moved yet. I just love talking to that man. And such a dreamboat!" The nurse grinned and over-dramatized the fluttering of her middle-aged eyes, reminding Dana everyone but she had seen Garrett. "So charming. That man and...mmm- mmm... such a dreamy voice!"

Dana couldn't argue with that; it sure worked for her. With a private smile, her face warm, she thought of the dreams that voice had inspired in her last night. She felt like fluttering right along with the nurse! Changing the subject to distract them both, she repeated her complaint. "I still don't see why I have to leave the hospital in a wheelchair, I could—"

"To hide your butt." The nurse sure knew how to shut her up!

Jen choked back a laugh, grabbed the handles and pushed Dana out the door as she was casting her goodbyes and thanks over her shoulder. All Dana's belongings were already packed in Jenny's car that was parked by the hospital doors. Dana would be back. Many times, of course, to do her therapy and see the doctors, but as soon as they crossed the threshold, she would be an outpatient, at last. She had been released into Jen's custody as negotiated with the doctors when Jen had drug her back to the hospital yesterday.

The doctors had insisted on keeping her overnight to observe and insure her flight hadn't done any damage, putting her through another whole series of x-rays and tests this morning, before letting Jen take her home—to Jenny's home. Her doctors had been pleasantly surprised with Dana's recent progress, but they put her wrist into a hardened cast first, regardless, making sure her fingers couldn't close or clasp anything heavy.

Like weights, for instance.

They didn't trust her out of their supervision to not push too hard and tear that shoulder again. The plaster cast would be weight enough for her shoulder to lift for now, they advised with smiles that had a lot of smirk in them. And she would, of course, wear her sling at all times, they said in that 'or else!' tone that doctors had perfected.

Dana had pretended she couldn't hear the doctors when they were advising Jenny of her duties as Dana's new jailor. She had to hold back her snort when Jen spoke so they didn't know she was listening, when Jen said, "Realistically, I figure I'll have only four or five days of good behavior from Dana before I lose control." She heard one doctor murmur something about that being enough of a slowdown with the speed she was healing. Then another mentioned the cast would restrict her, that Jenny need not worry. "I don't know," Jen responded, wryly, "I've seen how resourceful she is with hammers, that cast might not last long

Then the final hospital doors whisked open and Jen raced Dana outside, both of them laughing.

"I'm free!" Dana did an excellent imitation of a long jump, leaping from the wheelchair to the front seat of Jenny's car as if she still didn't quite trust the hospital staff to let her get away. "Free at last!" She grinned all the way to Jenny's home. Adding 'almost', later, under her breath, as Jen fussed trying to help her from the car and attempted to shepherd her right down the hall to bed.

Dana managed to dodge her and strolled out to the back yard. "Wow, this looks great, Jen! Can we eat dinner out here?"

Jen pointed at the outside thermometer that registered forty-eight degrees, "It is way too cold!"

"I guess," Dana relented reluctantly, unimpressed by the chilly temperature. She drew in and held a few deep breaths of the fresh, crisp air, before returning inside.

Before Jen could stop her, she was on the phone ordering pizza delivered for dinner. "Dana!"

"What? Its gourmet pizza," she stressed. "Have any wine? I feel like celebrating!"

"Do you promise to eat a healthy salad before your pizza?" Jen challenged.

"Sure."

"Are you on any medications?"

"No, mom, scout's honor."

Jenny attempted a scowl, but Dana melted her with her joyful grin. Laughing they broke out the bottle of wine and glasses. God, it had been a long time since they had been able to just relax and enjoy their friendship!

They lit the fire in the gas fireplace, settling on the floor in front of it, leaning against the couch with their wine and put a movie in the DVD player. Then proceeded to talk, and laugh, and talk some more, and completely ignore the movie, caught up in the freedom to relax together, until the pizza arrived.

After the last pizza crust had been munched and the movie restarted four times for lack of attention, they completely abandoned trying to watch a movie and Jen rose and brought Garrett's package over to Dana.

"Open it. Open!" Jen insisted like an excited child. "I can't wait! Do you want me to do it? I'm faster."

"No, that's okay" Dana smiled pretending not to notice Jen's impatience. She was determined to open it herself, one-handed, taking as long as she could. When the package finally spilled open, with just a book, a video, and a small envelope

156

inside, Jen seemed a little disgruntled, not seeing anything dramatic or romantic.

But Dana was ecstatic. "Look, Jen, this book is all about the Indians in Yellowstone going back 10,000 years! Oh look! He tabbed this ... it's Obsidian Cliff! Look it's in the book! Wow. He marked this page; I had no idea there were all those archaeological sites in the park ..."

"How wonderful. Open the damn card before I throttle you!" Jenny slapped her hand down firmly on the video about the geology of Yellowstone before Dana could pick it up to examine. "We'll watch it later. The card!"

The card enclosed a packet of photos, and a second smaller envelope. Dana read the note card and smiled softly, "Oh, how sweet!"

"Read it!"

Dana wanted to think about it longer in private, and just passed the card off to Jen to read for herself, while she picked up the stack of pictures. She thumbed through shots of a huge bull elk with all his girls, her cliff sparkling in the sunlight, a steep meadow with colorful grasses, and a breathtaking shot of an aspen circled meadow that seemed to just hang in the sky. She grinned at a picture he had taken of his beautiful appaloosa horse standing on an isolated dirt track with glorious fall colors in the background.

Jen read the note out loud.

Dear Lovely Dana,

I hope you'll enjoy the book and video, and that they make your next visit to Yellowstone richer. I hope that you will return soon and give the Park a chance to show you all its wonders. I've enclosed a few of them to tempt you.

I was able to get a few good shots of Obsidian Cliff. Jen mentioned you were disappointed you didn't get to stop. It's also marked in your book. I also enclosed pictures of one of my personal favorite spots that I'd love to show you sometime. It's a one-way dirt road that climbs up over the Blacktail Deer Plateau and follows part of the original Bannock Trail (see book). The pictures should show you why I think it's so special. Especially in the fall, on horseback.

In addition to the other items I am using to seduce you back, I've sent an annual park pass of your very own. It's good at any national park, but it's a gift I hoped that you and Jen would use to return to Yellowstone, and give it—and us—a second chance to enjoy that vacation you were so excited about. I'm hoping you will invite me along as your personal guide.

Please come back, Dana.
Love, Garrett


"That is so sweet." Jen looked up and noticed that while Dana seemed to be gazing at the pictures, her eyes were so moist that she probably couldn't see anything through unshed tears. "Dana?"

Unaware how tightly she'd held her emotions back in the semi-public environment of the hospital, Dana felt the floodgates release now. Safe, alone with her best friend, the wall of reserve cracked and burst in a swirl and rush of pent up feelings, tangled emotions pouring forth.

"It is sweet!" Dana turned and reached for Jenny's hand, "but so are you!" Now the tears welled and rolled silently down her checks and over lips that quivered attempting a smile. "It's because of you, Jen. You told him what mattered to me. That's how he knew. And you took care of me, and stayed by me, and gave me strength to get well. You are the sweetest, most special friend!"

Dana nearly choked Jenny, wrapping her in a tearful hug, as they cried and smiled and then cried together some more. Recognizing how close they had each come to losing a best friend, they knew how lucky they were to be here together, sharing things in a way they used to take for granted.


JEN MADE HER DECISION that evening, but waited until a week later to tell Dana. She had seen the "L" word on Garrett's card, though neither of the girls had discussed it.

When she saw the package from Garrett, she had hoped that he'd sent Dana something romantic. She knew he was totally hooked on her friend. She'd been very disappointed when she saw what he sent. Books and videos? Come on guy!

Then when she read his note and saw Dana's reaction, she realized that he had listened deeply, not just politely, to all she had told him of Dana's interests and their trip. He had absorbed it all, every detail, then acted. He hadn't just sent Dana flowers or chocolates, or things a guy might send any girl to woo her; he'd focused, with care and thoughtfulness, on what was special and specific to Dana. The more Jenny thought of it, the more she realized it didn't get much more romantic than paying that kind of attention to making someone happy.

He hadn't been shy about admitting he was trying to tempt Dana back, either; nor was he pushy. Just a clear and simple 'please come back' signed with 'love'. Jen sighed a little wistfully.

She was sure Garrett wasn't the type to throw that word around casually. He meant it; she'd seen it in his eyes and touch the last time he'd come to see Dana. But Dana hadn't seen it. Hadn't seen him. Did she know he was sincere, or did she just think it was 'sweet'?

That's why Jen had made up her mind that Dana had to go back to Yellowstone alone, without her. She owed it to Garrett to send Dana to him, give him the chance to take her, be alone with her.

Geez! The guy had saved Dana's life! He'd earned it! He'd be good for her—good to her. He deserved the chance to prove that to Dana. Even if it didn't work out for them as a couple, she trusted him with her dearest friend.

Of course, Jenny couldn't tell Dana any of this. Not only did she not want to mess up Garrett's chances, but Dana wouldn't go back without her unless Jen could convince her that she couldn't and didn't want to return. But Dana should. That would be the easy part, Dana was eager to return soon.

She pushed the button to open her garage and pulled in. Jen hoped she had the skills for the rest. Gathering up her belongings, and her nerve, she went in the back door, making sure to let her shoulders slump with weariness and dejection. With a disgruntled look on her face, Jen gave a loud and frustrated sigh as she tossed her purse, then herself, onto the couch beside Dana.

"Looks like you're going back to Yellowstone alone, girl. They won't give me any more time off from work this year. In fact, some new project's come up and we will all be working overtime!" Jenny gave another gusty sigh, truly grateful to get that whopper out, then took a quick peek from the corner of her eye, checking Dana's reaction to her performance.

Disappointed. "Are you sure?" Dana asked. "Do you think they might change their minds, Jen?"

Looking downcast, she gave her head a weary shake. "No way."

"Oh. Well then, we'll just wait 'til next summer vacation." Dana's voice was so soft and tinged with sorrow that Jen was starting to feel really cruel when Dana hopped off the couch, saying brightly, "You must be exhausted. What do you want for dinner?"

"Nothing that you try to cook!" Jenny rose defensively.

"Hey, I'm with you there. I stink as a cook; I just don't want you to have to. What I meant was do you want Italian, Mexican, Chinese, or Steakhouse. I'm buying."

"In that case," Jen grabbed her purse and keys, "there's an excellent Italian restaurant just a few blocks from here."

Now that Dana seemed convinced she had to stay put at work, maybe the rest of the plan would come to Jenny after dinner. This acting stuff was hungry, stressful work.

A DOZEN GLORIOUSLY fragrant and expensive roses arrived on Jenny's desk at work the next afternoon. The delivery service had followed Garrett's instructions exactly. When Jen opened the card attached to the vase, there was no signature, only two words inside. "Thank you!" Written over and over as many times as it took to fill the whole inside of the card.

Jen laughed and leaned forward to inhale the exquisite aroma. Apparently Dana had been chatting on the phone with Garrett last night. She'd meant to call from work today and give him a heads up, but had been too busy.

Clearly, he was a very clever guy—*for a blonde.*

# Chapter 13

"I HAD *NO* IDEA how traumatized Jen was from what happened back there!" Dana confided to Garrett on the phone. "I guess I was just so wrapped up in my own problems, I wasn't paying attention."

"Hard to pay attention when you're unconscious, Dana." Garrett reminded gently, a little puzzled himself by what she'd told him. "I do recall how she blamed herself, saying it was all her fault you got hurt. I told her then that it wasn't and you would never blame her. I don't know that she listened. That was back when she was afraid you weren't going to make it. So was I. But I figured she got over that once you got better."

"Yeah, she told me about that, we talked about it in the hospital. She seemed over it to me, also."

"You know, Dana," Garrett had to pause, feeling his throat tighten just to talk about that time, "It was pretty hard, ah, seeing you like that, at the accident." He cleared his throat. "We didn't let her get close enough to see much, but still ... it was bad." The raw sound of his voice proved it was worse than bad.

"I'm glad I missed that part, so to speak. I remember feeling fear for the little girl, a bump of pain, but that's all. Thank God."

Garrett couldn't speak. Dana was silent, for a while.

"Jen said it just hit her suddenly, like an emotional explosion. I understand that. I had an emotional meltdown myself when I got home from the hospital. I hadn't realized how much I was holding inside. But mine was relief, gratitude for being out, and with my friend. I felt free and safe, and very lucky. We had opened your package that night. So sweet and thoughtful, Garrett. Thank you. I was so excited, but I guess it struck Jen differently. We read your letter. She said that's when she suddenly freaked out and realized she was terrified to return to Yellowstone. I guess she had nightmares about it, also, but she didn't tell me this until now."

"Wow, hey, I'm really sorry. I didn't mean ..."

"Oh, I know. Don't be. Jen doesn't want you to feel bad. She wanted me to be sure and tell you that." Dana reassured. "But ... what I don't get is why, if she's so freaked, she pushed me to return right away, even alone? She insisted!"

Ah. Garrett was beginning to understand Jen's sudden revelation perfectly. His heart danced happily at the news. He managed to choke back a laugh, turning it into a thoughtful sounding "Hmmm" instead. He'd send that girl some flowers, at work, where Dana wouldn't see them.

"Garrett?"

"Oh, sorry, just thinking. What was that?"

"Why would she do that? It makes no sense!"

"We-e-ell, she probably wants you to conquer your fears, now. Not put it off. And ... She's afraid that if she comes along and freaks out, that ... ah, it might mess you up." Yeah, that sounded brilliant. "In fact, I bet that if you come out, have a great time, and get home safe and sound, it might really help Jenny." Even better. Leverage. "She'd probably be able to come out next summer with you, and face her own fears."

"You really think so?"

"I do. I really, truly do." It was a good thing Dana couldn't see the laughter in his eyes.

"I guess I can see the logic in that. I did really want to go back right away, but I can't drive for months, until I can use both hands, so—"

"I drive."

Dana's soft chuckle said she heard and appreciated the eagerness in his voice.

"Okay. I have an appointment with the doctor later this week, then maybe I could fly out there—"

"I'll be at the airport."

"—whenever it fits your work schedule."

"Which I'll reschedule. Just come, babe."

"I will."

They both paused to catch a breath, only to become more breathless as they realized that they would really be together, finally, for the first time. Soon. Alone. Eyes open.

"Oh, Garrett, take me—take me to Yellowstone." Dana's voice was a wistful whisper. "Take me to Obsidian Cliff. Show me all the wonders I missed and all your favorite places."

"I will, babe. Just come to me.," he promised softly. "I'll take you everywhere you want to go, everywhere you want to be."

HIS PHONE RANG just as he was rushing out the door; he'd already spent longer than intended cleaning his house—just in case. He checked his watch, then the display on his cell. Seeing the out of state area code, he fumbled to flip his phone open, praying it wasn't Dana calling to say she hadn't taken the flight he was heading out to meet. He held his breath after he answered and heard her best friend's voice, not breathing until he heard Dana was fine and on her way.

"Great. Thanks, Jen. I'm just leaving for the airport. I'll be sure she calls you—"

"Wait! Garrett! I just wanted to have a quick private word with you first." He picked up his coat and flipped the light switch while Jen paused gathering her thoughts. His hand halted on the door knob at her next words.

"Dana may seem a little, ah, cool toward you," she said hesitantly.

"What?" Did she mean cool as in cold? Had he heard right?

"Why? What have I done? Did I offend her somehow, Jenny?" Garrett dropped to a chair, confused, suddenly worried, clutching his coat and keys in his lap.

"Oh, no! No. That's why I felt I had to call. So you wouldn't think that, Garrett. She's just ... well, Dana just doesn't put herself out there. Her real feelings, I mean. All that flirting? It's like a shield. She can peek around it and see you, but you can't see into her, you know?"

"I don't expect her to jump into bed with me, Jen!" Garrett was annoyed with her implication while, at the same time, he had to admit he wasn't sure, privately, how much effort he'd put into holding back if Dana wanted ... well, he *had* just changed the sheets on his bed. But it had always been his plan to let Dana set the pace of any relationship.

"If I thought that," she was saying, "I would have come to chaperone, Garrett. I think you are a good guy, and so does Dana, and ... Well, she's not just flying out there to see Yellowstone, though she will probably act like she did. She hides, Garrett. She has good reasons to, but that's her story to tell you if she wants. I just wanted to warn you to be patient with her. But hang in there. Let her get to know you. Her emotions may seem cool or casual, but, I just wanted you to understand. But," Jen's tone changed from empathy to threat, "if you hurt her, your life won't be worth—"

"Hey, I wouldn't do that, Jen. I'd hurt myself first. I care about Dana. A lot."

"I know. I knew that. Just give her time, okay? I better let you go. Don't tell her I called."

Okay, nothing like a little added pressure and encouragement—or conditional encouragement with threats attached. Garrett had plenty of time to chew over Jenny's warning call, and let it psyche him out, on the drive down the pass to Bozeman.

He knew Jen was on his side, but ... Geez! As if he wasn't already nervous enough about their first real face to face, both awake, meeting! Nothing like increasing his fear of rejection before it even happened! Garrett was glad he'd put on his extreme deodorant that morning. He hoped it worked on nervous sweat as well as the ads promised. He should have slapped some on his palms, he thought, as he slipped a hand from the steering wheel to swipe it across the pressed crease of his best jeans.

Yeah, he'd dressed up a bit for her. Nothing much, still casual, but he looked and smelled much better than normal. Which he had pointed out to Corky on his way past the corral.

"See this is how you do it, you old rag. I'll get fancier, wear some khaki slacks, when I take her to dinner."

While he knew Jen just meant to warn him not to take coolness for rejection, somehow just thinking about it beforehand wasn't a companion he had really needed on the long drive to the airport. Well, he had been worried he might get too excited or get his expectations too high on the long drive.

No problem there, now! He switched hands and swiped the other palm dry.

He tried to switch his thoughts to the arrangements he had made for Dana, to calm himself. He'd already reserved a room at a hotel in Livingston for her. Optimistic, he'd reserved it for two weeks. She hadn't told him if she was planning to stay for more than a few days, but he didn't want to give her any excuse to leave soon.

He'd prefer to have her as a guest in his home, but, as they were virtual strangers, he didn't dare push that. I'm a stranger to *her*, anyway, he corrected, passing a slower moving horse-trailer. The only thing he felt he still didn't know about Dana, that *he* needed, was did he have a chance with her? A very serious chance?

She was a beauty, no question. Brave enough to rush a two-thousand pound male buffalo, no question, and thank god she was through with that! She loved nature and rocks, not malls and shops. Her personality sparkled and made him laugh. And she bounced. That was big. He wasn't thinking of her athletic skills, he was thinking of her spirit. She was one hell of a package! What would she think of him?

She was coming to him; she wanted him with her on her first return to the scene of the almost-tragedy. It must mean something. At least she didn't hate him, he could be sure of that.

But would she be coming to see him if it wasn't for the draw of Yellowstone? He knew showing her its attractions was his best in with her. He planned to wow her with sights and hoped some of the glory would attach to her guide. If he didn't screw-up, maybe he could hope for more.

He would play for keeps, if he could, not holding anything back by trying to act cool. But don't push, he reminded himself, thinking of Jenny's call again. Somehow he had to balance letting her see inside him, know him, know he wanted her, without seeming too needy, without pressure. He was making himself nervous again.

Arriving twenty minutes before her flight, he found a position in front of the bronze bear in the lobby. To make sure he got his girl, and some other dude didn't kidnap his prize from the airport, he had made a sign so Dana could spot him. Finding his hands damp, he switched the sign from side to side, constantly wiping his palms dry on his jeans. Good thing he wasn't *trying* to be cool; he was as nervous as a teenager with a bad crush.


OH MY, WHAT A cutie!

It had been important to Dana to get at least a quick look at her hero before he spotted her—a long look was even better.

She didn't call her ball cap pulled low over her eyes, covering all but her flame colored ponytail, a disguise. Neither was the knitted wool cape that hid her sling; it was just a convenient coat. That's how she justified it, anyway. Due to her handicap, Dana had been first off the plane, but she'd tucked herself in by a column on the balcony, letting the rest of the passengers descend first. Peeking over the railing to the lobby below, it hadn't been hard to spot him in the crowd awaiting arrivals. He was the hottest looking guy there—and the most charming.

Standing in front of a massive bronze sculpture of a bear, Garrett's thick hair was slightly shaggy, and more white than blonde. The sun-streaked color gleamed against his outdoor bronze on the lean and handsome angles of his face. A clean-shaven jaw had a firm male line; his nose was crisp and straight and lines in his cheeks promised smiles and possible dimples. As soon as the other passengers started down the stairs, she saw his head rise and a dazzling grin flashed those promised dimples. His blue chambray shirt was a lighter tint of the bright blue denim of his eyes.

What a doll! And the body! Dana almost groaned. He was long, lean and rangy, but muscled, not skinny. His shoulders broad, belly firm, and hips narrow where crisp, pressed jeans rested low and sexy, with a butt that had some muscle in it. She admired the corded strength of the bronzed forearms, visible under rolled sleeves, as he slapped a sign against his thigh, waiting and watching for her. She made out the letters. D-A-N-A. He was afraid she might miss him in this tiny little arrival lounge. How adorable was that?

Nerves started to prickle along her spine, butterflies skitter in her stomach, as Dana realized how much she stood to gain—or lose—on this trip. The guy she'd spoken with for so long, that was so kind, so thoughtful, fun and flirtatious, was also so handsome it was almost intimidating. Could she really be so lucky?

Dana had dated her share of men and fellow athletes, most of them seriously fit and handsome men, but had found most of them much less appealing on the inside. She'd already come to know this one inside, and fallen seriously. His presence in person was a knock-out punch.

Suddenly, she felt very shy and uncertain in a way that was unfamiliar—this man had her off balance from the start. But she had never been unconscious when she had first met a man, either! It was a weird and embarrassing first impression to make—especially when she hadn't been able to personally gauge his reaction.

Noting all the admiring smiles Garrett was getting from the females below, she shook off her discomfort, deciding she better get down there, if she wanted to stay lucky. You aren't the woman you once were, either, Dana, she was reminded, as she clutched the handle of her case with her one good arm and started carefully down the stairs. Keeping her head down, she watched every step, fearful of falling and being unable to grab something to save herself. A perfect metaphor, she acknowledged wryly, as she took a deep breath and went forward to meet Garrett, a friend and a stranger.

166

HE SPOTTED HER the minute she started down.

His breath caught, his heart stalled then plunged into a gallop at the wonder of it. She was here! Really here! Upright, moving, breathing, living, alive, and it was achingly beautiful for him to see. She descended the steps on slender mile-long legs, looking like a model, not a woman that had recently survived amazing odds.

Garrett tried not to gape. She was taller, fresher, more graceful, more of a presence, than even his dreams had made her. He'd easily forgotten she had an athlete's body, as she'd lain covered and still in bed, when he had focused on waiting for life to come into the pale and lovely face on the pillow. Even muffled under that cap and bulky cape, she drew attention, turned heads. Only the lowered brim of her hat, her slow and carefully balanced descent, gave any indication of her continued fragility.

And, hell! What was she doing hauling that bag with her! What if she fell?

Garrett started for the barrier, his sign forgotten at his side in his concern for her, just as she reached the bottom.

She raised her head and stepped out to stride straight towards him with a huge and happy smile on her face. His heart leaped a fence, then stumbled. Her picture had given him no warning of how dangerous that real life smile would be. Every male in the room, over the age of twelve, turned to see who the lucky recipient of it was. Clearly it was the hypnotized guy with the goofy grin on his face. But Garrett finally managed to draw a breath when she reached him and turned sparkling green eyes up to him.

"Hi," Dana smiled a little shyly, tilting her head, "I believe I'm your invalid?"

"No! I mean yes! Mine. No, not an invalid. Wow! You look fantastic!" He reached for her bag as she chuckled, seeming pleased he was feeling a little awkward, also. Taking her un-splinted arm he gently guided her out of the main traffic so she wouldn't be jostled, then he leaned forward to greet her.

"Is that a Montana custom?" She asked, flustered. "Greeting people with a kiss on both cheeks?"

"No," he grinned down at her, eyes blue as sapphires against the bronzed, honed face, deeply creased dimples framing his smile. "Usually it's just one, but I tried that, and it just wasn't enough, so I stole another. You must be addictive. God, it's so good to see you." His familiar voice dropped low and deep. "I've really been looking forward to this, Dana, especially your eyes."

Delighted, Dana laughed, "Well my eyes are glad to finally see you, also." Then she added more seriously, "Jenny told me how you kept asking me to open them. Thank you for that and well … everything."

"We were both getting a little scared of how long you were napping," he admitted. "It must have been beauty sleep, because you sure look terrific now."

A little embarrassed, she pointed at the piece of cardboard by his side, teasing, "Is that for me?"

"What? Oh, well," feeling foolish, he confessed. "I just made a sign. I was afraid...you never saw me... So you could find me before one of these other guys stole you and offered you a ride to Yellowstone."

Dana smiled. "I didn't need the sign. I recognized you. Jen had a paper from here with your picture. I'm surprised you could recognize me. Jen said I looked like road-kill in the hospital."

He grinned, but bit his tongue. The first times he saw her, Jenny was right.

"Well, I admit it was difficult since you weren't just a red-headed blur, charging a bison," he teased, then his eyes darkened, his voice soft and sincere. "I just knew you, Dana." He couldn't explain it better. He had just known she was for him, simply, instantly. He decided to welcome her again, with two more kisses on her cheeks, then holding her eyes, with a soft, breath stealing brush of his lips on hers.

"Ah," he breathed, enchanted, then he straightened and gave her a sheepish grin.

"See if you give me enough practice I can finally hit the target," he teased, suddenly remembering he was trying not to press her and had already kissed her five times in under five minutes. But man he was happy to see her so healthy! And here! She was still smiling, and not running to book a ticket back out of town, so maybe she was giving him a break out of gratitude. She had tasted like cinnamon and smelled like something fresh and heavenly he couldn't begin to name. He had to slow down, pace himself, give her a little space. He was damn glad to be with her.

Let's get your bags and get out of here."

HE HAD TAKEN HER to dinner in Bozeman, certain she was in dire need of some good food after her flight. Dana had been silent on the short drive from the airport—quiet and a little distant. Maybe just tired from her trip, or perhaps this was what Jenny had warned him about, though she didn't seem cool as much as calmly reserved. As he drove through the streets of the college town, he kept stealing glances at her, while she kept her eyes on the road ahead. He should be glad someone was; he could barely focus.

They were seated immediately at the restaurant, but as soon as they were shown their table, she excused herself to freshen up. When she returned and sat down across from him, they were face-to-face and private, at last. Her hat was gone, her auburn hair brushed and loosened to frame her face, her eyes were shielded, lowered to study her menu, a faint scent of crisp linen seemed to be more a part of her vital personality, than a fragrance. Then she raised those long-mysterious eyes to look straight at him, and the shock was physical. Seen, finally, so close and level and clear, he tried to fathom their exact color and realized they were not just green, he could not pin down a single name to call them. He felt like he had tumbled into a world of lush moss and ferns in the green-light of a deep forest canopy, with shafts of sunlight highlighting spring greens while striping the rest in emerald shadows.

"Garrett?"

"Yes?" He responded like someone that had been hypnotized.

"I asked if you knew what was best on the menu here?" She smiled.

He blinked. Freed, momentarily, from the spell of her eyes, he tried to figure out where 'here' was. Glancing down, he saw the menu in his hands, and checked the name and logo in the top corner. Right. Here!

"If you are a meat-eater, the free range Montana steaks are heaven." The place he just returned from. His voice felt dusty, as if he had been sitting with his mouth hanging open. He hoped not, but when he looked up at her, he kept his eyes from rising higher than her nose.

"You are frowning, is something wrong?" she asked.

"You had a path of little freckles over your nose. They're gone!"

"Oh," she grimaced, "Not much sun recently."

He had embarrassed her. "Sorry, I just missed them." Now *he* was embarrassed.

"Never fear, they will pop right back out in the sun." Brushing a curl from her cheek, she flicked those enchanting eyes back on him. "So why don't you just order me the biggest, best steak they have here. I am starved. I may never eat one of those quivering cubes of jellied fruit juice with carrots grated in it, again!"

169

Their laughter cleared the tension at the table and reminded them that they were friends, and not just awkward strangers.

Dana filled him in on her latest business decisions and arrangements as they enjoyed their meal. Garrett filed her in on Corky's latest horsing around and romances. She talked about how she had been worried she'd leaned too much on Jenny, then gotten in trouble for 'evicting' her from the hospital. They didn't refer to her hospital jailbreak. Garrett suspected it might still be a touchy subject.

He promised to take her to see the houses he was building, to take her around his home town up in the mountains, while she was here. They talked about the books and pictures he'd sent her and discussed the things they'd like to see the next day in Yellowstone. He told her about other trips he made there: where he'd gone fishing, where he'd seen wolf packs at dawn, and the first time he'd spotted a grizzly, unfortunately so close, that he had diplomatically traded his string of fish for a chance to back away.

When he glanced up at her, her eyes seemed to be studying his intently, reading the thoughts behind all his words. Good. He wanted her to know him. The sooner the better, he thought with mischief, because he wanted to steal a few more kisses. He almost grinned wondering how many more times he could get away with welcoming her to Montana.

They laughed, listened, explored and shared each other's stories and interests. At some point Dana had shifted closer, leaned toward him over the table as they laughed and spoke, the eyes that studied his held a hint of a smile in their green depths. They had shared so much over the phone that they found they were comfortable together, old friends in one way, relaxing naturally into finding new ways.

On the way out of town, instead of getting on the highway, Garrett decided to take a side trip first.

"I know it's late, but this is another way to connect to the highway, and there's something I want to show you first." He mysteriously kept his silence, then told Dana to close her eyes. He pulled into a parking lot and stopped, before he'd let her open them. Running to her door, he helped her out of the car grinning, then turned her around in his arms, laughing when she gasped at the sight behind her.

"Oh, my! Oh, Garrett! I've heard about this, seen a picture, but it's just so—"

"I know. And this is nothing compared to what's inside, especially with the new exhibit hall. I'll bring you down one day when it's open. Trust me, you'll want a whole day to explore this place." She leaned back against his chest and just gazed up, speechless.

Museum of the Rockies was engraved over the front of the massive building that fronted the now deserted parking lot. But that wasn't what had captured Dana's awe.

"Dana, I'd like you to meet Big Mike."

It was like being dropped into Jurassic Park. The night lights in the landscape glowed up at the massive, majestic creature that loomed above her on the lawn. Garrett just chuckled, enjoying her open-mouthed stare, pulling her closer against his chest, his arms around her waist, to steady and warm her in the chill evening air.

"Big Mike here is the world's first life-size bronze sculpture of a T- Rex skeleton. Pretty scary, huh?" He felt her nod. "It is fifteen feet high and thirty-six feet long."

It felt a lot larger than that when you stood under it and eyed the massive skull and teeth. it made one glad they didn't live back in the good old days, over sixty-five million years ago!

"This is part of the Montana State University that we are on," Garrett explained. "They have, as you can see, amazing opportunities to study archaeology, prehistory and geology. In fact, a professor from this school suggested the combination of some of those disciples and wrote a course text for geoarchaeology. Sounds like something designed for your interests, doesn't it?" He saw the spark leap in those green eyes, as she turned to him. "Since you mentioned you wanted to take some science courses, I thought you might want to check out this place. We could pick up a catalog when we come down for the museum." He could see the thoughts swirling behind her eyes, even though she didn't reply.

"You could take on-line courses, of course, but pictures aren't quite the same, are they?" He motioned back up to Big Mike towering over them, then pulled her back to the car.

Remaining quiet, he left her to watch the moonlight scenery as they climbed east into the Bridger mountain range, through Bozeman Pass, turning off the highway in Livingston.

Exhaustion had hollowed Dana's cheeks as he helped her out at her hotel, though she found a weary smile for him.

"I'm so glad I'm here. Take me, tomorrow," her voice was low and seductive, then she quirked a corner of her mouth in a tease, adding, "To Yellowstone. Will you Garrett?" She kissed his cheek and thanked him for the night.

As he drove away, Garrett had thoughts of taking her pretty much anywhere she wanted. Especially when she asked so nicely. It didn't sound like an order or a demand, the way Dana said 'take me' in that soft voice. With her emerald eyes locked on his, it sounded more like the sweetest of invitations. Maybe tomorrow, maybe whenever she was ready, she would let him make love to her. But her voice and eyes promised him it might be someday soon. But he was not going to rush her, especially after spending time with her today.

He was thinking that he'd trade soon, for always.

# Chapter 14

THEY HAD PLANNED ON an early start, yet Garrett was surprised to see Dana already waiting outside the hotel entrance for him. He grinned when he saw that she had cast off the cloak and cap that she had hidden under yesterday. She looked so vibrant and beautiful standing there, it made his chest ache.

Rays of the morning sun slanted in and seemed to delight in playing across the long curls that tumbled around her shoulders, bringing the flames to life, then spinning them into golden swirling shadows. She wore a heavy wool rolled neck sweater beneath a down vest of the same dark navy as the sling exposed on her left arm. A red bandana was knotted loosely at her neck. The last three feet of her height were nothing but long limbs, slender in comfortably worn denim. But the red laces of her hiking boots trailed across the concrete.

Her face glowed fresh and soft without makeup, only the soft shimmer of gloss on lips that smiled her delight to the whole world. Those eyes that so amazed him, sparkled in the sun like the dew on the grass, as she hopped over to the car laughing.

She had the passenger door open before he could get out.

"I hope you do shoes!" She smiled in at him. "I can almost dress myself, but I usually wear loafers. I forgot when I brought my boots that all the laces would be beyond my current skill level," she said with a carefree laugh.

Even as he stepped around to help, he marveled at her sense of humor in what must be a frustrating, if not depressing limitation. The seat of his truck was a little high for a one-armed climb, so he put his hands around her slender waist and lifted her onto the seat. Placing her boots on his thighs, he quickly hooked and threaded and laced the ties. When he had finished and glanced up to ask her if they were good and snug, he caught her watching him with a soft look that made the toes in his own boots curl.

"Perfect. Thanks!" She flashed a smile, then confided with a little shrug, "I'm so excited, Garrett, I feel just like a little kid."

He had wondered if he would see a shadow of fear, or at least apprehension in her eyes this morning, but only delight greeted him. Smiling himself, he carefully adjusted the seatbelt beneath her sling, and clamped it in. As he withdrew from the cab, he received a soft kiss on his cheek for his efforts.

Just a simple 'thanks' kind of kiss, but as he closed her door and rounded the truck he was feeling a little like an excited kid himself. When he climbed in his truck he rolled his window up to hold the subtle scent of her close.


THEY MADE THE DRIVE down to Gardiner with long stretches of comfortable silences, mixed with friendly conversation, easy in each other's company. Dana's eyes were eagerly roaming both sides of the river valley, scanning the varied rock faces and land formations. He could almost hear her trying to analyze and make sense of everything she was seeing.

Turning onto the main frontage road in Gardiner that bordered the Park, they pulled into a slot in front of the Paradise Valley Gallery. Dana wanted to stop and pick up a supply of postcards to send Jen daily, and select a few small works by local artists for both of them. She said the selections were difficult to make, but promised not to be too long as she was impatient to get into the park. Garrett browsed a different part of the store and then stepped next door to The Perk to get a couple of large expresso coffees while she completed her purchases. As they stepped back up to the truck, Dana set her purchases on the floor, then hesitated when Garrett came to lift her in.

"Something wrong?" He caught her slight frown.

"No ... I just, do you have a camera with you?"

"Sure." He reached into the glove compartment and tried to hand her his digital camera.

"Before we go in the Park, would you take a picture of me, Garrett? At the Arch? I need it from this side; I want the words in the picture. They're as simple and majestic as the gateway." He was already locking the car and guiding her across the road.

"I want the picture for my grandchildren, Garrett. That's what is so special about it. Someday they will be able to have their picture taken in front of it, for theirs."

They had left the car and walked down so they wouldn't block the entry road. Reaching out and taking her hand, he gave it a gentle squeeze, caught up in her emotions. It was a grand sight,

174

and a grand dream. Sometimes he saw it so often he forgot to appreciate that. He wouldn't again.

Especially since he hoped to share those grandchildren.

After the special memory pictures had been taken and they were back in the truck, Garrett pulled a small tissue wrapped package from his pocket.

"This is for you. Sorry it's not wrapped, but...," he handed it to her shyly, adding, "It's to remember this trip." He had planned to give it to her later, but now, when they were thinking of the future, seemed the right time.

He put the car in gear and pulled onto the road as Dana unwrapped the tissue. It was a necklace made of Montana Agate that she had fingered lovingly in the Gallery, then, reluctantly, passed by. Garrett had seen and silently purchased it for her.

DANA FELT A STING in her eyes, and a tightening in her throat at this, and all the other gifts, he gave so simply and thoughtfully.

She caught his eye as he slowed for the entry station. "Thank you. It's so lovely—"

"So are you, Dana." He turned and spoke with the Ranger showing his annual pass.

How did you breathe when someone said things like that to you? Dana wondered. Not as a flirtation, not as a line, just a quiet, seriously spoken comment that didn't ask or demand anything in return. He gave her compliments as casually, but thoughtfully, as he gave her gifts that had no great monetary value but were rich in consideration and warmth. His gifts made her feel special in a unique way, because they were so carefully tailored just to be prized by her. His words made her feel that each normal moment with her was a special occasion. God, the man was dangerous, adorable, and was scaring the hell out of her!

Dana needed to watch herself, before she melted into the fairy tale her hero was spinning, and keep a sharp, cool eye out for his flaws. He seemed way too good to be true so there must to be something seriously lacking in him. She'd try to remember to stay on guard. But it was hard to concentrate with a man she was so sensually attracted to that it made her lips ache to touch his. Then he said and did those things that made her stop breathing—

She should have made Jenny come with her.

No. That wouldn't have helped. Jen thought he was the most wonderful thing that had ever happened to Dana—even discounting the fact the man saved her life! Dana would be more than happy to jump the guy's bones just to thank him for that, but it wouldn't be gratitude. Oh no, it would be a flimsy excuse to satisfy her own growing needs and desire, and it *would* probably kill her. And she wasn't ready for this yet. She already felt too vulnerable, too out of control with all the drastic changes in her life. She knew better than to let a man that could make her forget to breath and think get that close—yet. She'd probably melt into a little puddle of mush right in his arms, she flicked a glance sideways, those strong, sexy arms ... Yes, she wanted him, but—

"What are you thinking?" He gave her a friendly smile.

"Oh, nothing, really ....," Turning her face to her window, she studied scenery as her face cooled down.

"I was just looking for wildlife." And she had better start looking *outside* the truck for it, she scolded herself firmly. She'd come to see Yellowstone. If she focused on that she could keep her thoughts disciplined, and keep him at arm's length—or keep herself from his.

"Based on the number of cars lined up beside that bridge up ahead, I think you're about to see some. This area of the river is a good place to see Bighorn sheep." He drove over the bridge and found a spot for them to pull off the road. Dāna plucked his binoculars off the dash holding them in her free hand, so he couldn't capture it, and more of her heart, this time.

"Those are probably uncomfortable around your neck with the sling and all, would you like me to carry them for you?" He asked courteously. He seemed unfazed when she declined and turned to lead the way back down the side of the road. The beige coats of the sheep blended so well with the steep hill that it was a delight for Dana when part of the hillside moved and turned out to be animals edging down to the river.


A GREAT CURLED-HORN male stood guard.

A protective instinct Garrett well understood, as they left and wound up through Mammoth and he took the road south along the western side of the Park. He had subtly arranged their first day so that they wouldn't have to pass the spot where Dana had been hurt—the spot that still made him shudder if he had to drive by it.

They detoured through the short loop of tumbled, balanced limestone boulders at the Hoodoos, then stopped to gaze in awe at the angular columns of basalt, formed by Mother Nature, that marched across the face of Sheepeaters Cliff.

When they pulled into the deserted informational turnout at Obsidian Cliff, Garrett took a snack cooler and blanket out from behind his seat, so his lady could sit and gaze at the Historic Landmark, and dream of its ancient story to her heart's content. He saw the paperback he'd sent that told of the cliff, peeking from her pack. Her pleased and peaceful smile as she sat in the meadow, where he had taken photos for her, was its own reward for Garrett.

"Thinking of your First Americans that mined that cliff for their tools and weapons?" he asked softly.

She put down her sandwich and smiled back, her eyes glowing mossy soft, and thoughtful.

"I was, but now my mind has slipped even deeper back in time, before anyone was here. I was thinking about the columns of basalt at Sheepeater Cliff. That lava flow would have needed to cool gradually to form those octagonal columns. Yet just a short distance away, here," she motioned to the cliff of volcanic glass before them, her eyes remaining on Obsidian Cliff as she continued quietly. "Here I see a great—huge! What is it? Two hundred feet high? This great flow of red-hot liquid hundreds of feet high is coming straight at us, and suddenly stops cold. Literally. It had to turn cold in a flash to turn into volcanic glass. They think it hit an ice sheet. That must have had to be even taller!" Her eyes turned back to his, but she wasn't seeing him. "This place, this park, is like the greatest sci-fi movie ever imagined!" Then seeming to come back to earth—or present earth, anyway—she laughed, "And we missed it!" Pausing a moment before adding, "Fortunately," though her voice sounded a bit uncertain about that last comment.


AFTER THEIR BREAK, they continued south past Norris. Dana straightened, alertly scanning both sides of the road, trying to soak up every detail. Before, with Jen, they had cut east across the park, so this would be new territory for her.

Much of this area had been ravaged in the Yellowstone Firestorms of 1988. Now trees had come back so thickly that seedlings were crowding onto the pavement to find some sunlight to grow. The trees weren't very tall, but it was heartwarming to see how densely the land had regenerated itself, as mile after mile of hills rolled with a green blanket of lodge pole pines.

"I was reading up about this," she motioned out the window, "how lodge pole pines actually *need* fire to grow." Comfortable in her scientific frame of mind, Dana shared the information she had learned, though Garrett already knew it. He enjoyed her enthusiasm and listened carefully as she continued.

"Apparently, even the geographic location figures in. Because Yellowstone is located at the east end of the Snake River Basin, the weather systems that blow through from the West coast make this a wetter place than most of its high altitude neighborhood. So to start with, fires don't usually burn as long or hard. Lodge pole cones normally wouldn't open for half a century except with a little help from fire. They have this protective resin that seals them. Normal heat doesn't open them, but fire melts the resin and pops them open to spread thousands of seeds. But, too much fire would have just burnt them up, so the moisture in the area matters. They've figured out that the tree needs to burn for twenty-five seconds to open that magic lock.

"Can you believe that? Too little time, the resin doesn't melt, too long and the seeds burn up. Blows my mind how complex it is. Oh, sorry, you probably know all this," her voice and excitement drained away. "I know I drive Jen crazy with my little speeches," she muttered.

"I know." He laughed.

He just laughed!

"I do know. I know you drive Jenny nuts. She told me. But I didn't know all that detail about timing and moisture. I found that fascinating. I use lodge pole pine in my home projects sometimes and you've given me a great idea. I'll have to try a little experiment. See if I can blow torch open some cones I have and start my own little tree farm on my property. They would make great little Christmas trees, and my horses could use more summer shade."


"ARE YOU SERIOUS?" Dana couldn't believe her ears.

"Sure." He shrugged.

See, she thought, that was the problem with Garrett. Not only did he not roll his eyes when she got off on one of her little lectures, but he also actually listened and thought about it, took her seriously. It was just way too easy to get addicted to someone like that.

When they parked at the Artist's Paint Pots, Dana literally bounced out of the truck.

"Excited?" Garrett chuckled.

"Very!" She grabbed his hand and would have drug him over the boardwalk to the trail, if he hadn't lengthened his strides to keep up with her.

The trail ran through the old fire zone, with some of the trees still only chest high, making it seem like they were wandering through a children's forest. Dana had just turned to ask him how much farther they had to go when the woods opened to the thermal basin at the foot of Paint Pot Hill.

Potholes filled with gallons of milky aqua paint, spotted splashes of clearly iron-enriched reds, and terra cotta, were mixed with transparent turquoise pools against the chalky white sinter of the surrounding ground. As Dana lingered on the boardwalk, fascinated with what earth could create, Garrett motioned to the hill above that had columns of steam rising from its top.

"The views are even better from up above, Dana, and there are geysers, also."

She nodded and motioned for him to start up the trail, as she waited for a last bubble to give a funny burp in a baby-sized soft aqua paint pot below.

Normally, she wouldn't have given it a thought, but half-way up the short climb, Dana found herself gasping for breath, her legs weak and knees shaky. Reaching a switchback, Garrett seemed to notice her struggle, and stepped down quickly to wrap his arm around her waist and boost her up the last ascent. Dropping onto a bench in front of a belching geyser, she tried to draw deep breaths, coughing, feeling dizzy and limp.

Garrett crouched down, kneeling in front of her, blocking the sulfur laced steam from her face so she could draw in some oxygen. "Hey, babe, even athletes get out of shape after a month or more in the hospital," he comforted, taking both her hands in his. She gave him a weak smile, but she was surprised and upset by her weakness.

"Give it time, Dana. There is one very important thing you are forgetting."

"You mean besides the fact that I am pathetically out of shape?"

Garrett bounced his eyebrows at her, sliding his palm slowly from her ankle up the back of her leg, leaning in close to her face. "Trust me, babe, there's nothing wrong with your shape!" His throaty voice only increased her breathlessness as he brushed his lips across her cheek, nibbled kisses on her jaw beneath her ear. Pulling back to give her some air, he added in a lighter tone, "Besides, you forgot that you are a sea-level girl, and we're in the six, or so, thousand foot altitude level in most of Yellowstone. Give yourself a break."

179

Rising, he pulled her up with him to a railing out of the sulfur steam, then turned her to face the view of the paint pots below. It was an amazing display of color, texture, and tone, and Dana felt a little better when she saw how small the people appeared now on the boardwalk below. Standing against the rail, she gazed out at the colorful palette below, then further out, to the viewpoint of distant unfenced meadows blending into rolling forests, logged only by past fires. Behind it all, distant mountain peaks formed dark pyramids beneath an endless sky. Garrett stood close behind her, looking out over her shoulder, sharing all the beauties of this unique and amazing land of Yellowstone with her.

She was aware of the warmth of his hard chest brushing her back, the solidness of his support, both physical and emotional. She leaned back a little to feel his arms circle comfortably around her waist, letting her rest sheltered against his strength. Instead of sulfur, now she was wrapped in his male scent. He smelled like woods, fresh winds and sage, and some subtle, spicy undertone. His smile was playful, his eyes carefully searched her face, as she turned her face up to his and reached a palm up to cup his face, silently nudging his head lower so she could rest her cheek against his. It felt good. He felt so right, and warm, strong and steady. She had no resistance to this generous and giving man. And, at the moment, she did not wish for any.

"This is all so beautiful," Dana sighed, content. "I'm so thankful you are sharing it with me, Garrett." His arms tightened in a silent squeeze of welcome and agreement. She nuzzled her face against his, turning to brush his cheek softly with her mouth, and offer him her lips.

He took them with a soft but serious hunger that had need leaping instantly in her belly. Her knees quivered, pleasure rippling down nerves, she sagged against him, his body bracing hers. Wrapped in arms that would hold her up, she opened to the passion as it crashed, shattered, washed over and through her, and even as it ebbed when he broke off this first real, brief but devastating—and very public—kiss. It left warm trickles to linger and caress her.

Gathered closer, her head settling in his shoulder, she felt him drop a quick kiss on the hair on the top of her head, as he held and steadied her until her breath returned and her legs were stable enough to start back down the trail. Swaying slightly, they gazed silently at the view, while their bodies and thoughts held the wonder of each other.

180

A large and loud group clambered onto the platform, breaking their reverie. Garrett preceded her down a short flight of steps to the trailhead, turning at the base he looked back up at Dana, worry creasing his face.

"Would you like me to carry you down?"

She looked down at him, her head angled to the side. His eyes looked like twin blue pools of sky. She narrowed hers a bit, considering. The amateur scientist in her was pondering whether the high-altitude was a factor responsible for giving Garrett's brief kiss such a sharp and dangerous punch. If that hypothesis was correct, if that's what a high-altitude kiss could do, then, Dana reasoned, it followed that high-altitude sex would be ... so deadly delicious! Paradise on earth? Hmmm.

Climbing down one step to be almost level with him, she reached out to trace a fingertip along the clean line of his jaw. Looking deeply into his eyes, she liked what she saw. Warmth, welcome, strength, she could see into them, into him. Her fickle, shifting needs and emotions shook her enough to have her reaching for her best defense—a bold, teasing step forward.

"Carry me in those big strong arms? I'm afraid I'd be unable to resist nibbling along this," her finger continuing to trace his face, teasingly sliding from his jaw, down his throat, "and you might lose your balance and fall."


HE JUST ABOUT DID. His throat dried to sage dust and all the blood vacated his head.

She seemed pleased to see him so struck and helpless; curling her hand up and around the taut muscles in his upper arm, she let him escort her down securely—though he thought she might just be the one steadying him!.

When they reached the truck and he was lifting her in, he saw a smug little smile on her face.

"What?" he laughed.

She just smiled and shook her head, saying nothing more as she settled so he could fasten her seat belt. As they drove toward their next stop, she gazed quietly out the window, her mind busy with private thoughts.

Unsure of the reason for her silence, Garrett wondered if he had gone too far, or not far enough. He had been open, responding naturally to her with his thoughts, feelings, affectionate closeness and kisses, but held his passions in check for when—or if—she asked for them. Then she had caught him off guard. He had wanted to dive in and stay down forever when she had given him that sweet mouth, that taste of her. He had managed to catch himself though, barely, to take a quick, mind-altering dip and scramble out before he scared her.

He hoped. Or before he lost all sense of time and place and they fell off the cliff, in public, into a boiling hot spring below, no less! Geez, Garrett! Steady, boy.

But hell, how was he supposed to keep his friendly guy side on when she could make him hard as a rock and forget to breathe with just the flick of a fingertip, or laughter in those long-awaited, and so worth it, glorious green eyes? She asked him to help her dress! Well, tie her bootlaces. How was he not supposed to be thinking about the undressing part all day? She just needed help and asked for it, fool! Get a grip.

She was probably sitting over there right now, worrying about his kiss. Thinking she had gotten much more than she had asked for, more than she'd planned on. More than she wanted? Sure, she flirted with him later, but that was probably just to put him at ease—not at attention—he scowled at his response. He was sure she had only teased a little so they wouldn't be uncomfortable with each other after that kiss. Dana would do that, make things easy and comfortable for the rest of the day. He'd never been with a woman *more* comfortable to spend time with.

He would behave. He would. He *could*.

If *she* would.

He was sure to redeem himself with the next stop he'd planned. It was perfect for a geo-goofy gal. He promised himself he would not act like a love-sick puppy. Well, try not, anyway.

He'd always been goal oriented, identifying then working hard and confidently toward what he needed to build the life he wanted. It hadn't needed a woman before to complete, but no woman had ever turned him inside out before like this one. She was one of a kind—his kind—and he would be a fool not to work for her affection. He just winced at the picture of himself as an overeager, awkward, ear-flopping puppy, charging and leaping at her. Covering her with sloppy kisses—well, maybe that part was okay.

No, he didn't have a problem being a fool for love, when it was the right love. He would just like to be a fool with a shred of dignity—though most women *did* have a soft spot for puppies ...

"Do you like pu...ah, waterfalls, Dana?"

"Love them. For their beauty and figuring out the geology of how they got there," she responded enthusiastically.

182

Garrett smiled to himself, he was about to hit the jackpot, but he kept his voice calm.

"Good. There is a very pretty one ahead that people have enjoyed from the roadside since it was built, but it has a new history, just recently realized, that I think you will enjoy.

Beside them the Gibbon River flowed calm and innocent along the left side of the road, serene beneath the green leaves of trees lazily hanging over its banks, gently sifting the dappled sunlight.

Then suddenly the river, along with its eternally peaceful scene, disappeared.

# Chapter 15

YELLOWSTONE SITS ON A SUPERVOLCANO, a volcano of such destructive force that it can change the global climate and threaten the very survival of its species; they are often known by the public as 'doomsday' volcanoes.

The last known explosion of a Supervolcano was at Toba, in northern Sumatra, about seventy-four thousand years ago. It was believed to be the 'final straw' tipping the world into an Ice Age, and one reason the modern human species might have thinned to just one genetic ancestral strain.

Yellowstone erupted—with super volcanic force—three times in the distant past. Exploding over two million years ago, over one million years ago, and most recently, six hundred and forty thousand years ago, and it is clearly still hissing, steaming, and hot tempered.

Multiple major lava flows covered the landscape so thoroughly since that last cataclysm of super eruptions that it wasn't even noticed that there was a thirty-five mile wide depressed caldera, from that ancient blast six thousand four hundred centuries past, until satellites looked down on it etched over Yellowstone in the 1960s.

Over time, more recent ash and lava flows had buried the clues, the evidence of that brutal crime, except in one spot where its remnants could still be seen—if not recognized—by the naked eye. Gibbon Falls.

Gibbon Falls sat quietly in the west while most of the crowds were seduced by the drama to the east at the Upper and Lower Falls in the Grand Canyon of the Yellowstone, where glaciers had carved majestically, and quite recently, relatively speaking, through lava flows. The lavas at Canyon were dramatic, chemically altered, cooked and weathered into exotic golden spires, ragged, rugged outcrops carved into castles of stone that gleamed gold, pink, and orange in the turquoise spray of picture perfect waterfalls, one hundred to three hundred feet tall.

But all that beauty and wonder, so avidly viewed from Artist's Point, had taken place *inside* the huge hole left by the great explosion, and was relatively *new*, geologically. All that existed previously at the Canyon site had been blasted into space as pulverized ash. So that prime attraction was newly built compared to what hid under this river's casual eighty-four foot drop that Gibbon Falls modestly offered from the roadside. It was not a golden scene, but a hard blasted black one, veiled behind the waters of a serene river that had fallen into chaos.

The deadly Supervolcano had hidden itself well, even after park roads were built, it had hidden in plain sight until a satellite photo revealed its secret. Waiting to be noticed, waiting for those that would respect and honor its worth in the discovery of clues to ancient times and events that would unlock secrets of earth's past caprices. Waiting to warn of what to expect and how to understand the shape of today's world—and predict its future. Waiting for those like Dana to see its terrible beauty.

The only known exposed, undeformed remnant of the actual ancient caldera rim, created the cliff the Gibbon River suddenly fell off. It looked like just another pretty little waterfall to most.

Dana stared at the water pouring over the fall as if she were trying to see through it to the end of the world, which, historically speaking, it certainly represented a damn good try at.

Garrett was beginning to recognize and enjoy that concentrated gaze. Despite the relative calm in Dana's face, he knew her mind was whirling with thoughts, studying details in the earth, putting herself back to events long past, projecting future implications, and absorbing it all like a huge, curious sponge that could never gather enough information. She must have been a challenge as a child asking her parents a million questions a minute.

Then he remembered.

She had been an orphan. Who had she had to satisfy that curious mind except herself?

Jenny had told him that Dana was a prodigious reader, tackling books on anything and everything that caught her eye, from popular novels, to dry technical science textbooks. She'd had so many questions and no one to devote the time to answer her as a child. Athletic, playful, friendly and easy to be around, she still had a quiet, serious reserve he'd never quite understood until now. It was an intelligent mind, one that retained the natural wonder and inquisitiveness of a child. She had nourished it privately and quietly beneath that lovely surface, and flawless face. Dana had depths a man could spend a lifetime learning, and a mind that would fascinate endlessly.

She turned, interrupting his study of her, and glanced over to give him an appreciative dropped jaw, her eyes wide in wonder, communicating silently—beneath the roar of the falls—her thanks for this treat, before returning to scan the view.

He grinned back. Yes, he knew how to enchant this woman! Leaning on the old stone wall beside her, testing its stability first, he was aware he was leaning out over the throat of a volcano. If he could just get it to blow up again, that should really impress her! No, just kidding, he apologized to the volcano gods. Bad idea. Very, very bad idea!

When Dana could finally speak, she edged behind his shoulder where she could talk in his ear, without shouting over the sound of the falls, never taking her eyes off the glistening black rim wall behind the cascade of water.

"I heard someone say, after watching a show about Yellowstone being a huge volcano, still alive, that she wouldn't ever come here, in case it decided to blow up on her vacation. She just didn't get it, probably a lot of people don't.

"They think that big means something like the Mt. Saint Helen's blast in my home state. They think it means incredible destruction to an area. People in a small close area killed, trees knocked down, floods tearing down bridges and riverside homes, maybe even the ash falling for several states. Or they think of Crater Lake in Oregon, which is an old caldera hole filled with water from when Mt. Mazama exploded and threw so much ash that they now use it to date soil strata far from there. But Crater Lake is only six miles wide, this rim is almost thirty six! Mt. Saint Helens' eruption was a thousand times, or more, smaller than what happened here.

"I told her she was crazy not to come see this place for that reason. If it had another explosion like before, it wouldn't matter if you'd stayed home or not. They've dug up twenty feet of ash from that ancient explosion in parts of California—and that's only so far. That kind of blast would cause a nuclear winter that would change the world and life on it."

Dana paused to chuckle. "So I told her she better hurry out and see all the cool stuff at Yellowstone before it blew and took her out at home, watching some dumb reality TV show!"

"And how did she take that dose of reality?"

"Oh, not well. Not well at all."

"Well, some people just prefer to think they can run between raindrops, I guess." Garrett replied wisely, hoping to make up for his earlier, errant and irresponsible wish.

AFTER SKIRTING THE GIBBON RIVER, the road was forced west along the caldera rim toward Madison Junction. There they would turn south and would be traveling inside the pit of the old caldera for the first time.

Keeping his eyes on the road, watching for his turn, Garrett cheerfully teased Dana.

"If you liked that, babe, then you're really going to love me for the next wonder I have to show you."

Glancing sideways, Dana studied his strong profile, his devastating grin, the thick sandy hair flowing in the wind from the open window. He was a good and decent man; a solid, responsible man. He was also a sweet and charming guy—not to mention seriously hot. Torn between asking 'Will I?' or 'What?' she realized she probably already knew the answer to the first question, but she would keep it to herself for now.

Garrett turned right off the main road onto a narrow one-way drive and looked over at her with that dimpled grin.

"Ready?"

"Yes. Yes, I am." For whatever you've got planned handsome, she added silently.


THEN HE PLUNGED HER from sunlight into a dark, narrow, primeval canyon of sound and fury.

It was like being taken from the placid world above through the gates of hell.

Steep, close, blackened walls loomed hundreds of feet on either side, blocking all but a narrow ceiling of distant light. Built of layer after layer of rhyolite flows, the hardened, blackened blood of the earth's bursting wounds and fury, laid down up to eight hundred feet deep as the caldera tried to refill itself until the last flow 70,000 years ago. The walls still held massive chunks of tumbled blocks and boulders, the bones of the earth's torn skeleton, in the welded clutch of glassy ash flows after the earth had cooled them—and her temper—only to throw out another layer of fiery agony. The Firehole River thrashed, thrusting, cutting, carving ever deeper into prehistoric rock, booming beside them, its power primeval in the darkness, its sound a repeated physical assault, thrumming on the senses.

As they drove up out of the deepest darkest womb of the canyon, they stopped to look way down sheer walls where the river

187

still raged, carving out caves and chewing its way downward. It was still stunning, still loud, but nothing like being down inside the churning, blackened tunnel-like maelstrom.

"Oh, Garrett! I think I need a cigarette after that!" Dana's shaky laugh and comment weren't referring to a need to smoke, but the after effects of her intense pleasure.

She was in love with the canyon. And the man that gave it to her? Well, she might be hanging out around too many falls, lately—she was starting to wonder if she wasn't going to do a little falling herself if she didn't keep her feet solidly on the rim!

She only made him drive the Firehole Canyon Loop two more times before she let him continue on to the next site, making him promise her another round or two on the return trip.

The sun was out and the wind had died down as they strolled lazily, hand in hand, along the half mile boardwalk that wound through a dozen or more geothermal features at Fountain Paint Pots. So tame seeming after the canyon, but still dangerous in its own way. All four of the Park's basic thermal type features could be found here, surrounded by a flat sinter plain rimmed with gray ghostly skeletons of trees that had succumbed to the acids and gases, yet refused to fall.

Unlike Mammoth Hot Springs, often called the fifth geothermal feature, where hot water rises through limestone—creating in essence, outdoor caves—all the other thermal features were caused by hot water rising up through volcanic ash with its silica rich chemicals, minerals, acids, and gases. Instead of creating deposits of chalky, marble-veined travertine, they produced fields—often floating— of crusty white silica sinter that hardened to grey-white deposits, commonly called geyserite.

At the Fountain Paint Pot Basin, and other park geyser basins, the difference was not in *what kind* of rock the hot, dissolving water rose through, but in *how the underground was plumbed* that distinguished whether it released pressure in bursts of water, hissing steam, bubbling springs, or brought up more mud that hot water.

Fountain Paint Pot, itself, was a burbling mud pot. Silex Spring seemed to bleed the yellow and orange trails of primal microbes from the brim of its turquoise hot spring, while a fumarole hissed gas at Red Spouter. Further out on the boardwalk loop were geysers of all shapes and sizes, each with its own personality: Jet, Jelly, Spasm, and the arrogant Clepsydra, along with several others.

"I've seen so many wonders in one day, I think I'm full, Garrett. I can't hold any more in my mind today or I'll lose some, and I want time to appreciate and remember every last minute."

"Boggles it, doesn't it? Tired, babe?"

She stifled a happy hum at the sound of that word on his lips. Jen was right. He gave it a softness that was sweet and sensual.

"A little tired," she admitted, "but I'm a lot happy, in a quiet way."

SO QUIET THAT on the return trip Garrett thought Dana had been napping until she asked him a question.

"What's the altitude at your house, Garrett?"

He smiled at her eternal curiosity.

"Not quite as high as here, but still above five thousand feet elevation."

"How *nice*," she lingered on the word. "So where *do* you live? In Livingston?"

"No just south of there. We'll pass it on the way back to town. We can swing in on the way, if you'd like. My horses would love to meet you. I've been telling them all about you. I have a place in Paradise Valley."

"Where?"

"Paradise Valley."

"How appropriate." He thought she murmured.

After no further response, Garrett took his eyes off the road for a minute, glancing over at her. She lay with her head against the back of the seat, eyes closed with a little smile just curving up the corners of lush lips. She must be dozing and dreaming happy thoughts.

He wasn't quite sure if she'd said yes to stopping at his place or not. If they went into town for dinner, he'd need to feed the horses anyway, before it got too late. Maybe she would wake by the time they got to his place. Then he could find out what was on her mind for tonight.

"TONIGHT? WELL, I WAS considering a little science experiment ...," she drawled, mysteriously, "but I'm too starved. It will have to wait until after dinner."

"Right, well did you want to go to a restaurant in Livingston, or should we whip something up here?"

Glancing around her, she sighed heavily. They were seated on his porch. Her feet were stretched out in front of her, she had a crisp, cold beer by the throat, a mountain range leaped from high prairie so close it seemed that, if she rocked forward, she'd crack her forehead on its granite. Surely God's country. Garrett's cozy log home and natural timbered wood barn, with its trio of sleek, pampered horses, said homestead with the emphasis on home, roots, and steadiness.

A soft wicker from one of the horses reminded her of Garrett saying he'd told them all about her, like they were his pals. If so, they probably recognized her when she arrived, she mused wryly. Telling each other 'that must be Dana, asleep, the unconscious one we've been hearing about'.

She sighed once again and turned her attention to the man beside her.

"About having dinner here? Garrett, I have a confession to make. I can't cook."

When he just turned to gaze at her without much alarm, she felt she better be more specific. "I burn water when I boil it, seriously, ask Jenny." That widened his eyes, now he looked concerned. "Except raw vegetables," she added hastily, "I can cook those."

He nodded calmly, then his forehead puckered a bit, his lips moved as if he was silently repeating her words to himself. Looking up puzzled, he asked, "With water? Do you cook the raw vegetables with water?"

"Yes, I turn water on and thoroughly wash the vegetables with it, then I cut them in sticks or chunks." She gave him a pleasant smile, leaned back to rock and take another sip of her beer.

Realizing she'd left something out, she added, "If they are carrots, I also peel them. I'm pretty handy with a peeler, now that I think of it."

Garrett waited, rocked a bit, took a sip of his beer, and asked, "Then what?"

"Pardon?"

"Then what do you do with the veggies?"

"Oh, my recipes? Well, I usually mix them all into a bowl, toss them for a salad. Or I arrange them on a platter around a plastic container of that dip you can get in the store, as finger food."

"Raw?"

"Yes. That's what I said I do. Raw vegetables."

"Right, you did." Garrett nodded, thought about that a bit, taking a few more sips of his beer, gazing out at the mountains.

"Can you cook potato chips and snack cracker trays, as well?" He tried to hide his grin.

"Oh course!" Dana laughed, "Anyone can do that."

"With sliced cheeses and meats?"

"Well, I guess, if I can find the slices at the store."

"That's ... amazing," was the only word Garrett seemed able to come up with, choking a laugh into a rough cough that didn't fool her for a minute. "They don't make your kind around here, Dana." He gave her a smile.

"Thank you."

"Well, then I guess we've got it made. Between your recipes and skills with the raw cooking and the fact I can make almost anything else on a grill or in a fry pan, we're set! But, we could just pop over to the Saloon in Emigrant. I just remembered they have a prime rib and prawns special tonight. It's mouthwatering!"

"It must be. Mine watered just hearing the words. I'm starved, let's go!"


WHAT THE HELL had he been thinking when he suggested they go to the Saloon for dinner?

Probably about Dana cooking him up a potato chip meal, or one of those veggie recipes.

Garrett felt like finding a wall to bang his head against to relieve the pain of his idiocy. From the minute they had walked into his local hangout, his pals, all of whom he was going to disown or kill outright, had kindly relieved him of his lady friend. They hadn't let him talk to his date alone, or even get close enough to speak to her at all, all night!

Just being sociable, trying to make her feel welcome, his friends—ex-friends—claimed when he complained, trying to edge into the circle surrounding her. They bought her drink after drink while they talked her ear off. Dana did such a good job pretending she was enjoying herself, that even he would have been fooled. If he hadn't convinced himself that she was probably just being polite, of course.

They hadn't given her back to him until almost closing time when she could barely speak or stand.

"So, what were you talking to those guys about?"

"Finding your see-crits." She told him with a pretty, if slightly silly, smile.

"My secrets?" He clarified.

"Uh-huh, need flawss." Nodding her head seemed to have made her a little dizzy, she clutched his arm for balance.

"And my flaws? Great! What did they tell you?" Whatever they said, he hoped she wouldn't remember by morning.

"Black hat said not as hansumm as him." Dana blew a raspberry and let go of Garrett to throw her arm out to the side, palm up. "Whadameye? Blind?"

Okay, he thought smiling, capturing her before her gesture sent her into the side of a car. It was okay if she remembered that.

He gave up trying to walk her out. Afraid she'd stumble and land on her bad arm, he carried her out to the truck. She mumbled away while he strapped her into her seat belt. Something about doing her 'hi-lad-dee-tood-spear-mint lay-der'. Then she'd passed out cold.

Thanks, pals!

He'd ground his teeth all the way to her hotel in town, thinking of inventive ways to get revenge on his friends. Ex-friends. He'd carried her up to her room, found her key, let them in and set her gently on the bed, though he probably could have dropped her without a whimper.

Poor thing, couldn't those dogs see she was an invalid, with her arm in a sling, her wrist in a cast? He noticed now they'd all signed it for her and hadn't even had the decency to leave any space for his name.

Now he was really pissed.

How could they get her so drunk; what if she'd fallen before he could catch her? And the hangover she'd have tomorrow, it just wasn't fair after all the pain she'd been through.

Poor little, beautiful, drunken sot.

He tenderly brushed the tangled auburn curls from her face. Dousing a washcloth in warm water, he washed it over her face and laid it on her forehead. He didn't dare try to undress her with that shoulder injury. He could probably get her jeans off, but he really didn't think he could trust himself with that. He just took her boots and socks off for her.

Getting a glass of water, he set it on her nightstand with her bottle of aspirin and left her to sleep it off.

Then he cursed himself and all his soon-to-be-dead friends, all the way back home. The hell of it was that it had been his bright idea. Tomorrow he'd find somewhere at least fifty miles from here to take her to dinner. The Old Faithful Inn should be about far enough, he hoped.

192

When he returned to the hotel the next morning, Miss Bright, Sparkling and Raring-to-Go wasn't out front waiting for him. Imagine that! He chuckled and went to find what was left of her.

# Chapter 16

SHE LOOKED BEAUTIFUL, regardless, he had to admit when Dana opened the door of her hotel room. Even if it was a little bit fuzzier and less lively kind of beauty. Fragile might be the word that would fit. Her pale skin seemed to have picked up some of the lovely tint of her eyes. Eyes that kind of reminded him of Christmas, now that he noticed the red and white stripes circling the deep green glazed centers. She smelled nice too, like lavender soap, coconut shampoo, and about a carafe of mint mouthwash.

"How you feeling, babe?" His voice was gentle, he tried not to laugh. He didn't laugh loudly, at least. Had to be considerate of that brittle little head. "I came up to see if you needed some help with your boots, but it doesn't look like you're ready for them yet."

Dana folded her arms across her chest, narrowing her eyes at the ill-concealed smirk on his face. Glancing down at the terry robe that wrapped nearly twice around her, stopping about eight inches from the floor, she seemed to be considering her exposed ankles and feet. "I don't know. It might be a new fashion statement. Fuzzy robe, sling, wool socks and hiking boots, it could work."

Well, he chuckled, at least her sense of humor had survived the night.

Slanting a thoughtful glance at him, she pursed her lips a moment, then said, "I'm not in the habit of sleeping in my clothes." Her face and tone were unreadable.

"I'm not in the habit of undressing women incapable of consenting," he responded to her unspoken comment about the night before.

"Ah, a gentleman," she said mildly, but looked mischievous.

"Yes, ma'am, always."

Garrett hadn't meant it as a challenge.

"Hmm." She hummed, her green eyes raking him with a look that was definitely not ladylike. He watched her pick up her boots and carry them over by the bed. Sitting down on the end of her bed she stretched out her feet and wiggled her naked toes at him.

"You want me to put your boots on *now*? How will you get your pants on?" He asked bewildered.

"Maybe I won't," she purred, giving him a very sultry look from under lowered lashes that made him highly suspicious. "My wool socks with this sexy little red band around the top, hiking boots ... nothing else. Don't you think it would make a funky, cowboy version of high heels, silk hose ... and a bright red garter belt?"

Garrett blanched, flushed, and sat down hard on the chair behind him as the image formed in his head. The hard fall conveniently snapped his dropped jaw closed.

"This—" he tried again. This time without the squeak. "This is revenge, isn't it?"

She could have just nodded at him. He didn't need her to give him that naughty smile with it. Hell, now she was crossing her leg, letting her robe slip open just enough so he could see a beautiful, shapely bare leg, all the way up to her ... damn, she stopped it at mid-silky-thigh. He cleared his throat this time, before trying to speak.

"Why are you torturing me? It's my friends," ex-friends, he thought, "that gave you the hangover."

She started that bare leg swinging slowly back and forth, like a hypnotic pendulum.

"You were the one smirking, big guy. Besides you're ... handy."

The voice and the look she was using on him was dangerous.

He felt his Adam's apple travel all the length up and down his throat as he swallowed. This was not a good idea. He could hear warning bells ringing all over. It wasn't just the revenge factor, but Garrett recalled Jen's warnings about how Dana hid herself behind her flirtation. Ever since he had picked her up at the airport, Dana had varied between warm and friendly, and politely quiet and distant. Except for that one moment in the park when she had reached for him and landed a slow, scintillating kiss on his lips that near burned his toes. But she was dizzy from the exertion and altitude at the time, so he didn't dare count that.

He didn't want to get caught in whatever game this was and get disqualified for the main prize. And this wasn't how he wanted to make love to her the first time. Tearing his eyes from her leg, he felt the rest of his body reacting and jumped to his feet, scooting toward the door.

"Thanks." He cleared the gravel from his throat. "I think I better wait for you down in the coffee shop."

She tossed back that gorgeous cloud of hair, leaning back to brace herself, one hand behind her on the bed, and very deliberately exposed another two inches of skin. She had a smile on her face as wide and dangerous as an open bear trap, just before it sprang closed on a cherished body part. He took another step towards the door.

"Besides, you are a lot cuter than all your friends ... Garrett."

How did she get her voice so low and hot, like that? Did she say cuter? He shuffled back toward her a few steps. Cuter? Okay. He would prefer more handsome, sexier, but—

"Ah, are you sure you don't need help getting dressed?"

"No."

"Okay." He turned back and reached the door, then paused, turning again.

"No, you don't need any help? Or, no, you're not getting— never mind." He yanked open the door and ran, calling, "See you down there," from the safety of the hallway.


DANA FELL BACK ON the bed and laughed so hard she was wiping tears from her eyes. She had certainly wiped the smirk from Garrett's face—even if she deserved it.

It was too bad she had a splitting headache and felt like she was about to lose the breakfast she hadn't even eaten yet, or she would have tripped him on his way out, and beaten him to the floor. He was such a doll! Sweet, but deadly sexy, with the manners of a gentleman, but his eyes had covered her with a look that told her he could probably rattle her teeth with his passion.

Ah, he was a keeper. Oh yes he was, Dana decided. For now, anyway, she waivered.

And wait until she told Jen about his reaction to her teasing! She started chuckling all over again until pain spiked in her head and she had to grab for more aspirin. You better feel better by evening, she threatened herself. She really wanted to do some serious experimenting on that man.

Managing to struggle into her clothes, she slipped her feet into her loafers. Down in the lobby, she stopped at the front desk before going into the coffee shop. Smiling sweetly at the clerk, she asked, "Tell me, what the altitude here is?"

"Oh, gosh, I'm not sure. Bud, do you know?"

"Oh, 'bout forty-six to forty-eight hundred feet, I think. Probably not much more than that."

"Thanks." Dana turned back around, got back on the elevator and went back up to her room. She added a few items from the bathroom and dresser to her bag then headed out, stooping to grab her boots and red-gartered wool socks.

Mentally she scratched the hotel off her altitude experiment list.


GARRETT WAITED IN the coffee shop, sitting over his untouched cup of coffee. Chin resting in his fist, the fingers of his other hand lightly drumming the tabletop, he beat himself up with second guesses and regrets.

Why had he run like that? Okay, she was just teasing him, but why hadn't he at least tried to turn it to his advantage? He probably could have changed her mind, she was, after all, in a weakened condition. Kissing her into oblivion, telling her it was a local cure for headaches? He could have at least tried. Had she wanted him to try?

Hell, all he'd been thinking about was having sex with her for how long now? He wanted her so much it was addling his brain. But he kept chasing after her by backing up! How was that going to work?

He'd never felt so mixed up and awkward with a woman in his life! He'd been feeling as queasy as she must, this morning, but for a different reason. He'd been happy she'd fit in so easily with his crowd last night. They shouldn't have taken up all her time, true; he was still angry with his pals about that. But on the way in this morning, he'd had a very unsettling thought gnawing at his stomach, one he just couldn't shake.

What if Dana had been getting bored to tears with just his company? What if she hadn't just fit in but been desperate for other people, anyone else, to talk to for a while? All night, actually.

Garrett lived a pretty quiet life; he was content with it. In just the small amount of time he'd been around a conscious Dana, she'd had an energy, curiosity, a vibrancy that amazed him—and she was still recuperating. Did he seem like an old slow fuddy-duddy to her? It was worrying him today—or scaring him.

197

What happened when he ran out of wonders to show her? What if he'd jumped her bones just now? Would she laugh, enjoy, then rack him up as just another fun fling on her vacation, then go home and forget him. He wanted her to love him, not discard him as a plaything. And he sure as hell didn't want to bore her, but he couldn't be anyone other than himself. Was he enough for this vibrant, fascinating woman?

And why was he beating himself up like this, he asked himself disgusted. She hadn't said or done anything really to show she was unhappy, just the reverse. But a guy could worry—or go loco, like he was.

He was glad he had the week off work. Dana, in person, was proving so much greater a distraction than the long-distance one. Whew, was she ever! If he'd even tried filling in a little time on the job these last few days, he'd probably have pounded a nail into his own head by now! Not a wise plan to be daydreaming with a nail gun in your hand, thinking of a particular redhead's mischievous smile and those need-to-be kissed lips—and those legs—

He groaned and lowered the coffee cup he'd just lifted to take a quick swig from a glass of ice water instead. Then another. Work. How were things going? Had he remembered to check his cell for any messages from his foreman this morning? Yesterday? Since Dana had arrived? Hell! Panicking, he fished his phone out of the pocket of his jeans and checked; blowing out a relieved breath, he saw there were no urgent messages his help had been needed

He silenced the phone, setting the ring tone to vibrate and slipped it back into the pocket of his jeans. With a wry grin he noted that he'd already been getting plenty of vibrations from that area since Dana had arrived. And it hadn't had anything to do with the cell phone in his front pocket, either!

Leaning back in his chair, he shoved his hand roughly through his thick but recently trimmed hair. He hoped his no-longer-covered ears weren't flushed red betraying all his wayward thoughts. Why did this one woman take away all his confidence and experience around women and make him feel like an awkward, anxious, lusty youth with his first girl?

"More coffee, Garrett?"

Covering his cup with his hand, he smiled politely answering, "None for me, Bess, thanks."

Just then, the object of Garrett's insanity sauntered into the coffee shop and turned a smile on him that made him feel like he had created the earth.

Maybe he didn't bore her. Where'd he get a dumb idea like that anyway? He rose, returning her smile and pulling out a chair for her.


BESS HAD SEEN the look that had broken over Garrett's face just before he had risen with a dazzling grin. She had turned and noted where it was aimed, spotting the tall redhead that, even in casual clothes and with one arm in a sling, moved across the restaurant with the beauty and athletic grace of a model or dancer.

Bess and Garrett had dated casually and playfully in high school and been pals ever since, like he had with other local girls. It was a small town and many women had angled for a dinner or movie date with the handsome and popular blond, one of the town's most eligible bachelors. But Bess had never seen that look on Garrett's face, or that smile on his lips and in his eyes. The man was a goner!

And judging by the warm joy in the smile the redhead returned, he was not only appreciated, but taken. Darn! Looked like she better spread the word around town that all the ladies might as well quit dreaming about this bachelor, Bess sighed to herself. He was taken, for good, it appeared.

And good for him, Bess thought with genuine warmth. Garrett was a very nice guy; he deserved the kind of smiles that woman blessed him with. She headed back to the kitchen for a new pitcher of coffee and to share the latest local news.


AS THEY LEFT the hotel Dana asked if they could run an errand before heading down to Yellowstone for the day. Garrett drove her to a local flower shop, not asking any questions until she came out with her arm full of long stemmed roses.

"For me? Gosh Dana, I didn't know you cared," he teased.

"You may have one if you will put it in the hatband of your cowboy hat, but I have plans for the rest. I've been meaning to do this and, after last night. I think I better pay my dues and do something good for my soul."

"Excuse me, miss," she said moments later, leaning over the high counter in the hospital reception area. "I have a problem. I brought flowers to thank all the nurses and doctors that helped and cared for me here, but, it's a little embarrassing, I have no idea who they are. I was in a coma when I was here. My name is—"

Before she could say another word, the woman's head suddenly jerked up from her computer monitor for the first time. She gave a little shriek, ran out from behind her desk, clasping her hands in front of her just before almost throwing her arms around Dana's injured shoulder.

"Oh, look at you! Just look! You look wonderful, Dana. I can't believe it! Hey, Julie, look! It's our buffalo attack girl! Doesn't she look just splendid! Hurry, go get the gang out of intensive care so they can see how fabulous she looks. Oh my, this is so exciting. I'm so happy for you! Is your friend with you? I thought that poor girl was going to cry herself to death, poor little thing. She must be so happy now. And look, here's Garrett, our local hero. Isn't he something? If it hadn't been for him there's nothing anyone could have done."

Dana grinned and nodded her agreement while Garrett's ears reddened, as he politely thanked the woman for the compliment. Smiling at the nurse, but looking up at Garrett with a teasing smile as she spoke, Dana said, "Well, I keep *trying* to show him my gratitude, but he's a little shy."

Garrett ears turned even redder.

By then more doctors and nurses were rushing into the corridor to see how 'their girl was doing', and letting out similar shrieks and joyous comments. Dana handed out tearful thanks with long stem roses to everyone, unable to believe how happy they were for someone they'd never really met.

Hearing all the commotion, Garrett's friend Bob, the hospital administrator, stepped out of his office. His face lit up with an immediate mile-wide smile. Garrett introduced him. Dana thanked him profusely for taking such good care of her and her friend, Jen, handing him a rose for his lapel.

"Is Jenny here with you?" Bob asked.

"No, I came to see Garrett," she stated, blushed, then quickly added, "And, of course, I wanted to get back to Yellowstone. Jen isn't ready for that experience yet, but Garrett is such a wonderful guide."


GARRETT BLINKED HARD, and bit back his grin at Dana's words, surprised to hear he had the top billing. There was nothing cool about the affectionate gaze she had thrown his way when she said that! Bob seemed to notice it also, giving Garrett a wink and a slap on the shoulder before saying his goodbyes and ushering his staff and himself back to work. Garrett was sure he walked out of the hospital at least two feet taller than he was when he walked in.

When he lifted her up into his truck she gave him a faint smile, saying, "You know, Garrett, even if you weren't my hero, I think you would be."

"Thanks," was the only thing he could think to say to that, as he grew another foot before climbing into his truck.

They'd barely gotten out of town when Dana gasped, and asked Garrett to pull over suddenly, pointing to the graveled fishing access at the upper end of Paradise Valley.

"Are you sick?" He pulled off the highway onto the gravel turn out.

"No. I just have to get a picture of this. I brought my camera today."

The two mountain ranges lining the east and west sides of the valley, stepped down in grassy benches and moraines to cradle the Yellowstone River cutting down the center of all the ancient glacial carvings.

Here at the opening to the valley—where the ranges almost joined—the river was tangled and spread out in heavy braids. Rocky islands divided the strands with brilliantly colored aspen and cottonwood, yellow against bright red willow brush, between the silver glittering strands of sun-rippled waters. Natural, unstructured, and defying its channel, the river sprawled fresh and free across and around heavy river rock and gravels.

Dana took several pictures. But, while still turned away from Garrett, shook her head and muttered.

"I cannot even imagine living here."

Just what Garrett had been afraid of! He could feel himself deflate back to the worried, insecure man that had questioned himself in the coffee house. The shorter one. He almost missed her next words.

"It's like being in heaven and not even having to die first." Tipping her head, she laughed, spinning in a circle, her good arm spread to encompass the scene.

Right. Just how Garrett had always felt about this place.

Seeming to regret her impulsive spin when her body stopped, and her head didn't, Dana stumbled over the river rock to lean against Garrett, wrapping her arm around his waist to steady herself.

"I am having so much fun here—"

Okay. Definitely not bored.

"—with you." She sighed and laid her head against his chest. "Thanks." She stretched on her toes and gave him a kiss on his cheek and headed to the truck.

Worrying was such a complete waste of time, Garrett thought, as he followed to help her in. He'd always believed that.

Settling behind the wheel, after cinching her in her seat belt, he leaned over and gave her a nice, sudden, solid, breath-stealing kiss on the lips. It was over before she caught up; her lips still hanging open helplessly when he pulled back on Highway 89, heading south, whistling through his teeth as he drove.

Passing the Saloon on their way south, Garrett chuckled when he saw Dana shudder as they drove by.

"Tell me, babe, didn't you enjoy your dinner there?"

"It was great. As you promised. But please don't mention food right now." She paused then turned to him, "I hope you don't think I always drink like that. That was about a year's worth for me." She rubbed her temple still in pain. "Maybe two years," she corrected.

"That's what I figured," he gave her a sympathetic smile," so I have an easy morning planned for you. We can see the sites from the car, then save our walking for this afternoon. How's that sound?"

# Chapter 17

"MERCIFUL. THANKS. A driving tour sounds perfect right now."

"Okay, I'll start your tour here. The sights don't all start down in the Park; there's a lot of cool stuff along the way.

"That dazzling pyramid on our left is Emigrant Peak of mining fame, where major volcanic action in the Absaroka chain took place about fifty million years ago. The whole valley has been closed in most of the time since then, until the river cut its way through. There are petrified logs, killed in those eruptions, all the way south from here to Yellowstone.

"On our right, see those chalky looking cliffs that have that dark rock rim mesa top? That basalt cap is from flows they figure date to around eight million years ago, probably all the way from an earlier Yellowstone area volcano. And, coming up soon, also on your right side, is a place called Point of Rocks. There they are, leftover parts from an ancient volcanic vent still sticking up like chimneys after softer rocks around eroded. They figure that's the same age as the Absaroka volcanoes."

"I'm impressed, did you study up for this?" Dana seemed fascinated by his knowledge of the scenery.

"Certainly! I even have cheat cards in my pocket. The minute I knew you were coming I went to the library and gave myself a refresher course," he grinned at her. "But, I'm actually pretty interested in the geology and history of the area myself. I'd just forgotten a lot of the specifics that I studied long ago."

Dana slowly swiveled her head from side to side.

Mountain ranges paralleled their course on either side— the Absaroka on the left, the Gallatin on the right. The Yellowstone River traveling beside the road, and occasionally underneath, meandered slightly shifting sides with Highway 89.

"Now here's an interesting spot and story. I mentioned the once closed valley, you'll note that this end is even narrower than the one you photographed. This is Yankee Jim Canyon. See that trail across the river barely wedged between the river and the cliff? That used to be the only way through the canyon. A smart guy named Yankee Jim figured how to get steady income during the mining rush days. He built himself a cabin and a corral on the trail at this narrow spot, and set up a toll for every one that wanted to pass, charging for every wagon, man and mule."

Near Corwin Springs, Garrett pulled down into a scenic viewpoint, promising Dana she'd love this view. Pointing across the river, he showed her the vertical red stripe on Cinnabar Mountain, called The Devil's Slide. The layers of strata had been tipped on end with the red streaks indicating two hundred million year old sedimentary rock layers. Thin, dark, hard, spiny rock ridges looked like the spiked back of a dragon, running vertically up the hill between the ancient red beds. An info kiosk told the history of the location and the miles of glaciers that once buried the spot where they now stood. More recently, the earliest railroad spur had been located near here. Park visitors got off at the former Cinnabar station, then took stagecoaches into the park.

A few miles further south they passed through Gardiner, under the arch, and entered the Park again, following the road east from Mammoth this time.

Garrett pointed out the blocked gravel road where the Blacktail Deer Plateau drive started. He told her he wanted to take her there sometime on horseback, show her where he had taken all the pictures he'd sent. The ones where the autumn leaves were almost as lovely and vibrant as the gold and crimson tints in Dana's hair, as Garrett casually described it, leaving Dana speechless again.

After they passed the caged Petrified tree, where the Blacktail drive exited, they turned south at Roosevelt Junction, saving the Lamar Valley for a later trip, sliding under hanging cliffs and columns of octagonal basalts before climbing up toward Mt. Washburn.

He talked about the moose he had spotted once in one of the deep, lush, tree and meadow studded valleys as they wound their way up and around a lazy series of switchbacks. Then as the pitch of the mountain grew steeper and rough rocks walls crowded them on one side, he told her to keep her eyes peeled for mountain goats.

"Okay, as long as you promise to keep *your* eyes peeled on this road. I just peeked out the window on my side and just about had a heart attack looking down on empty space for thousands of feet to treetops below. And these steep curves don't have guardrails. You are lucky I'm not afraid of heights."

"The girl that was a champion at flying through the air? Never." Garrett teased before wishing he had kept his mouth shut and not reminded her. He couldn't look away from the road to gauge her reaction, but he relaxed when he heard her laughing comment.

"Yes, but that was before I realized that I was mortal."

A gate barred the gravel road to the lookout atop Mount Washburn just before they went over the top at Dunraven Pass and, just as in a roller coaster ride, suddenly tipped straight down to a new open vista.


LIKE MOST TOURISTS, the first thing Dana noticed was a parking turn-out to the left, with its lovely ugly, green temporary public restroom perched at the upper end of the long parking area. It was a welcome sight after a long, nerve stretching ride over the mountaintop where there wasn't anywhere to pull aside, take a breath, or get relief.

"Whew! Pull over, cowboy. I'll be right back," she hurried off to get in line for the facilities, checking her pockets for tissues and hand-sanitizer in case they were out.

Garrett collected her when she came out and motioned her down the steep parking lot to where she could see his truck parked fronting a low stone wall. "I found us a more scenic spot down here. So tell me, Dana," he asked as they walked, "have you noticed something special about this place?"

"Well, I heard, while I was waiting in line, that it's a good place to spot grizzlies. They like the white pine nuts that can be found on this side." Her eyes widened, "Did you see one, Garrett?" She spun to look across the steeply slanting road to the grassy mountainside rising straight up behind them. Searching the clumps of pines, fallen logs, and blackened stumps, mixed with green and brushy patches for anything dark that moved.

"Not yet, babe," he laughed at her eagerness, "but maybe we will before we leave. But that wasn't what I meant. Guess again."

Turning back as they reached the car, she suddenly gasped, spotting the view over the low stone wall from the summit overlook. The ground dropped precipitously behind the wall, the Yellowstone caldera basin spread out as a vast space beneath them, with the sharp teeth of the Red mountains and Tetons rising clear and crisp on the far southern horizon. It was a breath stealing view.

"Oh, this *is* special!" she breathed. Slipping her camera out from the brilliant place she'd found to carry it, tucked inside her sling, she coaxed him into posing at the edge of the wall where she could capture the view behind him. He waited, patient and relaxed, as she decided just the perfect angle, while the wind ruffled and played with his thick golden hair. When Dana said 'cheese' he gave her a smile that was almost more breathtaking than the view, his laughing eyes bluer than the sky. She pretended to take several more shots of he Tetons in the background, she was enjoying *all* the scenery so much.


WHEN SHE FINISHED, he hailed a stranger to take a picture of the two of them together. Pulling Dana in front of him, he wrapped his arm around her waist. While Dana smiled straight into the camera, the photographer caught Garrett gazing down at Dana with a look that made him think they must be newlyweds on a honeymoon.

Garrett thanked the man then made her pose until he'd shot her from several different angles, most of them close ups. The hell with the mountains, Garrett privately thought, getting great shots of Dana's lovely face.

"Well, have you figured it out yet?" He asked when he was finished, handing her a cold soda from a small cooler. "Figured what's so special?" he asked, leaning against the car with a cat-eating-cream smile.

"You mean it *wasn't* this view?"

"Oh, that's special, all right, but this is something special for a geo-goofy girl like you. I'm shocked you haven't figured it out!" He mocked her, laughing, glad he had studied up to impress her today.

She pretended to scowl at him, demanding, "Give me a hint."

"Okay. Did you notice how long it took us to climb Mount Washburn?"

"Did I ever!"

"Well, there's the summit and pass right there, and we will be back down there in the basin in just a few minutes."

"Okay." She squinted at the pass and steep road, "so we come down the side of the mountain—" She tried to figure what his point was.

"Close!" His laugh was delighted; he knew he had her baffled.

"I give! Take pity on a girl with a hangover and just tell me, Mr. Smarty Pants." Then she raked her eyes down his jeans with a little impish grin, muttering something to herself.

"Inside."

"Huh?" Guilty green eyes snapped back to his. "Ah ... Inside what, exactly?"

"*Inside* the mountain, not *on the side of* the mountain," he told her patiently.

"We are actually coming down *inside* where the rest of Mount Washburn used to be. Your little supervolcano chopped it in half, Dana. Cut it right off and dropped it all the way down there." He was so pleased with the look on her face, he almost took a bow. He was making big points today impressing his lady. And, yeah, he'd caught her checking him out, but a guy wanted to be loved for more than his body. *Though—*


IF ANY OF EARTH'S FEATURES should be considered to have a little permanence, demand a little respect, a massive mountain should top that list.

Especially a towering ten-thousand foot bulky cone-shaped mass that had been built by the mysterious energy of a stratovolcano. Using fiery juices bursting from the soul of mother earth, it builds its profile over time—moments, days, decades, and centuries. It commands awe for its looming shape and size, respect for its unique origins, and—since the historic 1980 eruption of Mt. St. Helens—fear.

Old Man Mount Washburn was a massive and dignified stratovolcano, surrounded for miles around by layered-lava flanks like a chieftain in a spreading ceremonial robe. Dignified, respected since his rise to immense power fifty *million* years before with the Absaroka volcanic range, part of a fiery tribe. A monumental elder that should have lived a long life of peace and respect after the fires and battles of his youth had been extinguished. Extinct, aging, weathered, stooping a little lower with great age, but still able to rest on the laurels of wilder days, an elder of a distinguished class to be respected, if not worshiped.

Then that damned upstart Hot Spot slid into town—fresh from the Snake River Plain—young, undisciplined and reckless, building a Supervolcano so arrogant that it kept blowing the roof down over its own fool head! The damage from the eruptions was incredible, disrespectful, destroying what had taken tens of millions of years to build. The Great Rocky Mountains, forming the spine of the continental divide, had a huge gap blown right out of its back—pulverized to ash—and Old Man Washburn was chopped in half! Then that insolent upstart caved into its own crater and just lay down below hissing steam and spitting geysers up into the eyes of the once great ancients.

That was the chaos that was Yellowstone Park. And that didn't even count the Ice Age alpine glaciers carving everything up! It was too much, and then more and more piled on top, creating, destroying, over the top chaos as if it knew it was meant to be a famous place someday—earth's own extravagant showplace.


WHEN THEY CAME DOWN the remains of the mountain and neared the Canyon Village junction, Dana refused to accept Garrett's suggestion they turn west to Norris rather than continuing south. She didn't seem to buy his excuse of 'too much road construction'.

"I don't want to retrace yesterday, let's go this way. I haven't seen much down here."

Because you nearly died down here, darling!

"You're sure?" Garrett asked, warily.

"Yes." She stated simply, but firmly, as if there was no big deal.

Garrett respected Dana's request, though he was not comfortable about it. Just ahead they would have to drive past Dana's near-deadly spot. Garrett hoped to distract her—or maybe just himself.

"I have a story that might interest you. Have you ever heard about Waterfall Chasers?"

"No. Is that some kind of very extreme rafting trip? If so, Garrett, I don't think I'm quite up for that today." Her amused chuckle told him she was relaxed, not tensing up like he was.

"No, nothing quite that thrilling, though pretty dramatic in its own way. The Waterfall Chasers are these two guys that, come to think of it, remind me a lot of you. They have that curiosity about learning things that's amazing.

"These two, I think their names are Lee and Mike, were thinking that the Park was so massive—the size of two small states—and only about two percent of it was in public areas. So, hey, they think, there's a lot out there to explore! Given the geography, they figure there just have to be more waterfalls out there than the fifty or so people know about. So they set out to go—" He paused, grinning.

"Waterfall chasing," Dana said the words with a whispered wonder and reverence as if it was a quest for a holy grail. To her and the chasers, it would be.

He knew she'd love the idea. He glanced over and saw her elegant face lit up like she was having a religious experience, her eyes as bright as emeralds glimmering in the sun. He could tell she was just as excited about the concept of having a whole remote wilderness to explore as the romance of seeking out hidden waterfalls, maybe ones never seen by man or woman before.

"Can you just imagine what it would be like to go with them, Garrett?" Her voice was still soft.

"Sure," he laughed, only half teasing. "Mile after mile of trekking up and down mountains without trails. Footsore, blisters. These guys weren't young bucks, either. Biting bugs of all descriptions. Camping out in all kinds of weather with fun predators following you like mountain lions and bears—"

"Oh stop!" she laughed. After a moment's pause he could see her imagination fire back up as she added, "Still—"

"Yeah, still pretty damn cool to come around a corner and find one." He agreed. "And they did. They found one, then another, they found *hundreds* Dana! Some so amazing they would be worth a national park all by themselves. They found three even higher than Canyon's!"

"Hundreds?" she echoed, trying to absorb it. "I guess it figures, the chaos and ice age mountain glaciers would have chopped it all up."

"Yeah, hundreds. I think they now have mapped out about three hundred waterfalls in the park with a drop of fifteen to over three hundred feet high."

He left her to enjoy and digest that in silence as he made the turn off for Canyon Village where they could view the tallest waterfall in Yellowstone that the public could enjoy. The one that, after a famous painting by Thomas Moran was shown to Congress, had been instrumental in helping create the first national park—first world park.

The Lower Falls, in the Grand Canyon of the Yellowstone River, were three-hundred-eight feet tall and an artist's dream, even now that its record height had been broken, exceeded somewhere out there in the barely explored wilderness. It would only be a short walk from the parking area for Dana to get a look at the famous view at Artist's Point. The chemically altered and colored deposits from an old hot spring in the caldera would probably interest her, even though he knew she had already given her heart to Gibbon Falls.

"You're the best tour guide I've ever had, Garrett," she told him later. "That was fantastic."

He thought of mentioning other fantastic tours he'd love to take her on—very private ones—but managed to restrain his tongue. "My pleasure, ma'am."

# Chapter 18

EVER SINCE DUNRAVEN PASS, the roadside grapevine buzzed with word of a big grizzly sleeping near the road in Hayden Valley. Hoping at the time to avoid passing through that fateful route, Garrett had made light of the information, hoping to discourage Dana's interest in the news. They had passed several small clusters of cars and tourists off the roadside, cameras out, fruitlessly scanning everywhere, trying to figure why everyone else was stopped. As they drove slowly past, through the open window of his truck, the words that floated in were usually, "I *heard* that someone *thought* they saw ..."

Garrett snorted with laughter.

"I can't tell you how many times I've heard that; how many times I've seen tourists stopped taking pictures of blackened stumps or great big rocks in distant fields."

"I noticed all those big glacial erratics that were dumped out in the middle of meadows," Dana, ever the rock specialist, commented.

"Yes, but they take pictures because they think they are sleeping buffalo or bears, and probably proudly show off those vacation photos when they get back home. Of course, that *is* part of the magic of Yellowstone. Occasionally one of those rocks stands up and lumbers off! But most of the time it's just a rock that's drawn a crowd and excited rumors," he smiled, then quickly added, "Sorry, make that just a 'special' rock."

Dana flicked a grin at him, confessing guiltily, "You know, when we were here, Jen and I laid bets on how many cars we could stop if we just pulled over suddenly, got out, and pointed at nothing." She laughed, then sobered, "But we were afraid we'd cause a car accident playing a dumb joke."

"Good thinking," Garrett murmured, thinking Dana's long legs in shorts alone would have been enough to stop cars and cause a few wrecks.

They ended up traveling the road he had hoped to avoid, after stopping in Canyon for a quick view of the falls, and then for snacks. He was surprised when they rounded a curve in the Hayden Valley to find there were still droves of cars piled up beside an area with marshy lakes on either side of the road.

The grizzly must still be here!

Better yet, the grizzly was awake and could be seen moving on the far side of a pond. Garrett pulled over and managed to find a parking spot on a turnout, a safe distance, hundreds of yards, from the bear. But when they got out of the car to look, they lost sight of the animal.

Then the bear sat back up.

DANA'S ATTENTION WAS captured. And chilled.

The bear was in an open valley. There were no trees or cover except marshy grasses and low sagebrush. Yet the bear had crouched for a moment and completely disappeared from sight! If you hadn't just seen him, you never would have known you were sharing the open area with a grizzly bear! It seemed able to literally hide in plain sight. Dana felt a shiver run down her spine as she took in the expansive area that looked like a perfect spot she might pick for a pleasant hike and maybe a picnic beside the pond.

A picnic for the bear!

Which, according to the comments around them, was what it had been.

The bear had been feasting on a bison carcass, then laid down for a nice post-snack nap, while guarding its meal. It had just recently woken and started moving around, playfully rolling in the brush, sitting to lift a massive-clawed paw to scratch at an ear. It seemed completely oblivious to the fact that hundreds of cars and people were gathered on the road—clustered on a low bank just across the tiny pond—with cameras galore, and small children running about laughing and pointing.

Until a new car pulled off the road behind the bank of people, with a loud and yappy dog penned inside.

That suddenly caught the bear's attention!

Much to the crowd's delight, it stood up on its hind legs and looked straight at them, shifting its great wide dish shaped face to sniff the air, as it tried to track down the sudden source of noise and irritation.

Much to the crowd's horror, the bear dropped to all fours and headed purposefully straight at them!

It stalked right through the pond, toward the bank with all the exposed people, heading for the road and that dog. Never slowing, never stopping, even when it took an unexpected swim in deeper water. On it came, not yet rushing, but *very* determined.

People started backing up slowly, then more and more rapidly, trying to get back to their cars without turning their back on the bear. Some die-hard photographers—they hoped—remaining, glad to get such clear photos, seemed not to realize until it was almost too late that the object in their viewfinder was *much* closer than it appeared.

That was not telephoto!

That was real in your face grizzly bear, buddy!

Suddenly the bear lunged onto the road, startling people standing outside their cars. It hesitated a moment, then ran between them, mere feet away. It was a terrifying moment before onlookers realized it had rushed across the road, through the crowd, just wanting to get away from all the noise and pests that had accumulated while it was taking that nice, long nap.

No blood was shed. Only God knew why.

Jumping into the larger lake, it swam across at a speed that was a warning to never, *ever*, try to escape a bear by swimming. Climbing out on the opposite bank, far from roads and the public, it lumbered off. As the bear moved out of sight into the trees, Dana finally let out the breath she had been holding. Then, as the crowds and cars began to disperse, had an amused thought about what she had witnessed.

"What?"

"Oh, just a thought I had watching that grizzly. It reminded me of those old jokes. 'Where does a grizzly bear walk? *Anywhere he wants!*' But, more than that, an awareness that *here* the land belongs to the wildlife, to the grizzly. People are confined to the road and verges, and if they trespass too near, it's pretty clear who the boss is when he starts toward them. Almost like we are *his* zoo. Know what I mean?"

"A zoo is exactly how I would describe tourist season."

"Yes. It's madness, isn't it?" Dana agreed. "But, I meant, it's like we are the ones behind the bars, for his entertainment. When he's bored with us, he just strolls away and gets on with his life. I thought his indifference was just glorious."

"Yeah, well the last thing you want is a grizzly paying too much attention to you, but I know what you mean. It was pretty funny when he started walking through the water toward that bluff. That sure sent a chill through those viewfinders. Did you see how fast everyone cleared out?"

"Not fast enough!" Dana frowned. "This time it turned out okay, but I was afraid for a minute there that we were going to see blood. I think I know what caption I'm going to use for my photo of when he jumped onto the road in the middle of all those people that hadn't gotten in their cars yet."

"What's that?" he asked with a strange expression on his face.

"It's going to say, 'Okay, who's for dessert?'"

Garrett tossed back his head and laughed, delighted, then sobering, looked down at Dana with that same strange expression, shaking his head.

"What are you thinking, Garrett?"

"Just amazed at you, is all. How can you be so happy, relaxed and detached? I'd think you would be recalling your own brush with blood and danger?" He reached out to slide his fingertips gently across her cheek, letting her know of the caring that made him ask.

"I'm over it. Wiser for it. You'll notice I stayed *way* over here on this side of the pond to take my pictures. I'll try to keep my close-ups to telephoto lenses, from now on." She grinned up at him. "But you know Garrett," she sobered, "I didn't have a choice really. I wasn't just being foolish, and I sure wasn't looking for a buffalo photo op."

"I know that babe. I know." He wrapped an arm around her, drawing her gently to his chest.

"I'm so sorry," he murmured, "I was too far away to help." Nuzzling his face into her hair, his voice dropped, became rough and raw when he added, "I still have nightmares."

She snuggled into him, burying her nose in his chest, breathing in the scent and strength of him, feeling the beat of his heart, as she soaked up the sensations of being wrapped in the arms of the man that had turned tragedy into life and joy for her. Handsome, sexy, and with a lot of other attractive qualities, but what really drew her to Garrett was the warmth and steady comfort she felt with him. She felt safe, cherished; she felt she belonged with him. She wanted to laugh with him. She hoped to love with him. Just being in his company gave her intense, quiet pleasure.


HOLDING DANA CLOSE as long as he could, Garrett tried to hold tenderly—not clutch too tightly—though his memory of how she was almost lost to him forever made him want to crush her so closely that nothing could ever reach her through him; nothing would ever harm her again. Not wanting to scare her with the strength of his feelings he managed to release her when he felt her stir, trying to keep his voice light and friendly.

"Looks like we can get the car out now, ready to keep going, babe?"

"Absolutely! What's the next item on this amazing guided tour, Handsome?"

He had opened his mouth to tell her, but couldn't stop a pleased smile. "Think so?"

She lowered her lashes and swept him from head to toe, then breathed low and slow, "Oh, yes!"

Then she spoiled the effect by laughing and dragging him off to the car while he tried to recover from the feeling his whole body had been scorched.

"Was I just eye-raped?" He teased.

"Oh yeah. How was it?" the flirt replied.

"Whew! Good! Great! Better when there's not a crowd around though, I imagine."

"Now why would I just use my eyes, if we were alone?" Dana tossed over her shoulder before climbing in the car and shutting her door.

Garrett stood a moment, absorbing the implications, and seriously considered cutting the tour short and just taking her back to his place. But since he wasn't sure if it was his presence or the park's that was working its magic on her, or if this was just more playful flirting, he thought he better stick with what was working.

But those naughty green eyes sure sent him up in flames!

Climbing back into the driver's seat, he blew out a breath and reached to turn the air conditioning up a notch, hearing a low rumble of laughter from her as he did. He turned and gave her a wink and a grin, fanned his face theatrically, before pulling back onto the road.


GOD HE WAS CUTE! Dana thought. Maybe what she enjoyed most was the way he could be playful and hot at the same time, yet serious and thoughtful to match her moods—but none of it felt false. Yes, he wanted her to like him, but he was a naturally fun and likeable guy, like only a man comfortable in his own skin could be. She was hooked on the whole package, to tell the truth. She just didn't know how to tell him without playing at teasing. She'd spent her whole life needing—and never receiving—true caring and belonging; she didn't know how to express the simple words of love. She hadn't learned it as a child, and never felt it as an adult. Oh sure, she'd had plenty of public adulation—as an athlete—but that had only made her need to build a stronger barrier between her surface and private emotions.

Maybe I can just show him what I'm feeling, she thought. While I learn how to find the words to tell him. She smiled to herself, thinking about how she might go about searing his every nerve ending getting her point across. Getting a little overheated herself, she managed to resist turning the A/C up another notch and giving her very naughty thoughts away.


NEAR FISHING BRIDGE JUNCTION, they turned right to skim along the northern rim of Yellowstone Lake. The largest high-altitude lake on the continent, it was probably also the most seductively dangerous.

The *seduction* lay in its majestic beauty.

A break in the forested shoreline displayed a lush grassy bank fronting what seemed like a small sea, backed by the distant navy silhouette of a chain of mountains, so tall their peaks were coated in what appeared to be a thick white band of clouds, but was actually deep, new snow. The Absaroka Range, which Dana had so admired up north in Paradise Valley, again commanded the eastern skyline here. The combined textures and colors of all the tones of blue lake, sky, and distant peaks was sharply defined by the frame of green forests, then intensified by the white snow and clouds passing over the vast open expanse of water.

The *danger in the seduction* was the geology that simmered under and around; that had created this picture perfect lake.

Garrett mentioned that this north section of the lake was the area that had been hit by the swarm of a thousand small earthquakes just after Christmas in 2008. Over a thousand earthquakes under magnitude four was not unusual for Yellowstone—over a year—but not in just eleven days spanning the end of 2008 to early 2009. And, just a year later, in the last few weeks of January 2010, another swarm of over seventeen-hundred small earthquakes had hit on the other side of the park, centered half-way between West Yellowstone and Old Faithful. Only five to ten miles below the surface, neither episode was thought to be the movement of magma, just swarms caused through normal plate and fault shifting—but it sure got the public's attention.

It was hard not to shudder a little, even far from the quivering zones, Dana thought, if you knew about the configuration of the two older major lava domes.

The Sour Creek Dome lay behind them; they had just passed it on their east as they came out the bottom of Hayden Valley. The Mallard Lake Dome lay over on the western side just northeast of Old Faithful. The locations of these latest swarms seemed to echo those positions on just a slightly turned axis. The two older domes had seemed to breathe in and out over the decades, raising the land a bit, then subsiding. Yellowstone Lake had been tilted a few times from uplift at Sour Creek raising Hayden Valley and tipping the water to the south, drowning the base of trees on its remote southern lake shores. And especially since 2004, the lake seemed to be tilting more and more, dumping water into the southern backcountry.

That morning's local newspaper had a reassuring report about partnerships and protocols formed between the park, university scientists, the U.S. Geologic Survey, and the Yellowstone Volcano Observatory, in a joint monitoring and reporting service to study and keep an eye on the volcano and inform the public if danger appeared imminent. New real-time sensors were being installed in targeted thermal features to aid that effort.

Dana found it all fascinating and the powerful forces that shaped the earth thrilling, if unpredictable. She did, however, hope to experience a few real-time highly explosive events of her own—very privately with Garrett—before getting any other firsthand geologic demonstrations! But she must like to live dangerously.

They were headed down to West Thumb—a recent addition to Yellowstone Lake roughly 170,000 years ago—when it had exploded and created a small collapsed caldera of its own within the greater, much more massive ancient cauldron that rimmed the park. The newer collapsed caldera was tiny for Yellowstone, but still was about the size of the one in Oregon at Crater Lake.

One would think Yellowstone had been created by Hollywood the way everything about it was so extravagantly overdone! It had enough to see for a few hundred parks, and due to the shifting underground plumbing, a tendency to show a different face each time it was visited.

She had just read in a brochure, that Garrett gave her about West Thumb, that in 1991 geysers suddenly started spewing where there had only been springs known before—or since. Abyss

217

Pool had erupted for the first time in 1987 then again started erupting several times a day in the winter of 1991-1992 before returning to dormancy. Black Pool had heated and become blue, then erupted for the first time, also in 1991, then quieted down again but remained a blue pool. Lakeshore Geyser had done the reverse. Erupting up to fifty feet in the 1920s and 1930s, then for the last time in 1970. It now was barely distinguishable from the other cones that lined the lake side. Fishing Cone, where fishermen had once caught and then cooked their fish all in one smooth motion, now lay submerged, drowning in the ever tilting lake. Dana wondered what specific forces had triggered each of those changes.

Ever changing, ever amazing, beautiful, seductive, dangerous lands, she mused as she watched the landscapes along the shores.

And it had been visited since prehistoric times. She recalled there were a number of archaeological sites around the lake that documented the use of the area by hunter-gatherers since at least Late Paleo-Indian times—before about 6,000 BC— about eight thousand years ago! Fishing Bridge had sites from various periods, and the first pottery found in a documented dig in the park was excavated just west of West Thumb. There was yet another camp site along the lake that dated to over 4,500 years ago! Those were just a few of the ancient sites in the area. A recent joint study indicated ancient hunters may have crossed the frozen lake ice to hunt bears sleeping in their dens on tiny islands in the lake. She could hardly wait to learn the rest of the results gleaned from that joint effort.

The park's history, in the first people that had used this area, was as rich as its geologic one, though many knew little of its Native American history except for the chase of the Nez Perce and Chief Joseph through the park. That had happened just yesterday in relation to what had come before, and seemed even sadder to Dana because of it. At least now the native peoples could return to this park as part of the public it was designed to benefit, she thought wryly, and sighed.

"Tired?" Garrett asked.

"No. Just thinking about everything old and new and changed. Heavy stuff. I'm ready to get out and get some exercise to get my blood moving. I think it's safe now." She chuckled thinking of her hangover of that morning and how her blood had already been pounding when Garrett held her so close, after they'd seen the grizzly. She had needed to turn on her science and history mind just to cool herself down.

Now Dana was ready to get frisky—in a number of ways!

# Chapter 19

HANDS LOOSELY LINKED, just a few fingers entwined to recognize the heat that had been building between them all day, they strolled out on the asphalt pathway that led to the West Thumb geyser basin. After all she had learned recently of the significance of the area—as the last major eruption within the ancient Yellowstone caldera—Dana was surprised she was able to keep from breaking into a run to check it all out; but she didn't want to break the link with Garrett. That link was so simple, yet growing so intense, she felt that if she uncurled her fingers from his gentle clasp, it would be like unplugging an outlet and cutting off all the energy that flowed so warmly between them. The day was beautiful, the setting magical, and she wanted to savor it all with the man beside her—slowly and fully.

After all the other thermal features, she had expected this to be more of the same. Exciting for her interests, of course, but almost too much at one time to enjoy and appreciate properly. But Garrett had been enthusiastic about showing her West Thumb so her excitement had more to do with her growing fascination in spending more time with the man, the heat simmering between them, than needing to see more hot springs at the moment. Of course that was before he mentioned that it was a caldera within the caldera collapsed in Yellowstone Lake. And before her eyes scanned the far lakeshore, envisioning ancient encampments.

The scenery was spectacular. The air freshened with a breeze from the lake and dense forests on far shores, despite the underlying scents of sulfur and burp and bubble of hot spring gases. Dana gazed up at a sky so intensely blue it would have seemed hard, if not for the soft white cotton ball clusters of clouds that softened and enhanced it. The color was reflected deeply in the lake, making it only a slightly darker wave washed tint below. It would have been hard to distinguish the horizon between the two if not for the boundary of forest and mountains, a carefully created work of art by Mother Nature.

"Oh - my - God!' Her words were breathed out slowly, in absolute awe.

"Yes, he sure did show off here didn't he?" Garrett grinned.

"Or, she," Dana teased, then laughed, so delighted with the view, she could barely turn away. But when she looked up at Garrett, to smile her joy at him, her breath caught again, her heart stumbling at the handsome profile against the vivid sky. His thick golden hair fluttered in the breeze, bronzed face strong against the sky, the blue of his eyes like shards of it, but warmed by his happiness in her obvious pleasure. Yes, she thought, *all* the scenery was spectacular, all her air held magic.

"Having fun, babe?"

"Oh, yes! Though that hardly seems a big enough word for," she motioned around her, "for all of this!" She squeezed his fingers and leaned in closer to him to let him know he was part of her joy.

"I'm dazzled!" She turned and gazed directly in his eyes. "Thank you," she said softly, rising on her toes to give him a brief, soft kiss that barely brushed his lips before she turned to pull him along the path.

She stopped to lean on a rail on the outer edge of the loop. At first glance, she saw only a bland looking pond of putty. Then she noted its subtle but exquisite details. The bulk of the area was a pure soft tan. That was the color of both the water and the mud clay rims and fissured edges. Though deeply cracked, the clay looked quiet, soft, perfectly still at the moment, maybe eternally still. So still she could barely distinguish where the water met the bank. It had a sudden calming, quieting influence on her. She noticed a delicate individual bouquet of wildflowers growing beside the pond that was of the palest  aqua flowers she had ever seen.

Being a girl of the Pacific Northwest, Dana was used to— and preferred—her nature in the bold primary colors and darker green and blue hued brush of forests and mountains. She had never appreciated the fad with pastel southwest colored decor, but now she thought she might recognize where that appeal came from. Beyond the bank of the tan clay pond several flowering bushes spread low to the ground but were abundantly mounded in pale, flesh pink flowers.

You had to look carefully, quietly, to see the deep beauty of the softly colored, dainty flowers gracing the fat, flat texture of the lumped and cracked tan clay at Seismograph Pool. The serene and subtle picture, after so many hissing, steaming, bubbling and burping pots and pools, had a peaceful, thought provoking effect. She stood a long time and watched and thought, Garret quiet and relaxed a yard down the rail.

It turned her mind to questioning the reasons why he might have left her room that morning, when he hadn't needed to. She leaned on the rail a long silent time, before speaking, without looking in his direction.

"Garrett. Something I was wondering," she said quietly. "This morning we...you, ah..."

He froze, seeming to listen with breath held least he had made some fatal error.

"I mean, well you were such a—"

"Whuss?"

"—gentleman. So it made me wonder if ... well, if you had hoped that Jenny would come with me."

When he was silent too long, Dana picked at a sliver of wood on the railing, and spoke again, still not looking his way. "You two spent so much time together, became so close—" She spoke almost too casually.

"Jenny is a little sweetheart," he broke in. "She's an easy gal to love because she was so loyal to you, and because she reminds me so much of my little sister. She feels like a sister to me now." Turning toward Dana, he waited for her to raise her eyes and look into his before he told her, "My feelings for you Dana are not the least bit brotherly."

The grin he gave her after the sober statement, indicated exactly how wicked his feelings toward Dana were. She was relieved but not completely satisfied. They strolled a little further around the pond to see a different vantage point, before Dana ventured her next comment.

"You know, Garrett, when you first saw me in the hospital, I was pretty passive, helpless."

"Passive," she heard him turn the word over to himself, then choke back a laugh. "Yes, I'd say you were passive to the extreme, in a near-dead context," he agreed.

"Yes, well, my point is, some men are drawn to helpless women, to protect them, and ... well, I'm not really a passive woman. I may seem so at times as I study things, analyze a situation, but when I come to my conclusions, I act. I'm not helpless or passive, Garrett."

222

He raised his eyebrows at that, replying, "You know, I suspected you weren't the helpless type the moment I saw you charge that buffalo, Dana."

"Oh, right. I just wanted to be sure you knew the real—"

"Brave woman grown from a disciplined young, talented athlete, whose picture on the Wheaties box made me change cereal from my favorite Frosted Chocolate Loops as a young guy, just so I could stare at her? And now she's a successful self-made business woman—"

"You did?" Really?" She asked surprised and delighted.

"Yes, ma'am. Thanks to you I grew up to be a strong and healthy man—"

"And handsome!" She inserted, grinning.

"Why thank you, but to be honest, I remember my mom saying I would grow up to be as handsome as my daddy, so I'm not sure if the Wheaties get credit for that."

"Oh, that's sweet. Did your mom love your dad?" she asked wistfully. Garrett seemed surprised and puzzled by the question.

"She still does, and he still thinks she's the 'Best woman in the West'. That's his little joke. He told us as kids she was the best woman God ever made, but he doesn't want her to get uppity so he only gives her title to the west. They and my sister live out in the Southern Oregon and Northern California region."

Dana gave a happy, humming little sigh, unable to even imagine having a family like that.

"My dad raised me to be a gentleman, Dana," he seemed to get the drift of her questions. "And my mom raised me to not look for my strength by finding a passive woman, but a lively, independent, challenging one like her."

Dana looked at him silently, her eyes a soft and thoughtful green as she probed his for the truth they gave her, before nodding her understanding of all he was telling her.

"You'll love my family." He turned and led off briskly along the loop, leaving her with the words, "They said to tell you they are so glad and thankful you are well."

He told them about her?

Dana was shocked, then realized they must have known about his heroic rescue.

But they must also know she was here now!

What did they think of her? Did they resent her for endangering their son? Did they ask him questions about her? How much did they know about Garrett's gifts and invitation to her to come out? How did a family like his work? How much did they share? Did they worry about a woman taking advantage of their son? Well, not taking advantage *that* way, but worried he just felt too responsible for her? Come to think of it, maybe they *were* worried about her taking the other kind of advantage of him also— like she'd tried that morning. Oh dear, surely he didn't talk to them about things like that!

"Hey, watch that arm, babe," He caught her when she ran into his back. "What are you so deep in thought about?" He asked with a smile that said he already suspected he knew.

"Oh, nothing," She shrugged and turned to look ahead, then cried out. "Oh, oh! Look at those colors! It's like a modern art painting, all streams of brilliant colors flowing down a canvas of landscape, merging into that dark, navy blue ruffled lake. It's so stunning! Quick, Garrett, take a picture. Take a bunch of pictures!"

If the Artist Paint Pots and the tan pond on the far side of the West Thumb loop looked like artists' palettes, prepared to paint in pastels, with bright blues changed to tints of milky aqua, oranges blended into pastel clay, then this spot was where all the cans of unused boldly colored paint had been dumped out on the ground in their original intensity. They spilled across the upper beach to run down in rivulets and streams of cobalt, deep orange, bright yellows and greens to fall into the vast lake and wash away in its watery drain. West Thumb Basin was rich in a brilliant spectrum of color and filled with all of nature's different tones, moods, and textures, all merging with the midnight blue lake, in a frame of snow streaked mountains ranges. A recent eruption, less faded.

"That reminds me," Garrett had been taking in the mountains ranged beyond the lake, also. He took a dog-eared index card from his shirt pocket and studied it a moment before announcing, "There are twenty-three peaks in the park with an elevation over 10,000 feet and here, at West Thumb, the elevation is seven thousand, seven hundred and thirty-three feet." He looked up at her with a proud, if slight smile.

"I just noticed you have been interested in altitude," he added, "so I looked a few things up for you."

Dana blinked, bit her lip, stared at him a moment, glanced at all the people around them with a funny smile, and thanked him, trying not to giggle.

"That was very thoughtful of you Garrett." Green eyes sparkled at him. "Very thoughtful."

He was the best. Without a doubt.

And he'd done all that research not knowing the use she planned to make of *him* with the information!

Another wonder, she thought, as she turned to follow him toward the lake, watching his long legs strolling in front of her in comfortable old jeans that road those lean hips and cupped the muscles of that perfect male butt. The man sure could wear a pair of jeans!

Yes, he was a wonder—an adorable, thoughtful one—with a body that could give her the shivers at any altitude, and personality plus. Dana was so focused on her thoughts she nearly ran into that choice rear end again, when he stopped to point out one of the other interesting natural sights. Oh yeah, hot springs! She'd nearly forgotten all about the ones that were steaming and welling up—outside her own body.

GARRETT WAS PLEASED when Dana snuggled close to his side at the railing, surprised when she edged in front of him for a better view. But he almost bit his tongue when she gave a little wiggle back against his body in the tight space, making sure he knew she hadn't just wedged herself in front of him for the view of the pool.

With her soft curves planted against the front of him, he gritted his teeth hoping he would behave, desperately trying to remember what they had been talking about. It didn't seem that important at the moment. Especially not when Dana took his arm from the railing and curled it around her waist. He just stood there, silently holding her, staring down at the pool, breathing in the scent of her, feeling warmth and peace stealing through him, wishing he would never have to move. They belonged like this. Together. Joined. He had felt it from the beginning. And he had never felt like this with any woman before.

She squeezed his arm, tipping her head back to give him a soft, quick kiss under his jaw, then smiling up at him, hypnotizing him with some unspoken message in those glorious green eyes. She pulled him along to the next feature, keeping his hand in hers. She must feel it too, he thought. He hoped. He could dream she felt the same, anyway. All these sudden, little kisses—the lady sure knew how to express her appreciation!

That first small, soft 'thank you' kiss Dana had given him had shot through him like a thunderbolt, so unexpected, so sweet, so charged with the message in her eyes that locked onto his heart. It had taken him a breath or two to recall the crowds around him and calm himself. Then when she had implied it was Jenny he was interested in, he was stunned, wondering what had just happened. Still floating on her last kiss he felt like he'd just stepped down in a newly made crater, almost too jarred to respond. And that bit about wanting a passive, helpless woman? He had almost snorted. He had managed to bite his tongue when he mentioned his family. He wanted to nudge her, not terrify her, so he held back from letting on that he'd told his family that he *had* found that independent, challenging woman meant for him, and that he just had to catch her now, and pin her down. They were impatiently awaiting updates. He had to remember not to push her with the seriousness of his intent too soon, not wanting to scare her away.

He felt so off balance. Dana seemed to change from distant and thoughtful, even slightly defensive, to sudden eruptions of heat and joy. Serious one moment, flirtatious and naughty the next. He grinned. Now he thought about it, she was about as predictable as the geysers in this basin, a force of nature, and just as seductively dangerous. He wasn't sure if he needed a rule book, or a geologic map, to decipher her moods and keep those sweet kisses coming his way.

"I had planned to take you to the historic Old Faithful Inn for dinner tonight," for a very romantic dinner alone, Garrett silently added to himself, "but after stopping to watch the grizzly, it's getting a little late. We won't be able to hike the Upper Geyser Basin first, as I had hoped, so maybe we should save that for tomorrow." It had been worth the delay for Dana to get to see the grizzly. He rarely saw bears, even with all his trips to the park, and seeing a grizzly was even rarer.

DANA HAD PLANS of her own and had to think of something quickly. Luckily she had paid close attention to Jen who knew how to go about these things. She let a slight pout into her voice to match the one she hoped was on her unaccustomed lips.

"But I've never even seen Old Faithful Geyser yet. The most famous geyser in the world! I've seen pictures, but it's not really the same. Can't we loop back that way and have dinner and see the geyser, then come back again to hike another day?" She felt guilty like she was playing a trick on Garrett, but, really, it was for his own good. The man needed a little push—even a shove.

He didn't seem to notice the pout in her voice, his gaze was focused on her lips. He instantly agreed, turning west to head over the continental divide for Old Faithful.

"Anything you want, babe."

She was glad to hear it; she wanted a lot, actually.

226

# Chapter 20

"WHAT KIND of tourist would I be? Having been to Yellowstone twice now and not even having seen Old Faithful spout off yet?" Dana was thanking Garrett once again for bringing her here, as if she felt guilty about pushing to come. He was the one that should feel ashamed for his plan to hide her far from his local friends, he thought, as he pulled into the parking lot. But, bottom line? He didn't feel a drop of guilt. She was his.

The steeply pitched central roof of the century old historic inn was to their left as he guided her around the outer wings to the front where the 'world famous', as Dana reminded numerous times as they drove over Craig Pass, Old Faithful geyser sat in its own circular concrete outdoor viewing apron.

The concrete was currently covered with expectant tourists and a tall, dark, and handsome Park Ranger. Damn! Garrett managed to keep the curse to himself.

He just could not believe his luck! Who should he spy, after bringing Dana all the way down here to get her alone, but the back of the Ranger he least wanted to bump into. The last thing he needed right now was for Dana to meet the ranger that, like his nickname, all the women raved about and fell for. Or, for that matter, for his buddy to get an eyeful of *his* beautiful Dana. Absolutely no way was that happening! Especially not tonight, not when he had gone to such lengths to have a private, romantic dinner with a very special lady.

"Looks like nothing's happening right now," he quickly steered Dana into the nearby gift shop. "Let's pop in here first and find out what time the next eruption is scheduled."

UNAWARE SHE WAS being deliberately whisked from sight, Dana was glad to get a chance to browse a little while they waited. She found a few new postcards to mail to Jen, a long knit sleep tee with a grizzly bear imprint, then passed her eye over the books and DVDs on the park. He left her to shop and went to peek outside.

"We just missed it, I guess," Garrett appeared at her side, "the next one won't be for about another hour."

"Okay. Hey, look what I found. Just the gift for Gretchen. It's a DVD called The Complete Yellowstone. It's all about the park and looks like it has a lot of wildlife babies in it, and a special extra video on bears that won some award. Little Gretchen's vacation was cut short also, so this way she can see things she missed. But best of all, it has German subtitles, so her family and friends can enjoy it with her."

"That's a perfect gift for her, Dana. Let me get it for you," Garrett left her to browse while he went over to the cash register, glancing out the front windows trying to keep an eye out for Ranger Ravenwolf's location.

Still out there, damn!

"Hey, I've got a great idea," he suggested when he returned to Dana's side, standing with his back to the windows, blocking her from view. "Why don't we go up to the upper floor of the Old Faithful lodge? They have a veranda up there set up with benches to view the eruptions. We can take some Irish coffees out and get a front row seat and get the real historic flavor and view from there."

And my pal won't be doing crowd control anywhere near, thank you God.

"Sure. Sounds fun," she agreed easily.

Relieved, he quickly shepherded her under the portico through the red doors of the Old Faithful Inn.

DANA'S FIRST IMPRESSION of the inn was not what she had expected. It seemed very dark to her, including the ceiling that crowded down low over their heads. She stopped a moment, on the entry area rug, to let her eyes adjust from the brightness outside so she could begin to take in some of its details. All she could see was a big post. No, a tree trunk right in front of her, with a few candle-like lights around it. Everything else was a dark stain.

"Step forward just a few more feet," Garrett urged.

228

THOUGH CREATED FOR the public, the truth of the matter, in the early years of the Park's existence, was that only the wealthy could afford to travel to such a remote location by train and stagecoach to enjoy its wonders. Despite being in the middle of nowhere, a luxury hotel was called for to replace the growing number of tent camps and chuck-wagon style meals. And in 1900, luxury meant elegant, traditional clapboard or stone mansions—until the Old Faithful Inn was designed.

An early example of the rustic architecture and the Arts and Crafts Movement to follow, the architect wanted to create something to blend into, not ignore, its natural surroundings, with the use of simple, yet carefully handcrafted details and furnishings made of natural local materials. The luxury would come in the scale and magnificence of their usage and—at the turn of the prior century—in the hot and cold running water, electricity, steam heat and telephones provided for the guests.

It was this scale and magnificence that Dana stepped forward to appreciate, stunning even a century later. She realized she had been standing beneath one of the tiers of suspended balconies that encircled the central atrium, supported by tree trunk posts complete with curved branching arms that seemed to support each level of the open tiers. The upper tiers were railed by peeled logs and detailed, not in wrought iron, but the amazing bends and twists of smaller natural tree limbs.

Garrett had come to the Inn many times just to study the rustic architecture. For one of his client's he had done his best to recreate the peeled and twisted lodge-pole pine staircase, though it was truly an unmatchable original.

He watched Dana's eyes travel upward, her mouth slightly open, her eyes filled with appreciation as she looked up over seventy feet to where the light filtered into the darkness, intended to replicate light filtering through a natural forest canopy, then drop down to the rough chunks of local lava that shingled a massive fireplace that pyramided forty feet down to multiple great hearths at the central seating area. The simple wooden chairs were dwarfed by the five hundred tons of local lava they faced, like an indoor mountain created for their view.

"Okay," Dana drew the word out, sounding a little dazed. "It still seems a little dark from all the dark stain everywhere, but— whew! This is flat out amazing to think someone created this over a hundred years ago. That is all real wood and real rock ... and, just really cool."

229

"Wait 'til you see this staircase," Garrett guided her to an upper level, describing how he had tried to create something like it for one of his clients.

Stopping for steaming Irish coffees and biscotti at a coffee bar upstairs, they turned to face a wall of multi-paned windows and French doors that led out to the veranda, half of it covered under the steep roof, the veranda formed the broad deep cover for the porte-cochere entry below.

DANA WALKED OUT TO the open area, while Garrett pointed out the view to the Geyser Basins he wanted them to hike. Turning to look behind, and up, Dana saw the signature roof that graced all the photos and postcards she had seen of the Inn. She had to smile at the funny, asymmetrical arrangement of the rows and pairs of dormered windows, each with their pointed tent-like roofs. To her they looked like a bunch of eyes peeking out of the roof with eyebrows arched in surprise and delight at the scene, mirroring those of the guests below. And at the very top perched a rectangular box on the point of the roof where flags proudly waved that had once been a widow's walk used for viewing.

Turning back under the covered portion of the veranda, Garrett guided her to the left where a few rows of peeled log and wood-slatted settees formed a viewing area to watch the Old Faithful geyser eruptions. They took a cozy bench and shared in conversation with other guests, assisting to take pictures of other smiling couples memorializing their trips, before settling to enjoy being close and together, talking privately while they waited. He slipped an arm around the back of their seat, letting his hand curl on Dana's shoulder, inquiring if she was warm enough and comfortable.

Dana was plenty warm, and getting warmer, but she silently snuggled closer to his side, leaning her head against his broad shoulder. It felt like it was destined to rest there. Relaxed, happy, taking too deep a sip of her foamy Irish coffee, Dana accidentally got a glob of whipped cream atop her nose. Green eyes laughing up at his, she asked, "Do I look like a clown?"

He grinned down at the woman tucked to his side, then suddenly his eyes sobered, darkened, deepened. Leaning down, he slowly sucked the cream from the bridge of her nose, then focusing on the creamy lips below, slowly took possession. First with a gentle brush of his lips, then with a long, sweet, slow, softly drawing tender kiss, he spun her into sheer bliss, lost to the world around them.

230

Dana nearly missed the eruption—of the geyser—barely returning to earth in time, all the nerves in her body having sparked, hissed, boiled and gone up in a steamy burst of their own.

FOR GARRETT, no force of nature could match that of a kiss from this red-haired goddess. He tightened his arm around her, rested his lips in the scented hair on top of her head while his own head cleared enough so he could lead her down to dinner.

SHE PUT DOWN her menu and glanced around at the room. Garrett had suggested they might step over to the Snow Lodge, for a more elegant dining experience in its Obsidian Room, but Dana had preferred the historic Inn. The large fireplace anchored one side of the long log-cabin style room, with simple wooden tables and chairs, the backs and seats cross woven in wicker, that were lined up in rows on the wooden plank floor. So few people were about this late in the season that they still had a private corner, near a line of etched-glass wildlife panels, and the romantic mood they had sparked on the veranda lingered.

Taking a sip of her wine, Dana watched Garrett over the rim. Light glinted in his gilded hair that so handsomely framed his tanned face, the squared jaw that was as solid, she had come to learn, as the honor and character of this man. His eyes changed from the color of faded denim and sky, filled with laughter and warmth, to the dark denim of heat and desire she had just experienced when he had given her that wrenchingly tender and dangerously promising kiss on the veranda. He was strong, solid, honorable, fascinating and considerate, she'd need a ream of paper to list all his good qualities. And like his last name, Hearth, he warmed every part of her that longed to belong, to find a man that would be her one love, her home. A chill ran up her spine when she thought of how she might never have met him—except for a moment of fate, when he had saved her life.

He'd saved her, her handsome hero. It was hard to imagine now after being with him, getting to know him, how little that mattered in the balance sheet. Because that was just the kind of man he was. He saved people, helped people, cared about them and was considerate of their needs, whether he knew them or not, because he knew who he was. That mattered to Dana, it mattered a lot. With a little smile, she thought that he would be pleased to know that gratitude—paying a debt to him for her life—had nothing to do with her need and desire for him—except as

231

fate's introduction. And thank heaven for that. Raising her glass, she offered a toast.

"To fate."

"I will thankfully drink to that." Garrett smiled into the green eyes fate had finally opened to him, hoisting his glass.

She smiled sweetly back at him, then lowering her glass to the table, she let her smile, her lips and eyes, turn seductive as she trailed a fingertip slowly around the rim of her glass, her eyes locked on his. She watched his face flash into a broad, white-toothed grin, then saw him bite his lip, lowering his head to look at his arms braced on the table, trying to contain himself.

*Such a gentleman.* She would have to break him of that.

Reaching out with that fingertip, she trailed it slowly across the taut muscles of his forearm, pleased to feel the goose bumps she raised in reaction, before having to sit back so the waiter could deliver their plates.

"So, tell me about that hike around here you were suggesting." She prompted.

ON SAFER GROUND, Garrett took a deep, steadying breath and enthusiastically launched into a description of the local features.

"Well, the Biscuit Basin and Black Sand Basin aren't far away. You'll love Black Sand, it's named for its obsidian sands, but Upper Geyser Basin is the almost three mile loop that I was thinking of. And if you wish, we can continue another mile onto Black Sand by foot. There's also Geyser Hill and Observation Point right out front, and Mystic Falls Overlook trail is on the road north." He shared his personal information on the area and recommendations as they enjoyed a leisurely dinner.

"Why don't we stay?" Dana finally interrupted, pushing her plate aside.

"Stay?" Garrett looked up startled, not sure he'd heard right.

"Do you think we can get a room here without a reservation?"

"A room?" Garrett couldn't seem to get his brain to function.

"Yeah. I brought my toothbrush, just in case. Why don't you check what's available."

"Sure." He swallowed a deep draft of water and pushed away from the table, trying to saunter casually off toward the reservation desk, while he tried to figure out if she meant a room, as in one, or rooms for each of them. He almost turned back to get a clarification but reasoned that if she hadn't meant just one room, then she might think he was either cheap, or more likely trying to push her into something she wasn't ready for. Just to be on the safe side, he reserved two adjoining rooms, then made a quick call to arrange for his horses to be fed tonight and tomorrow morning.

"Did they have a room available for tonight?" Dana queried as he returned to their table.

"They had several," he hedged.

She gave him a slow, sweet smile, saying, "We'll only need one room, with one bed."

Ah. "You know, I better go make a quick call and check on work, make arrangements for my horses. Why don't you order dessert for us while I take care of that," Garrett suggested.

DANA NODDED, ORDERING a rich and filling dessert for Garrett, while her smile said she knew what she was having for dessert—something decadent—one very sweet, sexy, and slightly too gentlemanly guy.

He'd gotten them a simple room that still reflected the log-walled flavor of the historic inn, but not so historic that they had to go down the hall to use a bathroom. Dana was pleased with his choice. "Perfect!" She turned and burrowed into his chest and arms, holding him close for long moments before stretching up to whisper "Take me, make love to me."

They undressed each other slowly, carefully, like unveiling a rare, and valued present, their lips barely separating from each other's skin.

Shrugging the blouse he'd unbuttoned from her shoulders, Dana felt it catch on her cast, reminding her suddenly that she was not showing off the body she was used to. She tried to pull it back quickly while Garrett nibbled slowly under her ear, then down the pale column of her throat, but he caught her, stopped her.

"Please, Dana, don't cover up."

SEEING THE SHY, STARTLED blush on her face, her quick glance down at her scars, he recognized the source of her sudden shyness and embarrassment, so foreign to his self-confident lady. He knew it was time to bare himself completely and risk opening his heart to her view, as bravely as he asked of her.

"Dana, look at me, babe. Look in my eyes." When her wounded green eyes lifted to his, he told her, "You are so beautiful Dana, exquisite. You're a woman that has challenged life and survived. Please don't hide that, especially from me, babe.

"But..."

"Shhh," he breathed, pressing his forehead to hers. Locking her eyes with the dark denim of his. "You do not see what I see, babe. You do not feel what I feel. Let me show you." His lips began a soft, lingering, loving trail of kisses where a scar began on her shoulder. "Let me kiss it better, every inch, so you will know what I feel." Capturing her mouth again in a drugging kiss, he laid her on the bed, and covered every inch, every wound he could reach, and trailed his fingers along her cast down to her fingertips.

Eyes never releasing hers, he lifted her hand to his mouth, kissing and lightly sucking each fingertip in turn before returning to feast on her mouth again, trailing moist circles around her breasts, then leaving them waiting, to gently turn her and begin his slow, soft nibbling course along the stark, harsh scars across her back.

MOISTURE SEEPED from Dana's eyes to the pillow, the tenderness shattering. The orphan never had her childhood's cuts and scrapes kissed away.

Turning her back, on his elbows over her, his hard chest brushing, teasing, tightening the softness of her breasts, he cupped her face with both hands, lowered his lips to just a breath away.

"You need to know, I worshipped you!" His voice came out raw, powerful, the intensity and moisture gleamed in his eyes. She felt the sweet ache of the tender worship he'd lavished on every healing wound on her body.

"When I found you with that child cradled in your broken arms, trying to save her," he swallowed hard, squeezed his eyes shut for a moment, "Oh dear God, I worshipped you. When I realized you were still alive and I could try to save an angel like you... oh babe! I placed my hands on you, begging your blood to stay in you, for you to stay with me. It was the most intense, emotional bond I have ever experienced in my life!"

His words were spaced out slowly, so she would feel their strength in him, see the sincerity in eyes wholly focused on her. "I worshipped you with everything inside me. Became as one with you. Struggled with you for a life that was and is so important to me. Now that I know all of you, I realize you are more special than I could have ever imagined. You mean the world to me. So what you see as scars ... I worship. Oh my sweet Dana, they brought me you. How can I not honor them?"

And she saw the truth of his words in his eyes.

His mouth came down on hers with all the passion in his words and heart, all the strength of the emotional bond he felt with her, all the yearning possession he hoped to claim of her. Never had she felt a tenderness that was so achingly exquisite and painful. At that moment, Dana felt a long-tied knot inside her melt, unravel, flood her with warmth and a happiness she had never known existed until Garrett showed her, melting her body to match the melting knot in her soul, and tenderly taking her somewhere that could only be demonstrated by his love and passion.

Sometime during that night, she asked him not be so careful with her. Sometime during that night, she whispered breathlessly, "Don't be gentle. Take me with all you have to give. I won't break. You heal me, Garrett."

And sometime during that night, with all the sweetness and tenderness explored and expressed, they let raw passions soar, geyser to the surface, let the explosive forces build unchecked, raw heat boiling, rising, exploding in a shattering eruption that consumed them. Emptying the chamber of built up need and longing; leaving them melted liquid, to flow out together in a single molten mass, cooling, but covering all the landscape of their past separate lives; burying them under a new solid sheet of bedrock on which to build a future with each other.

All those passions found, joined, filling a chamber, simmering, steaming just below the surface, ready to erupt again, and again now the hot spot was formed, the chamber of shared feelings created. Slowly the little sounds of life returned, but the land had been forever changed and reshaped, with new depths and layers and history.

# Chapter 21

EVEN BEFORE HER EYES OPENED, Dana knew she'd been through a powerful personal quake—a massive upheaval and shifting of the ground that supported her life before last night—a series of quakes with aftershocks trembling through her body after each shattering event. She felt languid, liquid, still molten from the furnace of heat and passion, to find she had flowed over and around Garrett in a melded tangle of twined limbs. They had come to rest in a natural blend, unaware of where one began and the other ended, melded into one form. She breathed his earthy male fragrance, nestled over the steady rhythm of his heart, beating in time to her breath—in tune, in time, like one flesh. Yet so deliciously different! Reveling in her contentment, she felt the heat and strength, the texture and flavor, filling her senses with what had only been a pale hope, a dream, before.

Her lips lazily nibbled on him, nose nuzzled in the hairs on his chest, her arms curled to hold him closer. The dawn light drifted into the room fingering the flame colored curls mixed with the dark gold hairs of his chest, like a warm blessing, a benediction of the two entwined in harmony, in a moment of perfect happiness.

"Waking with the woman of my dreams still in my arms is heaven, babe." His voice was a soft, deep rumble in his chest.

"M-m-m-m," she hummed a soft chuckle. "You mean it's not a dream?" Snuggling closer, she drifted back into a pleasant doze with the reassuring beat of his heart, her hearth—her Garrett Hearth—beneath her cheek.

She had woken only for a moment, just to make sure her exquisite dream was real. Pressing her lips to his heated skin, she felt them curl in a naughty smirk, wondering if her private earthquake swarm of the night past had registered on any of those new sensors installed in the park. She fell back asleep with her smile lingering.

When Dana woke again, hours later, her source of heat was gone. Her head was resting not against the solid muscles of Garrett's chest, but on a pillow clutched in her arms. It still held the reassuring scent and warmth of him but she knew, before she even glanced around, that he was no longer in the room. It was late; she had slept in. She didn't worry.

It was much later that the panic set in.

Rising to head for a shower, Dana stretched lazily, feeling the sweet ache of a body that had been thoroughly caressed and sated. In the bathroom, she reached for a towel then paused to sort through a little basket of toiletries on the counter. Twisting the top off a small bottle of bubble bath, it released the scent of old-fashioned roses. She breathed in a drift of scent as sweet and dreamy as her thoughts and the smile they brought to her face. A shower seemed much too abrupt this morning, she decided. Dana wanted to wallow in a rose scented bath and let its waters lap lazily over her body as she recalled Garrett's touch. She wasn't ready to let go of that magic yet. Sinking down into the warm fragrance with a contented sigh, Dana brought back every moment, every memory, replaying all the sensations again.


LEANING AGAINST THE LOG RAILING in the crisp bite of morning, Garrett studied the steam drifting up from heated ground and beastly breaths that created a mystical scene beyond the veranda. Buffalo and trees floated to their knees in a steamy mist like a scene in a fantasy world—his fantasy world.

Last night all this guy's fantasies sure came true!

He couldn't resist that thought or resulting very male grin— or the shiver of doubt.

He woke that morning to the feel of Dana's lips against his chest, felt them curl up in a smile, heard her soft sigh, felt her breath brush and tickle his skin. Her soft fragrance soothed and owned him. He imagined he had reached heaven, his sense of well-being and happiness so utterly complete with her finally in his arms that everything that came before seemed like just mere existence, a mere marking of time until this moment. Love for the woman in his arms had overwhelmed him.

But would it last beyond this magical time and place? For her? Was all his good luck, all the magic, due to the influence of this fantasy land or to Dana's true feelings for him? Because magic it had been!

No woman had ever been what Dana was to him. Never had he wanted to take and give with such deep and demanding passion. Heat and passion that was all wrapped up in a lingering tenderness, happiness and so much more. He felt whole, complete

237

in a way he had never shared with a woman—in a way he had never known he had wanted or needed before.

"You're my world now, babe," he murmured to himself, "my fantasy come true." Taking a deep sip of his steaming coffee, denim eyes narrowed, he gazed beyond the misty fantasy scene in the geyser basin before him, to a picture of the private magic they could share.

He had been awake for a while that morning when Dana woke, momentarily. He stayed there awake for a long time after she had fallen back asleep. Though he was an early riser, he hadn't wanted to move until he absolutely had to; he had just wanted to lie still and savor the feeling.

Night after night he had dreamed of her. Occasionally nightmares related to her near death, but most often they were exciting sexual fantasies of her alive and vibrant in his arms. Heated dreams at night, distracted during the day with both soft and lusty thoughts of her. Always her... Yet even with all those high expectations he still was stunned by the shattering heat and explosive flame they had created together. Never could he have imagined a night like they had shared!

God knows he'd meant to be gentle, loving and tender with her. And he had cringed each time he felt the coarse-grained sandpaper of his big, clumsy hands scrape the soft, alabaster silk of her skin. But he had put every inch of his heart into loving and cherishing her. She had given him back a sweetness that near made a man weep. First she had whispered "take me" in that soft, throaty voice that curled his toes, and had been haunting his dreams, but later ... oh Lord, later!

Garrett snorted out a laugh and reached up to pull his collar away from his neck, already heating up just remembering how later she had demanded more. Seemed she'd been having a few fantasies about them of her own and wasn't going to put up with anymore of that gentle stuff. God what a woman!

He took in a deep breath of the crisp morning air to steady himself, bringing his thoughts back to that morning's sensations when he had lain quietly with all that soft, sweet female flesh wrapped so trustingly in his arms.

In all his dreams and wild fantasies, he realized he had never once fantasized what it might be like to actually sleep beside her, to wake to find her still holding him. He didn't know how to describe or pin down exactly how it felt, but it had been a kind of quiet wonder and peace that spread a glow of intense happiness inside him—almost spiritual. Whatever it was, he had wanted it to last, to wake that way every day. But he needed to be patient, not push Dana into giving more than she was ready for. She was his world, but that didn't mean she felt the same, though he swore he had felt it in her every touch, seen it deep in her eyes.

Glancing down at his watch, Garrett wondered if he should go take her some coffee and a cinnamon roll yet. Watching Dana as she had slept this morning, he had noticed the slight smudges under her eyes, the fragile look of her limbs. Lovely as they were, her arms and legs had lost the firm toned muscles of the athlete she had been. She needed to finish healing and rebuild. He felt guilty at the way he had been dragging her around trails, kept her on the go since she had arrived. She had looked so amazingly healthy when he had picked her up at the airport—and, he admitted, he had been so eager to use her interest in the park to woo her—that he had been thoughtless and selfish. She wasn't that long out of the hospital; she still needed lots of rest and time to recuperate. He had given her none, until this morning, when he had realized her exhaustion and left her to sleep as long as she could.

He was eager to see those green eyes open again, but afraid if he went up too soon he would crawl back in bed with her and show how selfish he could be, again. He'd give her a little more time. He needed to concentrate on how he was going to show her how much she meant to him today, while restraining himself and not acting so needy that he scared the hell out of her and ran her off.

More than one appreciative female eye had been focused on the broad shouldered, lean hipped, and so superb denim-clad male butt that was parked so picturesquely over the railing of the veranda over the vehicle entry of the Inn. But only one vacationing beauty had the brass to stalk across the wood floored expanse and sidle up next to the blonde hunk and try to claim him as her personal souvenir.

"Hey there handsome, what are you dreaming about? Need a little inspiration?"

Lost in his own world, Garrett didn't notice the teasing southern drawl aimed at him until a soft breast nudged his arm making his coffee jump in its cup.

"Whoa," he stepped back, "excuse me, ma'am. I was just leaving." He tried to move politely away from the brunette beauty, but she got a manicured hand on his arm.

"You're not going to run off and leave me all alone are you?" She pouted prettily.

"Yes ma'am, I most definitely am." He grinned into the predatory eyes. "My heart is already taken."

"Your heart wasn't the part I was interested in borrowing, big fella."

"Sorry," he managed to untangle his arm. "I'm the fully owned and permanent property of another lady, and I couldn't be happier about it." He turned and strolled back through the glass doors of the Inn, hoping his words were true, but recognizing that even if Dana didn't agree, there were no other women that could tempt her from his mind—or any other part of him.

Now the trick was just to be sure he didn't rush his fences and stampede his lady.


TOO MANY EMOTIONS. Too much need. The chill crept under Dana's skin as the bath waters cooled and the bubbles of rosy scent began to burst along with her happiness and the sweetness of her reverie. The first fault lines began to show as doubt began to make hairline cracks.

The practical, logical Dana had begun to sort, analyze and review the realities of her situation.

The reality was ... *She* had drug Garrett off to bed and jumped him!

She had instigated it, not him. She had taken advantage of a totally sweet guy that had invited her out to show her the park, and like the kind and caring gentlemanly guy he was, graciously he had ... well, accommodated her. Had he ever! But. That wasn't the point.

He was a guy, after all. Sweet and gentlemanly or not, guys were known to be very accommodating when it came to sex, whether it had been their idea or not. And that was the point. It wasn't his idea. Why hadn't he tried to get her in bed before? He'd talked a sexy story on the phone while she was in the hospital. He'd said all the right things to make her feel good and desirable then, and last night. But just how kind was he? Kind enough to sacrifice himself just to give her hope and desire for her future? The future she wouldn't have had if he hadn't saved her life to live with her terribly scarred body? Geez, how much could you ask of a guy?

Maybe he had just wanted to be a dear, close friend? She should have given more consideration to why he had shown such restraint. Had she pushed too far, too fast, put him in an

240

uncomfortable position? Had she lead him in a direction he hadn't intended?

Dana didn't really doubt his words or the beautiful passions they had shared the night before. He was a generous, giving, loving man; she'd come to know how much that was part of his nature. But she also knew he was the kind of man that would sacrifice for others, to protect, help, to heal. If he hadn't been, Dana probably never would have survived to be here—with him. And his love making *had* been *so* healing. Oh so very healing, and very, *very* hot! Dana couldn't stop the grin.

Face it girl, she told herself, how badly could you have harmed him with a night of hot, sweet, sweaty sex? So sweet, so hot, but for Dana—so very dangerous!

She loved him.

That stark fact stared her in the face and terrified her. She was *not* the romantic type—for a reason.

She'd fallen long before last night, but their heat together had welded it into a force and need she couldn't deny. But she would have to keep that secret to herself. It scared the hell out of her to realize she wanted to love, and be loved by him, so desperately, forever. And not all of Dana's scars were recent or visible. There lay the panic, the deep fears that shivered with this need.

Temporary love, temporary adoration. She'd had to build her life on that; she knew better than to expect too much, feel too much, need too much. How many times had she learned this lesson? She'd built a happy, healthy life with realistic expectations, enjoying the moments of joy, but never forgetting that happiness was provided by herself—alone. Life was steadier, safer when one didn't need, wish, hope, expect too much from others. Dreams should only be about things she could accomplish for herself. She knew better than to dream the dreams that she needed someone else to grant her.

Could she survive just loving him, without expectations?

She needed to get away, think things through, decide if she was brave enough to grab the moments and survive the ultimate, lasting pain. And she couldn't let her need for him show; she could not bear his pity.

Dana dried off and dressed. Her emotional shields were firmly in place when Garrett returned to her with his smiles and her breakfast.

"AH, WHAT A GUY! Is that for me?" Dana reached her one arm around Garrett's shoulder and gave him a quick, appreciative kiss on the lips. "Thanks," she smiled then grabbed the cinnamon roll and took a big bite. "Yum, this is great!"

She chatted with him while she ate, but he noticed something seemed off.

After all of the shared tenderness and explosive heat of their night together, Dana seemed to have gone dormant. Oh she was still sweet, friendly, caring, but it was the friendliness that warned him that the intensity of what they had shared might never have happened. Maybe it hadn't meant as much to her as it had to him. Maybe he didn't mean as much to her. He wasn't sure what had gone wrong, but when she had kissed him and smiled, he had gazed into those lovely green eyes and sensed the wall there. Last night he felt he could look down them to her soul. Today they sparkled with friendliness, but she had posted a guard.

Patience, he reminded himself, yet again. Give the lady all the time and space she needs.

*My* lady.

# Chapter 22

GARRETT WAS LYING ON THE BED, hands folded comfortably behind his head, chatting with Dana while she ate her late breakfast. Secretly he was hoping she'd join him there, gratify his senses, when she finished—that was clearly not in the cards.

"If you don't mind, Garrett, I'd like to watch Old Faithful erupt again. Close up this time. I want to hear the roar, feel the spray and gratify my senses. Okay?" Barely finished with her cinnamon roll, Dana gulped her coffee, dusted off her hands, jumped up, grabbing her bag and jacket, and was at the door ready to rush out of their room.

"O-o-kay." He graciously rose and took her things to help her out the door and down the dramatic gnarled limb-railed stairs. He silently, but reluctantly, checked them out of the room where they had created magic together.

While he was busy, Dana moved a few yards off and slipped into the open doors of a gift shop to purchase more batteries for her camera. Pausing on her way out to check the postcard display, she saw some that were different from any she had seen before. She lifted one she thought Jen might love, then slipped it back in its slot when she saw another that would be better. She was distracted from her selection when one of the attractive young women, browsing near her, nudged the other and muttered low and urgent.

"Eye candy alert! Two o'clock!"

Curious, she peered around the edge of the display to see what they were staring at.

It was . . . *her* man! The nerve! But seeing him suddenly from a distance, Dana was struck again by his rugged male beauty. He *was* gorgeous. Who could blame the women?

She restrained herself from raising her hand, murmuring "Me".

They were right; he was hot; she just didn't think of him that way—well, not only that way.

She saw him now as a deep, silky voice in her ear, big callused hands that could be gentle and comforting or wildly erotic. But most of all, when she thought of him she saw his eyes and lips, the emotions that flickered through those changeable blue sky eyes and danced in his smiles and cheeky grins. She saw the beauty of his emotions, his laughter, his mature and nimble mind, his kind generosity, his steady nature, all his passion for life and his fellow man—and all the passion he shared with her. Strong, steady Garrett had a heart bigger than all of Montana, so Dana forgot it was also packaged in a tall, built man, better looking than most Hollywood heart throbs. *Her man*. Right now, with his thick hair slightly ruffled by the hand he must have been dragging over it, he looked not only sexy, but adorable.

He was *so* going to break her heart into splinters when this temporary fantasy was over. But, even if she wanted to run before that happened, right now she had her turf to defend. Dana liked to think that fate had given her first dubs on Garrett. Thank goodness Jen had held her place while she was in a coma.

"Excuse me." Tossing her cards back in the rack, she shouldered in front of the women, blocking their view of her man as she strolled out to join him. She ushered Garrett outside before he got ogled all over by those women.

"SO, YOU WANT the authentic Old Faithful Geyser experience this time?" He grinned down at her, curling his arm around her shoulder to draw her closer, protect her from being jostled by other tourists hurrying to the viewing area. "By the way, how's your wrist doing? Okay? Feeling any pain?" He bent close to her ear to ask, and to draw her nearer. She smelled like his grandmother's garden, a warm and special childhood memory. But a scent that had never stirred him in the way it did now, drifting from the warmth of Dana's skin.

"My wrist? It is fine," she shrugged. "I should be the one worrying that I hurt you. Any bruises this morning from accidentally being clubbed with my cast?" She didn't look at him when she asked, but it was her first reference to the rough and tumble passions they'd shared last night.

Garrett grinned, encouraged. "Babe, just feel free to bruise me like that anytime you want." At her quick concerned glance, he hastily added. "No. I was kidding. No bruises. Honest."

She just nodded then turned back to give him an amused smile. "Are you saying you can take anything I dish out, cowboy?"

He laughed. "In a word? Yes! Make that two. Yes, please!"

"Hmm," she pursed her lips, studying his face for a few moments with an expression he couldn't read. "I'll have to think that over." Garrett wasn't quite sure if that was good news or not.

Sweeping his gaze around the colorful crowd, he checked for the best viewing spot, noting the ranger on duty. It was a woman. Good. At least he didn't have that to worry about, he thought, blowing out a breath, letting himself relax.

The crowd pleasing geyser was due to erupt shortly. Parents held on tight to their toddlers; the ranger kept a wary eye on everyone. Older children danced around their parents, little whirlwinds of impatience, spewing comments and questions.

"Daddy, I don't see nothing."

"Anything," the boy's father patiently corrected.

"Where's the fountain?"

"Can we go get the candy now?"

"When's it going to blow up, Mommy? Huh? Mommy, listen. It's not x-x-ploding! How come?"

"Look, that little boy gets to stand closer, why can't I?"

"Let's go see a bear! This thing doesn't work. Yeah, where's Smokey the Bear? Isn't he here?"

"When are we going to eat?"

"I saw a buffalo over there," a little girl pointed. "Can we go pet it?"

That last comment made both Dana and Garrett shiver and lose their amused smiles. They were relieved when they heard the mother patiently explain that buffalo were wild animals and very dangerous and they had to stay far, far away. Just like steam was dangerous, she added, and could burn her face off so they needed to stand back from the geyser.

"Can it killed me?" The chastened child asked, her eyes wide, lip trembling.

"Yes, but I won't let it, sweetheart, because I'll keep you close to me and safe."

"But when's it going to do something? It's broken, mommy!"

Then the slow wisps of steam drifting over the geyser thickened, and a few hisses and spits of water flared out. After some graduated, erratic spurts and burps of boiling bubbles, like an old geezer trying to rise up out of a chair, the old geyser finally got itself up and burst into the air. Rising higher and higher, it exploded from the vent, high into the sky with a gusty roar, fulfilling its promise as an ever faithful crowd pleaser.

Children shrieked with joy; babies hid their heads in their parents' shoulders, scared at first by the sudden explosion and noise, then turning to watch, patting dimpled hands together to show their pleasure. Adults tipped their heads back impressed at the power of this force of nature up close, except for the occasional scrooge who always had to grumble when it didn't last as long as he expected.

The ranger instructed the crowd on the mechanics of geysers: telling of the magma-heated rocks just miles below the surface, how circulating ground water was heated to boiling, how the tube like fissure of a geyser worked like a bottleneck to squeeze and not release the water, but force it up the tube so it had to explode into the air to release the pressure of all the trapped hot water and gases, then when the underground reservoir of water emptied, it stopped until it refilled and reheated to force its way up to erupt again. Each geyser was different based on the underground plumbing, some taking years or days between eruption cycles, but this geyser erupted well over a hundred feet high not only regularly, but often, spewing thousands of gallons of water every thirty minutes to two hours throughout its known history. Which is why it had earned the name Old Faithful.

Garret had placed himself behind Dana to watch the show, wrapping his arms around her waist and gently drawing her slender body back against his chest, his head resting on hers, breathing her scent, enjoying the special moment with her.

"Pretty cool, huh?" She tipped her head up, when it ended, her eyes emerald sparkles, smiling, sharing her appreciation with him.

"M-m-m-m, very," he dropped a kiss on her upturned nose. He wasn't thinking of the geyser but the lady he was holding.

Dana eyes dropped quickly, and instead of turning into him for a kiss, she eased herself out of the circle of his arms, glancing to either side, as if the crowd was the cause for distancing herself.

"So, where's this trail you were talking about?" Auburn curls captured the sun, but concealed her face, as Dana bent over to dig busily through her bag, finally coming up with a bottle of water, and standing to take a sip.

Garrett had folded his empty arms across his chest, thinking about Dana's quicksilver flips from hot, or at least warm, to, if not cool, distant. His little geyser had gone dormant again, and he didn't get what the deal was. Studying her as she tipped her face to the sun again to sip her drink, he looked at the line of her graceful throat, the sharp lines of her jaw, the prominence of

246

the delicate cheekbones, her alabaster skin looked like if she wasn't careful, her beautiful bone structure would breach it. She'd gone through hell, and her face showed she was doing a great job faking it. She was still a beauty, but she hadn't made it all the way back to glowing health, yet. Maybe it was just more noticeable today because her features and movements showed a subtle tension that hadn't been there before—or she was just tired from overdoing. Overdoing that he was guilty of causing—day and now, night.

"I don't know about you," he gave her a little smile, "but my legs are a little rubbery this morning." His eyebrows did a naughty dance to match the little leer in his grin. "How about we start out on an easier walk first. See how it goes. Geyser Hill is only about half as far as the Upper Geyser Basin walk. It really should be ashamed to call itself a hill, it's not that high unless you continue up to Observation Point. Still you're only going up a couple hundred feet. An easy walk and its jam packed with geysers."

"Sure. I'm game. Point the way."

Reaching out he captured her hand, weaving her fingers between his to make it harder for her to slip away. "Let me show you, babe. Right this way."

As they had strolled, hand in hand, around the geyser circle, passing by the lodge and cabins, Garrett noticed how bright the day had become. The mists of morning had been burned off by a sun that now pleasantly warmed, without overwhelming, the tangy air of a perfect fall day. Individual puffs of steam marked each thermal feature with their sinter surrounds gleaming silver in the light. Dana seemed more relaxed, enjoying herself, letting their hands swing gently as they sauntered along. He even coaxed a few dazzling smiles and laughter from her, so all was right again in his world; a world where everything seemed bolder, brighter, and fresher to his senses.

Even the ground felt more familiar and solid beneath his feet, though, he chuckled, according to Dana that was a geologically temporary condition. His smile felt like it was permanently etched on his face recalling that this fascinating, intriguing, and sometimes baffling woman, had given herself so generously to him—at least temporarily. He'd fix that. Gradually.

They took the bridge on the far side of the circle. The Firehole River glimmered with a thousand prisms of reflected light, as they started around the lower end of the Geyser Hill loop. They lingered by Anemone Geyser, enjoying its antics, deciding it must be one of the comics of the various geyser personalities. Every few minutes its pool filled with water, then it burped a few bubbles, erupted up ten feet, then drained back down its tube into hiding with a funny gurgle, before cycling out again every ten minutes, playing to its audience like a cheery jack-in-the-box. After laughing at its routine for a while, they turned to the other side of the walk to check out the next.

Plume Geyser erupted about every half hour, so while they had a few minutes to wait, Garrett wrapped his arm around Dana's waist, shared her bottle of water, before commenting casually, "You know you could stay at my house, instead of that hotel." Feeling her stiffen, he added, "There's lots of space for you to spread your stuff out, get it out of suitcases in my guest room, and it's a lot handier to the park." He saw the resistance in her eyes as she turned to him. *You are pushing her, buddy, back off*, he warned himself. "And, of course, it has its own private bathroom. Just an idea. Think about it and let me know."

Any response Dana might make was forgotten when a jet-engine roared to life behind them. Down by the river, a tall cone-shaped nozzle was loudly blasting water almost two hundred feet in the air.

"Wow, that's Beehive," Garrett said. He'd instinctively flinched like everyone else nearby. "I don't think it's ever gone off when I was here." They turned and tried to hold their position as everyone converged to see the event. "It only goes off once or twice a day. Did we get lucky! Look at that thing go! It's like a damn fire hose!"

They watched the five minute eruption with wonder, watching little rainbow prisms dance in the plume's spray. He tried to figure out what kind of velocity and volume of water the cone was pushing when Dana wrapped her good arm around him, ducking under his, to nestle her head against his shoulder. His mind blanked on everything else. She had come to him. She had come to hold him, without him having to pull her in. He preferred to ignore the fact that it was crowded and people were pushing in from all sides—she'd probably done it in self-defense. He tightened his arm around her and kissed the top of her head, keeping her close as they shuffled along the path. How appropriate, he thought. Next up was Heart Hot Spring. He knew that shimmer.

DANA GAVE IN to her feelings, letting herself off the leash a bit, to thoroughly enjoy the day, and this moment. She was wrapped in Garrett's heat and affection. He cuddled her close, kissed her hair, and invited her to stay at his home—in his guest room? He said she could put her *stuff* there, his body language indicated he didn't really want her to sleep there, but was giving her the choice. And no guy asked a woman to live, however temporarily, in his home, instead of her hotel, where it would be easier to keep her distant when he chose, unless ... Did he want her as much as she did him? At least for now? But could she keep her need from showing if she stayed with him? *No, probably not.* And it would be even more painful when she had to go home.

Gazing down into the colorful pool with the heart shaped throat, she determined to savor the romance of now, today, then give herself more space to think before she made any big, impulsive mistakes.

"That's two hearts you can count coop on today," Garrett whispered in her ear, snuggling his nose in her hair, taking a few quick nibbles on her throat.

"Pardon?" She tried to keep her knees from buckling and melting down into the spring.

"You can count this geyser heart, and mine, which you've stolen."

"Ah, Garrett, you are such a romantic!" She teased, turning to him.

"You're not, I suppose?" Rubbing his nose against hers, he dipped to steal a quick kiss from her lips.

"No. But with you I seem to turn into a big mush puddle." She confessed as he started to lean in to kiss her again when, glancing at the boardwalk over her shoulder, he suddenly jerked back, his eyes widening.

"Dana," he started urgently.

FOUR WORDS—maybe five—were all it had taken for Garrett's life to be screwed up royally!

# Chapter 23

HE HAD FORGOTTEN his own damn advice. Fool! He swore and cursed himself.

What the hell was wrong with him? Everything had been going along just perfect. He'd almost screwed things up when he asked her to move in with him. Now there's patient, go slow for you, Garrett, you idiot! But he had caught himself, made it more palatable, saved himself—or Beehive had. But even after that, *especially* after that gaff, Dana had come to him, reached for him and curled her arms around him. Everything had been perfect. So what did he do? Damn it!

There was just no excuse for rushing things like that and scaring the hell out of her. Well, he actually *did* have an excuse—a damn good one as far as he was concerned.

He'd seen a raven-haired ranger heading their way. His good 'ole buddy Ravenwolf would have sauntered up and, after saying hey to his pal, turned that lady-killing smile and all his charm on Dana and stolen *his* women right out from under his nose! It was no laughing matter. When they had hung out together, Garrett had watched him do it a hundred times to other guys. Ravenwolf had also stolen his share of Garrett's dates, without even trying. Oh, he admitted, there had been no malice in it. It was just that once a woman set eyes on Rave she seemed to simply forget any other man existed. It hadn't been a big deal then.

This was different. Dana was everything to him! So he'd done what any man would do.

Panic.

He'd rushed things and he had to admit he hadn't used a lot of finesse—or any finesse, really—but he'd followed all the basic steps first. Hadn't he? He'd courted her, sent her gifts, taken her places, bought her dinner, shown his respect, told her he loved her ... or had he?

The crowds parted around the tall man standing in the middle of the path, scraping his palms through his hair, and scrubbing his hands across his face, a little wild-eyed and talking to himself like a crazy man. They figured he was probably drunk or on drugs and gave him a wide berth, as he tried to recall when he had told Dana he loved her.

He was pretty sure he'd said it last night, or at least something close enough that she should have known that's what he meant. And he *had* made love to her, done the telling her without words thing. And hadn't he just told her that she had stolen his heart? Yeah, that was the same thing. Plus, he'd asked her to move in with him today, so he couldn't see how he had missed anything. There really shouldn't have been any reason for her to be so shocked and run off and hide in the ladies restroom, leaving him standing there at Heart Springs—what a joke. But his heart *had* been threatened—and he had sprung. She had run as if her life depended on it.

Just four words were all it had taken for Garrett to feel like his heart had been punctured and fallen down around his ankles, puddled and worthless like an old pair of briefs that had lost their elastic. He felt just as naked, exposed, and pathetic.

"I can't marry you!"

Those were the four words she'd gasped, shocked, and left him here. He would rather concentrate on whether they counted as four words, or more, than to let them sink in. After all, the words really meant she could *not* marry him. Five words. Somehow it seemed more painful as five words than only four. Tone, maybe he should focus on her tone of voice, instead of her words.

Had it seemed like a teasing tone? Maybe she had been teasing and that shocked choke and gasp, and deer-in-a-headlight eyes were just because she had suddenly realized—at the same moment—that she had to pee *really* badly. Emergency bad. No, that probably fell into the category of wishful thinking, or more like desperate hope. He was a fool. He was toast. And there was no getting around that.

And he had destroyed his life and hopes for nothing. Hell!

Rave had spotted him standing alone, waved, then taken a radio call and turned and headed back the other way. He didn't even have to be present to trash Garrett's love life. It was pathetic! No, you are what is pathetic, he muttered to himself.

Turning suddenly, to see if Dana had come back out of the building, he wondered why all the people around him scattered, and grabbed up their children.

DANA COULD NOT EXPLAIN the panic that propelled her to run from Garrett. She dodged into the restrooms, run into a stall, slammed and locked the door behind her before she had been able to think, or breathe. The hand she buried her face in shaking, her forehead cold and clammy; she huddled against the door thinking she just needed a few minutes to hide, get herself under control. She hadn't even thought ahead—or at all—of having to face him and explain herself when she came out.

She wouldn't think of that now. She couldn't even explain it to herself. She hadn't over reacted like this in such a long time. She'd made a point, a discipline, of hiding her reactions. She stifled a laugh that was more a sob. She was doing a damn good job of the hiding part right now! God!

Everything had been so perfect. They were having so much fun. The sun was shining, the sights were awesome, Garrett was so tender and attentive she thought she was letting go of her doubts and fears of this morning. They seemed silly when he kissed her by the heart shaped pool. She was in love. He was so romantic and sweet, and she had been so happy, until—

Too much happiness could be dangerously lulling, then the trap sprung, and the flashback of pain bit.

She thought she was over those panic attacks. Even Jen always commented how cool and calm Dana always was. Dana thought she had acted the part until it became real—mostly. Why had she let the pain of that small child flash into panicked action now? She tried to push away the childhood memory, one of her first, one of many, one she had never been able to shake, from that other sunny, happy, seemingly perfect day.

The house she had been fostered in had a big fenced back yard to play in with her best friend, Buster. The old brindled mutt had let her dress him in doll clothes and played Frisbee with her until he flopped panting in the shade, his tail always wagging. He loved her. The back porch led to a sunny kitchen. That day the lady did something new, she invited Dana to help her in the kitchen instead of telling her to go somewhere else to play. She got to stand on a chair at the counter, her hair in red pigtails, her body coated with flour as she helped make cookies for the first time. Dana felt so important, so wanted, she had been so excited and happy. She'd grinned up and asked the question she'd waited so long to ask, hope tight in her throat, ready to burst free in joy and laughter.

"Can I call you mommy now?" young Dana had asked.

252

Even now, Dana's stomach clenched as she recalled the moment—the answer.

"Oh sweetie, you don't really belong to me. You're just temporary. I can't be your mommy, but," hugging the child she assured her, "we have grown so very fond of you. You're such a good, sweet little girl. We'll miss you when you get a new foster family next week."

When she got her new family, the lady said she should call her "mother", but the little girl knew it wasn't true. Her friend Buster was left behind. He didn't belong to her either, and her new family didn't want a dog.

When she had gone to tumbling and gymnastics classes, they had wanted her. She would belong to a team. People smiled at her, wanted to talk to her and take her picture. People had been proud of her, strangers said they loved her. But there had never been anyone in the crowd that had been *hers*. And she had never asked any of the people she lived with again if she could call them her own. That hope had died until her roommate in college had told her that they would be sisters. Jen had adopted her—and, unbelievably, it had lasted year after year. But Dana had learned to live on temporary joy and affection. Expecting more terrified her. It was too painful, too scary.

SCARY. THAT IS WHAT the man pacing in front of the restrooms was. What was he muttering?

"The ring? Beg? Kneel?" Weird. And scary. Especially when one of his flailing arms snaked out and grabbed the arm of a passing woman.

"Excuse me ma'am," he had a desperate look in his eyes, and voice. "Would you marry a man without a ring?"

She yelped, backing against her husband, breaking Garrett's grasp.

"Hey! Get your own woman, buddy!" Her husband snarled at the much larger man, clutching his clearly pregnant wife, and hustling her away from that drugged out madman.

THE OUTER DOOR BURST OPEN with the sound of laughter as a group of women entered the restrooms, chattering.

"Did you see that big guy that was freaking everyone out?"
"The big, handsome one?"
"Yeah, but kinda glassy-eyed. Didn't you notice?"

253

"I noticed he had a really nice butt," another commented.

"What was he saying to that lady he grabbed?"

"I couldn't tell, but he sure scared the dickens out of her."

"Her husband should have popped him one."

"Are you nuts? The guy was twice his size!"

One of the women thumped the door of Dana's stall, startling her out of the past and into the present. Sounded like someone needed her hiding place; she needed to pull herself together.

"Hey! You about done in there?" She heard an impatient call. Waiting another moment to gather herself before she flushed and exited, Dana tuned into their conversation.

"Yeah. And you don't want to mess with a crazy, drugged out dude of any size. They can be dangerous," the chatter continued.

"Just my kind of guy," one teased, "tall, handsome, blonde, and dangerous!"

"True," her friends laughed. "And don't forget the nice ass."

They could have been talking about Garrett, Dana thought, as she stopped to wash her hands, and square her shoulders before leaving—except for the crazy part. She was clearly the crazy one. She tried to tell if her face was a mess, if the tear stains showed, in the metal sheet bolted to the wall that passed for a mirror. Slipping on sunglasses to hide her eyes, she pasted on the trademark performance smile that she had honed to face the world, and stepped out into the sunlight.

It only took a moment for her eyes to adjust and for her to realize they *were* talking about Garrett!

Rejoining him, they both felt awkward and pretended nothing had happened. Their conversation would have probably been stilted even if everyone wasn't staring at them. Dana led off briskly down the path toward the main buildings and parking lots, and Garrett stuffed his hands in the pockets of his jeans and followed.

"Dana," he ventured, speaking to her back, "I—"

"Sorry about that," her voice was as breezy as her stride, "nature called. I'm afraid I'm not feeling too hot. Ah ... woman stuff, you know?" She tossed the lie over her shoulder knowing it was guaranteed to make a man stop asking questions and was considered explanation enough for any sort of erratic mood or behavior.

"Oh. Right."

254

She could almost hear the embarrassed blush in his voice. She'd feel guilty later. Now she just needed to get some space for herself.


DESPITE HER BRISK PACE, when Dana marched them straight back to his truck, it was clear she didn't feel up to hiking the Upper Geyser Basin today. That was okay with him. It was her silence in the car that he didn't know how to break into, that unnerved him. They passed all the basins they hadn't seen yet on the west side, without Dana expressing any interest or comment. She just stared out the side window; he just drove.

Passing out of the park under the arch at Gardiner, he casually asked, "You starving? You must be. Want to stop here for a burger?"

"No thanks. Let's just head straight north. I'm sure you need to get back out to work at your job sites."

"Not a problem. My guys have it handled if—"

"No. I know I've been messing up your schedule. Besides, I'm pretty tired. I've been missing the daily naps I'm used to. Just drop me at my hotel, okay?"

Garrett couldn't argue with that, he had been worried about the same thing just that morning. "Sure. Tomorrow?"

"I thought I might check out Bozeman tomorrow. That museum you showed me—"

"Glad to take you, I've been wanting to—"

"No, that's okay. You get your work done tomorrow. I'll just go in and check it out myself. I'm sure you've seen it a thousand times, and I'd like to just piddle around and take my time exploring it." *Alone*. Her tone clearly said.

"How will you ... shall we swing by my house so you can borrow my other car?"

"No need. I can rent one for the day or maybe I'll decide to take the bus down so I can just sit and enjoy the scenery."

"Well, if you change your mind, I'd be glad—"

"I won't." Seeming to realize how harsh that sounded, Dana added, with a small smile, "But, thanks."

Garrett had an ominous feeling in his gut, but tried to keep his voice matter of fact when she hopped from his truck at her hotel, avoiding a goodbye kiss.

"Well, have fun babe, and feel better. Call and let me know how your Bozeman side trip goes."

He just hoped it wasn't one way. The airport was also in Bozeman.

# Chapter 24

"BOSS MAN IN there?"

"Well, I reckon you could say that," the subcontractor drawled, flicking the ash of his cigarette over the side of the metal steps attached to the trailer.

"Is that a yes or a no?" The laborer asked impatiently from a lower step.

"Well, there is a guy in his office chair that resembles Garrett, but I'm not sure he qualifies as being there," was the annoyingly slow, elusive response.

"Never mind," the young laborer clumped up the rest of the stairs onto the landing and reached for the door handle.

"Just don't mention the blueprints," the subcontractor warned.

"Hell, what do you think I need to discuss with him? There's a problem on the schematic for—"

"I mean, just don't point out he's been studying them upside down for the last hour."

IT HAD BEEN TWO days since Garrett had dropped Dana, kiss-less, outside her hotel. Just over fifty-one hours, to be more precise.

He hadn't called her that first night because he figured she would be sleeping and he didn't want to wake her up—or test her mood. He hadn't called her yesterday because he knew she was probably taking her time enjoying the museum—besides he'd asked her to call him when she got back. He had not called her last night because she was supposed to call him—but she didn't—so he just stayed up waiting later and later.

This morning he did not call her when he woke up on the couch, still waiting to hear from her. It was five in the morning and that was just plain foolish—and too needy. At lunch he did not feel he should disturb her figuring all the walking in Bozeman must have tired her out and she probably was sleeping in or napping—or intentionally ignoring him.

And he didn't call her twenty minutes ago because he remembered he had a friend that worked the hotel desk. Contacting him instead, he confirmed that Dana was still checked in—so there was hope, even if it was silent. He had considered calling Washington as his next move, and talking to her friend. But that seemed a little too high school to call up and ask Jen if Dana still liked him—not to mention the interrogation he would get.

He heaved a sigh and bent back over the blueprints rolled out on his desk, trying to look focused and busy, as one of his workmen clumped into the room in his muddy steel-toed work boots.

"Paul," Garrett acknowledged, then dropped his eyes back to his work.

"Boss," Paul returned the greeting edging up near Garrett's desk, then suddenly reversing himself, coughing in his hand, and going over to busy himself making a fresh pot of office coffee. Keeping his back to Garrett, he cleared his throat and asked over his shoulder, "Want some of this when I'm done? If you've got the schematics for the Johnson job, there's a problem we need to discuss."

"Okay." Swiveling in his chair, Garrett found the proper cardboard tube, and spread a new set of blueprints over his desk. Right side up, this time. Though he didn't notice the difference.

Paul brought over the coffees, sat down beside Garrett, and they spent the next hour going over job specifications and necessary change orders. Then the phone rang and Garrett was gone.

She'd left him.

He couldn't believe it or accept it. He wouldn't accept it. Not without at least some parting words, a parting kiss, an explanation—something!

Garrett was a man used to taking action to implement his plans and dreams and he wouldn't, couldn't stand aside and not try to win Dana back. He didn't want to pressure her, he'd never force her against her desires or will, but he sure as hell wasn't going to just let her slip away from him without understanding what had happened. Because he'd felt it, he'd seen it in her eyes, he knew she felt it too, they were so good together, she was so precious. No, he wasn't giving up without a fight, or at least a serious discussion.

His truck bounced hard, suspension chattering, as he threw up dust clouds on the gravel road that led to his house. When he had gotten the call from his buddy at the hotel and found out that Dana had checked out an hour ago and taken a cab somewhere, he hadn't needed to think it over for a minute. He would tear home, grab a few things he needed, toss a bale of hay into the pasture, then drive hell for leather to Bozeman before the next flight to Washington left. He needed his duffel and extra credit cards. If he had to, he would get on the plane with her to have time to talk to her—or follow after, if he missed her.

When he skidded to a halt at his front porch, his head was spinning with a mental list of everything he needed to grab and do in the next ten minutes. Waiting a moment, he let the billowing dust pass over the truck before he shoved his door open and jumped out. Charging toward the steps, the dust settled and he blinked hard and stared. That looked like Dana sitting in a rocker on his deck, a long-necked beer nestled against her cast, her free arm swinging to clear the storm of dust he had thrown on her.

He must be the luckiest idiot in the world. He could only hope. His hope faltered when he climbed the steps and almost tripped on her luggage lined up neatly on the edge of his porch as if poised to leap into the closest trunk headed out of town.

"Hey, babe. It's good to see." He leaned and brushed his lips across her cheek, before she could stop him. "Sorry about the dust," he could taste it on his lips. "I didn't know you were out here." The smile he gave her could have thawed the Artic.

Holding her cool beer against her cheek, she smiled shyly back at him as he pulled a chair up beside her on the porch. "I was just borrowing your fabulous view of the mountains. I had no idea a dust storm was rolling in," she chuckled, then fell silent, rocking a little as she gazed out across the sagebrush prairie.

She looked relaxed. He didn't think she was about to bolt right away, so he tried to relax also, rocked back in his chair, long legs stretched out, he studied the scenery with her for a while in silence, trying to figure out what to say, whether to hope or pray.

It was beginning to seem that the silence was going to sit there on the porch with them for eternity when Dana stopped rocking, and they both spoke at once.

"Are you—"

"Did you—"

They both laughed, then Dana encouraged, "Sorry. What were you going to say?"

"No, I'm sorry," Garrett countered, relieved. "Please go ahead. Ladies first." Glad he hadn't blurted out the question he was afraid to have answered, the one tumbling in his head like a caged hamster on a squeaky wheel. *Are you leaving me?*

"Okay. Um," Dana paused, bit her lip. She looked as if she hoped for a reprieve, unable to look in his eyes. "Did you mean what you said the other day? I mean, about letting me stay at your house for a while?"

"I did," he stated firmly, immediately. Then waiting for her to look at him, he added quietly, "I asked you for more than that, Dana."

"Yeah, she nodded, her voice whisper soft, her expression unreadable. Glancing down at her newly painted toenails then out toward the mountains, she added, "Maybe I can get back to you on that."

Garrett thought that over for a minute then said, "Fair enough." He let her off the hook.

Hoisting her beer, Dana took a big gulp, choked on it a bit, her eyes watering, then cleared her throat and lightened the awkward mood that was settling around them like the cloud of dust had earlier.

"Hey, thanks for the beer! You really should lock your doors," she grinned.

Garrett didn't respond right away, uneasily eyeing her luggage that was still outside though she had clearly gone in. He wondered if by staying awhile she only meant a few hours.

"You're not upset I just went in and made myself at home, are you?"

Yanking his eyes from the suitcases, he assured her, "Hell, no! I want you here, Dana." He just wished she had unpacked and made herself even more at home.

"Good, because I stole some apples, too." She laughed at the look on his face. "No, not to go with my beer, but to bribe your horses with. We had a most illuminating chat. They told me all your deep, dark secrets."

Garrett leaned closer, his face serious, his voice deadpan. "Don't believe one single word that Corky tells you. He is a back-stabbing, lying cur. He's that one that always looks like hell, and you can't trust him for a minute."

Dana laugh sounded delightful. "So that filly from Helena that you—"

"That is a bold faced lie! Corky's the one that got that filly in trouble."

"I see," she tried to stifle a giggle, seeming happy to get back to normal with Garrett. "Well, I'll take everything he says from now on with a grain of salt."

"Not if he gets to the salt, first," Garrett shook his head wearily, pretending disgust, before jumping to his feet. "Speaking of food, let me feed the beasts, then get cleaned up so we can have dinner."

"You're not going to make me cook to pay for my room are you?"

He almost suggested an alternate payment plan, then wisely changed his mind and grinned, "Darlin, I *would* make you cook me dinner but I'm fresh out of potato chips. I'll take you out as soon as I shower. Just sit there and relax and enjoy the view."

Before heading down to the corral, he grabbed Dana's bags and moved them inside the guest room. He didn't want them hopping off the porch and leaving while he was down at the barn.


A FEW MILES SOUTH on Highway 89, Garrett started laughing when he slowed for the light at Emigrant, and caught Dana's wide-eyed stare at the Saloon on their right. He had to reassure her that tonight he was not returning her to the scene of her earlier crime. Turning left off the highway instead, east past the gas station and general store, they slowed and stopped on the bridge over the Yellowstone River.

"What's up this way?" Dana asked while they waited for the small herd of deer to tiptoe across the end of the bridge and jump down the graveled bank for their evening drink from the river.

"Chico Hot Springs further up, but just over the river is the place we're going for dinner. Some friends of mine just opened a new bar and grill that's nicer than the Saloon and a real fun idea.

Crossing the bridge they turned right into a corralled-off parking area. Dana saw immediately that River's Edge was a lot more than just a local bar and grill. This place was designed for people who really loved the outdoors.

Not far from the willow screened banks of the Yellowstone River on one side, the other side and around the back was a large open area. To the left of the building was an outdoor dining area, with a big black iron barbeque that could roast a whole hog. Stretching behind that, Dana saw a volleyball game in progress on a grass court that seemed to sit at the feet of the massive bulk of Emigrant Mountain. In another area starting to catch the slanting

261

golden rays of the lowering western sun, guys were tossing horseshoes, and a basketball hoop had its own space.

"This is *so* cool!"

Dana took in the stunning scenery and simple pleasures the place offered, and recognized right away that this was a place of fun and community, a place that said you are family, unlike any other bar she had ever seen.

"It's special, all right. And wait until you see the inside. The food is fantastic and I have to tell you, it has the nicest men's restroom."

"What about the women's?"

"Never been there. Come on in, meet my friends. I've been hearing around town that the steaks here are as good as the fancy star-rated restaurant in town. I think I could eat two about now. Say, do you sing Dana? Karaoke?"

"Can't you just go outside if you want to hear a coyote yip and howl?"

"That bad, huh?"

"I'm an acrobat. I flunked chorus. How about you?"

"You'll just have to see if you can sweet talk my secrets out of me over dinner." He winked at her.


DANA HAD SHIED away from talking about anything too serious—like why she left and stayed away for days. Garrett still had no idea how long she planned to stay. But, during dinner, she shared a story with him about her first athletic competition that seemed meant to help him understand better.

"My first competition was very traumatic," she'd said with a wry smile, almost, but not quite laughing about it. "It was with all the other schools in our district. Not much, but it was the big time for me. I think I was about six or seven, and it was the first time I was going to be allowed to perform as part of our school team. I was ecstatic and terrified." He leaned close, arms folded on the table, watching her lovely eyes soften and drift off in the distant memory.

"I practiced every day for hours. I practiced when the coach told me to stop. 'Enough. The routine's perfect.' I never missed on the parallel bars. But, he never realized how important it was for me. I didn't want to win for myself. I wanted to win for our school, my team. Some of the girls thought I was too young, worried I'd screw it all up for them. So I practiced until I could do the whole routine in my sleep. I needed them to want me on the team, to belong with them. That was why I had to win."

She paused to glance down for a moment, then continued with a sad, half-smile on her face. "I did my warm-ups and did my whole routine flawlessly. But when the competition started and I had to do it for points, I started to feel the pressure. It had become so important to me that I shook and my palms sweated, even through the chalk. Everything went perfectly until I stretched out to grab the final bar to start my dismount. By then my palm was so sweaty, I lost my grip. I tried to grab, and there was nothing there anymore and I was falling."

Dana stopped to take a deep breath, finally looking back into Garrett's eyes. "I didn't get injured when I fell, but it was one of the deepest wounds I ever received, because the team lost the competition—because of me. They told me they didn't want me on their team, anymore. Coach overruled them, but ... it really hurt.

"Later I learned performance discipline and focus. I never really had stage fright after that, except for when something was personally very important, very special to me." Her eyes drilled her message into his. "Then sometimes I flinch from grabbing hold, afraid my hand might come up empty ... I'm working on it. Anyway," she seemed a little embarrassed, changing from her serious mood to a lighter tone. "Didn't you say something about how you could sing?"

"Well, just remember, I never promised to be good at it."

She never should have asked. Garrett's voice was enough to bring anyone to tears.

Dana was overwhelmed when Garrett got up after dessert and sang the most beautiful love song in a rich, schooled voice—and he sang only to her, blue eyes locked tenderly on green. It made her cry. She hated crying in public. She hated crying anywhere, anytime. And she hated that it made her love him so much that it felt like a dangerous pain was burning in her throat and chest. She barely managed to get the words out when he came back to the table.

"Take me home, Garrett. Take me home now and show me."

Show me how to trust, her heart whispered.

# Chapter 25

WHEN THEY RETURNED to his house—'*home*' she had called it—Dana disappeared into the guest room. Moments later Garrett heard her call to him through the door.

"What was that babe?"

"I said, 'Does this room come with benefits?'"

She stepped into the hall wearing the agate necklace he'd given her, her cast, and nothing else—except the pair of white wool socks she had teased him with before. The ones with the sexy red stripe like a garter around the top. The rest was all sweet, sexy, long and lean, scented female flesh. The alabaster skin, cloud of flaming curls, direct emerald eyes, all said the same as the words from the lush, sensual lips. "Take me."

Blood thrummed so loudly through his body, Garrett barely heard her confess a desire to experiment on him. He was too busy proving fishnet and heels were not as sexy as Dana's sense of style. He took her to his bed; he showed her with action instead of words.

He showed her slow, sweet, and gentle, softly whispering the words of the love song he had sung for her earlier, as he made love to her. Then tossing restraint away, he showed her more, pushing her up to a level of heat that burned with the power of his need, his love, his passion—she took him higher, further.

BEYOND THE MELTING POINT they burned, molten liquid in each other's arms, a boiling cauldron of flame rising under intense pressure and exploding into space. Dana held on with her teeth in his shoulder as they shuddered in completion, desperate to stay fused to him—bound to Garrett, bound to earth.

As they floated in a blissful aftermath, she murmured nonsensical words about passing altitude tests with bells and skyrockets and the Fourth of July, melting her down to her newly painted toenails. Finally managing to roll to where he had fallen, she nestled against his shoulder, planting little kisses to soothe the red mark where she had used her teeth, instead of her wounded wrist, to hang on for dear life. Wouldn't that have been some finale, she thought with a soft snicker, if she had swung up her cast and knocked her lover out? Of course then he *would* have to confess that loving her made him see...

"Did you see stars?" She whispered, before rising slightly, and bracing herself on his chest. She could feel his heart still hammering as she gazed down at him, smiling when he mumbled, "Galaxies."

"You have complained before, Garrett, that I am not very romantic..."

"Forget I said that, babe."

"And it is true. I am playful," she bounced russet eyebrows, "sometimes predatory with my lovers," she licked the bite mark, growling softly, then her green eyes locked on him, "but *never* romantic! You *are* a romantic though, Garrett," she stated with a teasing smile, tracing his lips with a fingertip.

"I already know you are the sentimental type. I mean how many guys have a horse named Flicka?" She asked, eyes sparkling with mischief.

"Maybe someone else named her?"

"Did they?"

"W-e-l-l no," he answered a bit sheepishly.

"Ah, you are sentimental! Will you confess to being a romantic? You sang to me," she pointed out. "I loved it," she nodded.

Garrett's gaze went to the ceiling a thoughtful moment. When his denim blue eyes came back to her, he raised his brows and said solemnly, "You know, babe, we manly construction types aren't supposed to confess things like that, so this has to be top secret."

"Cross my heart," she promised, crossing her bare breasts just to trip up his heart and tongue.

"Ahh ... but ... yeah. I guess I am the romantic type of guy. When it comes to you, anyway." Idly stroking her shoulder, Garrett let out a sigh, then shifted her to his side, lifting to grin down at her face.

"I'm afraid I have another confession to make Dana. You might as well know the rest of my secrets. This isn't the first time you've been the only female for me."

"It isn't?" First pleased, she frowned, confused.

"I think I told you I saw you on my Wheaties box when I was a young lad," his voice was soft and serious now, "but, I'm afraid I didn't tell you the whole truth about that." He smoothed a finger over the brow that arched at his words.

"You see," his fingers played with a curl near her chin, "I didn't think much of girls back then. In fact, I told my mom I hated a few that were always pestering me. I didn't want to hear they did it because they liked me. I sure didn't like them or their dolls and stuff. But ... well, you were on my cereal box and my mom used to watch you on TV. Once I saw you doing all those flips and stunts on that fake horse, those beams and bars and stuff, well ... I decided you weren't like most girls. You knew how to run and jump and fly around in the air. I thought that was pretty cool, so ... I talked mom into getting your box of cereal every time when we went to the store, even though I really liked Frosted Chocolate Loops better." His rueful smile charmed her.

"I still can't believe that!" Her delighted laugh choked off, her eyes blinking rapidly.

"I did. And it gets worse than that. Remember, this is all top secret. I liked to sit there and look at you while I ate my cereal, and I used to talk to you. Not out loud!" Shuddering, he laughed, then added, "Unless we were alone, of course."

HE WATCHED HER face grow still, her gaze become more intent as he ran the back of his hand down the delicate bone structure of her face, remembering the rounded contours of that younger face so well.

"I would tell you about this place I'd found by a stream, back in the woods. No girls were allowed there, but I promised to take you there. I'd tell you how you would like it a lot because there were rocks to climb on, and an old tree that had fallen across the water, and that we could take our shoes off and walk across it. But we had to be careful, because it was narrow and really slippery. But I knew you would be good at it. In fact, I hoped you could show me how to turn somersaults and cartwheels across it like you did on that beam on TV.

"And there was another tree limb," he continued, "that hung out over a pool and I told you we could jump from it into the water, or you could hang from your knees and swing and do all those neat things you do on TV there. If you fell in the water, I said I would catch you, though I figured you could probably swim because you always wore those glittery, swimsuit type things. I thought you and I could do a lot of fun things together, and," he paused, framing the words with the importance they had held for

266

him, "And I knew we could be like best friends," his blue sky eyes were soft and earnest.

"I figured it didn't hurt any that you were a girl, even though you were so pretty." The flush on his cheeks was that of the young boy, "because we could do so many things together. But I did kind of have a crush on you, I guess. I used to count the freckles on your nose." He brushed a fingertip across the real ones, grinning. "I still remember you had seventeen freckles in that picture. But I never had the nerve to mail you the Valentine cards I used to make for you." He saw the moisture well and brim in Dana's eyes.

Bending over, he kissed both the girl and the woman of his dreams. First, soft kisses for the girl then he deepened his possession of her lips with the passions he felt for the woman she had become. His girl, his woman now. He made love to her again with all the tenderness and need to cherish inside him. But she wept in his arms, sobbing as if she would go on until the rivers ran dry and a lifetime of tears were released.

Helpless to understand what he had done wrong, how he hurt her so deeply, Garrett just held her against his heart, stroking her soft, tangled curls. Whispering to her, "I'm so sorry, babe," he pressed kisses to her head, buried his face in the scent and softness of her hair.

When she finally wound down to shudders, and hiccupping sobs, finally hearing his words, she told him they were happy tears.

Of course! He should have realized that.


"NO, I'M CRYING because I'm so happy." Dana had nearly bawled the words out, choking, her red rimmed eyes welling. She had wanted to cup his cheek, be tender and reassure him, but she had needed to—very *un*romantically—grab for a tissue and loudly blow her nose. Then seeing the startled look on his face, her final sobs had blurred into a fit of watery laughter.

Then Dana felt the laughter fade inside her, replaced by some more poignant emotion. Her breath slowed. He was serious; he meant all this. If only she had known back when she was a child that there was a boy like him sacrificing his favorite cereal to spend his breakfast time talking to her, sharing his favorite place with her and planning to take her there.

She had never had a best friend to play with when she was little—not until college and Jen.

267

When he'd told her about the Valentines he made but never mailed and the freckles he had counted on her picture as a child, Dana had felt the shield around her heart quietly shatter, again.


"OH GOD," SHE swiped at her eyes, "you poor man. I'm sorry, so sorry. I'm not usually the crier. Jenny handles all that. But Garrett," now she did reach out to cup his baffled face with a slender hand, her eyes holding his. "You touched something inside me so sweetly," she whispered, "that it hurt too much to hold it in anymore." Brushing his face with her lips, she nestled back down beside him. "I promise I won't cry all over you again."

Folding her in his arms, he just held her tightly for a long while. Then he showed her the shoulder that was hers to cry on whenever she wanted, and made her laugh when he told her she had to wear that one out first, before she started on his other shoulder. They lay together quietly, closely, just soaking up each other's scent, and warmth, and comfort, before Dana was finally ready to speak.

Teasingly first, she began to open the rest of her heart to him.

"Back in my Wheaties days, most people only wanted my autograph. I did get some Valentines and cards and letters through a team fan club, but I don't remember anyone was ever kind enough to count my freckles for me, or—" She kissed the steady beat of his heart beneath her cheek, "or truly wanted me to be his best friend."

She gave him a sweet smile, leaning in to brush an even sweeter kiss across his lips. Rolling to her back, she settled her head against his shoulder and began to tell him her thoughts and feelings, sharing with him the parts of her heart that she had always shielded from the rest of the world.

"You know I was an orphan." Her voice was soft and matter of fact, but he listened carefully, knowing she was giving him something more intimate than their love making.

"I had pretty good places and most of the foster families I was with were good to me, if short term. When I was little, I always loved the fairy tales about someone that no one loved or cared about until they were rescued by someone they were special to. Cinderella. That was one of my favorites." Her smile felt weighed down.

"Not because people were mean to me, just ... well, the part about really belonging to someone, to have someone that belonged to me."

She continued in a voice that was softly wistful but never resentful. "When I was in grade school, I won a chance to go to a summer gymnastics camp, and that's when everything changed. That's when I learned how to make something be my very own. My talent made me special and gave me a kind of family that I could belong to. It gave me a confidence and control that I had never known and I devoted myself to it so I wouldn't fail and lose it all again, like I mentioned, I almost did at first.

"In college, Jen and I became best friends, my first best friend ever, and she's always been like my own sister, my family since I left the team. She is a wonder, as I am sure you have seen. But, I spent a lot of my life trying not to want too much for someone to love and belong to me. It was just easier to not be too disappointed that way.

"So I didn't dream the romantic dreams that many girls do. I dreamed of competitions and my career. I think the little girl that wanted to be Cinderella just secretly hoped that someday, someway, if it was meant to be, a handsome stranger would find her, save her, and show her about love. But it was a someday, later in the future, maybe never feeling, buried way inside me."

Dana opened her mouth to speak, gazing up at him with all her love for him in her eyes, then she snapped her mouth closed, biting her lip, catching herself just in time. She had almost shared her deepest longing, that her fairy tale would come true with him. She had been too caught up in the loving, the moment—that is what it was, all that it was, a moment—and she'd almost left herself vulnerable to be crushed again. She knew better than that.

Dana swallowed hard. Barely having snatched the last piece of her heart back in time, she recovered quickly. She was an old hand at that. Turning back to Garrett with a little laugh and teasing flutter of her eyelashes, she said in a low, sexy tone, "So. You are pretty handsome, stranger. Want to be my new best friend? Huh? I'll teach you how to cartwheel on logs and you can try to teach me how to be romantic."


GARRETT THREW BACK his head and laughed.

"Deal," he agreed, glad she didn't plan to run from the challenge. She may have taken one step back, but that was followed by two steps forward, wasn't it? And it sounded like she was going to give him a little more time for romance lessons, so he could wait. He had been disappointed when Dana had hesitated, but she had been too late. The words he wanted to hear her speak, that she had denied him at the last moment, had already spoken to him from her eyes. Trying to contain his joy, feeling his heart take a huge leap like it was clearing a fence, then settling himself, he kept quiet. Now that he knew he had hope he could let her have the time and space to come to him.

He wasn't about to make another idiotic mistake like before. Dana loved him, he knew it. He saw it in those green eyes, so soft with love and hope, before she had shied at the final jump, and turned away, pushing that wall back in place. She hadn't known love and belonging freely given. She didn't know she could trust her love, trust him. So he would show her.

But before they fell asleep, he had just one more thing he wanted to say to her—silently. Well, maybe two, but one of a different nature.

Rising, he gathered her socks from the hall and his bedroom doorway. Sliding her to the edge of the bed, he knelt before her and very solemnly and ceremonially, lifted one of her bare legs at a time and gently rolled each sock up her leg—as if they were as delicate as Cinderella's glass slippers. Grinning at the look on her face, he just winked at her and hoped that she understood the message he was sending. She was special, the only fit for him just as she was, in those silly, somehow sexy wool socks. Climbing back in bed he gathered her in his arms. He had another long, sweet, passionate, and nearly silent message in mind with her.

Only her name would whisper past his lips. The kisses and caresses he rained down on her body would fall quietly. The vow he made in his heart to give her all the love and attention she had been denied as a child would remain unspoken. He would love her silently and show this woman that he belonged only to her—heart, mind, and soul—until she was ready to hear the words. He didn't need to teach her to be romantic; he just needed to show her how to trust what she felt.

# Chapter 26

DANA HAD TO SHOVE Garrett to get him out of bed the next morning when his alarm clock shrilled to announce it was almost dawn.

"No," she had insisted, groaning, then chuckling. "Quit nuzzling my neck. That's not going to work for you this time, cowboy," though the shivers it was sending down her spine, and the quivers it was creating elsewhere, told her that if he didn't stop soon he was definitely going to make a liar out of her.

"Go to work. Let a woman sleep until a decent hour. Stop!" She laughed, then tried to adopt a firmer tone. "I know you have an appointment to bid a new job this morning, so get moving, pal."

He finally managed to pull his lips away from the sleepy warmth of her throat. He stared down at her, a puzzled line creasing his forehead.

"Caught you. I saw the note on your fridge," Dana explained, "so don't deny it." She gave him another nudge, but it was half-hearted. God, his eyes are blue, she thought. Even the haze of sleep couldn't dim their intense color, or their power over her. She quickly closed her eyes, to lessen the pull, adding, "Besides, I plan to sleep in lazily late, then take a disgustingly long, and hot bath—"

"I'll wash your back and—"

"No, you will be meeting your client." She tried not to picture those big, gentle hands, sliding slick and soapy across her body. "Then ... then," she shook her head, "where was I?"

"We were in the bath," he suggested.

"Ah. Then, after my nice, long, *solitary* soak, I plan to laze around in sweats and look at all the maps and books I picked up in Bozeman—"

"And unpack your clothes," he encouraged.

"—so-o-o I can study up on where I want my own personal, and very handsome, I might add, tour guide to take me next." At a look from him, she smiled and added, "And unpack and wash my clothes."

He seemed relieved enough by that last to roll to the side of the bed, convinced she wasn't trying to slip away from him again.

"You're sure? I can reschedule my appointment. If I tell him I have been roped to my bed by a sexy redhead, he'd understand. He'd probably send over champagne."

"Every day?" She gave him a knowing smile and patted his cheek. "Get to work. You are going to have to let me out of bed occasionally."

"Why?" He asked, almost seriously.

Dana just laughed and gave him a shove. "You work, I'll plan our next excursion. Which reminds me, I'd love to see the houses you're building. If you have time later today, why don't you pick me up at lunch and take me on a tour?"

"A tour ... with benefits?" He grinned, seeming to like the idea.

"Maybe," she teased with a very promising smile.

"Deal." He jumped up, energized.


AFTER HE FED THE HORSES, and showered, he made them both breakfast. But when he took it in to Dana, she had already fallen back to sleep. He stood there a moment, loving the look of her in his bed. Putting her French toast in the fridge with a note, he headed off to work whistling.

But his lunchtime benefits were delayed.

Dana had been too fascinated with his other skills. She asked questions all along the driving tour of completed, and now occupied, residences. Wanting to know all about what special problems had to be addressed with the extremes of heat and cold on the high mountain prairie. Asking about the feasibility of using wind or solar power in the area; asking if water was drawn from the river or from wells; wanting to know what kind of strata the wells were drilled through and how deep. She listened to each answer thoughtfully

When they got to the sites under construction, where they could go inside, she asked about the unique logs and woods he used in his homes, where they came from, how he created the satiny finishes. She ran her hands over the flawless workmanship on his custom cabinetry, and got excited over the dove tail joints. She stood a few moments at a massive carved front door special ordered for one house, amazed not at the design, but the fit, opening and closing it a few times, admiring the smooth operation

272

and snug fit with its framing. She oohed at smooth miters, and ahhed at rare-grained natural woods used on windows, doorjambs, and matching custom made interior doors; she praised the tile work on counters and shower stalls. Garrett couldn't have asked for a more appreciative and interested audience to the extra effort and quality he put into his homes.

When Dana noticed an elk-antler chandelier hung from the high open-beamed ceiling, where the chalet style windows framed a view of the mountain where the elk roamed, she appreciated the perfect natural symmetry and beauty of the balance of natural antler, wood, and stone, outside and in. When she asked where he had found the terrific chandelier, he had confessed he made it himself—a little hobby of his.

"You're an artist, Garrett! I hadn't realized before. Not just that piece, but the whole effect you create, its balance, all the details and craftsmanship and natural features you bring together with the setting to create homes for people. You don't just build houses, do you? You create homes with built in warmth and artistry. You *are* an artist. This is all so wonderful!"

She looked at him as if he was as unique and wondrous to her as ..., well, as a supervolcano or something! It was a very strange thought, yet gave him a very powerful feeling inside. He savored it a while, so touched by the heartfelt praise, he hardly knew how to respond.

"Thanks," he shrugged, "remind me to have you write some of my ads." But he ducked as he went out the door, sure he'd grown much taller.


"I WILL MAKE US steaks for dinner on my outdoor grill, and since you are the raw vegetable expert," Garrett reminded her with a kiss on the nose, "how about husking and washing some cobs of fresh corn and baking potatoes, and wrapping them in foil for me?"

Prep work done, they were sitting on the porch, waiting for the coals to heat, tipped back in their chairs, enjoying the serene dusk creeping across the high prairie. It was especially beautiful this time of early evening, as the Absaroka Range faced the west, where the sun was lowering behind the Gallatin Mountains. While the high prairie darkened, the row of jagged mountain peaks, with their late fall snow dusted tops, were featured and spotlighted in golden shafts of sunlight.

Dana watched as a small troop of mule deer made their way nonchalantly through the sage, heading for their path down the benches to the current level of the Yellowstone River. She liked to sit on this porch and muse about how this was once all filled by glaciers, then blocked into a huge lake as the waters melted, working the level down, bench by broad bench, cutting down to the lowest part of the valley for the present day Yellowstone River. The numbers scrolled through her head of the prehistoric past she had learned of at the museums: during the Triassic, Jurassic, and Cretaceous this was a shallow inland sea—sea level, so hard to believe—in the land and time of the dinosaurs, until *poof!* and sixty-five million years or more ago, and they were all gone; a hundred million years ago the Rockies lifted up; fifty million years ago the volcanic Absarokas spewed up Emigrant Peak and the ones she was gazing at; then the Yellowstone Volcano joined the rearrange-earth game about two million years ago. Sending up major explosive debris and lava flows every 600,000 years, or so.

But the last twenty-five thousand year time frame fascinated Dana the most. Ice sheets from the mountains entered and retreated through this valley. Their moraines and drumlins dropped gravel debris piles that were still visible in parallel ridges and whale-like humps. And most intriguing, somewhere in that time period man first came to the area—scholars argued over when exactly. It had long been thought it had to be only after the ice age, but new finds continually moved dates startlingly earlier—further back in time.

On a visit to the local Gateway Museum, Dana had discovered that only about thirty to forty miles up the highway had been one of the most significant finds in the country. She hadn't drooled, but it had been a near thing. When she saw the mural painted by the local school children about the Anzick site, her mouth had hung open in awe. She had been working her way around the displays of old stone points and arrow heads dating back hundreds, or a few thousand years, and then seen this—a story *almost thirteen thousand years* old! One of the oldest human burial sites in the US, covered in red ochre, with a huge find of Clovis point stone tools in the burial. And it wasn't the burial of a lone hunter, explorer, or trader that might have been ranging far from home. It was a child.

*A child!* Which meant a prehistoric family in a valley just north of here, estimated to have lived twelve thousand six-hundred years ago—even older than the famous Kennewick Man, by thousands of years. She'd been confused at first, seeing dates range from 11,000 to 13,000years, but that was because what was

274

known as the radio-carbon date had to be adjusted using other methods for a varied past earth climate. And as scientific knowledge and technology improved, it evolved just like humans and earth itself, so dates would constantly be refined now and in the future. Still that was *really long in the past!* Wow! Dana knew how rare a find like that was to the body of knowledge about the First Americans, and for their descendants.

Enchanted and fascinated, she tried to imagine what her prehistoric family would have felt, seen, and hoped for back then. Did they have any sense of being pioneers in a new land? What had happened? Had the child seen mammoths in the valley? Were ice age alpine glaciers still a factor, or had they melted back to the peaks? Her curiosity knew no limits. She wanted to find all the answers—personally.

There was such a wealth of prehistoric archaeology and unique geologic events abounding in the area. The secrets hidden and kept by the silent grasses and sages of the prairie and guarded by the parallel ranges of mountain chains, whispered on the wind to her, and had helped her make her first crucial decision—her first step in a new life and adventure for herself. That much needed personal goal to reach for and give her the anchor she felt she needed before taking other more dangerous steps.

She hadn't told Garrett yet. It was her dream, apart from him, but it would also give her a chance to explore their future together—if there was to be one.

Dana returned to the present when the deer family cut onto Garrett's property, much closer now. It would be a perfect picture to send to Jen. A record of this present, tiny, lovely moment in history.

She reached into her pocket to pull out her cell phone and the slight motion caught the eye of the deer. They paused with those silly mule ears up, facing her, perfectly posed for the shot she took with her phone. She took a few pictures, then after the deer moved out of sight, studied them for the one she would send Jenny.

Jen! She had forgotten to call and tell her she wasn't at the hotel! Sure enough, there were several missed calls from her. "I need to call, Jen," she told Garrett, apologizing for disturbing the serene silence on the porch.

"Hey, Jen, sorry I didn't call— Yeah, I'm still here, still fine."

Garrett sipped his beer and checked on his charcoal to see if it was hot enough yet, he had just sat back down and stretched out beside Dana when he heard her tell her friend, "You guessed right, Jen. He *is* fantastic in bed! And his butt? To *die* for—"

Geez, Dana! Garrett felt his face flush. Jumping up, he decided he must need to do something in the kitchen. He'd leave the girls alone to talk. Reaching for the door, he shook his head; he couldn't believe how women talked to each other! It was embarrassing, he thought, stepping inside and shutting the door behind him. Then he leaned against it and grinned. He had to admit it had tickled him down to his toes. Puffing out his chest, he swaggered over to the fridge and grabbed himself another long-neck beer. Fantastic, huh? And his butt? Fatal. *Huh!* Maybe he'd just eat his steak raw. He was feeling so manly he might just salt it with a few nails.


WHAT HE MIGHT find more surprising were the things the reserved Dana didn't tell her best friend, yet.

She told Jen she'd spent a few days, while Garrett was working, touring around the towns of Bozeman and Livingston. She told her how much she liked the museums, the college and the tree shaded lanes of porch-fronted old houses in town. She did not mention she had gone alone because she had run away, or that Garrett had popped *THE* question—or rather blurted it out of nowhere, to be more accurate. She did tell her friend that she had moved from her hotel to stay at Garrett's for a while, which she knew Jen would assume meant the rest of her vacation. But Dana did not mention she had made a major decision about her goals and plans for the future—or where those plans were located. It was too new to share just now.

Jen already knew Dana had gone to Montana to see more than just what she had missed at Yellowstone Park. It was only common courtesy to go and personally meet and thank the man that had saved her life, after all. Especially if he was as Jen had described: single, gorgeous, kind and considerate, with detailed bonus features. It had been impossible for Dana to get on with her life without knowing what kind of man had been calling her at the hospital, with that incredibly sexy voice and charming sense of humor. She had arrived at the airport convinced he was absolutely too good to be true, to seek out his flaws, and found someone more special that she had expected. Someone she needed more than she could imagine. That was a problem, if not a disaster.

She didn't tell Jen that she felt she had taken a flying leap off the high bar and gotten lost somewhere up there in the process of falling—captured by Garrett's love—and that when he released her, she was going to hit the floor so hard she might never recover. Or how it scared her. How in her bath at the Inn, after recalling the sweetness, how she had recognized the pain to come and felt fear, doubt, and a scary loss of control over her emotions. Or how, she'd felt the need to step back a bit, slow down, try not to get in any deeper—if that was possible. She didn't dare rest her future, her need, her happiness, on their relationship alone. She had needed to find the strength to just be, just accept all that she could share with Garrett—temporarily. But, she also needed something lasting, something that would belong to her, rest in her control, for herself.

Dana knew how to go forward, coasting on her own happiness. She'd done it all her life. There was safety there, if not as much pleasure. If she found her own new future, she could let herself find short term happiness with Garrett.

Especially after Garrett had asked her, no, *told her* to marry him? She still wasn't sure which it had been—except sudden and unexpected. And she had panicked and run, realizing the need for space and time to sort things out. Alone. She hadn't believed for a moment that he meant it. But she hadn't shared any of these feelings with her best friend, yet. Not now, not over the phone.

When Dana had gone off to spend time alone, she had worn the agate necklace he had given her, to keep him close as she had wandered the streets of his home town, and when she had taken another day to go to Bozeman, only a half-hour down the pass. She liked the college town immediately. She loved the Museum of the Rockies!

Wandering the halls of the region's geologic history, opening the drawers to pick up specimens of minerals and sediments she could hold in her palm, *feeling* the process, Dana touched and imagined the eons of time. The dinosaur hall was astounding. It might be easier to shrug off that dinosaurs lived a long time, ran the world, and suddenly died, when you just saw one long fossil or skeleton in a museum. Not here! Not *that* exhibit. Dinosaurs of all shapes and sizes in your face, surrounding you, humbling you. They were everywhere, literally tons of them, all the different kinds that owned this land together, including family groups with fossil shells and young. It brought home both the length and the shortness of time on earth, and its utter capriciousness as home to any species, no matter their number or

277

seeming power. It reminded Dana of how each life was precious, and had a story to tell the future.

She had stopped at a window that displayed the room where the staff prepared the fossils for viewing and for study. She watched them patiently brushing, chipping, and drilling them from their casts of sediment, so they could tell their individual stories.

"Who were you, and what did you do with your time on earth?" Dana had murmured, leaning against the glass, asking the fossil, and herself, at the same time. This. This is what I need. She wanted to unwrap the answers, unveil the mysteries, explore lost stories of the deep past and prehistoric families of an ever changing earth. She felt the same excitement she had at the Anzick panorama—this is what she wanted to do! This was the goal she wanted to work toward, earn for her personal fulfillment.

Subconsciously, Dana had been falling in love with the area and taken the ancestral bones found in its land as her own family. She had found a home she wished to savor, to study, to belong in, to build her future. And her home had a hearth to warm her heart—Garrett Hearth—a man to share with. At least for a while.

She had skipped out of the museum, telling Big Mike she would be back to see him later. Heading for the Montana State University registrar's office, she signed up for a winter quarter class on archaeology. It would be a start in the right direction. She would add geology courses in later. But she didn't tell Jen yet that she was going to test the idea of going back to college—for a Bachelor of Science degree.

WHEN GARRETT CAME back outside with a platter of steaks, Dana was just finishing up telling Jen about all the amazing stone and marble buildings in the small town of Livingston: the old stone schoolhouse that was now the Gateway Museum, the Carnegie style library, the surprising train station called The Depot, and the post office with its massive steps and—

"—a marble pillar! I kid you not Jen, it is amazing!" she said, as he stepped out the door.

Garrett could not believe they were still talking on the phone about the *same* subject—him! He turned to set the steaks on the grill, letting the heat and flames explain his flushed face, but they didn't hide his grin.

He was fortunate enough to have his teeth buried in a juicy corncob later when Dana said, "Wow! We are terrific cooks, aren't we?" Only the smile dancing in his blue eyes showed, when she glanced up, how hard he had to bite down to keep from laughing.

"We are a terrific team," he answered with an honest grin, when he was able. The harmony of their time that day had proved that. He could picture every day like this, beginning and ending with Dana as part of his life. "So, tell me. How was your trip to Bozeman? Did you say hello to Big Mike for me?"


SHE SMILED AND nodded, fondly remembering how the T-Rex had been one of her first welcomes back to Montana, thanks to Garrett. Then her smile widened when she recalled all the welcoming kisses he had disguised as a local custom. She hadn't really trusted him then; that was changing. She launched into the details of how she had fallen in love with his hometown and Bozeman, leaving out only her plans for the future, saving them for a special moment. When she told him about her surprise at finding there had been a Clovis stone point site just to the north, he knew of it.

"I have been meaning to mention that to you. I knew it would be right up your alley. They have some of the Clovis artifacts and the best pieces of the other oldest stone points found in Montana up in Helena at the State Historical Museum, along with mines up in that area where tourists can dig up gems and minerals.

"But the Anzick stone points are the most amazing things! I've seen them. They are knapped from banded and marbled colored stone with such skill that they look more like jewels than hunting tools. Maybe they were the precious gems of their time. Anyway, you will love it. Maybe we can take a trip up to the museum and mines in Helena, and—" Pausing in his enthusiasm, Garrett seemed to recall that Dana's remaining vacation time might be short. "That is, if you want, and have time, we can go."

Dana just smiled, thinking, *Oh, I've got all winter, cowboy!* But she said, "I'll make the time." Giving him no clue that she meant to extend her vacation.

"Great. Where do you want to go tomorrow? I cleared and delegated my work schedule so I am available for anything."

"Hmmm. Well, I think we should wake up with the alarm, and—' she gave him a slow, sultry smile, "—and *not* get out of bed for a while. Then we will need to soap each other's backs and ... such. Then we can head down to the park whenever we get dressed. I made a discovery on a geologic map I want to check

279

out. I'll tell you what and where tomorrow, if you are good. Very, very good."

HE PLANNED to be a pillar.

# Chapter 27

GARRETT HAD BEEN SURPRISED—and a little wary—when Dana asked him to take her back to the geyser basins around Old Faithful.

"Look what I discovered!" She shoved a map on the table where they were finishing their pleasantly late breakfast. It was a geologic map of the Yellowstone area showing seismic hazards, fault lines, and where earthquake swarms had peppered the area in recent years.

"Do you see what this is telling us?" Her finger tapped excitedly at a point on the map just off center of the wilderness area enclosed by the lower loop of the park road system.

He studied it carefully. "Ahh … No. Tell me what you found, babe."

"It's the edge!" Noting his blank look, she took a pancake, laid it flat on the table and slid a spoon underneath, upside down. Raising the spoon slowly while she held the edges of the pancake down with spread fingers, she asked, "Don't you see?" She seemed quite delighted with herself.

All Garrett could see was that life with this woman would never approach normal or boring.

"It's cracking around the lower edges. *That* is *probably* why the geyser basins are there." Then she slapped the mangled pancake down on her plate and drowned it in syrup, taking a big bite.

He wasn't sure if that was another clue, or not.

"Sure babe, but I'm afraid I still don't get it."

"M-m-m," she raised one finger, swallowing impatiently.

"It's the dome. The other dome. I want to follow this route down today." She traced the road south from Madison to Old Faithful along the west side.

"When the land rose up in a dome, like the pancake, the edges would have cracked in ring-like areas, maybe opening fissures. I haven't studied this, but I'm pretty sure that's why there is this string of geyser basins and hot springs along here. It's just my own guess, but I want to eyeball the landscape while we drive down, see it for myself, then come back and look it up. Maybe I'm right? Anyway, it's fun to try and puzzle out. And I still want to see that pool you told me about on the Upper Geyser Basin walk."

Still not quite sure what they were going to look at, the sparkle of excitement in her eyes was enough for him. He just needed to remember to keep his big mouth shut today, and smiling. After the morning they had just spent, the last part was a given.

IN ADDITION TO the resurgent Sour Lake Magma Dome rising between Hayden Valley and Yellowstone Lake, the other resurgent dome—known as the Mallard Lakes Dome—paired it in a lazy figure eight form to the southwest. The west side loop road from Firehole Lake Drive south to Old Faithful curving south, then looping east toward Isa Lake, roughly outlined the left side semi-circle of the Mallard Lakes Dome, geyser basins lining it's western rim. The large rough oval of the whole caldera boundary encircled both magma domes and most of the central sector of Yellowstone Park.

Dana liked to picture the dome as a raised peak with a long round skirt spread around it. Where the skirt touched the ground on the west side, geyser basins were strung along its hem like frothy lace. That's what she had pictured from the topographic map, but on the drive down the vegetation hid many of the clues she was looking for. The scenery—both inside and outside the truck—kept distracting her.

To demonstrate stretching to open steamy fissures, she had used a handy pancake, but in Dana's mind the geology of the region was much more fascinating and poetic. If she stayed on after winter quarter, she hoped to start working on some geology courses. Maybe they could tell her if her theory—no, she already knew that was the wrong term if she wanted to be a scientist—if her *guess* might be correct. Then maybe Garrett would pack into the wilderness with her to see up close the contours of the domes—someday—in a future that was looking ever brighter.

The weather was splendid when they started on the nearly three-mile round trip hike around the Upper Geyser Basin. The sun gave warmth without the blasting heat of summer. The crisp air freshened and mellowed the gusts of sulfur wafting through the basin and whitened the steam venting against a vivid blue, cloud puffed sky.

The Upper Basin trail ran from in front of the Old Faithful Inn on a northwesterly route along the Firehole River. An asphalt paved bike path ran straight from the Inn parking lot all the way out to Morning Glory Pool, but the bulk of the thermal features were on the boardwalk that cut right at Castle Geyser, wandered across the river, then looped back to intersect the paved trail at Grotto Geyser. The loop also allowed excellent viewing of the two popular sinter cone geysers that sat on corner lots that guarded each end of the boardwalk. Dana and Garrett decided to leave the pavement and take the raised boardwalk over the sinter fields around the thermal areas, then pick up the paved path again at Grotto and continue on to the end at Morning Glory. Evergreens lined the much wider paved path, and that would make for a pleasant stroll back on their return.

Castle Geyser welcomed them quietly, its shining white turret standing over ten feet, more visible between eruptions when it wasn't sheathed in steam. Due to the height of its sinter cone, and the time it would have taken to build the geyserite so high, it was believed to be one of the oldest geysers in Yellowstone Park.

"I sure hope there's no one under that!" Garrett took Dana's hand and guided her around onto the boardwalk.

Looking down at the damp and barren sinter field around the other side of the geyser, Dana laughed when she saw where he was pointing.

A lovely straw hat in perfect condition sat calmly about six feet out into the railed off zone around the geyser, as if its owner had just walked out and sunk straight down. As there was no frantic screaming, it was safe to laugh at the silly hat that had escaped its owner and sat on display, its crown a perfect miniature image of the massive cone beside it.

Taking a picture to chuckle over later, they moved on to admire the pie-crust scalloped edges surrounding the deep turquoise hot spring of Crested Pool, before moving onto the bridge that crossed the Firehole River.

Looking northwest from the bridge, up the lazy curves of the river, steam rose in spots along both banks, looking like a series of smoky campfires beside the waters. The horizon was a continuous high ridge of deep blue where the ancient caldera rim rose, reminding of the power of the past that had formed all these steamy basins. It was a serene vista on this fine day, but savage at the same time. The future still boiled beneath all this beauty, satisfied for now just venting gusting geysers for man's, and especially Dana's, entertainment and delight.

She hadn't yet seen anything like the next feature. Spasmodic Geyser was not erupting so they could clearly see its unique architecture and tint. Used to the jewel tones of the springs, and the opaque mud of many paint pots, these deep tan tones, with a slight dusting of powdery white along the edges, stood out in contrast. The subtle tones displayed the exotic texture of rounded formations like sponges or corals done in a beige that climbed down into a clear pooled crevice. Coral-like structures so far from any sea? Dana was intrigued; it would be another puzzle to research.

A throaty roar, then hiss, signaled a new geyser starting to leap into the sky, so she hurried on with Garrett. They'd heard that Grand Geyser was due to put on its show at any time. Even from a distance, the display was becoming more and more dramatic, exploding into the sky far above a tree beside the path that had to be at least eighty feet tall.

Realizing the people in the crowd, silhouetted in front of the huge gouts of spray were only about the size of large bugs, Dana asked, "How high is that one? It looks bigger than Old Faithful!"

"Old Faithful averages around one hundred thirty feet. That one can get up to two hundred feet when it's in a good mood."

She laughed, continuing to be amazed at the volume of the bursts, as they got closer to Grand Geyser.

"Well, I'd say it's ecstatic today!" She started to lope along the boardwalk, tossing an excited smile over her shoulder at Garrett, as if he'd arranged this just to make her day. When the geyser finally subsided, then gave one last burst as an encore, Dana clapped, unashamedly delighted with the show.

Strolling along, hand in hand, they passed more vivid pools and springs, crossing back over the river again. Dana detoured down a side extension of the boardwalk to study the collapsed circle of the massive Giant Geyser cone. As he joined her at the railing, she turned, brushing a stray auburn curl from her face.

"You know what this reminds me of? It looks like Mt. Saint Helens did after it blew up in 1980. A flat topped cone with one side completely blown out, and everything that was once rich and green, just a barren, desolate, ashy gray wasteland for miles around."

284

GARRETT JUST NODDED at her serious tone. He'd seen the pictures, they did look like this—only on a much more massive scale. Many lives had been lost in that tragic eruption.

They moved quietly back toward the main boardwalk. He wasn't sure if he was seeing sadness on her face at that memory, or if it was exhaustion. Pausing to pull his daypack from his shoulder, he dug for the trail map for Upper Geyser Basin as she moved on ahead of him. Pinpointing where they were on the map, he saw that the boardwalk would soon curve to the left before the next geyser, where it would meet the paved bike path in a T. They had been following the raised walkway loop through the area of unstable and dangerous grounds that wove between the geysers—where the sinter wastes could hide bogs and scorching pools of steam just beneath the surface. Once they reached the junction, they would be on solid ground again, and a wider pathway. They could turn right at the next geyser and continue on their hike to Morning Glory Pool, or if Dana was too tired, turn left and return to the Inn sooner on the bike path.

Glancing up, Garrett studied Dana, now several yards ahead of him. Trying to gauge her back and gait for signs of fatigue, he found himself intrigued instead by the subtle sway of her hips and those long endless legs. He smiled, enjoying the view, until he lost sight of her as she curved left behind a rare stand of dense evergreens that hid the Grotto Geyser and the junction with the bike path from view. He hurried to catch up to her.

COMING AROUND THE BLIND curve, Dana's eyes had fastened immediately on the geyser to her right, huffing declining bursts of spray over its ungainly cone. Trees trunks coated white had become trapped and tangled inside its cone in a powdery pile of rubble that reminded her a lot of the enormous dinosaur leg bones, like she had seen in the museum. Out of it all spouted noisy, hissing fountains. Glancing back over her shoulder, she wondered where Garrett was, not wanting him to miss this odd eruption.

Then she saw him coming.

Grinning, she flung her arm out to point at the last gasps of the gushers. He stopped just past the bend, started to raise his camera to get a shot of her on the boardwalk—

Then stopped and just stared. His mouth flew open, his arms lowered, and he seemed to crouch down slightly then freeze. Why was he doing that? Did he want her to pose? He looked more like he was about to leap at her. She pointed more urgently, trying to get him to look over at the geyser before it quit erupting.

285

OH, PLEASE GOD, NO! NO!

As he came around the bend to see her grinning, pointing, excited, she was far enough away, he had thought, to get a great full length picture of her with those lovely legs. She stood sideways on the narrow raised boardwalk, facing the geyser, with her head turned back to him, her smile caught and dazzled his eye more than any scenery. Lifting his camera to focus in on all of her with her arm out pointing—

His world had spun suddenly, horribly, then shattered.

He couldn't breathe. Or think. He started to yell. Then knew he couldn't. Bile rose in his throat. Adrenaline burst through his system. But he knew he couldn't move. *Should not* move suddenly. But every instinct screamed at him to lunge for her.

*Dana-a-a!* His mouth opened to yell in silent, helpless, anguish. She was halfway between him and the end, where the boardwalk met the bike path and solid land. On his right the geyser still hissed and belched spray, before him was Dana, and just to the right, and behind her, just beneath her pointing arm was a massive, two thousand pound bull buffalo!

It was much closer to her than he was, right behind her in the triangle created by the geyser and inside corner where the paths intersected, blocking everyone's passage. He was only vaguely aware of the crowds beyond, frozen, cringing behind benches, caught less than twenty-five yards away. Unmoving, they watched the bull take a steam bath near the geyser. Now horrified, they stared at the woman—completely unaware—less than two yards from the bull, though on the slightly raised boardwalk. It was obvious she couldn't back away. One step back and she would fall off the walk raised a foot above the unstable sinter bog to be trapped and sink, or be scorched. A step toward solid land was a step toward those hind legs edging the walk, blocking her from the bike path. A move toward him was a direct provocation in the line of that dark side mounted eye and curled horn, as the bull faced toward the geyser beside her.

Everyone except Dana was holding their breath. At the moment, the bull seemed immersed in his steam bath, either unaware of, or unconcerned with her. And she still did not know it was there!

And when she did? What? Panic? Screams of terror? How would someone that still bore the scars, still wore the sling—was

286

pointing with the damn thing!—of her last attack, react? *Oh, God, help her*!

He wanted to grab her and run. He knew the bull would charge if he did; getting to her fragile flesh before he could. He wanted to rail and wail at a world that could be so bitterly cruel and unfair. But that wouldn't help Dana. He had to think, calculate—

Then Dana quit pointing, dropped her arm to her side seeming confused, then turned her head to see what he was staring at. Garrett's gasp was lost in the one from the crowd. If Dana gasped, no one heard.

The movement of her arm had turned the bull's head to her, as she turned hers to see him. They stared at each other frozen for a span of time that seemed endless—or could be much too short. Like those brief shutter-like snapshots of time when all sound stopped, all breath caught, all motion stilled, and a memory seared into the mind for a heartbeat before chaos erupted.

Please God, don't let her scream, panic, faint, or move another inch! Garrett shook trying to figure what to do. He didn't have any room to maneuver! Why had he let her get so far ahead of him?

No one moved.

Her back was to him now. He couldn't see the expression on her face, though he could imagine the terror there. So far, Dana hadn't made a sound.

Then very slowly she turned just her face slightly, away from the bull, as if she was gazing at the geyser. Her profile showed a paler than alabaster mask, all emotion blanked. The bull blew a breath from its nostrils then turned its head slowly, also facing the geyser. They both stared at the geyser, motionless, watching each other from the corner of their eye, and pretending not to, for what seemed like three centuries to all who watched and waited tensely. It had to have been longer for Dana.

As the steam bubbling from the geyser lessened, the buffalo moved a few yards closer to the grotto. As hesitantly as the buffalo approached the sulfurous vent, the crowd on the opposite path, edged back further.

Sensing motion to his left, Garrett swallowed a shout as he saw Dana edging further away from him. The bull glanced over his shoulder at Dana. She paused. Again they stared at each other silently for another lifetime, before the bull swiveled that massive head back into the steam with a relaxed flap of its tail.

Dana sidestepped three more feet to her left, then stopped.

287

Garrett cursed silently. He was going to murder her when this was over. He shifted a yard to his left with her, hoping, if nothing else to get close enough to draw the bull to him, so she could escape. Then he'd kill her.

Damn that woman, what was he going to do with her? How the hell were they supposed to have time together, a future together, if she kept trying to commit suicide by buffalo, dammit! He was scared, desperate, and angry—at her, life in general, and especially himself for letting this happen. Again!

Dana, God help her, after remaining motionless and quietly studying the bull for a few more minutes, had just casually strolled behind the buffalo! Reaching the bike path, with an alert eye on the beast, she turned to the right. Why the hell didn't she go the other way, run away from it, when she could? Slowly, softly, but steadily she walked beside the buffalo again, heading toward their original destination. The big beast saw her, tipping its head slightly, following her with that big black eye, but stayed at rest in its steam bath.

He had wanted to lunge after her—at least run to get between Dana and the danger—but he knew he had to measure his steps as slowly and calmly as she had, to not irritate or attract unwanted, unpredictable behavior from the beast—or spook him toward Dana. Garrett was sure it could smell the fear on him if not for the sulfur steam. Fear for her, not for himself. Though that wasn't really true. If he lost her, there would be nothing left for him.

Slowly edging along her route, he was unable to even draw the bull's attention from her.

He finally was able to join her on the other side, well past the dangerous corner. Blowing a gust of relief when they reached the line of tourists on the other side of the bike path, Garrett had to sit down hard on a bench for a minute and just try to breathe. He was shaking. Violently. Bending forward, he clamped his hands between his knees. He didn't want Dana to see; he had just recalled that it was at this exact spot that a woman had been gored and killed by a buffalo in the recent past. He thought he might lose it or throw up the bile burning harshly in his throat.

A group of male bicyclists, leaning against a railing, nodded at Dana as she passed them. One calling out to her in a slightly accented voice, "You're a brave lady!" He saluted, laughing, indicating they hadn't been resting, but waiting, fearful of passing so near the buffalo.

"Not really," she replied with a faint, friendly smile.

Smile?

Noting the exchange, Garrett clamped down on his fears of losing a future with Dana, focusing on immediate concerns. Jumping up, he rushed to rejoin her like any territorial male. Good, he thought when she reached out to take his hand, dimming the smiles of the foreigners admiring her, glad his Dana wasn't as susceptible to a man with a foreign accent as some other women were. He had never figured out why, but he wasn't taking any chances.

"They must be on some kind of bike tour. Didn't they have charming accents?" His paragon commented casually, making his blood boil.

How could she?

How could she be thinking about things like that when she had nearly lost her life? Then he caught himself, just having gone from abject terror for her to burning with jealousy. Damn right he was jealous, but he had hold of the hand of the brave, if incredibly foolish, lady and he was keeping it—and had a thing or two to say to her, also! Giving that hand a tiny squeeze, Garrett strolled along, trying to bring his churning emotions under control. His heart was still thumping away hard in his chest. Whether it was all from fear and panic at Dana's first confrontation with a buffalo since the injury, or spiced by something else, jealousy, need, love—

He knew he was ready to give all of himself to this brave and courageous woman. If she wanted to cut his heart out and feed it to that bull, he'd hand her the knife. He had felt it from the start, and now he needed to act, before he lost her forever. He was hers, but was she his? Did he dare act, open his mouth again, and watch her run from him … again? He was, for the second time, thinking of proposing ring-less, though he wanted Dana to pick her own rock. He had no idea what her favorite mineral or gem was—though his favorite would be the color of her eyes.

*Rings? Gems?* Where had his mind gone? His thoughts spewed around such inconsequential things, still panicked. What was important was that he wanted to give her his life! Not just a ring. He wanted the gift of her life to belong to him—though how the hell he would keep a woman alive that seemed to draw buffalo horns like a magnet, would be a challenge.

Dana stopped suddenly, pointed and whispered, "Look Garrett, is that a coyote or a wolf? Over there, just across the river, inside the very edge of the tree line."

He stared at her a moment, then looked in the direction that she had pointed. Her face was so calm, awed by this sighting, just like any other tourist, on any other day. He was dumbfounded. And after she had just faced what should have been her greatest fear! It all seemed too surreal.

"Coyote," he muttered, then found a laugh for the disappointment on that lovely face.

When they reached another bridge over the river, where high dirt banks and trees surrounded it instead of sinter fields, Dana asked Garrett's help in getting down. She wanted to get a closer look at the rock and strata along the embankment, but didn't want to skid and fall with a cast on one wrist. *Now* she was being cautious! Instead of taking her arm he just smiled, lifted her in his arms, and carried her. Setting her down on a flat rock beside the river, he seemed oblivious to the stares of others, including Dana's puzzled gaze.

"Hey, thanks," she whispered.


DANA WAS NEVER carried like that. Like a child—even when she was one! It made her feel weird. Weird and warm, and kind of ... not helpless, but rather ... *cherished*.

Later, when they finally got to the end of the trail, an observation deck framed the gorgeous finale, the famed Morning Glory Pool.

# Chapter 28

MORNING GLORY POOL gained its name and its fame from its resemblance to the flower, with the long, slender throat of its crater welling up in intense blue to spread out over the pool like opened flower petals. But over the years, its fame had led to a lessening of its blue glory. Too many tourists tossed coins and other debris into the pool, despite signage, and damaged the circulatory system, lowering the temperature, along with the intensity of the blue it could produce. Bacteria and algae formed—where it hadn't been before—creating more orange, yellow, and green tones encircling the once bluer pool. Still special, but not as unique as it was once.

Standing on the decking beside the pool, between wisps of steam, you could look right down into the deep crater of the pool. It looked so deep and mysterious, you could imagine it as a watery tunnel connecting to the next world. Benches, intended for seating, provided an even better standing platform for an excellent unobstructed view and photographs into the pool's blue depths.

After all the other visitors took their pictures and paused to admire the view, they drifted away and left Dana and Garrett alone beside the colorful pool.

He stepped up onto the bench and helped Dana up, careful of her injured arm, slipping her in front of him, so they could both look into the pool. Wrapping his arms around her waist, he pulled her snug against his chest, inhaling the fresh scent of her hair, as he rested his chin over her good shoulder.

Today the geologically formed flowering trumpet was multi-hued in tints from vivid cinnamon tones, to greens and tonal blues. Steam ghosted over the surface, giving a momentary clear view into the deep tunnel, then drawing a silky veil back over itself, to seduce viewers trying to probe its mysteries.

They stood a long time, without words, just enjoying the view and the quiet moment together. Garrett soaked up the joy of feeling her warmth and life in his arms. So precious to him, so fragile, so easily lost, so dear.  He needed this woman in his arms, his life, always.

Pressing his cheek against the warmth of hers, he felt her shift and relax against him, accepting and enjoying his hold, which became more and more intimate, as their bodies molded together. Speaking softly in her ear, trying not to shudder, he finally told her of his terror at seeing the buffalo near her, his amazement at her calm reaction.

"I know how fearless, how brave, you are babe. You don't need to prove that to anyone. After all, it's been documented by the media," he teased shakily, before adding soberly, softly, his breath warmly brushing her ear, "Babe, if I had gone through what you did before, and saw that bull in my path, I would have turned around and run away screaming! Well, not screaming, but scared sh...Silly! Like all those other guys were. How *could* you do that? Even brave as you are, how could you do that?" Garrett's voice was soft, incredulous, and the hurt in it clearly said "to me?"

Dana didn't answer at first; she just rocked gently in his arms.

Sighing, he tried to temper his words, his fear.

"I guess if anyone knew if it was going to attack, it would be you. You're the only one I know that has experienced it, but— how could you *know*?"

"I didn't know, Garrett," was her simple answer.

"But—"

"I looked, waited, and after it moved there was more space. I know how fast they are but, I really didn't have any choice. I never saw it until I was on top of it. Besides the odds were worse, I figured, the longer we stayed in such close proximity."

Odds? She was calculating odds? God love her!

"So I let it see me behind it; let it decide if it was bothered. It seemed not," she explained calmly.

"But Dana, you can't expect a wild animal to think or show attitudes like a domestic animal might. They're wild, unpredictable, and well, I guess you know that, hell, but ... What if it had attacked? How could you face that again, honey?"

Dana managed to turn to face him, without letting his arms release her. She nuzzled into his chest, clasping her good arm around his waist. Looking up at him with those glorious green eyes, she asked him back, seriously, "How could I not, Garrett?"

He could no more answer her than he could breathe with her pressed to him.

"Garrett, I was kind of happy when I saw the buffalo."

"What! What? What if after everything, you had been ... killed?" He had to say it, not sugar coat it. Now was the time for honesty.

"You don't understand, Garrett. I would die more surely from constant fear than if the buffalo had killed me today. I will not live a fearful life. This was my chance to know that." Her voice was soft and sincere.

He gazed down at the eyes so close to his, their green depths more amazing, more mysterious, than the depths of the pool beside them. He tried to plunge into those eyes to find the answer to what gave her such spirit, such courage. How could he ever let her out of his life? How could he keep her? His lips gathered hers, joining softly, naturally, before the thought to kiss, to act, had even formed. Had he bent to her? Had she risen to capture him? Their lips had decided on their own to join, to be together. The tenderness of the kiss ached, it belonged, and it owed them both. Its intensity ebbed and flowed between them, tender depths shifted to hot, deepened lust, then slid into love and trust, roaring back to passion, hotter, harder, the longer it lasted.

They survived without air. This fate shared, this inevitable joining.

Tears had run down Garrett's checks the first time he had touched Dana—for her pain. Love now surged through his soul, to burn moistly in those same eyes, to dampen those same checks with a joy, and sizzling passion, as they touched again, bonded again, in love this time.

"Dana, you're not ever leaving," he whispered urgently against her lips.

I WILL NOT LIVE a fearful life.

Lost in that moment, and the depths of his arms and eyes, Dana had not heard the false echo of her own words. But, was not her fear of loving alone, or being loved temporarily instead of belonging, living fearfully, failing to trust? She realized she had to live up to her own words. She could no longer live in fear, afraid to grab for this love. She couldn't let something so vital slip away. She could not let Garrett slip away.

Ah, she loved this man, this handsome, sexy, romantic man, all tough strength and open, giving heart, wrapped up in a bundle of laughter and humor.

She leaned back from him a bit, pulling in a deep breath, "That reminds me ... I guess I could, well, *probably* marry you. You know, if you still—"

293

"WHAT? REALLY? YES!" Garrett stuttered, shocked. "Are you sure?"

"Sure," she shrugged and smiled. "Why not?"

Garrett could actually feel the joy flooding into his heart. Did she mean it?

"So unromantic, my darling Dana!" He complained, laughing, delighted, folding his arms even more tightly around her.

I guess I could probably marry you?

But least she change her mind if he mentioned that, he murmured instead, "Aren't you supposed to say 'yes, darling' or 'forever, my love'? Instead of 'sure, why not'?" He was smiling, hugely, almost giddy, but he still feared he might have misunderstood her intentions—he needed to be crystal clear on this.

"I promise I'll get on bended knee when my arm is free, and I give you your ring," Dana reassured him, her smile and eyes warm with tenderness and laughter.

His heart started beating again at her promise, at the love he saw filling and opening the depths of her eyes and heart to him.

"Sure, why not?" He shrugged, then threw back his head, joining her in a joyous roar of laughter that made tourists venturing to see the hot spring smile just to hear them.

"She proposed to me!" Garrett explained, exultant, with a grin so huge it nearly split his face.

Dana gasped, her mouth rounded in denial, before she just nodded and expelled a laugh.

"Yes, I guess I did. I told you about my fairy tale. You are my handsome savior, so live with it, cowboy!"

"I've been waiting to hear that." He gave her a scorching kiss to seal the deal.

The tourists took a picture of the beauty of their loving embrace. Then shyly asked them for an email address to send it to them.

"For your grandchildren," the elderly Asian couple explained.

Smiling and bowing, they left the tall, handsome, American couple alone by the amazing pool that captured and blended the jewel tones of their eyes, shining with love for each other. A wondrous, glorious love, beside the shimmering depths and wonders of Morning Glory Pool. Captured in, and for, eternity.

"I HAD TO PROPOSE to him to get him back in bed," Ms. Unromantic joked to Jenny over the phone, the next day. Dana's voice sounded as casual and breezy as usual, so Jen was sure she hadn't heard correctly.

"You what?

"Yeah, but Jen, he is *so* worth it!"

"Did you say 'propose'? As in marriage?"

"I thought at first it was the high altitude at the Inn, but he is even better down here, which is lower."

"Dana! Dammit! Don't you dare start any science stuff with me right now! Are you getting married to Garrett?" Jenny demanded.

"Oh! That reminds me. You need to take the week of Thanksgiving off. Did you and Garrett pick out cabinets? He said to tell you he ordered your kitchen."

"What?" Jenny nearly shrieked with frustration. "Wait! His house does not have a kitchen?"

"Well, of course it does, silly." Dana laughed. "I meant another kitchen."

"You don't even cook, Dana! What do you need two kitchens for? Never mind. Don't answer that! God, you make me crazy! Let me make this simple. Proposal, ring, wedding? Yes or no?"

"No. But we're going to mine one ourselves later in Helena."

"What? Dana! Oops ... sorry I have to go. Bye!"

Dana pulled her phone away from her ear and frowned at it. Jenny had hung up on her! How could she hang up when she was giving her the most important news in her life? Muttering, she went inside to complain to Garrett, but found him talking on his cell phone.

"I know ... I'm very lucky! Thanksgiving Day. No, it's for the cabin I'm finishing as a model. Yes, she told me. It's not a deal breaker. I can cook," Garrett raised laughing eyes to where Dana stood listening. "Listen, don't book a hotel, that's what the cabin is for. We want you to have a place here to stay anytime, so I'm putting the kitchen you liked in it. I'll use it for a show model when I don't need a guest cabin. Sure, thanks again. See you soon, bye."

"Did you call Jen? I was talking to her—"

"And driving her crazy, so she called me for the facts." He scooped his frowning lady onto his lap.

295

"I have a good idea," he kissed her nose, "why don't you drive me crazy instead. I know of a little science experiment I'd like to practice on you. I'm trying to perfect my process. I believe I can start a chain reaction," he nibbled her ear," that can result in an exquisite explosion." Rising, he carried her down the hall to his laboratory, whispering sweet ways he'd like to blend their chemistry in her ear.

ONCE GARRETT WAS ABLE to breathe again, after recovering from their experiments, he asked Dana the question he had been afraid to touch. He was even more afraid to ask now that he knew how much her sport had substituted for the family she lacked.

"Will you tell me, babe, what your injuries mean to your career?"

He asked it simply, stroking a hand lightly across her damaged shoulder down to her wrist. He wanted to give her the choice to share as much or as little as she wished.

He was amazed how directly she faced the future.

"It may never heal right, Garrett."

"Babe, I have to tell you this, it has been giving me nightmares, and it is only fair that you know the truth before we take the next step." Pulling in a deep, shaky breath, he found it hard to look directly in her eyes, as he confessed.

"I am responsible for the extent of damage to your wrist. I should not have moved it. I knew I was injuring it more when I pried the child from your grasp—"

"Stop right there!" Dana's voice shook with a sudden anger he had never seen from her before. "Don't insult me, Garrett. Or yourself. No one forced me to try to save that child. And you knew it. If you had thrown away that child's safety, or even caused her another moment of terror being clutched to a bleeding woman, do you think I would have ever forgiven you? I was ready to sacrifice my life for her. And I would have if not for you. So forget this asinine guilt over my wrist!" Blowing out a huge burst of air and the last remnants of her frustration, she cupped his face and made him look in her eyes. "Okay. That's over, permanently. Agreed?"

He nodded, started to open his mouth to speak, but she covered his lips with her fingertips.

"Listen, it is really important to me that I can talk about the status of my injuries without worrying it is going to make you uncomfortable. Don't take that freedom away from me, please. Let's go back to what I wanted to share with you." She curled down against his shoulder again, waiting for his arm to come back around her.

"As I was saying, my wrist may never heal right. We just don't know yet. I've had months to realize and accept that, but I know I will be okay, whatever the outcome. I started so young, do you realize that I have been an athlete for over twenty years? A whole career! For so long, my life was all about that discipline and focus. I've been very lucky and happy with that, but now I want other things. So many other things." She placed a kiss on his throat, before continuing.

"After the accident, all I could think about at first was how my body had failed me. It was a disaster, who would I be without it? Then I realized that I'd been given a second chance, a second life, my broken body was my freedom in a way. It forced me to think about going out and grabbing what I want now, with both hands. Well, one and a cast," she laughed ruefully. "It changed me, you changed me, and you are the first thing I wanted to grab with my new freedom."

"Got me, babe." He kissed her softly, seriously. "What else do you want? How can I help?"

"Well, I might even start another studio and classes here, part time, but I want to take classes of my own first. A Bachelor of Science degree is my goal."

"Wow, that's terrific! Go for it, you're a natural. But, another studio here? Can you still do that?"

"I could with some trained employees. For years I've been videotaping my performances, and a series of training demonstrations. They're better than doing it live, because no matter how good I was," she chuckled, "I could never master stop action or slow motion to demonstrate a point. So I could make it work, if that's what I decide to do."

"My business is going great, Dana. I'd like to see you treat yourself first, and get that science degree. But, I was wondering, it must be amazing flying around on the bars like that, won't you miss it? Isn't there some surgery that could get that back for you? So you can fly again?"

"Too soon to know, Garrett. Maybe. Maybe not. But it will be okay. Even if I can't fly, I can still leap. After all, there's nothing wrong with my legs."

"No, there's not a thing wrong with your legs," he growled running his palm up bare silky skin, shifting her on top of him. "Let's discuss this leaping a little more, could I have a demonstration of technique?" He nibbled on her neck where she was most ticklish. "Maybe another little experiment you want to try out on me?"

"You just wait, my love," she laughed. "When I get this other hand free," she paused to playfully bite his nipple, then lowered her voice to a sultry threat, "I'll still show you a thing or two about flying."

She completely forgot to tell him she had already signed up for a course in Bozeman—until a pleasantly long time later.

*EMAIL To: Gretchen - Germany*

*From: Dana -U.S.*

*Subject: fairy tales come true*

*Dear Gretchen- Thank you for your letter and best wishes on my recovery. You asked about the nice hero man that saved us. Have I got a surprise for you! What girl doesn't dream about the knight in shining armor, the handsome hero that rescues her? Not that we modern girls aren't independent and can't take care of ourselves, still, it is romantic to have a fairy tale come true, isn't it?*

*Well, I am sending you my new address. I am moving so I will be near Yellowstone Park for your next visit there. (I still hope I can show you my rainforest, too, someday.) I am moving because I am going to marry the man of my dreams, that wonderful, handsome hero of ours, Garrett Hearth! Can you believe it? I'm so lucky!*

*We thought that what could really make our wedding more like a fairy tale come true is if you could be our honored guest, and our flower girl. We know it is short notice and you probably won't be able to make it, so don't feel bad, but I want you to know you will be beside us in our hearts and minds. We love you. Tell your folks we would love to have you all as our guests, anytime.*

*Love, Dana*

*PS. Garrett asked for your email address, so I think he may write you also.*

*EMAIL To: Gretchen – Germany*

*From: Garrett - U.S.*

*Subject: Luckiest man in the world*

*Hey little sweetheart, Garrett here. I guess Dana told you she made me the luckiest guy alive. We both want you here, if you can come, but I know it's hard to arrange so fast, and I have to tell you honey, I can't wait any longer to lasso my brave, lovely little filly. We set the date for Thanksgiving, just weeks away. Dana thinks it's so I won't forget our anniversary, but it's the other way around. I am so thankful to have her become my wife that the day that I married her will always be Thanksgiving Day to me, so why confuse things with two of them?*

*Anyway, here is what I wrote to tell you, to promise you. If you can't get back to the states, don't worry. I promise that you will get to be our flower girl someday, even if it is years from now when you are older. You are the reason Dana is in my life, and she is the love of my life. I'll probably want to marry her all over again every year, but I will wait until you can come back and be our flower girl to marry her again. That's a promise.Bye doll, Garrett*

DANA FINALLY GOT BACK on the phone with her best friend the next day.

"You hung up on me, Jen! I can't believe it. I'm telling you my most important news, and you hang up!'

"And how exactly was I supposed to *know* it was important news when you were speaking in gibberish?"

"Well, I was excited." It was probably the first time Jen had heard a pout in Dana's voice.

"God, I guess! Hey, congratulations, honey. I am so excited for you, Dana!"

"Yeah, pretty amazing, huh? I get three dreams for the price of one! I get a great guy, I'm going to study archaeology and geology at Montana State, and I get to go study it all at Yellowstone Park all the time, just down the street. Three for one!"

"Dana, do not be flip. Don't play cool with something like this. This is me, and I won't put up with that bull," Jen warned, furious with her best friend.

Dana's voice immediately softened as she let loose a lifetime of needing to love and belong to someone of her own.

"Oh, Jen, I do love him. I love him so much it makes my throat burn just to say it, to know it. Garrett is the man whose eyes I look into and see nothing but love and happiness. Yes, he comes with bonuses, but—

"I can see my whole world in his eyes, Jen. I can see it clear down to his soul. Someone I can love and trust until the day I die. Someone who loves me way more than he should, but I'm taking him with both hands, and keeping him."

Even as she scolded Jen for starting one of her crying jags, Dana felt the tears of pure happiness welling in her own eyes—her heart full and finally freed by belonging to one oh-so-special man.

# Epilogue

THE HUGE FRONT DOORS of the barn had been flung open. The horses had been moved to the neighboring filly's place for the day, much to Corky's delight. Every nook and corner had been cleaned to a sparkle before space heaters and card tables of refreshments were set in the openings of the stalls around the outer walls. The hay in the half-loft had been moved back to accommodate the stereo system and speakers and room for a few favored local musicians.

A flower strewn and scented altar was the focal point of the area below the loft, facing neat rows of muslin draped and ribbon-bowed folding chairs, set on either side of a narrow aisle on the broad scoured wood plank floor. Baskets filled to overflowing with fragrant bundles of sage leaves mixed with dozens of yellow roses and spicy, bronzed seasonal flowers and leaves, trailing colorful streamers of autumn colored ribbons, hung from hooks all around the barn walls that were normally utilized for tack.

Large white canopies had been erected in a line from the mouth of the barn back to where a large barrel barbeque was parked at the opposite open end, throwing off heat along with the spicy aromas of the coming feast. The canopy posts were all decorated with flowers and fall leaves, adding their own fragrant spice, with windbreaks hung along one side, the semi-open arched pavilion was comfortably warm despite the location and lateness of the year.

The weather seemed to want to bless the wedding as well.

The sun had invited itself to join the festivities dressed in its finest blue coat embroidered with just enough soft clouds to spread a blanket to keep crisp from being chill, and snow flurries had been detained up north and would be unable to attend. Many of the guests had preferred the open area between the barn complex and the house's front porch, where they could enjoy that sun, looking out over the vast high prairie and the majestic mountain ranges that lined either side of the valley. Earlier a small herd of mule deer had passed through the fields, pausing with their

Y-shaped heads turned curiously to check what all the to-do was about at Garrett's place, delighting the out-of-town visitors, before continuing on down to the river.

All their guests had moved into the barn now, and settled down. The handsome groom and his best man moved solemnly up to stand beside the altar; the bride's party was assembled at the threshold of the barn. Everything was in readiness to begin.

Dana could just be seen ready to enter, a tall, slender vision in satin and lace, with her wild red curls partially tamed, dripping dainty spirals of ringlets from beneath a seed pearl cap, around her elegant face.

Waiting at the head of the aisle, she inhaled the spicy aromas, gazing around at the seated guests she spotted the dozens of yellow roses in the flower baskets along the walls. Stunned because, except for her bridal bouquet, such expensive out-of-season flowers had not been part of the original design. Feeling warmth steal though her, moisture seeping into her eyes, she knew who must have ordered the last minute surprise to the design. It could only be her soon-to-be husband—reminding her of the yellow roses he had sent her in the hospital—messengers of his care and feelings. She knew it wasn't Jen. Jen would never have been able to keep it a secret or surprise without exploding.

Garrett had done it. Her sentimental, romantic, tough, strong, steady, handsome guy.

So thoughtful. Like the lace-covered sling to match her wedding gown, he had asked a local gal to make for her arm. Dana heaved a deep sigh of pleasure, as she gazed down where he stood beside the altar. He would belong to her, and she to him—the bliss of a lifetime she had been afraid to wish for. And he would make a romantic out of her yet, she smiled to herself. What woman could resist with a man who so cherished—while always respecting—her. Looking forward to all that lay ahead for them, she took a moment to remember all that lay behind. Her thoughts drifted dreamily to their first night of love making ... the tenderness, then the explosive passions they had shared until they had melded into one hot—

Dana felt a tap on her shoulder, and opened her green eyes, letting the memory of that first incredible night fade. Garrett had taken her to altitudes that couldn't ever be measured on earth!

Smiling, she looked up to send a blazing smile down the aisle to her future husband. To her surprise, Garrett was scowling back at her!

This time the tap was more of a shove in the back, as Jenny stage whispered in her ear.

"Dana, wake up! Are you going to stand there forever! Garrett's getting impatient. And who's that raven haired hunk that showed up as his best man?"

"His friend, a ranger at Glacier. We will still go there next year, like we planned, you know. Now hurry, go on ahead," Dana whispered.

Glancing down a moment, Gathering up her bouquet, her smile, the edge of her skirt, and all her hopes, Dana stepped toward her future, seeing Garrett's face instantly break into a huge welcoming grin.

Poor guy. She must have daydreamed so long he thought she had changed her mind.

Not a chance!

She felt like skipping down the aisle behind Jen, eager to forever join her special man. He was her hero, and she was his.

When she reached him, his hand stretched out for her. Green eyes met blue with a sparkle of delight and a tender loving sigh. They were home now.

And there they joined. Beyond the buffalo, not far from the amazingly pool in Yellowstone where they had exchanged their 'sure-why-nots', and where they would return many times.

And their 'forever afters'?

Well, they did live in Paradise Valley, after all.

According to Dana, it was a *blissful* altitude

# AUTHOR'S NOTES

First a warning: DO NOT TAKE ANY MEDICAL ADVICE FROM DANA!

This is a work of fiction, but much of the science was carefully researched, *except* for anything related to the medical sciences. I frankly didn't want to be told that I couldn't do something I wanted in that area of the plot. Though I do have a Creative License, I hate feeling guilty when I have been directly told "No". Here is a list of the areas I frantically waved that license: all things medical, the restroom at the geyser basin, and those high-altitude experiments of Dana's? Those are definitely just for fun and laughs (as far as I know).

The "Buffalo Road" locale exists in the park, just not where I placed it. I was actually trapped in traffic by a bear sighting at the real location, watching the huge herd of buffalo on the opposite side of the road, when this story idea reached out and grabbed me. With a file cabinet full of story starts, I had never intended to write about Yellowstone—but I found it *impossible* to resist.

The prehistoric geology and archaeology of the area were carefully researched. I did my best to sort through various theories and ever changing and improving knowledge to present that information accurately, but in as simple and fun a manner as possible. I have no science degrees, just a great curiosity and fascination, and wanted to share a more playful, user friendly version of my amateur studies. All errors are mine alone—except Dana's guesses— that pancake business is totally her thing!. If you would enjoy the more technical details, some of my sources and references for further reading are at the back of this book.

I also need to clarify what I wrote about Gibbon Falls. When I first visited Gibbon Falls, the Supervolcano story of Yellowstone was just becoming known to the public and the location was as I described it. It has now changed after years of construction, its story now given the importance that was hidden from our knowledge for so long. At Canyon Visitor Center there is now a map table that tells the Supervolcano story also. (Jealous) But I wanted to capture that *moment in time*, mere years ago, when a great scientific discovery still sat quietly concealed before our eyes—before we forget how little we still know and understand our earth, and how many surprises there are still to explore and uncover.

No matter how many times you visit our national treasure, Yellowstone's appearance and personality are ever changing. I hope it is just one of the new friends you made on this journey.

Thanks for the trip. Bett

PS - One final flash of that creative license; I do know they are actually American Bison—not Buffalo—but where is the romance in that?

# ABOUT THE AUTHOR

Bett lives in the beautiful Pacific Northwest near what is now known locally as the Salish Sea and just an hour—or so, depending on the ferry lines—from the Olympic National Rainforest. Just a short drive in any direction brings plenty of scenic inspiration. But on a trip to Montana she found herself falling for Yellowstone, and its irresistible story. As the first National Park anywhere, it deserved to be first in her National Park Road Series.

Bett seems to think, however—*or prefers to think*—that "Author's Photo" means a photo taken by the author. The one on the back cover is one of her favorites from her many research trips to the park. She calls it "Life on Earth" because it reminds her of a space shot of earth, but it is a photo of the streams of life's primitive microbes flowing into the lake, taken at West Thumb in Yellowstone.

Buffalo Road is her first published story, with many more to come. I hope you enjoy Dana's personal journey and this trip through Yellowstone National Park, past and present.

To see more "author photos", leave comments, or when this book will be available in paperback, or when the next book in the series is ready.

contact by email : Bett@bettboneauthor.com

# Coming Next

GOING TO THE SUN ROAD
A Glacier Park Love Story
Book 2 in the National Park Road Series
 by Bett Bone

Journey to Glacier National Park in NW Montana on the historic landmark Going To The Sun Road-
Please email bett@bettboneauthor.com to request notification of publication of eBook and paperback release dates.

# buffalo road references

Alt, David D., D. W. Hyndman. 1986. Roadside Geology of Montana. Missoula: Mountain Press Publishing Co.

Breining, Greg. 2007. Super Volcano: The Ticking Time Bomb Beneath Yellowstone National Park. St. Paul, MN: Voyager Press/MBI.

Christiansen, Robert L. 2001. USGS Professional Paper 729-G: The Geology of Yellowstone National Park: The Quarternary and Pliocene Yellowstone Plateau Volcanic Field of WY,ID,&MT. USGS.

DeVoto, Bernard,editor. 1953/1981. The Journals of Lewis & Clark. Boston, New York: Houghton Mifflin Company - Mariner Book.

Finley-Holiday Films. 2011. "The Complete Yellowstone DVD - 2nd Edition - English with German,French,&Japanese Subtitles." Whittier,CA: Finley-Holiday Film Corp.

Janeski, Joel C. 2002. Indians in Yellowstone National Park. revised. Salt Lake City: University of Utah Press.

Lahren, Larry A. 2006. Homeland: An Archaeologist's view of Yellowstone Country's Past. Livingston: Cayuse Press.

Levin, Harold. 2006. The Earth Through Time-8th Ed. Hoboken: John Wiley & Sons, Inc.

MacDonald, Douglas, and UofMontana. 5 year study MYAP update report Feb 2016. NPS Archaeology Program: Projects in Parks:MYAP-Montana Yellowstone Archaeological Project at Yellowstone Lake. University of Montana/Yellowstone NP Cultural Resources Staff Joint Project.

National Geographic Channel DVD. n.d. "The Secret Yellowstone (inc waterfall chasers)." National Geographic.

National Park Service, U.S. Dept.of Interior. 2010. "Yellowstone Nat'l Park News Releases: RSS." yellow 2010 news. www.nps.gov/yell: Yellowstone National Park .

Owsley, Douglas W. Jantz, Richard L.:editors. 2014 Smithsonian Institution. Kennewick Man: The Scientific Investigation of An Ancient American Skeleton. College Station: Texas A&M University Press.

Tankersley, Kenneth B. 2002. In Search of Ice Age Americans. Salt Lake City: Gibbs Smith.

Tarbuck, E.J, F.K. Lutgens. 2002. Earth: An Introduction to Physical Geology -7th Ed. Upper Saddle River: Prentice Hall.

Travel Brains, Inc. 2005. *Yellowstone Expedition Guide.* www.travelbrains.com: Travel Brains, Inc.

Whithorn, Doris. 2001. *Images of America: PARADISE VALLEY on the Yellowstone.* www.arcadiapublishing.com: Arcadia Publishing.

Yellowstone Association. n.d. *"Individual informational brochures available at each feature in park, ex:Canyon, West Thumb,etc."* Yellowstone National Park, WY: www.yellowstoneassociation.org.

Yellowstone Volcano Observatory/USGS. 2010. *Protocols for geologic hazards response by the (YVO)Yellowstone Volcano Observatory-Circular1351.Aug.* http://pubs.usgs.gov/circ/1351/index.html.

www.ingramcontent.com/pod-product-compliance
Lightning Source LLC
Chambersburg PA
CBHW020410260626
47156CB00007B/2323